DESERT BLOOD

The Juárez Murders

Alicia Gaspar de Alba

Arte Público Press
Houston, Texas

This volume is made possible through grants from the City of Houston through the Houston Arts Alliance.

Recovering the past, creating the future

Arte Público Press
University of Houston
452 Cullen Performance Hall
Houston, Texas 77204-2004

Cover design by Giovanni Mora
Cover graphic art "Las muertas de Juárez reclaman justicia"
by Segundo Pérez

Gaspar de Alba, Alicia, 1958–
 Desert Blood: The Juárez Murders / by Alicia Gaspar de Alba.
 p. cm.
 ISBN 978-1-55885-508-3 (alk. paper)
 1. Americans—Mexico—Fiction. 2. Pregnant women—Crimes against—Fiction. 3. Mexican American Border Region—Fiction. 4. El Paso (Tex.)—Fiction. 5. Adoption—Fiction. 6. Lesbians—Fiction. 7. Mexico—Fiction. I. Title.
 PS3557.A8449D47   2005
 813'.54—dc22   2004055417
                                                                    CIP

♾ The paper used in this publication meets the requirements of the American National Standard for Information Sciences—Permanence of Paper for Printed Library Materials, ANSI Z39.48-1984.

8 9 0 1 2 3 4 5 6 7   10 9 8 7 6 5 4 3 2

A las "muchachas del sur"
—con respeto.

To the "girls from the south"
—with respect.

Hay muertas que no hacen ruido, Llorona
Y es más grande su penar . . .
"La Llorona"

The U.S.-Mexican border *es una herida abierta* where the
Third World grates against the First and bleeds.

Gloria Anzaldúa,
Borderlands/La Frontera: The New Mestiza (1987)

It is in pornography that the basic meanings of sex crime are
distilled—the female body fetishized, displayed, sacralized,
only so that she can be hated, possessed, profaned, sacrificed.

Jane Caputi, *The Age of Sex Crime* (1997)

Life, after all, is not a Hollywood mystery. There is no resolution, no evil madman to blame it all on. The perfect murder is,
it turns out, unusually easy to commit, especially when the victim is no one "important," an anonymous figure—and Juárez
has plenty of those.

Sam Quiñones, "The Maquiladora Murders,"
Ms. (May/June 1998)

Disclaimer

The serial sex crimes, or femicides, which are the subject of this novel, are true. An epidemic of murdered women has plagued the Juárez-El Paso border since 1993. All of the main characters in this story, however, are fictional. Any similarities to living or dead people are purely coincidental. Some of the suspects and public figures that appear in this book are taken from periodical and television reports. Their names have been changed, but identity markers remain, such as a character's national origin or nickname. The victims are a composite of real-life victims. Some readers who are familiar with the "maquiladora murders" may recognize certain details about a given crime and find that they don't match "what really happened." Because this is a fictionalized account of true events, I have taken liberties with chronologies and facts. I have also added a metaphorical dimension to the story, using the image of American coins, particularly pennies, to signify the value of the victims in the corporate machine; the poor brown women who are the main target of these murders, are, in other words, as expendable as pennies in the border economy. Let me stress that, to my knowledge, none of the bodies of the actual victims was ever found to have had American pennies inside them.

Also, because there is, as yet, no solution to the murders, only theories and speculations, the line of investigation offered in this book is based on four years of research into the crimes and a lifetime of personal experience in the social, political, economic, and cultural infrastructure of the U.S.-Mexico border that makes it possible for such crimes to take place with impunity.

The press has described these crimes as "Jack-the-Ripper style serial killings." The bodies of the victims were immolated, mutilated, dismembered, or beaten beyond recognition. At least ninety of those murdered women were also raped. Tragically, as of this writing, ten years after the epidemic started, and over 350 bodies later, the crimes remain unsolved. More tragic still, the killings continue. In 2003, for example, twenty-two more female bodies were found raped and murdered in Juárez, among them that of a six-year-old girl who'd been stabbed multiple times and had her eyes removed.

It is not my intention in this story to sensationalize the crimes or capitalize on the losses of so many families, but to expose the horrors of this deadly crime wave as broadly as possible to the English-speaking public, and to offer some conjecture, based on research, based on what I know about that place on the map, some plausible explanation for the silence that has surrounded the murders.

I am from El Paso, a native of that border, I join the ranks of those who believe silence=death. *Madres*, protect us. *C/S*

Los Angeles, California, 2003

I

THE ROPE TIGHTENED AROUND HER NECK, and she felt her belly drag over sand and rocks, the wound on her breast pricked by sagebrush. She was numb below the waist, and her face ached from the beating. One of them had given her an injection, but she could still move her arms and wedge the tips of her fingers under the noose. They'd stuffed her bra into her mouth, and the hooks in it hurt her tongue. When the car stopped, her head slammed into something hard. The pain stunned her, and she was crying again, but suddenly, she felt nothing in her arms. The numbness spread quickly up her spine. Her jaw, her belly—everything felt dead.

They shut off the car lights and let her lie there in the dark, inhaling the fumes coming out of the tailpipes. Her tongue tasted of metal. All she could do was blink her eyes. The stars looked like the city lights, and for a moment she felt like she was hanging upside-down, all the blood rushing to her ears, making her face hot.

She remembered the ride at the fair. The Hammer, it was called, and the other girls had warned her not to get on, said she would throw up, but she didn't. She'd fainted, instead, and woke up in the back of this car with a man hitting her face and another one she recognized from the factory pushing a syringe into her stomach.

For a second her eyes were seared by a sharp light, and then she saw their faces, like large silver coins, so bright she didn't see what was glinting in their fists until they were on top of her.

The drug they had given her made her feel like she was under water. She could not feel the blades slicing into her belly. She saw blood splashing, heard the tearing sound, like the time she'd had a tooth pulled at the dentist's office, something torn out by the roots, deeper than the drug. Felt a current of night air deep inside her, belly hanging open. She tried to scream, but someone hit her on the mouth again, and someone else stabbed into the bag of water and bones—that's all it is, the nurse at the factory once told her, a bag of water and bones.

They were laughing, but she could hear someone singing, a woman's voice singing, *sana, sana, colita de rana, si no muere hoy, que se muera mañana.* Heal, little frog's tail, heal; if you don't die today, may you die tomorrow. It sounded like her own voice.

2

IVON CLOSED THE MAGAZINE and leaned back against the leather headrest, feeling queasy. Reading on airplanes didn't bother her usually, but that article on the murdered women of Juárez had unsettled her. "The Maquiladora Murders," it was called, by a male freelance writer, which she found surprising for a piece in *Ms*. She opened the magazine again and stared at the picture: a close-up of a woman's legs half-buried in the sand, skin the color of bruises, white sandals still on her feet. A dead woman's body. 106 dead brown women. She couldn't figure out what upset her most: the crimes themselves or the fact that, as a native of that very border, she didn't know a thing about them until just now.

"The temperature in El Paso is a cool 98° this evening . . ." the captain joked about the weather. "We're going to begin our descent soon . . . may experience a few bumps. . . ."

The plane lurched into a patch of rough air. Her stomach muscles tightened. The nausea had gripped her hard. Maybe it wasn't the article. Maybe it was returning to El Paso after two years away, and knowing that her mom was not going to approve of the crazy plan that Ivon had concocted with her cousin, Ximena. The inevitable confrontation with Ma. Or maybe it was just claustrophobia from sitting in the back row of a crowded airplane next to a chatty cowboy.

At LAX she had gotten the last window seat, and no one had sat beside her the first leg of the trip, but then a tall guy in a camel-colored cowboy hat boarded in Las Vegas, walked all the way to the back of the plane, and decided he wanted the middle seat next to her.

3

"Mind if I take that seat?" he smiled, showing a chipped front tooth. His Texas twang surprised her. In his striped polo shirt, he looked more like a rich kid from Beverly Hills or Palm Springs. More like a golfer than a cowboy, or maybe a surfer on steroids.

Ivon shrugged. "Whatever." She lifted the magazine to her face and pretended to read. Plenty of other middle seats he could have chosen, but no, he had to take up some of her space. Right away she felt her chest close up, and she had to concentrate on taking deep breaths and letting go of her annoyance. The business-suited woman in the aisle seat stood up to let him through, curling her lip at him behind his back.

He settled in and buckled up, then placed his hat on his lap, coddling it as though it were made of glass. His arms and elbows claimed instant ownership of both armrests.

Ivon couldn't help noticing the bush of white-blonde hair on his forearms or the watch he wore on his right wrist: a gold Patek Phillippe chronograph with three dials. Ivon collected watches. She knew the price of a piece like that. Ten grand, at least. The five-hundred-dollar titanium Tissot that Brigit had given her for their fifth anniversary seemed cheap in comparison.

"You live in El Paso?"

"Not anymore," she mumbled, not looking up from the page she was reading.

"Going home to visit?"

She glared at him. Bloodshot eyes, blond stubble on his tanned face, blond hair shaggy around his face. He smelled of rank whiskey.

"I guess you could say that."

She turned her attention back to the article, reading about a certain Egyptian chemist who'd been arrested in 1995 for allegedly killing at least one of the women himself and masterminding the murders of seven of the others through a gang of accomplices called Los Rebeldes. *Many of the young women had been raped, several were mutilated, and a large number had been dumped like worn-out machine parts in some isolated spot.*

Ivon jotted that sentence in her dissertation journal. The dead women of Juárez had nothing to do with the topic of her research,

but she was beginning to think this issue would have made a much better project for the dissertation.

"Don't mean to be skimming over your shoulder," he interrupted again, "but are you reading about all those girls getting killed across the border?"

"Trying to," she said.

"Sure is a damn shame they still haven't caught the killers after all these years."

Yeah, and I'm ashamed I'm just now finding out about it, by reading this article, she wanted to say, but it would have been too embarrassing to admit that kind of ignorance to a complete stranger.

When the flight attendants came around with drinks, Ivon asked for a Diet Coke. He ordered a double Jack Daniels.

"Mind holding my hat so I can take out my money?" he said.

Ivon held the hat by the crown, not sure why he didn't just put the thing on his head and stop fussing with it. The straw was glazed hard, and the hatband was a miniature leather belt tooled with turquoise studs and silver conchas. The initials JW were worked in gold in the tiny buckle. Inside the rim it said Lone Star Hat Company and gave off a heavy odor of sweat and cigarette smoke.

"Fifteen-star hat," he said, handing a twenty-dollar bill to the attendant. "Cost me a pretty penny, and it itches like hell."

"Mm-hm," she stared at her magazine. When was this guy going to get the hint that she wasn't interested in conversation?

"Care to join me?" He offered her one of the little bottles of whiskey.

"I don't drink," she lied, digging into her bag of peanuts.

He took the hat from her, put it on his head, finally, and poured both bottles of Jack into his plastic cup of ice.

"J.W.," he said, holding out his hand.

"Hi," she shook his fingertips. She didn't usually shake hands like that, but she didn't want to encourage the guy. She raised the magazine to her face again.

"Sorry," he smiled, "I know you're trying to read. I just get nervous on airplanes."

"It would be nice if I could finish this article before we land," she said.

"I'll shut up," he said, and sat back, sipping his cocktail. Ten seconds later he was looking in her direction again.

"Ivon Villa," he read the address label off the cover of the magazine. "8930 Palms Ave., Los Angeles. Is that near the airport?"

"Excuse you," she said, scowling at him over the magazine.

"You don't look Mexican." His blue eyes looked bleary. "I didn't mean that as an insult. Sorry. It's just that you don't have an accent, or anything."

The plane dipped and bounced and the flight attendants rushed through the cabin picking up half-empty cups and other trash. He left her alone and chugged what was left of his drink before the flight attendant took his glass.

"Bet you fifty cents I can guess what you do for a living," he said.

She ignored him. He was just some racist white man on the make.

"You're a model, right? Or in the movie business."

What was it about straight guys who liked to pick up on butch women? She rolled her eyes and shook her head. "You lose. Not enough roles for lesbians in the business."

That snapped his attention span. "That was a mistake," he said, his cheeks and neck coloring a bright pink. The whiskey had already glazed his eyes.

"Don't worry about it," she shrugged. "I'm going back to my reading, now."

"Can't you see the lady wants to be left alone?" the woman in the aisle seat told him.

"I sure as hell apologize, ma'am." He took his hat off and coddled it in his lap, again, staring straight ahead.

Ivon ran her finger over the text she was reading: *Life, after all, is not a Hollywood mystery. There is no resolution, no evil madman to blame it all on. The perfect murder is, it turns out, unusually easy to commit . . .*

"Flight attendants, please secure the cabin for arrival."

He fished for something in a front pocket. It slipped out of his hand, landing between his jeans and her chinos. She retrieved it and gave it back to him. A roll of pennies.

"Almost forgot your winnings," he said, and a little whistle of air escaped through the gap in his tooth. "Fifty cents."

"It's okay. You keep it."

"It's yours," he insisted. "We had a bet."

"Really, I don't want it. I wasn't taking your bet seriously." Ivon stowed her journal and the magazine, zipped up her backpack, and buckled up again.

The plane plowed through the usual gauntlet of air pockets on the landing. Settling back with a clenched belly, she raised the plastic screen on the window and looked out at her hometown, the lights of the valley glowing under the huge pearl of a full moon.

Unless it's twilight, the only thing you see when you fly into El Paso is the desert—the brown, pachydermal, sagebrush-stubbled skin of the desert. But at twilight what you notice right away is the sky, the green veil of sky that stretches between Mount Franklin and the Guadalupe Mountains. From the plane you can't see the boundary line, the cement riverbed that separates El Paso from Juárez. The borderland is just one big valley of lights.

You can't see the chain-link fencing of the Tortilla Curtain, or the entrepreneurs in rubber inner tubes transporting workers back and forth across the Rio Grande, or the long lines of headlights snaking over the Córdoba Bridge—one of the three international bridges that keep the twin cities umbilically connected. For the locals on each side of the river, the border is nothing more than a way to get home. For those nameless women in the sand, those tortured bodies she'd just been reading about in the Ms. article, the border had become a deathbed. For Ivon Villa, it was the place where she was born. The plane landed with a jolt.

She had to wait for J.W. to fix his hat just right over the bald spot at the crown of his head before she could get out of the seat. He stepped aside to let her go first.

"Catch ya later, alligator," he said, winking at her and tapping the brim of his hat.

Ivon nodded but didn't speak to him. She was feeling nauseous again, like she had a swarm of butterflies hatching in her belly. For a few seconds, the thought of backing out of this crazy plan occupied some real estate in her brain.

3

"IVON! IVON! OVER HERE!"

It was her little sister, Irene, showing off her swimmer's body in a midriff and cutoff shorts, bright yellow earphones wrapped around her neck like a choker. She was standing next to her cousin, Ximena—both of them waiting for her at the gate. Irene was holding a helium balloon that said "Congratulations on the New Arrival."

"Hi, Lucha!" Ivon gave her sister a tight hug. Ivon called her "Lucha," for the popular Mexican *ranchera* singer, Lucha Villa; Irene called Ivon "Pancho," for their revolutionary ancestor. Their mother hated those nicknames, especially Ivon's.

"I can't believe you spilled the *frijoles*," Ivon said to Ximena. "I thought I told you it was a secret. Sure you didn't put it in the family newsletter?"

"Hey, don't give me any ideas," Ximena said. "Besides, I didn't tell *them*, I just told her. What's the fun of secrets if you can't share with at least one family member?"

Ivon narrowed her eyes at her cousin. Ximena gave her a bear hug. She was the oldest of Ivon's cousins, over the hill and then some, she liked to say. She stood nearly six feet tall and at least two hundred pounds thick. She tousled Ivon's hair. "Little Ivon is gonna be a momma," she said, crowing out a big laugh. "Never thought I'd see the day."

Irene kissed Ivon on the cheek and offered her the balloon. Ivon didn't take it. All she needed was to run into people she knew and have them think she'd had a baby.

"Can you hold it for me while I get my bag and stuff?"

8

Irene shrugged and pouted all the way to the baggage claim. "Where's Brigit?"

"She'll come out later, once we get this thing squared away."

"Yay! I get to be an aunt, finally," Irene said, linking her arm in Ivon's. Her brown-black eyes sparkled. Ivon was taken aback by how beautiful her sister had grown in the last two years.

"But this isn't gonna change anything, is it? I'm still coming to live with you guys, right, if I get in to Saint Ignatius?"

"Maybe," said Ivon, pinching her sister's cheek, "people shouldn't count their ducklings before they hatch. How's Ma?"

"I didn't tell her you were coming, if that's what you want to know."

"You better not, or you'll be sorry, *ésa*," Ivon poked her sister in the belly, grabbing a thin fold of skin between her fingers.

"Ouch! Don't pinch my *lonjas*," Irene cried out, laughing. She held out her right hand so that Ivon could see her graduation ring. "Like it? I got my zodiac stone on it, see? Ma wanted me to get the school color, but I wanted turquoise." Irene tilted her head as she admired her ring. "Looks nice with the gold, don't you think? I've been working for Ximena since March so I could help Ma pay for it."

"Working for Ximena? Doing what? Paying her bills on time?"

"That's right," said Ximena. "She's my personal assistant. Keeps me on track."

"Uh-huh," said Ivon, grabbing her sister's hand, "let me see that ring again." Irene's hands had lost their adolescent pudginess, and her long fingernails were painted a dark red with little gold stars appliquéd to the tips.

"I hope you're still graduating in December," Ivon said. "No boyfriends distracting you, I hope."

"¡Ay, sí!" said Irene. "You know I'm gonna be valedictorian, and I made captain of the swim team, too. Someone had to change the reputation of the Villa name at Loretto Academy."

Ivon had been kicked out of Loretto in the eighth grade. She'd been caught one day at lunchtime smoking pot in the bell tower of the convent.

When they stepped outside the airport, the blast of heat nearly choked her. Just like walking into a sauna. The rubber soles on her Doc Martens felt gummy on the scorched pavement. The sky had changed to indigo in the time it had taken them to come downstairs and collect her suitcase.

"Here we are," said Ximena, as they approached a white Chrysler van she had parked in what Ivon called a "chaired position." A handicap permit hung off her rearview mirror.

"How'd you manage that?" asked Ivon, pointing at the permit.

"Just lucky, I guess. Sorry about all the junk," she said, stacking newspapers and file folders to make room for Ivon's luggage. "This is my home away from home."

Ivon lifted her bags into the back, on top of a row of battered banker's boxes, then piled into the front passenger's seat and strapped on her seat belt. Even Ximena's perpetual patchouli scent couldn't mask the smell of cigarette smoke and old bananas that emanated out of the hot upholstery. From the crumpled-up paper bags all over the floor, Ivon could tell Ximena spent a lot of time in that van.

"Let me guess," said Ximena, cigarette already dangling from her lips as she headed for the parking lot exit. "You need a place to stay, right? Your mom's place isn't an option?"

"That's a good guess," said Ivon.

"How come?" whined Irene. "I wanted you to stay with us."

"Maybe later in the week, Lucha. I need to get my bearings. This is all kind of crazy, and I just cannot deal with Ma right now."

Ximena reached for the lighter and lit her smoke. "Hey, you want one?"

Ivon shook her head. "Brigit made me quit."

"Good for her," said Ximena, sidling up to the airport cashier to pay for parking. "Here's the thing. Grandma Maggie's house is available until a week from Friday. As you may or may not know, since you never respond to my e-mails, we're having our big family reunion next weekend to coincide with Father's Day."

Ivon cut her eyes at Ximena.

"Don't worry," Ximena continued, "I'm not going to point a gun to your head and make you go, even if you haven't been to a reunion since Grandma Maggie's funeral, but . . . if you're around, and stuff, and you might be . . . who knows how long all these arrangements will take . . . it's Father's Day, you know? I mean, think about it. Some of our old geezers, hell, your own grandpa, might not be around much longer."

"Don't guilt-trip me, okay? I don't need both you and Ma doing that," said Ivon.

"There she goes," Ximena said, looking into the rearview mirror at Irene. "What did I tell you? Two minutes, max, and Ms. Thing here is gonna be sitting on the Pity Pot. Get off it, *prima*. Your poor mom's doing the best she can."

Ivon winced at Ximena's rebuke.

"So, like I was saying, Grandma Maggie's house is free right now. All I use it for is my office and to hang out sometimes, so you'd have the place to yourself for a few days. We can figure out what to do after that, if it ends up taking longer than a week or two, I mean."

"A week or two?"

"Who knows? I mean, this girl could give birth tomorrow, but we'd still have to arrange a court date for the adoption, and even my friend, the judge, can't tell me how long that might take. You're here for a while, girlfriend. That's why I'm saying, might as well hang out for the reunion. The XYZ Club could, you know, get high and watch *Xena*. I've got killer weed."

"Drama!" said Irene. "What's the XYZ Club?"

Ivon reached over and smacked her cousin's leg. "Shut up! You're worse than a soap opera." She changed the subject. "So what's this girl's name? Is she okay?"

"Cecilia. She's had some . . ." she stopped suddenly and pounded the horn. "Hey, move over, fuck-face," she yelled out at the low-riding Impala in front of her. "Fucking *cholo*, get a motor or get off the street! Anyway, what was I saying? Oh yeah, Cecilia's had some complications, but everything's okay. I took her to the clinic and she checked out fine."

"What kind of complications?"

"The girl's been wearing a girdle, you know, so they can't tell she's pregnant or else she'll get fired. She stands up all day at the factory, and it's made the baby ride too low, or something like that.

But like I said, the baby's fine, Cecilia's fine, it's all good."

"She'll get fired if she's pregnant?"

Ximena turned to look at Ivon. "Well, yeah, the factory would have to pay maternity leave. That would cut into its profits. Take your birth control if you want to keep your job."

"Are you shitting me?" Ivon took mental note of this detail for her dissertation.

"Company logic is there's plenty of girls lining up for your job," said Ximena. "More supply than demand, you know. They don't need to hang on to anybody who's pregnant and can't fulfill her quota."

"That is so fucked up."

"So how 'bout it, Sir Ivanhoe? Grandma Maggie's Deluxe Resort?"

Ivon hadn't heard that nickname since they were children. "That's cool. That's perfect, actually. And when do I get to meet Cecilia?"

"Tonight," said Ximena. "We're going to pick her up outside her factory after her shift." Ximena checked her left wrist. She never wore a watch, but was always checking the time anyway. "Let's see. She's got the second shift, so she punches out at midnight."

"Midnight?" said Irene. "Dude, that's late. Can't y'all wait till the morning?"

"Up to you," Ximena said to Ivon, "but she is expecting us to pick her up, so she'll probably miss her bus. Poor thing lives out by Puerto Anapra. I guess I could go over there by myself and drive her home."

"What are you talking about? I'm dying to meet her."

"Can I come?" said Irene.

"No," Ivon and Ximena said in unison.

"You guuuys."

"Not tonight, sweetie," Ximena said, looking into the rearview mirror. "Let's let your sister meet the biological mother of her baby by herself, okay?"

Mother of her baby . . . the words made Ivon feel suddenly suffocated by the heat and the smoke inside the van. Even the open window didn't help. She picked up a file folder from the dashboard and started to fan herself.

"You guys decide on a name yet?" Irene asked.

"Either Dierdre or Samuel Santiago."

"Dierdre?" Irene and Ximena echoed.

"Don't ask me. That's Brigit's New Age stuff." Ivon reached over to turn on the radio, not surprised to find it already tuned to an oldies station playing "Suavecito." All El Paso stations played oldies.

"I never met a girl like you in my life . . ."

It never failed. Whenever she was in El Paso, something always reminded her of Raquel, the woman who'd snapped Ivon's heart in four pieces, one piece for each year they'd been together. She tried to think of something else, but the song brought her back, like an MTV video digitally connected to Raquel—her black eyes and full red lips, the *suavecito* movement of her hips on the checkered dance floor of the Memories bar.

"Hey, Ivon," Irene interrupted. "While you're here, maybe we could go to the fair in Juárez. Ma won't let me go with any of my friends, and I've never been. It just opened last weekend. Will you take me?"

One thing about Irene: she sure was an obedient child.

"We should all go," said Ximena, "as part of the extracurricular activities for the reunion, I mean. Good idea. Hold on." She swerved into the parking lot of Pepe's Tamales in Chelmont and brought the van to a sudden stop. "Be right back. Can't have tequila without tamales."

"Tequila?" said Ivon. "I thought we were going over to Juárez."

Ximena checked her wrist again. "We've got a couple of hours. I'm starving. You still a vegetarian? Oh, sorry, that's someone else. Be right back."

"Aren't you scared?" Irene asked when they were alone. "About the baby, I mean?"

"I don't know." It embarrassed Ivon to admit her yearning was stronger than her fear. "It'll be nice to have someone to clean out the litter box and unload the dishwasher when Brigit and I get too old to bend over."

Irene laughed. "Goofball," she said. Then, as an afterthought, "Ma's gonna flip, you know? I mean, dude, she's really gonna flip."

"Tell me about it." Ivon was realizing she hadn't eaten all day, and her stomach was starting to growl in anticipation of the tamales.

"What're you gonna tell her? You *are* planning on telling her, right?"

"I was thinking of bringing the baby over, you know, all wrapped up with a little cap on his head, and saying, 'Guess what, Ma, meet your first grandkid. Brigit and I adopted him from some *maquiladora* worker in Juárez.' Can you just see the size of cow Ma's gonna have when she hears that?"

"I'm serious," said Irene. "Ma's had so many cows with you, I feel like I live on a farm. Ximena told me about the time you hitch-hiked all the way from here to that women's music festival in Michigan right after I was born."

Ivon yawned. "No biggie. Everyone used to hitchhike back then."

"Ma says you were jealous I came along. Says you were running away."

"That's bullshit. Anyway, I think it was the tattoo that really messed her up."

Ivon had gotten a labrys tattooed on the back of her neck her first year of grad school at Iowa. It had supposedly depressed her father so much, he had taken up drinking again after fifteen years of being sober. It had also, somehow, caused his death. That's what Ma said.

"You wanna see something really cool?" asked Irene. "Check me out."

Ivon turned around to look at her sister. She didn't see anything at first, but in the yellow light of the Pepe's Tamales sign she saw that Irene was sticking out her tongue and there was something shiny in it.

"Don't tell me you got pierced?"

Irene put her tongue back in her mouth. "Cool, huh?"

"Oh, God," Ivon said, snapping a hand over her eyes. Her students in L.A. didn't pierce their tongues just to look cool. There was a sexual reason behind it, a same-sex sexual reason that Ivon did not want to know about right now.

"Well, what do you think?"

"What does Ma think?"

"She hasn't seen it, yet. Just had it done a couple of weeks ago."

"Eagle-eyes Ma hasn't seen it?"

"I think I'll show it to her while you're here."

"Oh, great. That'll be another thing she'll blame on me, you watch."

"I know," said Irene, giggling. "So, what's the XYZ Club?"

"Oh, just a stupid little club we formed when we were kids that only those of us whose names began with an X, a Y, or a Z could join."

"But your name begins with an I, like mine."

"That's before I changed it, officially, from Y-V-O-N-N-E to I-V-O-N."

"Bet Ma loved that."

The driver's side door opened, and Ximena thrust two bags of tamales into Ivon's lap. For a second, the aroma of moist cornmeal drowned out the stench of bananas. Ivon's mouth started to water.

"Okay, we're all set," said Ximena. "Half a dozen red, half a dozen green chile and cheese. I hope y'all didn't want any."

She backed out of the parking lot and peeled rubber.

"Shall we drop off the kid now or give her some dinner, first?" Ximena asked.

"You guys are so mean."

"She's a growing kid, probably needs to eat first. You can go and drop her off by yourself, later, while I unpack. I'm not going anywhere near Ma's house. She can sense me within a two-town radius."

"Loud and clear," said Ximena. "Okay, so here's the deal. My friend—he's a priest—is going to go with us tomorrow, so he can be there when you meet Cecilia's folks. She lives with an aunt and the grandmother. It's always a good idea to have a priest present, makes folks feel less awkward, less like they're committing a sin. You got the goods?"

"I got the goods."

"Cash?"

"I know who I'm dealing with, okay? D'you think I'd offer them a check?"

"Just checking. Anyway, you're gonna have to give some of that to this priest."

"Oh, he gets a cut, too?"

"I thought you said you knew who you were dealing with? Of course, he gets a cut. Doesn't the church always get a cut?"

"How much?"

"Two, three hundred, at most. And don't forget the *mordida*. Just in case someone tips off the police and you get stopped on the way out of the clinic, you got to have some bribe fare, no more than fifty or sixty bucks, probably."

"Shit, Ximena. You should've told me this before. All I brought is exactly 3K for the girl. Now I'm going to have to go to the bank tomorrow."

"Look, that's the way things work over there. I don't make the *pinche* rules."

"Right. Sorry."

They passed the veil-shaped chapel at Loretto Academy, where she had gone to grade school. Ivon had kissed a dead body in that chapel. The old nun who used to be her fourth-grade homeroom teacher, Sister Ann Patrick, keeled over one day in the cafeteria, and everyone at the school was forced to attend her funeral. The kids in her homeroom were supposed to go up to her casket and give her a kiss on the forehead.

"Oh, and another thing," Ximena was still talking. "Get another fifty for the nurse who's gonna fill out the birth certificate. The priest knows someone at the maternity ward at Fort Bliss."

"Dude, this sounds like so sleazy," Irene said.

"Welcome to the real world of the border, baby girl," said Ximena, driving toward the huge lighted star on Mount Franklin, an El Paso trademark signifying hope.

4

Two voices were playing ping-pong in Ivon's head right now—her mother's and the little boy's. Strangely, the little boy's was winning, but her mother's was a seasoned player, accustomed to being shoved in the background, to sneaking up from behind with an ace or a guilt trip.

—Dad, the little boy insisted, *I thought you were gonna supervise me in the kid's section. I'm starting to feel kinda lonely.*

— *En martes,* her mother's ace flew out, *no te cases ni te embarques.*

It was a Tuesday, and according to Mexican superstition, her mom's second religion, it was not a lucky day for weddings or journeys. Well, Ivon wasn't getting married—been there, done that, six years ago in a Unitarian church in Iowa City—but here she was, embarking on the journey of a lifetime—parenthood—and about to meet the girl whose baby she was going to adopt. Ten to midnight, on a Tuesday.

Over the past six years, Brigit had kept trying to convince her that they needed a baby—talking about biological clocks and what-not—but Ivon was a Taurus, daughter of a man who considered himself a great-grandson of the hardheaded Pancho Villa and an Apache woman, and she did not bend or break easily.

Last August, Ivon had landed her first job as a visiting professor in Women's Studies at Saint Ignatius College in Los Angeles. The dean, a Jesuit priest who as a rule did not like to hire ABDs, had given her twelve months to finish her dissertation, *Marx Meets the Women's Room: The Representation of Class and Gender in Bathroom Graffiti (Three Case Studies).* (The dean hadn't thought much of the topic at Ivon's interview, finding it a little too frivolous for a Ph.D. candidate, until she explained that public bathrooms are a

17

type of exhibition space in which the bodies of women and the graffiti they write and draw on the walls—a closed discursive system of words and images—can be read semiotically to analyze the social construction of class and gender identity in what Marx called the "community of women.") After defending the diss., she'd be promoted to assistant professor step one, a tenure-track position with a higher salary and an office she didn't have to share, and she'd be on the way to job security, but only if she finished. Job security, or rather tenure, meant they could buy the house they were leasing in Palms, a three-bedroom bungalow with wood floors and a little orchard of orange and lime trees in the backyard.

Her dad had always said you weren't anything in this country unless you owned your own house. Dissertation, tenure, real estate—that was the order of things. Kids were distracting, not to mention expensive. Ivon had never known poverty, but she'd grown up in a neighborhood of latchkey kids and mothers on welfare who cleaned houses in secret so they wouldn't lose their food stamps. She couldn't see herself being a parent, she said, without the time, the money, and the space she needed to really provide for a child. And anyway, if Irene ended up going to Saint Ignatius and moving in with them, they wouldn't have any spare room. Those had been the most persuasive arguments against Brigit's biological clock, until Ivon heard that little boy in the bookstore last Christmas.

Dad, I thought you were gonna supervise me in the kid's section, I'm starting to feel kinda lonely.

Ivon had laughed out loud, and a woman standing at the end of the Home Improvement aisle turned to look at her.

"How cute," Ivon said to the woman.

"He's my son," said the woman. "He loves coming to bookstores." The woman smiled at her and turned back to the row of books she was perusing.

Ivon never even saw what the little boy looked like, but that's when she knew. She couldn't explain how or what she knew. But all of a sudden Brigit's broken record about raising a family finally made sense. The *not enough time* motto of Ivon's just couldn't hold up next to *he's my son*. What she did with her time, how much time she had left, who she spent her time with—these were the things that mattered. She realized you could make up money, but you couldn't make up time. She had never told Brigit about the mutual fund her dad had left her in his will, which had been growing a healthy interest for the last eight years, waiting to become the down payment on her first house. You couldn't grow time with interest. And time was not renewable. Ivon was thirty-one and Brigit thirty-six. By the time their kid went to college, Ivon would be just shy of fifty, and Brigit would be near retirement age. No wonder Brigit's alarm was blaring.

Ivon didn't even wait to get home but called Brigit on the cell phone from the freeway. "I want a boy," she said as soon as Brigit answered.

"What?"

"I want a boy who's going to want me to supervise him in the kid's section of the bookstore, who's going to feel lonely because I'm not standing right there next to him."

"What?"

"Brigit? Are you deaf? I'm saying I want a boy. You know what I'm saying?"

"Oh my god! Ivon! Are you sure? What about Irene? What about your dissertation?"

"Irene can baby-sit. And we won't be the first couple to have a baby and finish a dissertation at the same time. Besides, I only have a couple chapters left, anyway." That wasn't exactly true. One chapter was a case study she hadn't even gathered data for yet, and the other was the conclusion, but Ivon didn't think Brigit needed to know every gory detail of her dissertating life.

"A boy? Really?"

"Is that cool with you?"

Brigit wanted a girl, dreamt of giving birth to a baby girl that looked just like her, with blue eyes and dark hair, a girl she was going to name Dierdre, in honor of some Celtic goddess that Brigit believed in, until she was diagnosed with diabetes just before leaving Iowa. Now she just couldn't see passing the disease down to her baby. If and when she had one. She'd been saving for an adoption ever since.

"Yeah, sure, I mean a baby's a baby, right?"

"I want to name him Samuel Santiago, after my dad and my grandpa."

"Oh my god, Ivon! I can't believe you're actually saying this! Am I dreaming? You really want a baby?"

"How long will an adoption take?"

Brigit had done all the research on private adoptions and gay adoptions, had even looked into county adoptions, where the county paid you to adopt a kid rather than vice versa. Those kids were messed up, emotionally, but Brigit didn't care.

"Could be months by the time we do the class and get our home visit."

"Let me call my cousin, Ximena," Ivon had said. "Maybe she can hook us up with somebody in Juárez."

"You think?"

"She's a social worker, Brigit, she works with at-risk youth. Maybe she knows some girl who wants to put up her baby for adoption."

No response.

"Brigit?"

"Is that legal?"

"Why wouldn't it be? Ximena's a social worker, that's what she does."

No response.

"How much do we have in the savings?"

"Five thousand dollars, almost."

"That should be enough."

"God, Ivon, suddenly I'm the one who's scared."

"Tell me about it."

"I mean, are you sure? Is it really that easy?"

"Women are always giving up babies in Juárez."

I'm starting to feel kinda lonely, Mapi, she could hear Samuel Santiago already, *come supervise me in the kid's section.* Mapi, a combination of Mami and Papi, because Ivon was going to be a little of each.

En martes no te cases ni te embarques. Her mom's voice wouldn't give up, kept hitting at the same weak spot that Ximena had attacked earlier, with her own barrage: *This is a lifetime commitment, Ivon. Are you sure you and Brigit are going to make it? You've settled down, right? I can't tell you how many kids I've had to place in foster homes because their parents break up and neither one of them wants the child. Don't make me regret helping you,* prima.

The night air was laced with diesel fumes. Ximena had parked across the street from the Phillips *maquila* in the Benavídez Industrial Park, and after waiting fifteen minutes, she'd gone inside to see what was keeping Cecilia. Ivon got out of the van and leaned against the hood to watch the activity outside the plant. Buses moved in and out of the gated lot, their yellow headlights beaming on the golf-course-like lawn that wrapped around the factory. The workers arriving for the midnight shift streamed out of the buses and filed into the fluorescent lights of the lobby. All women, they looked like clones. Same lipstick. Same blue smocks. Same long dark hair. Lines of other young women—the thinner ones in jeans and baby-tees, the plumper ones in skirts and loose blouses—carrying purses and plastic shopping bags, waited to board the same buses, to be shuttled back to their respective *colonias.*

Twelve years ago, Ivon had taught English as a Second Language at this same plant, and at RCA, TDK, and Sanyo. That's how she'd met Raquel, working for her brother's language institute to help pay her undergraduate tuition at UTEP. Her students were all Mexican men, all mid-management personnel who needed to communicate with their *gringo* bosses.

"*¿Quieres un* ride, *güera?*"

She hadn't paid attention to the black Suburban idling up in front of her. The driver reached his tattooed arm out and almost touched her.

"*Ven acá,*" he said. "*¿Qué vendes?*" The other men in the car hooted and called her *mamacita.*

She fixed the driver with her stare and said, "*Chinga tu madre, buey.*"

The driver slammed one hand into the other, pointing an index finger at her—the Mexican equivalent of flipping someone off. "*¡La tuya!*" he spat, and the others called her *puta* and said she should fuck her own mother. The tires squealed as the car tore off down the avenue.

"Five minutes in Juárez and you're already pissing off the natives, huh?" said Ximena, crossing the street.

"I *am* a native," said Ivon. "Asshole asked me what I was selling."

"You don't look like no native to me, homegirl, wearing shorts and leaning against the car looking all sexy in your California tan. *Te miras muy* Hollywood."

"Yeah, right. You'd think they've never seen a woman in shorts. So? Where's Cecilia?"

"Her line finished early and she punched out. The security guard said someone picked her up. Shit, we came all the way out here for nothing."

"Do you think she's okay? Maybe it's the baby. What if she went into labor?"

"I checked. She didn't go to the infirmary, just got off early. It happens."

"Now what?"

Ximena opened the door on the driver's side. "Now we go home, *ésa*."

Ivon walked around the van and climbed into the passenger's seat.

"We'll go to her house tomorrow morning," said Ximena, starting the engine. "I'll pick you up at nine. We can do breakfast over on this side. Sanborn's makes a mean plate of *huevos rancheros*."

"Shouldn't we go by her house now and make sure she's okay?"

"She lives in a *colonia* way out in Puerto Anapra. Wild horses couldn't drag me there at night, *ésa*. No roads, no electricity. Just a black hole of danger, especially for women."

Ximena's van bolted over the speed bumps in front of the factory.

Ivon buckled on her seat belt. "Got a bone to pick with you, Ximena. I didn't know about all the women being raped and killed in Juárez. Why didn't you tell me about it? I had to read about it in *Ms.* magazine. These crimes were already happening in 1996, when I was here last, and you didn't say anything about it then, either. I'm all ignorant about this shit."

"Hell, any time you come to town it's like a doctor's visit, *prima*. You're in and out the door, practically, because you're so done with this place. I didn't think it mattered to you."

Ivon sat quietly. She had to admit her cousin was right. She had abandoned her hometown, coming back only when she had to, for some family-related ritual, and leaving as soon as it was over.

"You still should've said something," Ivon insisted. "It's not even on the news."

"*Ms.* magazine, huh? Well, it's about time somebody covered these crimes. Other than those stupid little newsbytes they publish in the *El Paso Times*, nobody's interested. People think of it as Juárez news, not El Paso news, like the two cities weren't fucking Siamese twins. Leave it to white women to scoop a good story."

"Hey, they're doing us all a favor. At least somebody in this country is paying attention."

"Oops, I keep forgetting you have a *gringa* girlfriend. No offense intended, okay?"

"I just can't believe there are a hundred and six bodies, already, and it's not plastered in every newspaper in the country."

"Is that what the article said? A hundred and six? That's impressive. Somebody's doing their research. It's more like a hundred thirty-seven by now."

"A hundred and thirty-seven slaughtered women on the U.S.-Mexico border and nobody knows about it? What's that about?"

Ximena made a sharp left onto La Ribereña, the long boulevard that parallels the Río Grande and leads to the Córdoba Bridge. "And that doesn't even include the ones who've gone missing. We're talking hundreds more. And some of them—I bet you *this* wasn't in the article you read, since it's a big secret—are American girls from El Paso and Las Cruces."

"Chicanas?"

"Mostly, yeah. Same profile. Teenagers with dark skin and dark hair, slim and short, coming over to party, like all of us used to do back in the good ole days when Juárez was safe. My friend, the priest who's coming with us tomorrow, he's formed a nonprofit on this side, Contra el Silencio, it's called, and once a month, the group organizes a *rastreo* over here . . ."

"A what?"

"*Rastreo.* Means body search. They're looking for bodies."

"Isn't that a little morbid?"

"I know, but what're you gonna do? The police aren't looking for them, so it's mostly families and friends of the missing girls who go out and walk the desert. I've been out a few times, myself."

Ximena took a swig of water out of her water bottle. "Police are pissed as hell. They say we're trampling crime scenes and messing with the evidence, but the truth is, folks have taken matters into their own hands because the supposed task force they set up to investigate the murders—they're a bunch of assholes. Treat the families like shit. And a lot of the girls don't even have families here. They're called *muchachas del sur* because so many of them come from small towns and villages in the south. Their families never even find out they're missing. Or worse: dead."

Ivon shivered and rolled up her window. She didn't know what to say. Ximena lit a cigarette and Ivon watched the headlights of the few cars driving the Border Highway across the river on the El Paso side. She wanted a smoke.

"So has this Contra el Silencio found anything?"

Ximena nodded, releasing a stream of smoke against the windshield. "We're looking for the American girls, but you never know who or what you're going to find."

"Have you seen one of those bodies with your own eyes, Ximena?"

"It's not pretty, I can tell you that. Frank, I mean Father Francis, found one last summer under a pile of tires near the brick plant. Luckily, I had a house visit and didn't make it to that one. The girl's face and fingertips had gotten burnt off, but her hair was intact. She was unidentified for nearly six months until they were able to i.d. her by her teeth. She wasn't one of ours, she was from Torreón, nineteen years old, had a six-month-old kid, and she was attending a computer school after her shift at the *maquila* so she could get a better job. A sister of hers back home finally realized she was missing."

"How could her hair be intact if the rest of her face was burnt off?"

"Frank says the killers must've used a blowtorch. Also, she was raped with a garden hose. It was in her anus as well as . . ."

"Damn," said Ivon, feeling a queasiness come up in her throat.

"What we found in February, I was there for that *rastreo*," Ximena continued, shaking her head. "They weren't even bodies, just bones and clothing scattered across a radius of like 300 yards in Lomas de Poleo. People were really freaked out, let me tell you. Someone in the group found a plastic Mervyn's bag that had a trachea and a bra inside it. Someone else spotted a spinal column in some weeds, and then a skull turned up with a silver tooth in it engraved with the letter "R." We found a pelvis, another skull, another bra, a red sweatshirt that had four holes in it . . . I mean it was horrible. I myself dug up a pair of size 5 women's jeans and a black tennis shoe that still had a part of a foot inside it."

"Jesus!" Ivon shivered again.

"Yeah, it's pretty fucking dangerous around here these days. And Lomas de Poleo, where Cecilia lives, is where they found a lot of those bodies, so we'd be driving into the dragon's lair if we went there tonight."

Ximena reached over to squeeze her cousin's leg. "I know you like jousting with dragons, Sir Ivanhoe, but we're going home sweet home to polish off that bottle of Hornitos."

"Hey, I agree with that statement."

Ivon reached over and hit the button that automatically locked all the doors. Under the glare of the full moon, the street looked almost surreal. No traffic at that hour, except for the white and green buses taking the *maquiladora* workers back to their shantytowns on the outskirts of the city. Ximena shifted her headlights to high beam.

"Oh shit!" Ximena braked suddenly. The tires squealed on the asphalt, and Ivon's seat belt tightened against her neck. A bright-eyed creature stared at them in the middle of the road. Behind them, a bus blared its horn. The creature jumped. The bus swerved and drove around. They both heard the knocking of the creature's skull under the bus.

"What was that?" said Ivon.

"A jackrabbit, I think."

Ivon's mother would've said it was a sign.

5

GRANDMA MAGGIE'S RAMBLING TWO-STORY HOUSE stood almost directly under the shadow of Mount Franklin and across the street from the church of Our Lady of Guadalupe on Alabama, where Ivon, like all of her fourteen cousins, had made her first communion and attended the weddings, baptisms, and funerals of the Cunningham-Rivera-Morales-Espinosa-Villa clan. The last funeral had been two years ago, for Ximena's maternal grandmother, a gypsy fortune-teller their grandfather had met in Spain whom everyone called Grandma Maggie.

Don't mess with me, Ximena used to say when they were kids. She was the eldest and the favorite of Grandma Maggie's grandchildren. *I've got the blood of a bullfighter and a gypsy in my veins. I'll either kill you or curse you if you get in my way.*

Grandma Maggie had left her house to Ximena, who used it as a kind of halfway house for runaway teenagers during the nine months of the school year. It was her way of making a difference, Ximena said. The only permanent resident of the house was Grandma Maggie's hundred-year-old tortoise named Yerma.

Ivon padded down the driveway in her flip-flops to pick up the morning paper. The sharp sunlight glinting off the white rock of the xeriscaping sliced into her eyes. She was two shots away from a hangover. After they'd gotten back from Juárez, they'd watched *Xena* reruns until the tequila ran out and Ximena passed out on the couch. She wasn't anywhere in the house when Ivon opened her eyes that morning.

Standing on the edge of the driveway, she could see clear down to the Chamizal, a Mexican flag the size of a football field flapping in the morning breeze. She noticed that the smog hovering over the border was thicker than usual, like a heavy brown pall that stretched across the valley. Toxic fumes from ASARCO, she thought. The only time the smelter wasn't contaminating the environment was at Sun Bowl time, when it suspended operations to keep the nearby university football field clear of smog.

It was just past seven, but the heat was already so thick it shimmered off the asphalt. The next door neighbor watering her geraniums waved at her. Ivon waved back. By the time she got back in the house, her back felt like it had been ironed under her tank top.

She sat down at the kitchen table to drink her coffee—nothing but yucky Folgers in the fridge, she was going to have to find a Starbucks somewhere—and scan the headlines. Yerma ambled into the kitchen, her claws clicking on the hardwood floor, and plopped down at her feet. Ivon fed her a piece of banana with her medicine hidden inside it, as Ximena had showed her last night, and the tortoise swallowed it whole. Yerma stared up at the helium balloon that Irene had tied to the doorknob of the back door last night. *Congratulations on the New Arrival.* Her stomach felt jittery again this morning.

"You're up early, Your Highness," Ivon said, stroking Yerma's scaly head. "That stupid phone call wake you up, too?"

According to the caller i.d. display, the call had come from prison. She'd picked it up just in case it was one of her cousins needing to be bailed out. "If you accept this call, please press one," the recording said, but the prerecorded voice said something that sounded like "chimney," and Ivon didn't recognize the voice and to her knowledge didn't have any cousins named Chimney. Must be one of those runaways, she figured, and slammed the phone into the cradle.

"Hey! You just got a call from someone in prison," she called out to Ximena, but her cousin didn't answer.

Ivon burrowed her head under the pillow until her alarm rang an hour later. It didn't surprise her to find a note from Ximena on the kitchen table: *Couldn't sleep. Went home to change. Pick you up at 9 sharp.*

Ivon sipped her coffee, enjoying the sound of the church bell calling people to morning mass. The bells reminded her of that summer she lived in San Miguel de Allende with Raquel. For a minute, she allowed herself to indulge. Raquel had been accepted to the art school there, and Ivon had tagged along with her camera and visions of becoming a famous photographer. She had just finished high school, and anything was possible. She took pictures of burros on cobblestone streets, of balloon vendors in the plaza, of pigeons on the steeples of that ancient church. When she got back, she submitted them to *National Geographic*. She never got a response. She sent them to the *El Paso Times* and got a cute little rejection slip: *Trite, but thanks anyway.* That's when she decided to go to college. Clearly, she didn't have what it took to be a photographer.

She started to fold up the *Borderlands* section, when a tiny story caught her eye.

Another woman murdered in Juárez

The body of another young woman was discovered on the Mexican side of the Anapra hills near Mount Cristo Rey late Monday night. The victim was allegedly beaten and raped. She is believed to be a 15-year-old assembly plant worker who was reported missing by a family member five days ago.

The mounting body count has prompted Mexican law enforcement officials to seek the assistance of the FBI in profiling the victims. See related story on B3.

"Anyone home?"

The man's voice startled her, and she realized she'd left the front door wide open and the screen door unlatched. She glanced over at the clock on the stove. It wasn't even eight, yet.

"Hold on, let me get my husband," Ivon called out, heading for the phone.

"It's Father Francis," the man called.

"Ximena didn't tell me you made house calls."

She peered into the living room and saw a balding blonde man in jeans and a black turtleneck standing in front of the door in a pool of bright heat.

"Good morning." Father Francis spotted her. "Ivon, right?"

"Where's Ximena?"

She felt something cold crawl down the sweat on her spine when the man reached over and opened the screen door. "May I come in?"

"You know, I'd feel better if you didn't. Ximena's picking me up at nine o'clock. She didn't say anything about you stopping by."

"Shimeyna had an accident," he said, mispronouncing her cousin's name.

"What?"

"Last night, or rather this morning, on her way home she plowed into an electric pole or something, trying to avoid hitting a pedestrian. Nothing major, just a concussion and some bruises, but she won't be able to drive today."

"I passed out. I didn't even hear her leave," said Ivon.

"God protects that cousin of yours," he said, making the sign of the cross over himself. "This happened just before she got home. On Lee Treviño."

"Well, what happened? I mean, was it her fault?"

"I think she was under the influence. Did you girls do any drinking last night?"

Ivon was still standing in the doorway of the kitchen. The empty bottle of Hornitos tequila sat on the kitchen table.

"A little," she said.

"I thought so. The person was apparently an illegal, and jay-walking to boot, but since Shimeyna was under the influence, the police said she was responsible. And since it's her third offense, they impounded her car and hauled her off to jail. We're going to need to bail her out."

Ivon remembered the early morning phone call. "Oh shit! Jiminy!"

"Excuse me?" said the priest, still waiting for her to tell him he could come in.

"It's Ximena's nickname. Jiminy Cricket, that's what we used to call her when we were kids. I got a call this morning from prison but didn't know who it was. I didn't hear the name right, so I just hung up."

"That's what she said. And that's why I'm here. Mind if I come in?"

"Oh, sure, sorry. But I'm nowhere near ready to go. You want some coffee?"

"You sure your husband won't mind?" he said, winking at her as he made himself comfortable on the plaid sofa.

"Coffee's in the kitchen," Ivon said. "I'm going to jump in the shower." She had an aversion to serving men, all men, including priests, cousins, colleagues. The only man she'd ever served coffee to and warmed tortillas for, and only because her mom made her, had been her dad.

Her cell phone rang just before she stepped into the shower. "Hi, Bridge," she said into the receiver, taking the phone into the bathroom and locking the door behind her. Brigit had to tell her about the latest foibles of Harvey Milk, the cat, who always got into fights with the neighbor's cat, and how the neighbor, a self-identified member of the NRA, had come over toting his shotgun and promised to turn Harvey into dog food if he messed with his cat again.

"Sweetie," Ivon interrupted, "I really don't have time to talk right now. The priest is here, he's waiting for me to get ready so he can take me to meet the girl."

"What priest?"

"Long story. I'll call you later, okay?"

"Ivo-o-on," Brigit whined, "tell me what's going on."

Ivon summarized, leaving out the jail part. No sense getting her all riled up. Brigit was a rule follower, and that kind of information would not go down well. "Now I really have to go, okay? Love you. Wish me luck."

Ximena had laid out a stack of fresh towels for her last night, a new bar of Irish Spring soap still in its box. Ivon showered quickly, not bothering to shave her legs or blow-dry her hair. She pulled on a pair of loose linen pants, threw on a t-shirt, then changed her mind and chose her white guayabera shirt instead, stepped into her Doc Marten sandals, and she was ready to go, wet hair moussed back behind her ears. She decided to add a touch of lipstick just to defuse the looks she was bound to get from people not used to seeing a woman in a guayabera. With the three grand in her money clip tucked into her front pocket and her cell phone in hand, she walked out into the living room again.

Father Francis was reading the paper, holding a half-empty mug of coffee.

"Fifteen years old," he said, looking up at her, eyes narrowed. "She was just a child, and they gave her a job over there, cost her her life." He shook his head, opening the paper to an inside page. "This is an example of how they like to insult our intelligence. Look at this." He pointed to a headline that read *70 Deaths Unsolved in Juárez.* "Seventy deaths? The death toll is almost double that number. Who do they think they're fooling?"

"I've always said people lie to themselves in this town," Ivon said. That's one of the things that had driven her away. People like to pretend they can cover the sun with one finger, while the truth is shining all over the place. People forget things in El Paso. Someone's father can get drunk on an Easter Sunday, climb Mount Cristo Rey with a pint of rum in his pocket and a gallon of it in his liver, trip on his own drunk feet, roll down the hill and break his neck, and folks will go, *pobrecito, Samuel Villa was such a good man, he loved his family so much.* Or the relatives will look you over, from your Doc Martens to your chinos to your tank top and the tattoo of the two-headed ax splayed on the back of your neck, and say, have you gained a little weight, honey? Are you married, yet? *Denial is not a river in Egypt,* her father used to say. But nobody gets it. Nobody gets anything in El Paso. That's why Ivon had it in mind to take her little sister away from this lithium-loaded city where nothing and nobody ever changed.

"Ready to go?" Father Francis got to his feet.

"Look," Ivon said, squaring her shoulders and pinning her eyes on the priest, "all I have is three thousand, for the girl. I can get you your cut later, after I go to the bank."

"Actually, Ivon, you're going to need five hundred to bail out your cousin, and another hundred and fifty for the car. She said she'll pay you back."

"She wants me to post bail?" Ivon laughed in amazement. "She's too much!"

"That's Shimeyna for you," said the priest, walking out the screen door. "She operates on favors and debts."

"What is she? The Godfather?"

"I believe that is her favorite movie," he chuckled.

6

GRIDLOCK. The drive downtown from the bank in Chelmont should have taken no more than ten minutes, but it was still morning rush hour on Montana Street, and for a moment, Ivon felt like she was back in L.A. on Sepulveda Avenue. When had El Paso grown so much, she wondered, that even the surface streets were jammed at this hour?

The El Paso jail was located two blocks away from Ivon's favorite gay bar, the San Antonio Mining Company, which had held its ground over the last twenty years. The other gay bar, now called the New Old Plantation, popular with all the cool heterosexuals in town who liked to say they went dancing at a gay club, was just around the corner. Jail and queers—that pretty much summed up how folks in El Paso felt about Ivon's kind. Certainly summed up how her own mother felt.

Father Francis drove his Toyota twice around the block looking for a parking spot and finally pulled into a red zone in front of the fire station.

"Wait here," he said, "in case you have to move the car. I'll go get our alcoholic friend in there. Can I have the money, please?"

Ivon didn't like being told what to do, and she especially didn't like the priest passing judgment on her cousin. What did he know about Ximena's life? She dug the envelope of bills out of her pocket and nearly tossed it at him.

"Be sure to get a receipt," she said. She called home while she waited but after four rings she got the voice mail—Brigit must have already left for work. A policeman came by and rapped his knuckles on the windshield.

"Parked illegally, sir," he said, whipping out his citation book. She squinted at him. For a second, the young man in blue looked exactly like Leonardo DiCaprio. She squinted at the name on his badge. Cunningham.

"Patrick? Is that you?"

He bent over and peered into the open window. "*¿Prima?*" He smiled. "Hey, it's been years. What's up?" He punched her lightly on the shoulder. "I didn't know you were coming to the reunion this year."

Patrick was Ximena's younger brother and Ivon's sidekick when they played cowboys and Indians as kids. The last she'd heard, he was going to Border Patrol school. Or maybe it was the police academy. She got out of the car and gave him a hug.

"Sorry about calling you sir," he said sheepishly.

"Don't worry about it, I get that a lot. But look at you. Still tracking outlaws?" she teased him, punching him over his badge. "I thought you were gonna chase wetbacks."

"Nah, family gave me too much grief about it. Called me a sell-out and stuff. You look good, girl, how's life in the ivory tower?"

"Kicking my ass. Hey, did you know your sister's availing herself of the detention facilities?"

"Again?"

"You mean it's happened before?"

"Let's just say I'm not surprised. What did she do this time? Last time she was leading a picket outside of Safeway after they fired all their illegals."

"Hey, Ossifer!" Ximena yelled out from the steps of the detention center. "Are you spreading vicious lies about your big sister?"

Father Francis brought up the rear.

"How does she do it?" Ivon mumbled under her breath as she watched her cousin maneuver between the cars on Overland Street. "How does she keep her job if she's a regular here?"

"You've heard of Judge Judy and Judge Wapner, right?" Patrick muttered back. "We've got Judge Anacleto. He plays dominoes with my dad and the old guys. He expunges her record so nobody finds out, and she keeps her job."

"Hey, Jiminy," Ivon said to Ximena, smiling apologetically.

Ximena shook her head at her. "I can't believe you hung up on me, *prima*," she said, then ducked down to kiss her brother on the forehead.

"Sis," he said, blushing. "Can't keep away from Captain Baca, huh?"

"Don't tell Mom and Dad."

"Do I ever?"

"Lighten up, Paddy," she said, pinching his cheek. "We gotta go. Oh, can you get my van out of the pound?" She handed him her car keys and the receipt. "Just leave it at Grandma Maggie's. Oh, and don't forget you're on airport duty next Friday."

Patrick gave Ivon a hug and a kiss while Ximena opened the door behind the driver's side and piled into the seat. "Let's go, Frank," she said to Father Francis before pulling the door shut.

They paid the toll at the downtown bridge and headed west on La Ribereña.

"See that?" Father Francis pointed to a telephone pole painted with a black cross on a bright pink rectangle. "Each one of those crosses that you see stands for one of the murdered women. You see them all over the city, one for each dead woman and girl."

Ivon wanted to take a picture of it, but then berated herself for thinking like a tourist. Not a tourist, Ivon, said the ABD voice inside her, it's called research. She still wasn't comfortable in the skin of an academic.

Past the downtown traffic of buses and *rutera* vans, bicycles and taxis, pedestrians and barefoot Tarahumara women with babies slung on their backs in bright *rebozos*, the boulevard narrowed to a one-lane street as soon as they entered the *colonias* section of Juárez, the squatter colonies. The neighborhoods closest to the downtown area had been incorporated into the city decades ago and now they had paved streets and electric poles and running water. Here, the houses were made of cinder block, painted in exotic colors like lime green and lilac, and they had fences and iron bars at the windows, and SUVs squeezed into the tiny driveways.

Further west, directly across the border from the exotic Bhutanese buildings of the university in El Paso, the houses got shabbier and shabbier. Shacks made of wooden pallets and old tires, corrugated tin roofs. Here and there an *Abarrotes* store or a dance hall with beer logos and naked female torsos painted on the wall. They passed a junkyard of rusty, gutted cars and old red buses. A clump of trailers that Ximena said was a public school. In front and behind them, it was mostly buses and bicycles circulating up and down the unpaved streets. Some of the buses were public transportation, others had "Transporte de Personal" written on the side. One of them said "Viaje Especial" on the back.

The ASARCO smokestacks presided over the whole desolate terrain.

"We've gotten a donation of garage doors," Father Francis was saying, and Ivon realized he was speaking to her.

"Sorry, I spaced out. What about garage doors?"

"Habitat for Humanity," he said, yanking the car sideways to avoid hitting a kid trying to skateboard on the dirt road. "We use the garage doors to build houses in the *colonias*," he said. "We're always looking for volunteers."

"Give it a rest, Frank," said Ximena from the backseat.

"So what am I supposed to say to this girl?" Ivon turned around and asked her cousin.

"Don't say a thing," Father Francis said. "Shimeyna will go in first and talk to the girl and her family, and if they agree to everything, I'll take you in to meet them. Whatever you do, do not tell them you're a . . . you're a . . . you're not . . ."

"Cat got your tongue, Frank? He means don't go saying you're a dyke, or they'll never agree to let you adopt the baby," Ximena clarified. "They'll think you're a pervert or something."

"They give a shit about that? They're living in Hell's Kitchen, here, and they give a shit what I do in my private life?"

"It's not a matter of privacy," said Father Francis, "it's a matter of religion. These people are very religious, very traditional. Poverty only strengthens family values, it doesn't take them away."

Ivon bit her tongue and stared out the window.

"Okay, so I'll go in and talk to them," Ximena continued, "feel them out, massage their guilt and stuff like that. They're very humble people, but they've got their pride, you know, and this is still their decision. I don't think they're going to change their minds at this point, but it's a formality that they meet you and approve of you. You have to give the money to Frank beforehand, though. He's the one who'll take care of the money matters after you and I walk out of the house."

"Wait, they get the money before I get the baby? I don't think so."

"I guess that depends on you," said Father Francis. "Do you want the baby to be born here, in one of these hovels, with one of their so-called midwives kicking rats away from the bed, or at a clinic, where she can at least get a clean bed and a doctor?"

"You don't give them the whole fee right now," Ximena clarified again, "just enough to help them with the deposit at the clinic, the doctor's fee, that kind of thing. A thousand should do it."

"The nurse's fee," added Father Francis.

"The nurse's fee?"

"She's the most important player, here," said Father Francis, swerving into a tiny washboard lane under a sign that read *Agua para Puerto de Anapra será realidad*—Water for Puerto de Anapra will be a reality.

"She's the one who'll write the names and place the baby's footprints on our Fort Bliss certificate. Without that, we can't get the baby across the border. Think about it."

"So I'm supposed to pretend this is *my* baby, like I'm the one who had it?"

"She catches on, fast," said Father Francis sarcastically, looking into his rearview mirror. "I guess that Ph.D. comes in handy at a time like this, doesn't it?"

Ivon turned to look at Ximena. "What the hell? Why's he being so rude to me all of a sudden?"

"Shut the fuck up, Frank," said Ximena. "Don't pay any attention to him. He gets nervous, that's all. Like he hasn't done it fifty-two times already. Don't worry, we can get the whole thing legalized on the other side. The certificate is just to get the baby across the border."

Father Francis pushed the knob on the radio. It was tuned to a Juárez station.

"Over here's where they found some of the bodies," he announced as they passed a section of trash-covered dunes. "Lomas de Poleo, Pollen Hills, they call it. A couple of little boys found a human skull buried in the trash they were sorting. Police found the bodies of twelve women here and the remains of several others."

"Jesus, what a place to live," said Ivon.

"Don't blame Jesus," said Father Francis. "It's not like they have a lot of choice. They're squatters. Puerto de Anapra is one of the cheapest *colonias* in which to live."

The irony stung Ivon like a rock on the cheek. Water for Puerto de Anapra, the sign back there had said. A port without water. Not even the Rio Grande came to this godforsaken place. The sudden piercing shriek of a train whistle gave her goose bumps. On the horizon to the right, the Santa Fe rail lumbered across the desert. Just north of the border highway, beyond the tracks, she could see the white buildings and gleaming parking lots of Sunland Park Mall. The bumpy drive, the heat, and the dust were all giving her a headache.

"You okay?" Ximena asked her. "You look kinda green around the gills."

Ivon shook her head. "Didn't get enough sleep, I guess."

"Here we are," said Father Francis, pulling up in front of a flat-roofed plywood and tarpaper shack. There were people milling all around the place, men in cowboy hats, women with black shawls draped over their heads, battered pickups and cars with mismatched doors clustered in the chamiza on each side of the house.

"What's going on? They having a fiesta or something?" said Father Francis.

"It's ten in the morning, Frank," said Ximena, heaving herself out of the car. "Something's weird. I'll be right back," she said, and slammed the door.

Ivon watched her cousin meander through the crowd, shake hands with some of the men, exchange kisses with some of the women. Someone said something in her ear, and Ivon saw Ximena's shoulders go up as if the hackles had just risen on her back.

Ximena turned toward the car and for a split second, Ivon saw fear in her fearless cousin's face, then she turned back and ducked into the shack.

"You can give me the money, now," said Father Francis. "Don't let anyone see what you're doing."

Ivon counted out ten one-hundred-dollar bills. Father Francis watched her.

"You get two-fifty of this, right? What's Ximena's cut?"

She handed him the money, and he slipped it into his shirt pocket. For the first time, she noticed the scabs and scratches on the back of his hand, the calloused knuckles and nail-bitten fingers.

"I take three-fifty, actually. Two-fifty for Contra el Silencio, one hundred for the birth certificate. Ximena doesn't take anything. Angel service, she calls it."

"Is this how you make ends meet, Father?" Ivon said, pushing her money-clip back into her pocket. "I mean, this isn't something you do through your church, right? This is your own racket?"

"Ximena and I are just trying to help these young women. They can't afford another mouth to feed, they make five dollars a day in those American factories, and their food coupons don't last the week. They have to work eleven hours just to buy a box of diapers and four hours to buy a gallon of milk. Children are running around addicted to gasoline and paint by the age of five, that is, if they don't get run over by a bus or mauled by a wild dog or simply die from dysentery or malnutrition. We're just trying to help clean things up around here. Which is a lot more than some people do for their own community."

They were quiet for a moment, and Ivon had that nauseous feeling in her gut again. All those people turning to look at the car were making her nervous, but it was the animosity she was suddenly feeling from this priest that she couldn't tolerate.

"Look," she said, turning to face Father Francis and look him squarely in the eye, "I don't know why there's this friction going on right now between us. I'm sorry I'm asking really dumb questions, okay? And I'm really sorry that I haven't lived here since 1989, and that I haven't been back since 1996, and that I don't know shit. Okay, that's been established. What I need is to be brought up to speed on what's going on. Can you, like, not give me a hard time, please? This adoption thing is very scary for me."

Father Francis raised both hands as if to surrender in an argument she didn't even know they were having. "Ximena's right. I always get panicky when we do these things and I can be an asshole when I panic. Sorry." He pounded his chest once. "Mea culpa."

Ivon didn't realize how upset she was until she saw her hands shaking. "So tell me about your organization," she changed the subject. "Ximena didn't say much about it."

"These adoptions are Ximena's thing. I help her out because she gets me donations for Contra el Silencio . . . you know, one hand washes the other . . . but we're basically a nonprofit. Other than advocate for the missing girls, we also picket the courthouse and the offices of the *Times* and the *Herald Post*, protesting the silence of the authorities and the media on these murders."

"I don't get it," said Ivon. "Why the silence? You'd think this was big news. If only to sell more papers. People love the morbid stuff. Especially when it makes Mexico look bad."

"You really don't know what's going on in your own backyard, do you?"

He reached into the glove compartment and took out a pack of Winstons, offering one to Ivon. She declined. He lit one for himself and threw the pack on the dashboard.

"The victims," he said, smoke billowing out of his nose and mouth, "the lost ones. Not all of them have been *maquila* workers from Juárez. There are four girls from El Paso that we know of . . . they disappeared in 1996 . . . two women from Las Cruces and another woman who was a journalist from Holland . . . she was investigating the crimes on her own. Well, guess who just recently went missing? The Las Cruces women—they were sisters, by the way, supposedly involved in narco-trafficking—were found shot to death wearing house slippers and robes, their bodies dumped at the racetrack out by San Agustín. A few months later, the Border Patrol found the raped and beaten body of one of the El Paso girls, a sixteen-year-old sophomore at El Paso High School, on the riverbank by the black bridge near ASARCO. And two months later Contra el Silencio found another girl buried under a pile of tires near the brick plant. Did Shimeyna tell you about that?"

"Yes," said Ivon, swallowing hard, "she told me about the bones, too."

He took three quick puffs off the cigarette. "Did she tell you about how the other bodies that turned up in these hills here in Lomas de Poleo had the right breast sliced off and the nipple of the left breast mangled or bitten off?"

"I get the picture, okay?"

Father Francis threw the cigarette butt out the window. "The rest of our girls haven't turned up, and nobody's looking for them . . . officially, I mean. The FBI has no evidence of malfeasance, they say. They can't get involved without evidence. Girls ran off with their boyfriends—that's the line of the judicial police over here. The activist groups that run *rastreos* on this side are only looking for the Juárez girls. That's why I started Contra el Silencio, for the friends and relatives of the American girls. But the media, or rather, the mayor, doesn't want people in El Paso to know what's really going on. So once in a while, I get these little threatening phone calls about minding my own business. Goes with the territory, I guess."

"Here she comes." Ivon watched Ximena as she extricated herself from the crowd in front of the house and made for the car. In one hand she was clutching a crumpled piece of paper. Her face looked white as chalk. She got into the car, breathing hard, as if she'd just run a few blocks.

Ivon and Father Francis both turned to look at her.

"Well? What happened?" asked Father Francis.

"You okay?" said Ivon.

Ximena stared straight ahead, eyes watery, chin trembling. "She's dead, you all. Cecilia's dead."

Ivon felt her face grow cold. "What?"

"She didn't come home from her shift last night, and some guy on horseback found her body inside an abandoned car out by the airport this morning. Stabbed to death and with a rope around her neck, like she was dragged. Still wearing her smock and her nametag."

"I thought you were picking her up," said Father Francis.

"We went to the factory, Frank, we were there before midnight, but she'd left. She punched out early and the security guard told me someone gave her a ride."

Father Francis pressed his hand over his mouth.

"Sick fucks," said Ximena, suddenly. "Sick fucks running loose in this city." She slammed her hands against the back of Ivon's seat, and started to weep. "Son of a bitch! Frank, if I'd picked her up earlier . . ."

"Shimeyna, you couldn't have known."

"And . . . and the baby?" Ivon felt as if a vice were squeezing her chest.

Ximena covered her face with her hands and wept.

Ivon felt the breath drain out of her lungs.

"What animals!" said Father Francis, opening his door.

"Where are you going, Frank?" said Ximena.

"Don't they need a priest in there?"

"They're at the morgue. Cecilia's grandmother and her aunt. The police took them to identify the body."

"By themselves?" said Father Francis, turning on the ignition. "Two women alone in a police car in Juárez?" He floored the gas pedal and the tires spun a cloud of dust around the car.

"They wouldn't try anything, not with all the witnesses that saw them leaving," said Ximena. "Say a prayer for her, Frank, while you drive. Say it out loud, please."

"Dear Father," Father Frank intoned, after making the sign of the cross over his face, "we ask you to bless the ravaged body of our friend Cecilia and the innocent soul of her unborn child. Take them unto your bosom and comfort them, and may they rest now, forever, in the valley of your perfect love."

Ivon felt the tears spill down her face. "We have to find out who picked her up last night," she said. Something was cutting into her vocal chords, and she knew it was the voice of the little boy—*Mapi*, he kept calling her, *I'm starting to feel kinda lonely.* "I want to go talk to that security guard. I want to know what he saw."

Father Francis looked at her and rolled his eyes. "You think he's going to tell you anything? He's probably in on it. For all we know, he's the killer."

A traffic jam had formed on the main road. The boy on the skateboard they had passed earlier was sitting in the middle of the road hugging the skateboard to his chest. Cars had pulled over willy-nilly, and a line of buses stretched up the hill that led out of Puerto de Anapra.

Father Francis rolled down his window and called out to a group of girls.

"*¿Qué pasa?*"

"The bus hit that boy," said one of the girls.

"Is he hurt?"

"*No le pasó nada al buey,*" said another girl. "He's always riding that *chingadera* in front of the buses." The girl pointed at her temple. "*Le faltan canicas, es un baboso.*"

"Father, why have you forsaken us?" Father Francis muttered as he cranked up his window and turned the air-conditioning to full blast.

Someone tapped on the windshield and startled Ivon. It was a boy on a bicycle holding up four old Barbie dolls with singed hair and high-heeled shoes, their shiny dresses cut high on the hip and low on the cleavage.

"*Maqui-Locas,*" the boy said, flashing a gap-toothed smile at them. "*Muy cheap!*"

[handwritten annotation] → of us, themselves, 'cheap' — pennies/coins

7

OUTSIDE THE CITY MORGUE, a protest was in progress. A group of about fifty women in black, holding posters that read ¡Ni Una Más! No More Assassinations and Stop the Violence against the Women of Juárez, End Impunity, stood in a line in front of the building. People in the crowd carried bright pink signs with black crosses painted in the middle and pictures of young girls inside each cross. Television crews were out with their cameras and reporters. Police cars had gathered in the parking lot. A stream of black smoke issued from the chimney of the morgue. The hot morning air stank of turpentine and cinder.

A policeman came up to the car as Father Francis pulled into the parking lot.

"Váyanse, no hay servicio."

"¿Hay paro de trabajo?" asked the priest. Ivon realized he spoke with a Castilian accent.

"Estas viejas escandalosas," the policeman gestured at the protestors over his shoulder. "It's not a strike, it's these crazy women wanting attention, that's all." He spit at the ground.

"We're here to be with the family of the girl they found this morning," said Ximena. The policeman shook his head again. "No se puede pasar. No dejan pasar a nadie, las cabronas. Esa familia estuvo aquí hace rato, pero ya se fueron."

"What did he say? He talks too fast," said the priest.

"He says they won't let anybody pass," Ivon translated. "He says a family was here earlier but that they're gone."

44

"*¿Por qué hay tanto humo?*" asked the priest. "*¿Queman los cuerpos?*"

"No, they're not burning the bodies," the policeman said. "It's the clothes. They had it all piled up in the patio, and it got infested with rats."

Ivon translated again for Father Francis.

"But that's evidence," said Ximena.

The policeman ducked down to peer into the backseat of the car. He took off his sunglasses and narrowed his eyes at Ximena. "Evidence of what, señora?"

"*Gracias, venga,*" said Father Francis, shifting the transmission into reverse.

"Watch it, Frank!" Ximena cried out.

A redheaded woman with a microphone and a bearded man toting a video camera had suddenly scampered up behind the car.

"*¡Me lleva la chingada!*" the policeman cursed, and walked away.

"Excuse me," the redheaded woman called out in English, waving at Father Francis. "Excuse me." The woman stepped up to the window on Ivon's side. Her freckled face was flushed a bright orange. "Good morning, my name is Rubí Reyna. I'm the cohost of the show *Mujeres Sin Fronteras* on Channel 33." She spoke flawless English in kilometric speed. She smiled, and Ivon was surprised to see that she wore clear plastic braces over bleach-white teeth.

"You're the Contra el Silencio group, aren't you?" Rubí continued. "One of the protestors pointed you out."

"They are," said Ivon.

Through the windshield, she was watching the police harass the women in the line.

"What can we do for you, Mrs. Reyna?" said Father Francis. "We're in a hurry."

"Please," she smiled again, "call me Rubí." She took a pink business card out of her purse and handed it to Ivon.

Ivon passed the card on to Father Francis.

Mujeres Sin Fronteras

*Where women have no borders, no boundaries,
and no checkpoints.*

Lic. Rubí Reyna and Sra. Clara Apodaca,
Executive Producers

Walter Luna,
Director of Photography

Channel 33
Cd. Juárez, Chihuahua

"We're doing a special series on the murders," Rubí said, her jade-green eyes sparkling. "I've just finished a segment on the forensic examiner . . ." She touched her hand to her heart. "My respects to that woman. That one airs Friday morning, along with some footage from this protest here. On Monday we're doing a point/counterpoint discussion with Dorinda Sáenz and Julia Del Río, followed by an insider's look at a *rastreo*. Don't you think that's a tremendous idea? I think it'll be very informative for our audience, not to mention boosting our ratings, but none of the groups here will let me film their searches. *Voces* won't even return my calls, and the segment's airing on Monday."

Finally, she took a breath, smiled, and continued. "I was hoping I could persuade you to let us, my husband and me, attend your next walk and talk to some of your people on camera. I believe you have a search scheduled this Sunday. *¿No es cierto?*"

"How are you going to get the special prosecutor and the founder of CARIDAD in the same room together?" asked Ximena. "They hate each other's guts."

"Donations," said Rubí. "Is there any other way? If you don't get a chance to see tomorrow's show, I'd be happy to send you a copy of the tape."

"I'd like to see that," said Ivon right away.

"She's a professor," Ximena offered. "She teaches Women's Studies in Los Angeles."

"Is that right?" Rubí's eyes widened a little. "I should interview you."

"We can't have a whole crew following us around, Mrs. Reyna," Father Francis said. "It would be too disruptive. And we'd have to get everybody's permission to let you do any filming. Some of our members will refuse, I can tell you that right now."

"A crew?" Rubí gave a tight little laugh, and the bright desert light reflected off her braces. "Don't I wish, Father. I have a coproducer, Clara Apodaca, and my husband Walter Luna, here . . ." She looked at the cameraman and he waved at them. "Walter volunteers to film all of our footage on his days off, and we have one camera guy at the station. That's the entire crew of *Mujeres Sin Fronteras*. It's called the probono budget, which is all we get on Channel 33. And don't worry about the permission thing, either. I have release forms for everybody who wants to appear on the segment, and only those who sign the forms will be filmed. I'm a professional, Father. I have a journalism degree from la UTEP."

"I'll talk to the group," said Father Francis, handing Rubí's card back to Ivon. Ivon tucked the card into her shirt pocket. "If they agree, I'll call you."

Rubí's hand rested on the open window. Ivon noted the manicured nails, painted a pearl white, the diamond tennis bracelet and diamond-studded wedding band. "I was wondering, *padre*, if you could use a bus to transport your people back and forth across the border?"

"A bus?" said Ivon. She glanced back at Ximena, who arched her eyebrows.

"My father owns Transportes Reyna del Norte. He just changed the model of his buses, you see, and he's got a few of the old ones he's going to donate to the Maquiladora Assocation. There's nothing wrong with them, they're just the old model. I was thinking I could ask him to donate one to your organization in exchange for letting us attend your *rastreo*."

"Not a bad exchange rate, Frank," said Ximena.

Father Francis cleared his throat. "Well, sure, we could use a bus. Folks would rather not drive their cars across if they didn't have to. But I still have to ask the members, Mrs. Reyna. I really can't make that decision on my own."

"Do you know what happened to the girl they found this morning?" Ximena asked. "She was a friend of ours."

"The pregnant girl?" Rubí pressed her lips together. "Poor child. They . . ." she covered her mouth with her hand and looked like she was about to cry, ". . . they violated her as much as they could, and they stabbed her in the belly so many times, they almost sliced through the baby's neck."

"Dear God, what inhumanity!" Father Francis said, crossing himself.

Ivon felt the bile coming up in her throat. "Did you see her?" she managed to ask.

Rubí shook her head and wiped the corners of her eyes with a tissue.

"No, I came to interview the medical examiner for the show. . . . She didn't want to do it live at the station, so we had to prerecord it. She's working on the girl's body right now."

"Can we see her?" asked Ivon.

Rubí frowned a little, not sure what to make of Ivon's request.

"Ivon was going to adopt her baby," Ximena explained.

"¡Ay, qué triste! ¡Qué pena!" Rubí said, the jade green of her eyes misting over. She squeezed Ivon's shoulder. "They killed your child, too, then," she added.

Ivon hadn't thought about that.

"I can get you in there, if you really want to see her. But they're doing the autopsy. Do you think you can handle seeing an autopsy, or do you want to wait?"

"I can handle it," said Ivon, getting out of the car. Ximena got out, too.

"Park over there," Rubí told Father Francis, pointing to a black Jaguar, "behind my car."

They waited for Father Francis to pull his battered blue Toyota into the lot.

"Are they really burning the clothes in there?" Ximena asked.

Standing between them, Rubí lowered her voice. "The official story is that the School of Medicine next door was complaining about the smell, and that's why the mayor ordered the clothes to be burned. But the medical examiner told me that they found traces of a virus on the clothes."

"What kind of virus?" asked Ivon.

"God knows, but they say it's deadly, so they had to burn the clothing."

"What kind of virus lives on clothing?" Ivon couldn't let it go. Maybe it was an outbreak of the plague they'd had in New Mexico a couple of years ago. What was it called? Hantavirus?

"Who knows?" Rubí shrugged. "They make up a lot of lies around here."

Father Francis caught up to them, carrying a black satchel. He raised his right arm and blessed the line of protestors. The line separated to let them pass. Over the door of the morgue it said *Amphitheater*. Mexican sense of humor, Ivon thought. The smell of turpentine and burning cloth wafted through the smoky foyer.

"*Mire, señorita*," Rubí explained to the receptionist, "these women are the victim's cousins from El Paso, and this is her priest. They need to see the body."

"Please sign the register," the young woman said. She waited for the three of them to write in their information, then gave them each a visitor's tag and a nose mask.

"*¿Huele muy feo, eh?*" the receptionist warned, "*el cuerpo ya se estaba descomponiendo, así que usen sus mascaritas.*"

"What did she say?" asked Father Francis.

"The body was decomposing already, Frank," Ximena said. "Use your mask."

"Dear Lord."

They followed Rubí Reyna past the small reception area and down a dark hallway that ended in a grey steel door. Ivon felt her heart hammering. She had never been in a morgue before. She held her mask tightly over her nose and mouth as they entered.

"God it stinks," murmured Ximena.

An older woman in a white lab coat and two assistants in bloodstained scrub suits looked up from the corpse they were working on. The woman was clearly displeased by the intrusion until she saw Rubí Reyna.

"You're back already?" she said.

"This is the Contra el Silencio group," said Rubí. "They knew the girl."

The doctor lowered her eyes. "*Lo siento*," she said, and went back to work.

Behind them, bottles of chemicals and broken skulls lined the rusty metal shelves. Bones were heaped inside plastic trash bags on the floor.

"The medical examiner's name is Norma Flores," explained Rubí in a whisper. "We went to high school together a thousand years ago. Salvador Peñasco and Laura Godoy are interns from the School of Medicine. Junior, I mean Salvador, and my husband play golf together. *¡Ay, qué tonta!* I should've brought Walter in here to film the autopsy."

Ivon couldn't move. She was standing less than five feet away from the body of the girl who was going to be the mother of her child. Her head was turned sideways, facing Ivon, the eyes a milky red, the mouth wide open. The body was marbled green and yellow, the skin loose, the hands curled inward, toes pointed. Dark rope burns on her neck. The thick flaps of the torso were folded back, but it was easy to make out the puncture wounds, one, two, three . . . Ivon counted seventeen black gashes—vertical, horizontal, perpendicular, diagonal, she'd been stabbed by more than one person, clearly—between the pink and yellow tissue on the inside.

Ivon closed her eyes for a moment, not permitting herself to dwell on the number of wounds, forcing the little boy's voice out of her head. When she opened her eyes again the girl's head had been turned in the other direction.

"Why is the skin green?" Rubí asked. "Is that a normal color for a dead body?"

"It's a normal color for a body that's been inside a closed car in forty-centigrade heat for more than eight hours," the medical examiner explained. She was separating the long black strands of Cecilia's hair while the interns lifted the organs out of her torso and laid them on a butcher block at the end of the table. "We're lucky the head didn't explode."

The head flopped in Ivon's direction again. The medical examiner pulled a roll of duct tape out of one of her pockets, stretched out a long piece, and cut it with her teeth.

"What's the tape for?" Rubí continued.

"Since the neck was broken, we have to tape the head down or we can't work on it." She straightened the head, ran the middle of the tape across the forehead, and tucked the two ends under the edges of the table.

"Junior," the medical examiner called out to the male intern.

Ivon stared at his large, sinewy hands as he wriggled them into a fresh pair of gloves, thick veins bulging through the latex. He tied on his green scrub mask and went to stand beside the examiner.

"This is the cutting line. You want to remove the hair at the top of the head here, just pull it off the scalp like this. It comes right off."

She tossed a thick clump of hair into the metal barrel that served as a trash can.

"And then make your incision from ear to ear and pull the scalp down. Be careful when you cut the skull. The brain might be liquefied already."

Ivon pinched her nostrils to keep from heaving.

"You okay?" Ximena said in her ear.

Ivon nodded, trying to convince herself that she was just watching an operation on television. She'd seen brain surgery and open-heart surgery and bone marrow transplants. As long as she didn't let herself smell anything, as long as she didn't dwell on the fact of the baby, she could stand it. She wasn't expecting the intern to use a hacksaw to cut the scalp.

Father Francis had removed a white stole, a Bible, and a vial of holy water from his satchel and started his blessing ritual. The medical examiner frowned for a second, made eye contact with Rubí, and rolled her eyes slightly.

"*Doctora* Flores," called the other intern. "Can you look at this, please?"

The doctor went to look over her shoulder.

"I think these are gallstones," said Laura Godoy. From the mass of organs she was cutting apart and weighing—lungs and heart and liver—a handful of small black rocks rolled onto the butcher block.

"That explains all the yellow discoloration on the skin," said the doctor. "She probably had jaundice. *Pobre muchacha*, at her age. Probably never even knew she had it."

"Are they real rocks?" asked Ximena.

"Put on a glove. You can touch one if you want."

Ximena snapped on a latex glove and felt one of the gallstones. "How can the body make rocks?" She held it out to Ivon. "You should feel this."

Rubí Reyna covered her mouth and rushed out of the room.

"She must've been in a lot of pain," added the doctor.

Ivon turned her attention back to the head. She couldn't think about Cecilia's pain. The jagged screech of saw-tooth on bone had stopped. She heard a sucking sound as Junior pulled off the skull-cap. She watched him peel back a layer of what looked like wax paper to reveal a gray-green brain inside.

"The brain is mush," said Junior.

"Use this," the medical examiner instructed, handing him a regular soup spoon.

With a scalpel, he loosened the brain from the skull, scooping it out in pieces with the spoon. He placed the pieces in a metal dish and handed the dish to Laura Godoy to weigh on the balance.

Ivon walked over to the medical examiner, and asked, "Where's the baby?"

Norma Flores was collecting the gallstones in a plastic cup. In another plastic cup, Ivon noticed something that looked like coins: blackened, corroded coins mixed with pennies.

"What?" said the medical examiner.

"The baby? Where is it?"

The medical examiner shook her head. "Nearly destroyed. We autopsied it already."

"Was it a boy or a girl?"

The doctor glanced at Ximena.

"She was going to adopt it," Ximena explained.

"*Inocente criatura.*" The doctor yanked off a glove. "It was a boy, a really little thing, not even three kilos, but he was perfect, ten toes, ten fingers, a head full of hair."

Samuel Santiago, she thought, feeling her chest flutter. The name of her father and grandfather, her son's name, her son who was going to call her Mapi.

"How much is that in pounds?"

"Tiny," said the doctor, pulling off the other glove, "about six pounds."

"Was he cut up really bad?"

"*¡Bestialmente!*" the medical examiner hissed. "Butchered, like an animal. Luckily, he had the umbilical cord wrapped around his neck, or else all the sharp force trauma would have cut off his little head completely."

I'm starting to feel kinda lonely, Mapi.

Ivon felt herself grow clammy. She realized the room had started to spin.

"Dust to dust," she heard Father Francis saying, but the gaping hole in Cecilia's head was filling with stones. Her toes and fingers were uncurling.

8

THE FIRST THING SHE NOTICED WAS SMOKE, and, for a moment, she was afraid they were still inside the morgue surrounded by the smoke of the burning clothes. She knew she had lost it in there, but couldn't remember anything else. But then she felt movement, felt a swath of sun on her face. She opened her eyes and saw she was lying down in the back of the priest's car. Through the windows she could see sky and telephone poles, an occasional tree. She sat up, feeling hungover.

"She's alive," said Ximena. Both she and the priest were smoking.

"How are you feeling?" asked Father Francis.

"Couldn't be better," said Ivon, becoming aware suddenly of the pain over her left eye. She touched her forehead and felt a lump there. "Ouch!"

"Scared the shit out of me, *prima*," said Ximena. "Thought you'd had a stroke and died, the way you just dropped to the floor. Hit your head on the edge of the autopsy table when you fell. Nearly brought the organs down on top of you."

"That's not funny, Ximena."

"Doctor said you probably gave yourself a concussion. Said we should take you to the hospital to check you out."

"I'm not going to any hospital," said Ivon. "I'm fine." Under the smoke she could smell something else. She sniffed at her armpit and realized the odor of the dead body was in her shirt. She caught a deep whiff of it and nearly gagged. "Fuck, I stink. I need to take this shirt off."

"We all stink," said Ximena. "Don't worry about it."

"I don't want to smell it on me all day."

54

"We're taking you to your mom's house, okay? You can hang out there, take a shower, change your clothes, and I'll pick you up later tonight for Plan B."

"What're you talking about, Ximena? I want to find out who did that to Cecilia. I want to go talk to that security guard at the factory. He must've seen who picked her up."

"I have an afternoon mass," said Father Francis. "We have to get back."

"Can you drop me off? Where are we now?" Ivon looked out and tried to orient herself. Juárez had grown so much, it was hard to know where she was anymore. But then she saw the Río Grande and the Franklin mountain range to her right and realized they were on La Ribereña again, heading west, past the Chamizal.

"Wait," she said, "isn't the Córdoba Bridge behind us?"

"Frank takes the downtown bridge," Ximena said, throwing her cigarette butt out the window. "It's just around the corner from the church. Frank thinks it takes less time to get across, even though . . . ," she raised her voice at Father Francis, ". . . Juárez Avenue is under construction and it actually takes *longer* to get across than it would to drive from the free bridge to downtown."

"I'm going to rent a car," said Ivon. "I need my own wheels."

"Look, *prima*, I know you want to find out what happened and all, but trust me, that's a dead-end street. And I do use the pun on purpose. It's dangerous. Nobody knows anything. Nobody will tell you anything. There's no use in you going around asking questions. You'll just get yourself into a mess of trouble, and that's not what you're here for. Let's stay focused, okay? You're here to adopt a kid. Now, I have a plan B, but I have to work a few things out first . . ."

"Can you really be that callous?" Ivon interrupted. "I mean, you knew Cecilia. You know her family, she just got slaughtered. Don't you give a shit?"

"It's not about giving a shit or not. Of course, I give a shit! It's just that I live here, okay? I know what kind of sick fucks we're dealing with and I know you don't want to be involved in any of it. We don't want to mess with those fucks. I know it hurts, and I know you're pissed . . . we're all fucking pissed."

Ximena's face had grown red and the veins were starting to show on her neck.

"Calm down, Shimeyna," Father Francis said.

"I know." She reached out for the pack of Marlboros on the dashboard.

"Give me one," said Ivon. She'd been on the tobacco wagon for over a year, but right now, she was pissed off and she needed a smoke. Ximena handed her the car lighter. She coughed on the first pull.

They were approaching downtown Juárez now, and the bridge loomed like a concrete hill in front of them. She could see a line of people crossing the bridge on foot. She remembered doing that as a teenager, walking over to hang out on Juárez Avenue, at bars like the Kentucky Club and Faustos, clubs like El Noa-Noa—none of them carded, and the drinks were cheap. For ten bucks, you could get wasted and still have some money left over for one of Fred's famous *tortas*, ham and avocado sandwiches on Mexican bread, laced with jalapeños and slathered with mayonnaise. She couldn't believe she was thinking about food after what she'd just seen.

"We're in luck," said Father Francis, "it's a short line. Who has a quarter?"

Ximena rooted around in her purse and pulled out a crumpled piece of paper. The paper crackled as she unfolded it. "Shit, you all, look at this!" She held it up. It looked like a newsletter of some kind, with three columns and a photograph in the middle.

"What's that?" said Father Francis.

"Cecilia's cousin gave it to me this morning. I forgot all about it. She said Cecilia had found it on her machine last Friday when she came back from her lunch break. The grandmother showed it to the police, but the police blew it off, said it was probably a prank someone was playing on her at the factory."

"Let me see," said Ivon. The blue ink was runny and blotched, so the writing was almost illegible, and the face in the picture looked more like a mimeographed skeleton than a person, but part of the title was clear: *ichy's Diary. Volume 3, No. 1.* The year was blurry, but the logo under the title was very clear. A pentagram inside a circle.

Ivon took the sheet and held it up against the window. There was some writing under the picture, but the only word she could make out was *trematode*. At the bottom of the page, as the fifth numbered item in a list titled "Look What's Inside," the handwritten message You're Next!, the words inscribed in inverted crucifixes. Along the bottom left edge of the paper, in tiny typescript that was surprisingly clear, part of a web address: *http://www.exxxtremelylucky—*

"It's in English," said Ivon. "And there's a web site, too, extremely lucky something, with a triple x."

"It's pornography, Frank!" said Ximena, striking the priest's arm.

"Trematode. What's a trematode?" said Ivon.

"Give me that!" Father Francis turned around in his seat and snatched the page out of Ivon's hands. "Where's it say trematode?"

"Right there, under the picture."

"Dear Lord." He wiped the sweat off his upper lip with the back of his wrist.

"What is it, Frank?"

The car behind them was laying on its horn for them to take their turn at the toll booth.

"Richy's Diary," he said, filling in the missing letter in the title.

"Who's Richy?" Ivon and Ximena asked at the same time.

Ivon watched the priest's Adam's apple move up and down under his black collar.

"Pay the toll," he said.

Ximena handed the quarter to the attendant, and they drove up the slope. At the top of the bridge, sitting between the two flags, was one of Ivon's favorite views of downtown El Paso: tall bank buildings against the slate gray mountains and a bluebonnet sky. She loved this place. She hated this place. Always, the same contradictions.

Suddenly a man's face appeared in the window on Ximena's side, and all three of them gasped. A man in a wheelchair selling Mexican lottery tickets.

"Fuck off!" said Ximena. The man shrugged and rolled himself to the next car. "Well, Frank? What's the story?"

"He's the only person I've ever heard use this word," Father

Francis said softly. "I was there. I heard him when he said it. I was at his trials."

"Who the fuck are you talking about, Frank?"

"Richard Ramírez," he said. "Hence, Richy's Diary."

"The Night Stalker?" said Ivon.

Father Francis nodded. "Precisely. El Paso's most infamous native son."

"Isn't he dead?" said Ximena, taking the page back.

"He was sentenced to death row, but I don't think they've executed him, yet. I heard he was getting married to some woman from Los Angeles a couple of years ago."

"How come you know so much about this guy, Frank?"

"They gave him nineteen life sentences," he continued as though he hadn't heard Ximena's question. "One for each murder he committed. The year of the trials was my first year in El Paso. I ministered to him in prison."

"You're shitting me, Frank."

"It's true. His family was part of our congregation. They asked me to go with them to Los Angeles and talk to him, hear his confession, and forgive his sins."

"Frank! I can't believe you never told me this."

"The Night Stalker has a newsletter?" Ivon asked.

"Probably has his own web site, too. Anything is possible on the Internet these days," said Father Francis. "For all we know, he could have computer access in San Quentin."

"Why would somebody be using his picture for a porn site?" Ivon persisted.

"Richy loved three things: cocaine, Satanism, and pornography."

"Oh my god, Frank, you just made all the hair on my head stand on end."

They pulled up to the customs booth and the three of them chorused: "U.S."

"Bringing anything back from Mexico?" the INS officer asked, grimacing as though he had just smelled something foul.

"Not a thing, sir," said Father Francis.

Just evidence of a murder, Ivon thought.

9

THE AQUA-BLUE ALUMINUM SIDING on her mom's house looked more weathered than usual. The house itself seemed to have shrunk since the last time Ivon had visited two years ago—she hadn't even come home for Christmas. But the garden looked lush, as always, an oasis of green lawn in the middle of the desert, daisy and geranium beds, an arch of red and yellow roses framing the small front porch. The shrine to Our Lady of Guadalupe her dad had constructed in the yard when Ivon had turned fifteen was festooned with a shiny Christmas garland. She spotted her mom in her red bandanna, hunched down by the honeysuckle bush on the side of the house.

"I have a couple of long meetings back to back, but I can pick you up around six," Ximena said, as Father Francis pulled his car up in front of the chain-link fence. "Seven at the latest."

"It's okay, I'm just going to stay a little while and then I'll get Irene to drop me off at Grandma Maggie's. I really need a shower and a nap."

Her mom had gotten to her feet and was staring at Father Francis' car, shielding her eyes with a gloved hand.

"Okay, see you at Grandma's place later. I'll know by then if we can see this other girl tonight," Ximena said.

"I mean it, Ximena," said Ivon, "I can't even think about this adoption thing right now. I'm going to find out what happened to Cecilia, with or without your help."

"She's right, Shimeyna," Father Francis said. "We have to do something about Cecilia. At the very least we should make time to be with the family."

Ximena shook her head. "You know my policy on this, Frank. I stay out of it to protect my family, and you know that."

Ivon opened her door and stepped out of the car.

"Don't tell Tía it's me," Ximena called out. "I can't talk to her right now. Floor it, Frank!" The car sped off with a squeal, leaving Ivon blinking on the sidewalk.

"Ivon?" her mom called out, hurrying to the gate, slipping off her gloves. "*M'ijita*, is that you? *Ay Dios mío*, I can't believe you're standing there, *como si nada*. When did you get here?"

Her mom squeezed her between her arms, and Ivon squeezed back, tighter than usual. She held her breath to keep from crying as her mom kissed her face and fussed about how skinny she looked.

"You don't smell so good, honey," her mom said, wrinkling her sunburned nose and making what Irene called her *fuchi*-face. "But you look just like your dad in that shirt." She sniffled, wiping at the corners of her shiny green eyes with a lace-edged hankie she took from her apron. "So handsome. And with your hair like that, it's almost a spitting image of your dad when we were first together."

"But *he* wouldn't have liked it, would he, Ma?" Ivon couldn't resist goading her. "Or did you forget that Dad was always getting on my case about the clothes I wore and how I looked more like a *joto* than a girl."

"Don't talk badly about your father, *m'ijita, que en paz descanse*. Why don't you bury all that resentment? He's not around to defend himself, anymore."

"You're right, Ma, I'm sorry. I don't know why I said that. I guess I'm just really tense right now. How are you? What're you doing crawling around in the bushes?"

"I was making lunch and I saw this gopher run across the yard. That's what's making these huge tunnels under my lawn. *Mira nomás*. I'm putting poison in all the holes. Who was that who dropped you off, *m'ijita*?"

"Just some friends. What's for lunch?"

Her mom put her arm around Ivon's waist as they walked to the porch. "It's so strange, you know. Your sister asked me to make *albóndigas* today, as if she knew you were coming."

"My favorite," said Ivon, kissing her mom on the cheek.

"Where's your luggage? Don't tell me you left it in your friends' car?"

"It's at Grandma Maggie's, Ma. Don't get mad, okay? I stayed there last night because of something I had to do with Ximena today. But that's over, so here I am."

Her mom narrowed her eyes at her. Ivon could tell she was seeing right through her. "*Pues sí,*" she said, "I guess it must be more important than your own family, whatever you had to do with Ximena. We haven't seen you in two years, but . . ."

"Where's Irene?" Ivon interrupted, awkwardly.

"At work, *m'ijita.* Where else? She'll be home for lunch. How long are you staying?"

"Let's go inside, Ma, I have to talk to you about something that *is* very important, actually, and it *is* my own family."

"Go on in," her mom said, making her *Juchi*-face again. "Wash up. I don't know if it's you or something out here, *pero algo huele podrido*, like something's rotting, and you smell like cigarette smoke, too. When I talked to Brigit on Mother's Day, she said you had stopped smoking. I hope you haven't taken up that nasty habit again, *m'ijita*, look what it's doing to your grandfather. I'll be in as soon as I finish with this poison. If you want, make the lemonade or warm the tortillas."

She was upset, no doubt about it, but Ivon felt too weak and tired to take her on. Her mother's house always smelled like cilantro and beans and floor wax. The living room was bright with the early afternoon sun, but the dining room and kitchen at the back of the house were cool and shady. Two places had been set at the kitchen table. A *molcajete* brimming with freshly made *pico de gallo* sat next to a vase of daisies. Two pots boiled on the stove, one with beans, the other with her mom's famous meatball and zucchini stew. A stack of her mom's flour tortillas waited to be warmed on the *comal*. On the counter by the sink, a handful of lime wedges sat next to a metal lime squeezer, a jar of white sugar, and the same round pebbly pitcher her mom had been using since Ivon was in grade school. She looked out the window at the backyard and spotted Samson, their old German Shepherd, sleeping in his usual place under the pomegranate bush. Ivon took comfort in all of it.

She was home, in her mother's kitchen, where order and cleanliness reigned, where the next thing to be done had already been laid out, the steps clearly indicated—warm the tortillas, make the lemonade, sit down to eat lunch. This is how she'd grown up, her uniform laid out on the chair before she went to bed, shoes polished by her dad, book satchel waiting by the front door, the cereal bowls and the cereal set out on the table the night before. This is how she liked to live her own life, now that there was no Ma to defy, now that she didn't have to prove how independent she was by going against her mother's grain at every opportunity. She washed her hands in the immaculate white sink—the faint smell of bleach still emanating out of the porcelain—and started to juice the limes.

I should call Brigit, she thought, but couldn't bring herself to explain anything just yet. She couldn't handle Brigit's disappointment on top of her own.

"So what's going on, *m'ijita?*" her mom said behind her. Ivon hadn't even heard her come in. Her mom had a feline quality about the way she moved around the house—neither Ivon nor Irene could ever tell when she was nearby.

"Why didn't you let me know you were coming? You in trouble or something? Did you and Brigit have a fight?"

"Just the opposite, Ma." She decided to plunge right in, but kept her back turned as she finished making the lemonade. "We're having a baby."

"*¿Que qué?*"

"You heard me, Ma." Ivon placed the pitcher under the tap and filled it with water, eyes focused on the rusty swing set in the backyard. "We're having a baby. I mean, we're adopting a child. That's why I'm here. Ximena was going to hook me up with a girl in Juárez who wanted to give up her baby, but . . . ," she choked back the sudden knot in her gullet, ". . . but it didn't work out, so I guess there's a plan B or something."

Her mom didn't say anything.

Ivon poured two heaping scoops of sugar into the pitcher, not wanting to turn around and look at her mom's reaction, already feeling the tension in her neck. She took a wooden spoon from the utensils drawer and stirred the lemonade.

She heard her mom lifting the lids on the pots, checking the food. The silence felt like a plastic bag around Ivon's face. She kept stirring the lemonade. Outside, Samson sat up suddenly, as if he'd heard something familiar. Then he let out a little bark and hobbled over to the gate, wagging his tail. Irene was home.

"Does your sister know?" her mom said, finally.

"Yes, Ma, she knows. Ximena told her." Bravely, she turned around and took the pitcher to the table.

Her mom was staring at Ivon as though she were an alien.

"Hi, Ma, I'm home!" Irene called out. "You should see all the traffic on Paisano. I guess everyone's going over to the fair in Juárez. Ma?"

"We're in here, *m'ijita*," her mom called over her shoulder. "Your sister's here."

Irene ran into the kitchen. "Pancho!" she squealed and threw herself into Ivon's arms. "Wow! I can't believe you're here. When did you get here?" She was pretending she hadn't seen Ivon the day before.

"Give it a break, Lucha," Ivon said. "I told her already. She's gone into shock."

"I'll tell you what gave me a shock," her mom said, arms akimbo, "was watching this girl come home after her curfew last night, smelling like beer. Was she with you?"

"Yes, Ma, she and Ximena went to pick me up at the airport. I didn't let her drink more than two beers . . . it wasn't like a big *borrachera* or anything."

"*Pues*, that's all we need, to have the two of you wind up alcoholics, like your dad. Wash up," her mom told Irene, "and warm the tortillas. Ivon, set another place for yourself and get some ice into those glasses. I'll be right back."

They waited until she'd left the room before looking at each other. They cracked up.

"*Se le volaron*, huh?" Irene lit the burner under the *comal*. "She looks so mean."

"She's in denial, I think. She hasn't said anything about the baby thing, yet." Ivon took a straw placemat out of a drawer and set her usual place at the table.

"What stinks?" said Irene, imitating Ma's *fuchi*-face. She uncovered each pot to check the smell of the food, then smelled the tortillas.

"Must be the trash," Ivon said.

"Dude, what happened?" Irene flipped a tortilla onto the hot *comal*. "Tía Fátima called and told us about Ximena's accident. Is she okay? Did you guys go to Juárez, after all? Did you meet the girl?"

Ivon shrugged. "It didn't work out, and I don't want to talk about it, okay? I think Brigit and I are just going to bite the bullet and do it the old-fashioned way: wait for L.A. County to place a kid with us. I think it's probably safer that way."

"Not to mention legal. Damn, I didn't know Ximena was into all that. I mean, it's like she's trafficking babies or something."

"Don't say that. She's not doing that. She's helping out those poor women in Juárez. There's a lot going on over there that I haven't paid a lot of attention to, and it's horrifying, and Ximena's right in the thick of it. Made me sick. I feel like going home."

"No way. I thought you were gonna take me to the fair."

"I'm not going home *today*. There's some . . . research I have to do, and I'm going to stay as long as it takes. We can go to the fair on Friday if you want."

"Go where?" her mom appeared suddenly. She had changed her blouse and brushed out her grey hair and applied her usual shade of lipstick, a frosty coral pink that her father used to say set off her green eyes.

"To the fair, Ma," said Irene. "Ivon's taking me to the fair, since you won't let me go with my friends."

Ivon had taken the ice-cube tray from the freezer and was popping a few cubes into each glass.

"Bunch of *cholas*," her mom said. "Going over there to flirt and get into trouble, *nada más*. I hope you're going to find better people to socialize with when you go to UTEP. I thought you'd find a good crowd at Loretto . . . that's why I sent you there, instead of Father Yermo, pretty penny it's costing me . . . but no, you had to go and pick the *cholas*."

"My friends are not *cholas*, Ma. They're not into gangs or drugs or anything. They're on the swim team, like me. Just cuz they got tattoos doesn't automatically make them *cholas*. Ivon's got a tattoo, and you don't go calling her a *chola*."

Ivon glanced up and saw her mom give Irene a warning look. Ivon's tattoo was a taboo subject in her mother's house.

"I didn't know you were going to UTEP." Ivon steered the conversation in another direction. "I thought you were going to apply to schools in California."

"And, what? End up like you?" her mom snapped. "Worst mistake we ever made was letting you follow your cousin Mary to that Iowa college. Your poor uncle Joe never knows where that girl is these days, *vagabundiando* around México on a train, writing embarrassing stories about the family. You two should have stayed right here. la UTEP's a good school. All of Fátima's kids went to la UTEP, and they all stayed in El Paso, close to their family, where they belong. You, you go off to college and turn into one of those women libbers, *o lo que sea*, and then you move to Los Angeles, and I never see you. Now you want Irene to leave me, too."

Her mom caught her breath. "She's all I have left."

Ivon and Irene stared at each other. That's how things started around here. Her mom's matchstick temper could flare up at any moment. Ivon shook her head and turned around to pour the lemonade.

"Ma, why are you yelling at Ivon?" said Irene. "She's not forcing me to do anything. I'm the one who wants to go away. I'm going to law school, remember? la UTEP doesn't have a law school, and, anyway, my counselor says la UTEP sucks."

"Don't use that kind of language in this house if you don't want me to slap your face. *No te hagas la chiflada* just because your sister's here."

Ivon's face had gotten warm and she knew she was about to lose it.

"She's deflecting," Ivon said to Irene. "You know Ma likes to do that when there's an elephant in the room that she wants to pretend isn't there. Why don't you just say what's really on your mind, Ma? About this adoption thing, I mean."

"It's all part of the same thing. I am not deflecting," her mom said. "And stop using those big words like you don't think I know what they mean. Hand me those bowls, lunch is ready."

"No, Ma, I am not going to hand you any bowls, okay?" Ivon pulled a chair out and sat down. "You're going to sit down with me and tell me how you feel about this."

Her mom stood with her heels together and her hands fastened to her hips. "*Now* you want to know how I feel about this, when you've already gone and made your decision, *tú sola?* How do you think I feel? *Es una vergüenza.* That's all you do: embarrass me in front of the whole family. It's not enough that you went away to college and turned into a *marimacha* with that Women's Studies degree, or that your father took up drinking again because of you. Now you want to bring a child into that . . . that immoral lifestyle of yours? *Es una vergüenza.* You should be ashamed of yourself. *That's* how I feel about it. Satisfied? Now give me those damn bowls."

Ivon buried her face in her hands. Her hands were trembling. Her whole body shook with rage. She wanted to smash those bowls against the wall. She took deep breaths to keep from crying. She would not bawl in front of her mother.

"That's the meanest thing I've ever heard you say, Ma," said Irene. "I thought you were proud of Ivon. You're always showing off about your daughter the Ph.D. who lives in Los Angeles. Now you're suddenly ashamed of her because she wants to have a baby in her life? What's wrong with that? Who cares what the family thinks? I don't care. Ivon's not hurting anybody, Ma. You always say that your kids' happiness is all that matters to you, but look at you, look at the shit you're saying. It isn't fair that you're blaming Ivon for Dad's drinking. What? Are you going to blame her for his death, too?"

Ivon knew what was coming, but she still winced when she heard her mother slap her sister's face. She turned around and grabbed her mother's arm before she struck again. "Don't hit her in front of me, I've told you that," Ivon said through gritted teeth.

Her mother yanked her arm away, eyes blazing. "Don't you dare talk to me like that. Who do you think you are, the man of the house? I'm still your mother. And your sister is not going to be disrespectful in this house."

"Let's get out of here, Lucha."

Irene swallowed back her tears. "Okay," she said.

"Go ahead," her mom yelled out behind them. "Take her away from me. Turn her into a Pancho just like you. ¡*Manflora*! ¡*Marimacha*! ¡*Sin vergüenza*!"

10

"YOU'RE DRIVING MOSTAZA?" Ivon asked, feeling a shiver of deja vu at seeing her dad's 1978 mustard-yellow El Camino in the driveway.

"Uncle Joe finally finished rebuilding the engine," said Irene.

"Only took him five years," said Ivon.

"He talked Ma into giving it to me for my sixteenth birthday."

Ivon had learned to drive in that car, had spotted the yellow leather seat during her first sexual experience with a girl from the volleyball team, had spent hours driving around with her dad after arguments with Ma. It wasn't just any El Camino, Dad would say. It was the last of the original El Caminos, the Sun City Car Show award-winner for Best Overall Ride of 1982, the same year Irene was born. And her dad had made her promise never to run away again.

"You wanna drive?" Irene dangled the keys. Her eyes looked wet.

"Not right now." Ivon's head had started to throb where she'd hit herself on the autopsy table, and her vision was blurry. She slid into the passenger seat. The tears in the yellow leather upholstery were mended with duct tape. The seat belt didn't work.

On the radio Selena was singing "bidi bidi boom boom." Irene raised the volume.

From the corner of her eye, Ivon could see her mom watching them from behind the screen door. "Let's scram before she sends her evil monkeys after us," she said.

Irene squealed the tires out of the driveway. "Where to?"

"I need a big, tall drink."

"Me, too. I know a place near Fox Plaza where they won't card me."

"Isn't there a supermarket near Grandma Maggie's house?"

"There's a Furr's on Copia."

"Let's go there. I can get beer and stuff to eat for the rest of the week."

Irene wiped the tears off her face with the back of her hand while she drove. "Dude! That was *so* fucked up! She was *so* . . . whatever."

"I knew it," said Ivon. "I knew she was going to have a cow when I told her about the adoption." One day in town and already Ivon felt like she'd never left.

"She had a buffalo, not a cow," said Irene. "I've never heard her go off like that. I can't believe she was calling you all those names."

"You haven't known her as long as I have."

"I'm not staying here, Pancho. Even if I don't get accepted to Saint Ignatius, I'm coming to live with you guys as soon as I graduate. I've had it with her madness."

At the supermarket, Ivon asked Irene to pick up a gallon of drinking water and to espresso-grind a pound of French Roast coffee beans while she got the groceries she needed. A carton of eggs, a block of Monterrey Jack, a dozen corn tortillas, a can of salsa, a small bottle of olive oil, two six-packs of Lone Star, a jar of Bufferin. All the essential food groups.

She was at the checkout line waiting for Irene to show up with the water and the coffee when she felt a tap on her shoulder.

"Ivon? *¿Eres o no eres?*"

She recognized the scent of the perfume before the voice. She twisted around and felt a twinge in her neck.

"I thought it looked like you."

It was Raquel. Ivon stared at her as though she were an apparition. She hadn't seen Raquel since she left El Paso eight years ago. All of the times she'd been back since then, she had never run into Raquel anywhere, not even in Juárez when Ivon went to Sanborn's or the *mercado*—their two favorite places. Suddenly, here she was in the Furr's Supermarket on Copia, of all places, acting like a local.

Except for the thick stripe of white running down the middle of her long black hair, Tongolele-style, Raquel had not changed. She was still slim and elegant, and the charcoal-black of her eyes was still arresting. Ivon felt afraid suddenly and didn't know why.

"What's the matter?" Raquel asked. They spoke only in Spanish. "You look upset. Am I upsetting you?"

"You gave me a heart attack," said Ivon, laughing. "How are you? What a surprise." She didn't know if she should give her a hug, and decided against it.

"I'm doing well. I'm married now. And you?"

Ivon shrugged. "Good, good. I'm married, too." She held up her left hand to show her the silver wedding band. She didn't see a ring on Raquel's finger.

Raquel glanced at Ivon's cart. "Looks familiar," she said, "still eating nothing but eggs and *quesadillas*, I see. Drinking that bad beer."

"It's so weird to run into you, after all these years. Did you move over here?"

Raquel shook her head. "Not a chance. You know me. I've never liked living on this side. My husband wanted to buy me a condominium here in El Paso, but I used the money to renovate my mother's house, instead."

Ivon felt her belly contract at the word *husband*. In Raquel's handbasket Ivon saw a package of Kotex pads, a box of crayons and some coloring books. Did she have kids, too? Ivon wondered. Raquel followed her gaze.

"These are for my brother's girls," she said, answering her unasked question.

"How are they, your nieces?"

Raquel smiled, and the tender look that came into her eyes disarmed Ivon. "The oldest one, remember Myrna? She's in high school, already. Chachi is in seventh grade, and the little one's in third. I think you were gone by the time Karina came along. The three of them are going to summer school here at Loretto. I pick them up after school and drive them back to Juárez. Gabriel, my brother, doesn't like for them to carpool."

There was an awkward silence, and Ivon wondered what was

taking Irene so long.

"So is your brother still running that language school? Frontelingua, right?"

"Can you believe it? After all this time. We're practically the only ones left now, still offering English classes to the *maquilas*."

"It's doing well, then?"

"Thank God. We have our own building now, right behind the art museum in the Pronaf. And we've expanded. Actually, we do computer training as well as teach English."

"Computer training? That's smart."

"You know Gabriel, always looking for a good business deal."

Yeah, I know Gabriel, thought Ivon, remembering all the times Raquel's brother had threatened to beat her up if she didn't leave his sister alone. The irony, of course, was that Ivon was eleven years younger than Raquel, and it had been Raquel who'd done all the courting while Ivon was still in high school.

"Did you hear me?" Raquel said.

"Sorry," said Ivon, "I'm having a hard time focusing today."

"I was asking you if you still like photography. They have a show at the museum that you might like. Hand-colored black-and-white photographs of Indian villages in Chiapas and Oaxaca. The photographer's a friend of ours. He just graduated from the art institute in San Miguel. Remember San Miguel?"

Ivon avoided the bait. "Sounds interesting," she said. She checked her watch.

"You should come see the show."

"I'm only here for a few days, on business, you know. And then there's my mom . . ."

"How is your mom?"

"She's fine. Gardening, cooking, killing critters in her yard. Always busy."

Irene appeared suddenly beside Ivon. "There you are. Remember Irene?"

The tender look came back into Raquel's eyes. Her dimple showed when she smiled. "*¿A poco ésta es la garrapata?*" Raquel reached over to hug the girl.

Irene scowled. "And you are?"

"Raquel Montenegro. I used to be your sister's . . . friend."

"Oh, her friend," said Irene, nodding, "as in her friend friend, or her girlfriend?"

Ivon watched the stiffness creep into Raquel's face. That had been the issue that had broken them up, after all, Raquel's unwillingness to leave the closet because of the fear that her brother would reject her and not allow her to come near his daughters. Not to mention the fact that she had affairs with men on the side.

"Her friend," Raquel said primly.

"Why'd you call me a *garrapata*? I'm not a tick."

"Just an endearment that stayed with you since the day you started kindergarten. Ivon and I dropped you off, and you wouldn't let Ivon go when we walked you to your classroom. You were crying so hard, and you had your arms *and* your legs wrapped around her like a *garrapata*. It broke my heart. The nuns had to pull you away."

"You were so scared, I think you pooped your pants, *mensita*," Ivon said.

Irene laughed. "Really? I don't remember any of that."

"I guess Ivon doesn't talk about me very much," Raquel said.

Ivon was next in line. She turned around and unloaded the cart. She did not want to hear any more of the conversation, anyway. An odd queasiness had started in the pit of her stomach, a type of jitters that she hadn't felt in a very long time and that only Raquel could produce.

"Guess what?" Irene interrupted her distress. "Raquel says she's going to the fair tonight. You wanna go? You wanna meet her there?"

Ivon looked at Raquel, and Raquel held her gaze.

"Since when do you go to the fair?" Ivon asked.

"Actually, Gabriel and the director of the museum rented a booth together, and my brother wants me to watch the Frontelingua table tonight for a few hours."

"Is your husband going?"

"He lives in Chihuahua and only comes down here once a month."

Why is she telling me this? Ivon wondered.

"Is yours?"

"Excuse me?"

"Is your husband going to the fair with you?"

Ivon frowned at her. "I don't have a husband," she said, "and no, my wife isn't going either. She's in Los Angeles."

Raquel's eyes flashed, and, for a second, she creased her lips in that hoity-toity way that used to irritate the shit out of Ivon.

"I can get you in for free," said Raquel. "Meet me at the entrance at nine."

"Sure," Ivon said, shrugging. "Why not? See you there."

She asked the checker to throw in a pack of Camel Lights, paid the bill, and grabbed the plastic bags.

Irene gave Raquel a kiss on the cheek. They were old friends, now.

"See you at nine," Irene said to Raquel.

"Grab the water, *ésa!*" Ivon said. She did not turn around again, but knew that Raquel still had her eyes on her as they walked out of the store. Once, Ivon had believed Raquel put a spell on her with those black eyes. The curse of *los ojos negros de Montenegro,* that's how Ximena had described it long ago.

"She's nice," said Irene, taking the wheel again. "I think she still likes you. How long were y'all together?"

"Four years."

"How come you broke up?"

"None of your beeswax, okay?"

"*Ay, ay,*" said Irene, taking the shortcut across Memorial Park. "So what do you wanna do? You wanna kick it and just chill?"

"Don't you have to go back to work?"

"Yeah, but Ximena's got meetings on Wednesdays. There's nothing for me to do but sit there answering the phone. She won't care if I take the rest of the day off."

"I don't think so, Lucha. You have no idea what a fucked up day it's been for me. That little incident with Ma, that was just icing on the cake. I'm really wiped. All I want to do is take a shower and a long nap. Just drop me off at Grandma Maggie's right now and pick me up later, around nine so we can go to the fair together, okay?"

"Nine? My curfew's at ten."

Ivon checked her watch. Ten past one. All that gore in just half a day.

"Okay, come over after you get off work, then, but we're not going anywhere until it gets dark. It's too hot. Just tell Ma you're spending the night here. Which reminds me . . . I have to call Brigit. She doesn't know I'm staying here." She felt in her pockets. "Oh shit! I forgot my cell phone in the priest's car."

"I can get it for you when I go back to the office. The church isn't far."

"Shit! I hope Brigit hasn't tried to call me."

"You think she's gonna mind that you're meeting Raquel at the fair?"

"What Brigit doesn't know isn't going to hurt her, so don't go saying anything if you happen to talk to her, okay? And tell Ximena she better not spill the beans about Cecilia, either."

Ximena's van was in the driveway at Grandma Maggie's house.

"What's *she* doing here? I thought you said she had meetings," said Ivon.

"Me, too."

Ivon had been looking forward to being alone.

"Want me to help you unload the groceries?"

"I don't need any help. Just go back home, patch things up with Ma so she'll give you permission to go to the fair later. And don't answer back. You know how much Ma hates that."

"See you at five-thirty, then," Irene said, dejected.

"Call before you come, okay? I may still be asleep."

"Hey, what *about* Cecilia? Is she okay?"

"Believe me, you don't want to know."

"I'm not a kid anymore, Ivon, in case you hadn't noticed."

"I'm fifteen years older than you are," said Ivon. "To me, you will always be a kid."

Irene made a face at her, laughed and leaned over to give Ivon a kiss. Ivon put her arms around the girl, holding her tightly for a moment. She was just one year older than Cecilia, Ivon realized. Cecilia could have been her little sister.

"Eww," said Irene. "It's you. You're the one who stinks."

"Told you I needed a shower," Ivon said, getting out of the car.

"Dude, I'm so happy you're here. I've missed you."

"Yeah, yeah, just cause I'm taking you to the fair."

"¡Marimacha!"

"¡Chola!"

II

IVON LUGGED HER GROCERY BAGS and the jug of water into the house. Ximena was splayed out on the recliner watching an episode of *Xena*.

"Taking the day off?" Ivon said. She tried to keep her irritation in check.

"I cancelled. I'm just too messed up about today. Needed some time to myself."

"Join the club," Ivon said, passing in front of the television.

"So what're *you* doing back so soon? Thought you were hanging out at your mom's for awhile. How'd it go?"

"Where should I start?" Ivon called out from the kitchen. "Cow Central? Or Ex-Lover City?"

"Say what?"

"Never mind." Ivon dumped the bags on the kitchen floor. "Hey, did you find my phone in the car, by any chance?"

"Yeah, I put it in the bedroom. It was ringing off the hook, so I turned it off. I figured it was Brigit, so I didn't pick up."

"Miracle," said Ivon. She stuffed everything she had bought, except the aspirin and the cigarettes, into the empty refrigerator. "You want a beer?"

"No thanks, I'm on the wagon today."

Ivon popped a couple of Bufferin back with some beer. In the adjoining laundry room, she stripped off her clothes and threw them all into the washer, setting the temperature to hot and adding an extra splash of liquid detergent.

Naked, she walked past the living room.

"There's a sight for sore eyes," said Ximena.

76

"I'm getting in the shower," Ivon said, taking her bottle of Lone Star with her. She saw her cell phone on the nightstand and turned it on; sure enough, there were 6 new messages on her voice mail. She definitely could not talk to Brigit right now.

In the shower, she sat on the tiles with her knees drawn up to her chest and let the warm water wash over her while she finished her beer. The salty taste on her lips told her it was more than water running down her face. The water turned cool. She took the loofah sponge hanging from the faucet and scoured herself from forehead to feet. Shampooed her hair twice. She needed to scrub the scent of death off her skin but could not remove the image of Cecilia's body from her mind, a permanent stain in her memory.

After she was dressed, she plopped down on the sofa with a fresh Lone Star and her pack of Camel Lights. Now Ximena was watching a *telenovela*. The digital clock on the cable box told her she'd been in the shower nearly an hour.

"Feel better?" Ximena said.

"Cleaner, anyway. I couldn't get that smell out."

"Yeah, I scrubbed down myself. You didn't say anything about my outfit."

Ivon looked at the yellow tent of a housedress she was wearing. "*¿Y eso?*"

"Grandma Maggie's clothes," she said. "I keep forgetting to leave my own stuff here, and that's all I could find. Ugly, huh?"

"I've seen worse." Ivon took a long pull from her beer. "Where's the turtle?"

"Tortoise. She's not a turtle. Her name is Yerma and she's out back cooling down in her little pond right now. Someone left her inside the house all day and she almost suffocated."

"I didn't know what to do with her. You didn't tell me I had to leave her outside."

"I know, my bad. Poor thing is so old now, I really should have her put down."

Ivon guzzled some of her beer. "Shit, what a day!"

"Tell me about it."

"What am I going to say to Brigit? I can't even bring myself to hear her messages, much less call her. I feel so numb. And the crazy part is, I'm starving. Even after what we saw."

Ximena pulled her pack of Marlboros out of the side pocket of her dress and lit up. "You didn't have lunch at your mom's?"

"No. I decided to drop the atom bomb and tell her about the baby. So we got into World War Three instead of eating."

"¡Ay! You told Tía about Cecilia and the baby?"

"All I said was that Brigit and I were adopting. Way more than enough. Oh, and get this, we leave the house, right, before Irene gets her face slapped off—she's in it, too, trying to defend me against the homophobic wrath of Ma . . . So Irene takes me to the grocery store down on Copia, and guess who I run into? Raquel."

"Montenegro?" Ximena coughed into her hand. The living room had filled with smoke, and Ximena got up to switch on the swamp cooler.

Ivon nodded. "*Los ojos negros de Montenegro*, remember?" The cigarette was making her dizzy, so she stubbed it out in the ashtray.

"Talk about a blast from the past. No wonder you look like puke warmed over."

"Thanks," said Ivon, peeling the label off her beer. "I haven't seen this woman in eight years, and suddenly there she is behind me at Furr's, telling me the story of her life and inviting me to go to the fair with her tonight. Irene was ecstatic."

"Told you the story of her life, huh? What did she say?"

Ivon took a long sip of her beer. "She says she's married now, and that her husband lives in Chihuahua and she only sees him once a month . . ." She belched. ". . . but I don't believe it, she's not even wearing a ring. Same old Raquel, always lying about something."

"Maybe she just wants to make sure you don't put a move on her."

"Right," Ivon said, rolling her eyes. She belched again.

"And she invited you to go to the fair? Just like that?"

"I think Irene sort of invited herself, really."

"Well I got news for you, *prima*, you may not make it to the fair tonight. You have a date with me this afternoon. You're going to meet Elsa, mother of Jorgito."

"What? Who's Elsa?"

"Plan B, remember?"

Ivon chugged the rest of her beer and set the bottle down on the coffee table. "I don't think so, Ximena. I really can't deal with anything else right now. I'm traumatized. Aren't you? I could've lived a full life without seeing that autopsy, not to mention all the other shit that happened today. All I want to do is zone out in front of my computer and work on the dissertation until it's time to take Irene to the fair. Knowing me, I'll end up online looking up that web address we found."

"What web address?"

"In that 'Richy's Diary' thing."

"Shut up. You have to let that go, Ivon. You're not here to solve Cecilia's murder."

"I can't get it out of my mind, okay? We were right there. She was probably getting killed while we were waiting for her outside the factory." She felt herself choking up and held her breath for three counts. "What I can't figure out is those coins."

"What coins?"

"At the morgue. Next to the gallstones."

Ximena shook her head. "I didn't see any coins. Sure you weren't hallucinating?"

"They were right there. They looked like corroded pennies or something."

"You need to eat, girlfriend. You're starting to sound delirious. Come on, let's go get some lunch so you can get your wits together before you meet Jorgito."

"Ximena, listen to me. I'm serious. I don't want to go through with this adoption thing, anymore, okay? I've changed my mind. Brigit and I can get a kid from L.A. County. It'll be less hassle, and I won't have to explain anything."

Ximena changed the channel on the remote. "I already told Brigit about Elsa."

"You did what? I thought you said you hadn't picked up."

"Not your cell phone, but when the phone rang here at the house . . . I *am* allowed to pick up the phone in my own house, *¿qué no?*"

"Brigit called here? How did she get this number?"

"I think she talked to your mom."

Ivon laughed nervously. "Great! Now I'm really worried."

"Sounds like your mom gave her an earful about how much you resembled your dad. She told her you smelled like cigarette smoke, too. Brigit's afraid you've taken up smoking again."

Ivon laughed even harder, and the tears squeezed out of her eyes. "Could anything else go wrong today?" she said.

"Sure," said Ximena, "you could meet Raquel at the fair and lose your heart again."

The cell phone rang. They looked at each other and cracked up.

"I'm gonna take it in the bedroom," said Ivon, taking a deep breath.

"I'll bring you another beer," said Ximena, pushing up from the recliner. "Might as well have one myself, while I wait, it's gonna be a long conversation, I bet."

Ivon sat cross-legged on the rumpled bed, pillows piled on top of each other. She was sure she'd straightened the bed before she left that morning. The pillowcase smelled of patchouli, so Ximena must have taken a nap.

She picked up the phone on the third ring. "Hi, sweetie."

"What's going on, Ivon?" Brigit was already in tears, she could tell.

"I know I owe you a big explanation, okay, but I never imagined things were going to turn out like this. I thought I could just, you know, come pick up the baby and go home. I didn't know about all these murders."

Silence. Not even a sniffle. "What murders?"

"Didn't you talk to Ximena? Didn't she tell you?"

"Someone got murdered?"

Ivon shook her head. Ximena walked in with a bottle of beer, and Ivon covered the mouthpiece. "Didn't you tell her about Cecilia?" she whispered.

"Hell no! I told her about Elsa."

"Christ, you could've told me!"

"Can't win for losing," Ximena mumbled on her way out.

Ivon took another deep breath and spoke into the phone again. She decided to try the professorial approach. "There's a story about what's been going on here in the latest issue of Ms., if you want to check it out. Some maniacs are targeting young women who work at the twin plants in Juárez. No one seems to know why or who is responsible, but over a hundred girls have been kidnapped and tortured and killed. It's like an epidemic. The girl whose baby we were going to adopt was murdered last night. The baby, too." She thought it best not to go into more graphic detail.

"Oh my god, Ivon. What happened?"

"She got stabbed to death. We didn't know anything about it until we got to her house this morning. That's why I haven't called you all day. I've been too upset. I didn't know how to tell you." She left out the part about the autopsy. Brigit would freak out if she knew Ivon had seen that.

"That's the most horrible thing I ever heard, Ivon."

"I just want to go home."

"What about Elsa?"

"What *about* Elsa? What did Ximena tell you about Elsa?"

"Ximena said she's really sick and has a three-year-old little boy named Georgito, but Elsa doesn't have any family there and she's been having a hard time providing for him because she's been so sick. She needs someone to take him. Ximena said she was going to take you to meet Elsa today, so you could meet the boy."

Good ole communicative Ximena, Ivon thought.

"I thought you wanted a baby, Brigit. A newborn."

"Well, sure, that would've been my first choice, but a three-year-old is still a baby. It's not like he's all grown up. And besides, you said you wanted a boy."

"So what's the matter with her, why is she so sick?"

"Ximena didn't say."

"Hold on." She covered the mouthpiece and called out to Ximena.

"What?" Ximena yelled back. "I'm watching the news."

"What's the matter with Elsa? I mean, why is she so sick? Has she got AIDS or something?"

Ximena popped her head in the door. ""It isn't AIDS, and it isn't contagious."

"Not AIDS, not contagious," Ivon said into the phone. She left the mouthpiece uncovered so Brigit could hear what Ximena was saying.

"Elsa got some injection at this *maquila* she was applying to a few years ago. You know, they make them do a pregnancy test when they apply for a job over there . . . and they make them take birth control shots and stuff . . . but she got pregnant so she didn't get the job. After Jorgito was born, she developed these weird tumors. Doctors thought it was a really bad case of endometriosis or maybe even cervical cysts, but it turned out to be ovarian cancer. She's at stage four, and the chemo she gets over there, you know, it's not like those social security clinics get the latest technology. That stuff makes her sicker than the cancer. Way sicker. She doesn't have much time."

Ivon shook her head. "D'you hear all that?" she asked into the phone.

Silence.

"Brigit? You there? Did you hear what Ximena said?"

"Poor Georgito," said Brigit, sniffling again. "His mother's so sick, and he has no one to take care of him. Ivon, we can't leave him there. What would he do? What's going to happen to him when she dies?"

"Brigit wants to know what'll happen to the boy if Elsa dies and we don't take him?"

Ximena shrugged. "Same thing that happens to all poor orphans in Juárez. They end up begging on the bridge, getting rounded up by some child prostitution ring or running drugs back and forth across the border. No big mystery on that one. And it's not *if* Elsa dies, it's when. She doesn't have much time."

"We can't leave him there, Ivon," Brigit said again.

"Is he okay?" Ivon asked Ximena. "I mean, there's nothing wrong with him, is there? His mother's not like a big boozer or an addict, right?"

"He's probably got worms in his belly from eating dirt, maybe lice in his hair. He's a little pale and not too big for his age. But other than that, he's a cute little boy. Smart as hell, too, taught himself to speak English from watching TV. And the best thing is I can get adoption papers drawn up on him right away because of Elsa's illness. She can write a letter declaring you to be Jorgito's legal guardian, and we don't even have to go through the Concilio de Familias or anything. Elsa can straight-up hand him over."

"Ivon, don't you want to go meet him?" Brigit said. "Poor baby."

"Okay, okay, I'll go meet him. Okay?"

"I should be there with you. This is way too much for you to have to handle on your own. You want me to come?"

The image of Cecilia's body came to mind.

"No," said Ivon. "You stay there. It's way too weird around here."

"Tell her to go shopping," Ximena said. "For toddler's clothes and stuff."

"D'you hear that? Ximena says you should go buy toddler's clothes."

"Oh my god, Ivon, she's right. I was expecting a baby, not a toddler. We don't have anything ready. We don't even have his room ready."

"Exactly," said Ivon, making the okay hand gesture to Ximena. "You get his room ready, and I'll call you when it's all over to tell you when we're coming home."

"What room, though? I was going to put the crib in our bedroom. But he needs his own room, he's three years old, and all we have is your study or the guest room. Which one?"

That was a good question. Ivon hadn't thought about giving up her study.

"You decide."

"You sure?"

"No, use the guest room. I'll call you when it's over. Don't get all worried if you don't hear from me tomorrow."

"Tell her you're staying for the reunion," Ximena whispered.

Ivon shook her head emphatically. Ximena shrugged and went back to her television.

"I don't want to do blue or anything stereotypical like that, okay?" Brigit said.

"Well, don't go making his room pink, either," said Ivon. "Or yellow."

"How about red and black?"

Ivon laughed. "Yeah, with a farmworker flag draped over the bed."

"Ivon, we're going to have a son."

"I guess so, huh?" Ivon said, and suddenly her voice tightened. *Mapi,* she heard the little boy's voice again, *I'm lonely, come supervise me in the kid's section.*

"Hurry, hurry, you're missing it!" Ximena called out.

"Gotta go, Bridge, Ximena wants me to see something on TV."

"Ivon, you didn't really start smoking again, did you?"

"Bridge, please. Is that what my mom told you? Did she tell you we'd had a big fight when I told her about our plans? That she called me all these horrible homophobic names?"

"She did sound kind of angry."

"Yeah, no shit. Pulled her Lydia the Dragon Lady routine."

"Does she know about all the other stuff, the murder?"

"Can you imagine? She'd keel over."

"Get over here, Ivon! Look at this!"

"Okay, sweetie, I better go, Ximena's practically falling off her chair over here."

"Ivon, what does *mujer*—hold on, I wrote it down—*mujer llega* mean? I know *mujer* means woman, but I don't think I've ever heard that expression. *Mujer llega.* Doesn't *llega* mean arrive? Your mom said you were a *mujer llega,* just like your dad. An arriving woman? It doesn't make sense."

Mujeriega, womanizer. Ivon's mom was still judging her by her old ways.

"I'll explain it to you later, okay? But don't call my mom anymore. She's on a rampage. We don't need to encourage her right now. Talk to you later."

Ivon hung up and hurried to the living room.

"Shit, you missed it!"

"I couldn't get her off the phone. What'd I miss?"

"They just interviewed Bob Russell on the news, about the murders."

"Who's Bob Russell?"

"An ex-FBI dude they brought in to help the pigs in Juárez with profiling the victims. He's written all these books on serial killers."

"What'd he say?"

"He says there's evidence to suggest that some of the girls were murdered by a serial killer. He says it could be a guy from El Paso crossing over to commit his crimes because he knows there isn't a death penalty in Mexico. He also said the same shit the police have been saying for years. That the victims are leading loose lives and putting themselves in danger."

"Oh, so it's the victim's fault, huh?"

"Is it any wonder those maniacs are still at large?" Ximena pressed the power button on the remote and turned off the tube. "Okay," she said, standing up. "So is everything cool with you and the little woman?"

"You mean how do I feel after being railroaded by the two of you?"

Ximena chucked her on the chin. "Maybe some *carnitas* will make you feel better. I know this great place on Mesa that has the best *carnitas* in the world. The pork practically melts in your mouth. Then I'll take you to meet your future kid. Even your mom's gonna love him."

"Don't even mention my mom right now." She thought about calling Irene to let her know she wouldn't be making it to the fair, after all, but she'd find out soon enough. Irene would just want to tag along with them, and Ivon did not want to deal with that.

"How much is this gonna cost, Ximena? Do I have to make another bank stop?"

"Just give her a thousand dollars, that's a lot more than she would make in a factory in six months. She doesn't have much more time than that. Maybe a little extra to cover the funeral expenses."

"Damn," said Ivon, "this is the second kid I'm thinking of adopting whose mother is either dead or dying."

"Yeah, lots of women are dying in Juárez these days," said Ximena.

12

ELSA LIVED AT THE BACK OF A GREASY SPOON called El Rinconcito near downtown Juárez. Elsa's grandmother, Doña Hermelinda, a hunchback who shuffled around in slippers with a stained, threadbare apron over her housecoat, ran the restaurant. The old woman hovered by the stove, frying thick *gorditas* and smoking a hand-rolled cigarette.

"*Pues está muy enferma*," the old woman said in a gravelly voice, "my granddaughter is very sick. That little boy sucks all her strength out."

"She's nursing him?" Ivon asked Ximena. "He's taking in her chemo?"

"She doesn't have any milk, are you kidding?"

"Go on back," said the woman, ash from her cigarette falling into the frying pan. "She's back there, watching television. That's all she does all day. If it weren't for this restaurant, we would both be out on the street. *Esa muchacha*. What a mistake it was for her to come here. She was supposed to take care of me, *y mira nomás*."

"Sympathetic, isn't she?" said Ivon.

"Tired is more like it," said Ximena. "Poor old thing's been supporting Elsa since she moved here from Zacatecas."

They walked past the four metal tables of the dining area, only one of which was occupied by a man in a parking attendant's uniform, behind a pair of folding screens that separated the living area from the restaurant, past a stone sink crammed full of dishes, cockroaches swarming over the dirty plates, past a door with a running toilet behind it, through a corridor so dark it felt like a tunnel, and into a dim room with two beds, a rocking chair, a television, and an electric heater. Even in the dimness Ivon could see the water stains veining the ceiling. The plaster peeling from the walls. Mounds of clothing covering the floor and the top of the beds. The whole place smelled of grease and mothballs.

Elsa slept in a nest of clothing. The little boy sat on the edge of the bed, sucking his thumb and watching television. He wore nothing but briefs and a knitted cap.

"*Hola,* Jorgito," said Ximena, squatting down to give the boy a hug.

The boy kept his eyes on the tube and his thumb in his mouth. He was watching cartoons with the sound turned off. The black and white images looked grainy.

Elsa opened her eyes. "*Ay,*" she said, trying to raise herself, "*qué vergüenza, me quedé dormida.*"

"Don't worry," Ximena told her, going over to help her sit up. "We just got here. We were talking to your grandmother out front. This is my cousin, Ivon."

Elsa leaned back against the wall, smoothed her hair down, and offered her hand to Ivon. It felt cold and bony. "Please sit down. Can I offer you a *refresco? ¿Tienen hambre?*" she asked, smiling. In the blue glare of the television, her teeth looked skeletal. The dark mole that nearly covered her left cheek looked more like a black hole swallowing her face. Probably skin cancer.

"No, thanks," said Ivon, finding a clear space on the edge of the other bed, "We just had lunch." The thought of having anything to eat or drink in this place turned her stomach.

"She wanted to meet Jorgito," said Ximena, perched in the rocking chair.

"Jorgito, *m'ijo,*" Elsa said to the boy, "*apague su tele y venga a saludar. No sea grosero.*"

Jorgito took his thumb out of his mouth and turned to look at Ivon. For a second, she was thrown off by the anger she perceived in the boy's dark stare. Suddenly he smiled. Dimples. Rotted front teeth. "*Hola, cola,*" he said, and turned back to his cartoons, doubled over in laughter.

"¡Jorge! ¡*Grosero!* He's so spoiled," Elsa apologized. "But he's a good boy. He's well-behaved when he's not showing off like that.

He doesn't give me any trouble."

"Isn't he hot with that cap on?" Ivon asked, feeling the sweat already beading on her nose and down her spine.

Elsa glanced at Ximena, then back at Ivon. "He hits his head against the wall when I go to the doctor. He has bruises."

"Can we see?" said Ximena.

Elsa swallowed and then nodded.

"Come here, *flaco*," Ximena said to the boy, tickling him under the arms. The boy giggled and went to her. She tickled him again, under the chin, then yanked off his cap and tickled him behind the ears. He got angry at that and was about to smack her, but Ximena caught his hand in midair and tickled him under the arm.

He pulled away from her. "Give it back!" he said, ". . . or I'll bite you."

In the glow of the television his head had the shape and the color of an eggplant. Ivon felt the goose bumps rise on her arms.

"That's more than just bruises," said Ivon. "Do you hit him?"

Ximena gave her a look, but Ivon ignored her.

"He hits his head when I leave," she said again. "And sometimes my grandmother hits him when he plays near the stove."

"What does she hit him with, a frying pan?"

Ximena gave her another look. Elsa didn't answer.

The boy yanked the cap away from Ximena and shoved it down on his head, eyes shiny, like he was threatening to cry.

"What happened to his hair?"

"It hasn't grown in. Doctor said it's from poor nutrition."

"*Ven acá*, Jorgito," Ivon called to him. "I have something for you." She had asked Ximena to stop at a gas station on the way over so she could buy him a toy. She had gotten him a little blue truck with a Chevron logo.

He saw the flash of something in her hand and toddled over. He was bowlegged and his head looked much bigger than the rest of his body. He smelled of urine.

Ivon hid both hands behind her back and asked him to choose a hand.

"That one," he said, pointing to her left side.

"*¿La izquierda?*" Ivon said, pronouncing the word slowly, "let's see." She showed him her empty left hand, wiggling her fingers against his soft pale belly. He chuckled. She put her hand behind her back again.

"Which hand?"

"*La 'quielda*," he said again, almost getting the word right.

Ivon shifted the toy into her left hand and brought it forward. "You're smart, you win!" She opened her palm and showed him the little truck.

He took it in both hands and stood there, staring at it. His fingernails had not been clipped or cleaned in a long time. She looked down. Neither had his toenails.

"What do you say?" his mother prompted.

Jorgito looked up at Ivon, boring his eyes into her like he was trying to figure out who she was, what she wanted from him. "*Gracias*," he whispered, flexing his shoulders.

"You're welcome," Ivon whispered back.

"Her name is Ivon," said Ximena in English. "Can you say Ivon, *flaco*?"

"'Von," he said, flashing the dark little squares of his front teeth at her.

Ivon stuck her hand out and said "*mucho gusto*," but he came up to her and kissed her cheek. Ximena laughed. Ivon blinked back tears.

"Go play with your toy in the kitchen," Elsa said, "and stay out of your *abuelita's* way. I don't want you bothering the customers or going near the stove."

It was the way he walked off into the dark tunnel separating the bedroom from the kitchen that broke Ivon's resistance. He was not afraid of the dark. He was not afraid of the grandmother who hit him. She heard his bare feet slosh through a puddle of water and realized the floor of the passageway was wet. It was no place to bring up a child. Brigit would've said something about the conditions he was living in, but it wasn't Elsa's fault, or the grandmother's, either. They were doing what they could to survive their poverty and Elsa's illness. That's what Jorgito was, already at three years old, a survivor.

Both Ximena and Elsa were watching Ivon.

"What?" Ivon said.

"Do you like him?" Elsa asked.

"Sure, he's a cute kid," said Ivon. For some reason, her heart had started to hammer in her chest.

"He's my reason for living," said Elsa, "but I know that I can't leave him with my grandmother. Who knows how long she'll last after I'm gone, and she's not . . . well . . . you know, she's not very patient with him, and she . . . this is so embarrassing . . . she drinks sometimes and that makes things worse."

"He's had some pretty severe beatings," said Ivon.

"It's not all her fault, he really does pound his head on the wall when I'm gone."

"Probably terrified that you're leaving him with her."

"Yes, maybe that's it. *Pobrecito, m'ijo.*" She started to cry.

"What about the father? Doesn't he . . ."

"There is no father," Ximena interjected. "She hasn't been with anyone. It's still a mystery how she got pregnant."

"What? You're saying Jorgito was immaculately conceived?"

"I don't know," said Elsa, wiping the tears off her face with the back of her hand. "It happened at the factory where I was applying for a job. They gave me a pregnancy test and told me I had to wait a few weeks so they would know for sure that I wasn't pregnant. And then I got pregnant, so I couldn't work."

"Some pregnancy test, huh? She was probably raped."

Elsa pressed a hand over her eyes and shook her head.

Ivon switched to English. "But how could she be raped during a pregnancy test? I mean, that's just a urine sample, isn't it?"

"Listen, you have no idea the kinds of things they do to women at some of those *maquilas.* They give them birth control shots, they make them show their sanitary napkins every month, they pass around amphetamines to speed up their productivity. Hell, they've even got Planned Parenthood coming over to insert Norplant, which basically sterilizes the women for months. What's to prevent some sick fuck from raping them during a so-called pregnancy test?"

"*¿Estás segura?*" Ivon said to Elsa. "Are you sure you didn't have sex with anyone? That some man didn't take advantage of you?"

"I swear by the life of my son that I have never been with a man. I was only sixteen years old at the time. My grandmother would've killed me if I had done that."

"But it could have been rape, you could have been forced to have sex."

"No," cried Elsa, "there was no sex. I swear by my mother, by my son." She started to cough, and dark spittle came out of her mouth that she wiped up with a piece of clothing from the bed. "He said it was a pregnancy test. The nurse took my temperature, and *el doctor* asked me all kinds of embarrassing questions, like did I have a boyfriend, when was the date of my last menstruation . . . *y luego, pues* . . . he put something inside me."

"Something like what?" asked Ximena.

"I don't know. He said I had to have a pelvic exam, like all the others, and that he had to take something out of me to make sure I wasn't pregnant."

"So he put something inside you to open you up . . ."

"*¡Un fierro feo!* The metal was so cold."

"You've never had that kind of exam before, have you?"

She coughed again. "*Me dolió mucho*," she said, "and I was so afraid it would smell bad down there. He told me I had to come back in a week so he could do another exam."

"Another one? The same thing?"

"Not really. They took my temperature in my mouth and . . . you know . . . back there. And then he put something else inside me, something different. I don't know what it was, but it was sharp, almost like a needle. It hurt so bad, I could feel myself bleeding. And then he told me I had to lie with my legs up for fifteen minutes. The nurse watched me to make sure I didn't put my legs down."

"Ximena, it sounds like she was inseminated," Ivon said, in English.

Ximena went to sit beside Elsa. "Elsa, did you tell anybody what he did?"

"No. He said to come back six weeks later. Too many applicants, he said, that's why it took so long. But when I went back it turned out I was pregnant, so I didn't get the job. A woman I met at the bus stop, who had just gotten fired from the plant for being late, told me that the nurse had told her that this man was making experiments *para un anti-conceptivo.*"

"He inseminated her, Ximena, to test his contraceptive."

"God almighty," Ximena crossed herself.

"What factory was this, do you remember?" Ivon asked.

"No," she said, too quickly.

"Elsa, please," said Ximena, "if you remember you have to tell us. We think he must have done something to you to make you get pregnant."

"I told you there wasn't any sex."

"I don't mean sex, Elsa. It sounds like he inseminated you artificially."

"I don't understand. What does that mean?"

"It means he put sperm inside you, probably with a syringe of some kind, and impregnated you. You must have been ovulating," Ivon explained.

"I don't understand," Elsa said again.

"If it's true that he was testing a contraceptive, he probably made you pregnant to see if his drug would be effective."

"You have to tell us where this was, who did this to you, Elsa?" said Ximena.

Elsa started to cry again. Deep sobs that shook the bed. "You won't take Jorgito if I tell you. He won't have anyone to take care of him."

"Of course, she'll take him," said Ximena. "Won't you, Ivon?"

They were both staring at Ivon again, and she felt lightheaded all of a sudden. This was it—the decision of a lifetime. She closed her eyes and waited for the little boy's voice to speak to her, to say something about feeling lonely and wanting supervision in the kids' section, but the little boy was silent. All she heard was the sound of plates in the background and the old woman's voice scolding Jorgito for something. The old woman would probably beat him to death once his mother had passed. Brigit would never forgive her. Then her mother's refrain crept in. *Manflora. Marimacha. Sin vergüenza.*

"Of course," she said, exhaling, "I'll take him, but only if she tells us who did this to her and the name of the factory."

Elsa made the sign of the cross and mumbled a prayer over her clasped hands.

"Tell us, Elsa," said Ximena, placing a hand on Elsa's arm.

Elsa pressed her lips and her eyes shut and took a deep breath. "It happened at the ETC plant in the Benavídez Park," she whispered.

"ETC? What's that?" said Ivon.

"His name was Dr. Amen."

"Dr. Amen?" Ximena looked horrified. She gripped Elsa's arm. "The Egyptian?"

Elsa hiccupped, eyes full of tears, and nodded. "I saw it on the news when they arrested him. It was the same man."

13

"WHO'S THE EGYPTIAN?" Ivon asked for the twentieth time since they'd left Elsa's place. Ximena would not answer. She looked catatonic behind the wheel. By the time they reached the line for the downtown bridge, she had already chain-smoked three cigarettes.

"I mean it, Ximena. Talk to me, goddammit! Tell me it isn't that chemist they arrested for the murders."

Ximena looked at her suddenly. "What chemist?"

"I read about some Egyptian chemist in that *Ms.* article. What was his name?"

"You wanna get a drink?" said Ximena. "I can't tell you about the Egyptian without a drink first." She swerved out of the line and forced her van into a parking spot on a side street.

"It is the same guy, isn't it?"

"Amen Hakim Hassan, that's his name. Come on, let's go to the Kentucky Club."

It was Happy Hour and the bar was packed with tourists drinking Corona beer. A polka blared from the jukebox. They sat at the bar and Ximena ordered margaritas.

"Well?"

"I wish Frank were here. He'd be able to summarize the story better than I can."

"I don't want a summary, Ximena. Don't you think I deserve to hear the whole story about the biological father of this kid I'm supposed to adopt?"

"We don't know for sure he's the biological father. It could've been anybody's sperm."

"Like maybe they have a little sperm bank at the factory? Give me a break, it was his fucking sperm, Ximena, and you know it."

"That poor little boy," said Ximena.

The bartender brought two salt-rimmed champagne glasses and poured their drinks with a flourish. There was something familiar about him that Ivon couldn't place. She knew she'd seen him before.

"So what did the article say about the Egyptian?" Ximena asked. She put both hands on her glass, but didn't drink from it.

"That he was arrested for preying on young women he picked up in the downtown clubs. That he was paying some gang to commit more killings for him while he's in prison, and they think he's the mastermind behind the crimes."

"Did the article say he had assaulted this prostitute that he had locked up in his house, but she escaped somehow and reported him?"

"Maybe, I don't remember all the details."

"One of the theories behind the crimes is that there's a black market on human organs, and they target young women because they're healthy, they haven't developed bad habits yet that will have a negative impact on their organs. According to our sources, some of the bodies were found with their insides carved out of them. And since those bodies were all found near areas in the desert that are used as landing strips, the theory goes, those healthy hearts and livers and whatever else the human organ market needs get harvested fresh from the kill and taken away immediately on helicopters."

"That's ridiculous. That requires a sterile environment at the very least."

Ximena finished her drink in one gulp and wiped the salt off her lips before continuing. "Our source has also discovered that some of those girls that were hollowed out had gotten fired because they were pregnant, and then coincidentally, they ended up dead."

"Like Cecilia."

"Uh-huh. That prostitute who escaped from the Egyptian and got him arrested said that he had been giving her injections to keep her from getting pregnant. When she refused to take them any more because the contraceptive was making her sick, he went ballistic and wanted to kill her. He accused her of sabotaging his career."

"I don't believe it."

"I don't blame you." Ximena signaled the bartender to bring another round. "It's fucking unbelievable."

"I don't believe you would keep all this information from me, Ximena."

"And why would you need to know that? What does that have to do with the price of babies in China?"

"Cecilia was obviously at risk, just for being pregnant. If I'd have known . . ."

"What would you have done? Smuggled her across the border and taken her to live with you and Brigit in Los Angeles? Or maybe you think I should've done that, taken her to live at Grandma Maggie's maybe, is that it?"

The bartender brought two more drinks. Ivon polished off her first one and handed him the glass. Ximena was right. What could she have done to protect Cecilia?

"So you're saying this Egyptian guy likes to impregnate women so he can use them as guinea pigs for his contraceptives?"

Ximena shook two cigarettes out of her pack and offered one to Ivon. Immediately, the bartender was there with a lighter. "It gets better," said Ximena. "Frank had a contact at one of the *maquilas*, a nurse that used to work at ETC. She told him she used to help Dr. Amen, as she called him, perform pregnancy tests on some of the girls who came to apply at the factory."

"Not all of them?"

"Well, yeah, all of them had to take a pregnancy test, but apparently there were some he chose to test for something else. He made her take saliva samples, not just urine samples, and he gave them pap smears himself. She had to keep meticulous charts about their periods and ovulation cycles. I guess he thought she was stupid and didn't know that he was doing sexual things to these girls during their physicals."

"So he *was* raping them?"

"Whatever gynecologists do. Except he wasn't a gynecologist.

He wasn't even an M.D."

"Did the nurse ever tell anybody, other than Father Frank?"

"When the Egyptian got arrested, she quit ETC and went to work somewhere else. Frank lost contact with her."

"Did Father Frank ever say anything?"

"He couldn't. The nurse told him all this in confession."

"Did she ever see the Egyptian actually inseminating these girls?"

"No, but she knew what he was doing. Remember, she was monitoring their cycles."

"To see how long they would take to incubate?"

"Sounds like it."

"She didn't tell you who they were, I suppose."

"One of them was Elsa."

Ivon stared at her cousin in disbelief. What else was Ximena not telling her? "You fucking knew?"

"I didn't know he had inseminated Elsa. I thought he'd probably raped her and she didn't want to admit it."

"Either way, Ximena, you knew the kid you were asking me to adopt came from the sperm of a pervert and possible serial killer."

Ivon hadn't felt the urge to hit someone in years.

"Whatever he did to her probably gave her cancer, too," she said.

Ximena shrugged. "It's possible."

"Fuck you, Ximena. You bitch."

"I deserve that, okay. I'm sorry. But we're talking about an innocent child here. We don't even know for sure Hassan's the father."

"Yeah, for all we know it could be Father Frank!"

Ivon pushed her stool back and stalked off to the bathroom. She needed to put her hands in water or she really was going to punch something.

The bathroom reeked of pine disinfectant. She turned on the tap and let the cold water trickle over her palms. What fucking nightmare had she walked into? Nothing in the world could convince her to follow through on this adoption thing now. Brigit would never accept Jorgito under these circumstances. No matter how many heartstrings he pulled on Ivon, she wouldn't be able to keep this information from Brigit. That's it. She was going home. She would not stay another day in this hellhole. She'd have Irene drive her to the airport and she'd fly standby on whatever airline could get her to L.A. tonight.

Once her hands had cooled down, she sat in one of the stalls a long time, reading the graffiti. In between the usual *So-and-So Sucks Pussy* and *X Loves Y* she found something that chilled her blood. Someone had scrawled that old saying of Mexican president Porfirio Díaz: *Poor Mexico, so far from God, so close to the United States.* Underneath it, somebody else had written in red nail polish and shaky lettering, *Poor Juárez, so close to Hell, so far from Jesus.*

Even as angry as she was, Ivon recognized a gift from the gods. Talk about the representation of class and gender in bathroom graffiti! Violence against women, the economic exploitation of the border, even the politics of religion. She could use Juárez as her third case study. With Cecilia's murder and Elsa's story about medical testing and illegal insemination at the *maquilas*, the chapter could write itself.

Was this cold-blooded, she wondered, to do a case study on a girl she'd just seen at the Juárez morgue and another who was dying of cancer? Or would it help her understand what was going on in her own hometown? Eight years ago when she'd left El Paso, she vowed she'd never live here again; things were stagnant here—nothing ever changed. Even as a child, when people asked her what she wanted to do when she grew up, she'd say, "leave El Paso." She thought she knew everything there was to know about this place. The truth was things *had* changed, and she didn't understand any of it—not the murders, not the silence that surrounded the murders, not even the context in which the crimes were committed. All she knew was that this had fallen into her lap. How could she turn her back on this chance to do something?

That would mean staying, though, and getting more rather than less involved in this nightmare that Juárez had become. She would have to research the crimes, read whatever had been written about them over the last five years, on both sides of the border, maybe she'd even find something online. She would have to talk to Cecilia's family, go to the *maquiladora* where the girl had been employed and speak to her coworkers, snoop around the infirmary of ETC. Did she really have the energy to do all this homework?

It's almost the middle of June, she reminded herself, you have a little over two weeks to meet your deadline and keep your job. Here, at least, was a real idea, a problem she could explore, a concrete direction for her research—something she had not had since they'd moved to L.A. Job-tenure-real estate, she reminded herself. Think of your house. Think of the Irene plan. How was she going to provide a roof over Irene's head if she didn't keep her job? After that little scene at Ma's house earlier, Ivon knew it was more urgent than ever to get her sister away from those backward Mexican ideas Ma kept trying to instill in the girl about being a good woman.

Okay. Decision made. She stood up and straightened out her clothes. She would stay and talk to people and do the research she needed for a new case study based on that graffiti. She'd start tonight, as soon as they got back to Grandma Maggie's house. That was all. No babies, no adoption, just the dissertation.

14

It was early still, in Mexican time, when Irene pulled into the fairgrounds in Juárez. She had no problem finding a parking space close to the main entrance. She stopped the El Camino behind a big truck that said LONE R★NGR on the license plate.

She was so mad at Ivon. She couldn't believe Ivon hadn't called her. Patch things up with Ma, Ivon had said, we'll go when it gets dark. Yeah, right. As soon as she saw Ximena's car in the driveway, she should've suspected Ivon would just shine her on, like she always did around their cousins. All she was was "the little sister." Well, they had a date with Raquel, and Irene intended to keep it. She didn't need Ivon to take her to the fair. She had her own car, her own money, and she knew how to drive in Juárez. She was going to meet Raquel there, and that was final. Raquel would take care of her, show her around, maybe tell her more about when she was a kid, back when Raquel had been Ivon's "friend."

Raquel was standing with a group of men by the ticket counter. Standing right next to her, holding her hand, was a girl about Irene's age, wearing a short black dress and black platform sandals. Irene looked down at her white jeans, striped T-shirt, and blue suede Skechers, and felt underdressed.

"Sorry I'm late," said Irene, kissing Raquel on the cheek. "I was waiting for Ivon, but I guess she couldn't make it."

"I'm not surprised," said Raquel, but Irene could tell she was disappointed. "At least you're here." She spoke to the men. "*Muchachos*, this is Ivon's little sister, Irene." She pronounced the name in Spanish. "And this is my brother's friend, Saúl Méndez. He's the photographer being featured at the museum of art. And this is his brother, Paco."

They looked almost identical, except the photographer had a mustache and Paco looked like he pumped iron. They took turns shaking hands with Irene.

"*Mucho gusto*," each one said, "*para servirle.*"

There was a formality about it that made Irene want to laugh.

"And this is Junior, or rather Salvador Peñasco, and his *chofer*, Chuy."

"I've never met anyone who had their own driver before," Irene said, shaking Junior's hand. The driver flashed gold-capped teeth at her. She couldn't help staring at all the tattoos on the driver's arms and hands; she could even see tattoos around his neck.

"He's a junior," said Raquel, "you know, a rich boy. His father owns an industrial park. That's why he has a *chofer.*"

He was tall and skinny, had closely cropped hair, and was wearing a wife-beater and baggie pants. He looked more like a gangbanger than a rich boy.

"My niece, Myrna." Raquel still wasn't finished with the introductions. "She's meeting her friend Amber here later, and I thought it might be a good idea for you to get to know each other. They'll show you all the best places for girls your age. I promised to keep Saúl company while he signs copies of his photographs. So I won't be able to join you until the museum booth closes."

Irene got the picture right away. Raquel had brought her niece along to entertain her while she and Ivon had the night to themselves.

"Cool," said Irene, in English. "You do speak English, right?" she asked Myrna.

"Of course," said Myrna. "If you prefer." She said something in lightning speed to the men, and they all laughed politely. The guy named Paco told her to behave.

They stood around a little longer, like they were waiting for something. Irene wasn't sure if they were expecting her to get tickets for everyone, but then the men left and Raquel went up to the ticket counter and got free passes for her and Myrna.

"It's too bad Ivon didn't come," Raquel said, as they passed through the turnstile. "I even have tickets to the *palenque*. Pepe Aguilar is singing tonight. She used to love the *palenque.*"

But Irene wasn't thinking about Ivon anymore. Finally, she was at the fair.

"Wow, this is like a real carnival," she said to Myrna, head turning in every direction. "It's almost as big as Western Playland."

She noticed Myrna rolling her eyes at Raquel, like she was some kind of dolt or something. Whatever. This was the first time Irene was on her own like this and she wasn't going to let any Juárez chick's attitude bring her down.

The front part of the midway was crammed with booths and tents representing every kind of business in Juárez, from the electric company to jewelry shops and shoe stores. She followed Raquel and her niece to the *Museo de Arte e Historia* tent, where a leather-topped table and some leather chairs stood in front of a television flashing images of Aztec pyramids, Diego Rivera murals, and folkloric dancers. A woman's voice droned on and on about the importance of art and history in Mexican culture. The guy named Saúl was already sitting in one of the chairs, laying out a spread of black-and-white photographs on the table. In a corner of the tent stood another table piled with video- and audiotapes. A banner hung off the red tablecloth that read Instituto Frontelingua. A woman in a maid's uniform was walking around with a tray of drinks in one hand and a plate of Swedish meatballs in the other. Myrna helped herself to some meatballs, but Irene didn't want to get any food in her teeth, so she just took a soft drink.

A handsome blonde man in jeans and a tan cowboy hat came in to look at the videotapes piled on the Frontelingua table, and Raquel went over to talk to him.

"You girls have a good time," Raquel said to her niece. "Meet me back here at eleven, and we'll all go to the *palenque* together. The second show's at midnight."

"What's the *palenque*?" Irene asked.

"The best part of the fair," Myrna told her all snooty-like. "It has a casino with card tables and roulette, and there's cockfights, and a big concert every night. But they don't let women in by themselves."

"And they shouldn't," said Raquel, "especially not pretty young girls like you. Go on. Have a good time. But be careful, there's always some thief or *rabo verde* waiting to take advantage of you."

Irene followed Myrna out of the tent. "What's a *rabo verde?*" she asked.

"A pervert," said Myrna, rolling her eyes again.

"Look, do you have a problem?" said Irene. "You don't have to baby-sit me, I can take care of myself."

"Just don't say anything. You sound like a *pocha.* I don't want people to think I'm a *pocha,* too."

Pocha. Irene hated that word. Even Ma called her that at times. Was it her fault she spoke Spanish with an accent? Could she help it if she was born in El Paso, if the nuns forced her to speak only English at school? Even the *mexicanas* at her school had to speak English.

They wandered around the midway without talking to each other. Irene noticed that all the girls her age were as dressed up as Myrna. A lot of them walked hand-in-hand with boyfriends. Everyone spoke Spanish. She felt tongue-tied and awkward all of a sudden, sure that everyone could tell just from the way she was dressed that she was from the other side. *Pocha.* She fumbled in her backpack and took out her CD player and headphones. She had this really big need, suddenly, to listen to Tori Amos' "Black Dove," which she thought of as her private birthday song.

"She was a January girl," she lip-synched the song.

Myrna tapped her on the shoulder, but Irene ignored her.

"By the woods, by the woods, by the woods . . ."

Myrna tapped her again.

"What?" said Irene, lifting the headphones off her ears.

"You want to buy something?" Myrna said. "They have really nice silver jewelry from Taxco over there, or if you want a purse or a wallet, that booth over there has the best leather stuff. But you have to bargain with them, or else they'll think you're a tourist or a *gringa* and charge you whatever they want."

"I thought you said I shouldn't say anything."

"I'm sorry, I didn't mean to hurt your feelings. I'll bargain for you if you want."

They went to the jewelry booth and Irene selected a silver yin-yang ring for herself and a matching one for her cousin Gaby. She spotted a square-link bracelet she thought Ivon would like, and a silver rosary she could give to Ma for her birthday. Myrna haggled with the woman until she got the price down to twelve dollars. For everything.

"Wow, thanks!" said Irene, slipping the plastic bag with her purchases into the denim Universal Studios backpack that Ivon had sent her back when she had started high school.

"Let's go see the games," said Myrna.

They walked into the games area and watched people playing at the Wheel of Fortune table, throwing darts at some *lotería* cards on a corkboard, aiming at green plastic soldiers in the shooting gallery. Rows and rows of stuffed animals in pastel colors lined the shelves at each station. Irene was good at these games and always won something at the church bazaar, but she felt too embarrassed to say she wanted to play.

"Shoot down *La Migra*, here's your chance!" the boy who ran the shooting gallery crowed out. Irene laughed.

"*Ándale, güera, quítate o te van a confundir con La Migra.*"

"*Baboso,*" Myrna said to the boy.

"*¡Me la rayo!*" the boy called out.

"What'd he say?" said Irene. He had spoken too fast, and all she'd heard was *güera* and *migra*. *Güera* was another way of saying *gringa*.

"Let's get out of here," said Myrna. "Are you hungry?"

From the tone of their exchange, Irene could tell whatever he'd said had not been nice, and Myrna had tried to defend her. She didn't press the issue, but the awkwardness came back. She was beginning to understand why her mom was always saying, "I don't want you going over there by yourself or with your *chola* friends. People are completely different over there, even if it is just across that dirty puddle of a river." She felt like everyone was staring at her, thinking she was a *vendida* or something, because she was from the other side. She looked like them, same color of skin, same Mexican features and, yet, she didn't belong. She was an American. To a lot of people that meant sell-out.

The games were flanked by concession stands, *taquerías*, and bigger restaurants that offered tables under tents and live musical entertainment.

"I could use something to drink," said Irene.

"Let's get a *michelada*."

"What's that?"

"It's like a margarita, only with beer, it's really good."

Myrna led the way to a beer stand and ordered two *micheladas*. Irene watched the guy pour Carta Blanca beer into two glasses of ice and spice each drink with lime juice and salt. He placed the frothy beers in front of them, and she was amazed that he didn't ask for their i.d.

"My treat," said a male voice behind them, in English, and they both whirled around at the same time. It was the same man in the cowboy hat Irene had seen earlier at the Frontelingua table. He raised his hat to them, smiling, and handed the beer vendor a five-dollar bill. "A *Dos Equis* for me, *por favor*."

The bartender poured his beer into a plastic glass.

"We can pay for our own drinks," said Irene.

He ignored her and looked at Myrna. "I was just talking to your aunt over at the language school table," he said, his voice low and sexy, "and she asked me to keep an eye on you two."

He took his glass and raised his hat to them.

"That's nice," said Myrna, fawny-eyed and smiling stupidly.

"My pleasure," he said, toasting with her. He turned to look at Irene. "You're related to Ivon Villa, aren't you?"

"How'd you know?"

"We met on the plane," he said, winking. "Saw you there at the airport waiting for her."

"Oh, yeah?" she said, but she wasn't interested in conversation. She could see the ferris wheel and the lights of all the other rides. *Ranchera* songs and house music blared out of sideshow loudspeakers and clashed with the noise of carnival music and auctioneers. She wanted to get going.

"Well, thanks," she said. "Ready?" she yanked on Myrna's arm. Myrna gave her an irritated look.

"*Adiós*," Myrna said to the guy. "*Gracias por la michelada*."

"Y'all are welcome," he called out behind them.

"I hate that," said Irene. "Can't guys see two chicks walking alone before they try to home in on you?"

"I don't mind," said Myrna. "Why do you think I come to the fair?"

They sipped their drinks as they walked. *Michelada* became Irene's instant favorite drink: cold, salty, limey, fizzy, a real thirst-quencher.

"I have to get some nail polish," said Myrna.

Irene followed her to a booth that sold beauty products. They sampled different colors of nail polish. Irene applied green and blue to one hand, lavender and black to the other, trying not to cover up the little stars she had paid so much for when she'd gotten her last manicure. Myrna said all those colors looked too *naco*, which Irene figured meant tacky, and used the same salmon-pink color on all of her nails. They tried on different shades of lipstick, sprayed perfume on each other, and tested a variety of hair sprays. Irene was beginning to feel a little better. She offered to pay for Myrna's stuff, but Myrna didn't let her.

"I don't need your money," said Myrna. "My dad makes a lot of money. You don't have to pay me for showing you around."

"Sorry, I didn't mean it like that," said Irene.

Each one paid for her own products. Myrna bought nail polish and perfume. Irene got two shades of nail polish and matching lipstick.

"You want to get on some of the rides?"

"Sure," Irene nodded. She couldn't figure this Myrna out. First she was drama, then she was cool, then she was rude, then she was defending her. Irene decided to go with the flow. You're at the fair, she reminded herself. It would've been better if Ivon were here, but she couldn't live her whole life depending on her big sister.

Irene wanted to ride the ferris wheel first, then they got on the Hammer, on the Spinning Teacups, on the Flying OBNIs (which she learned later stood for UFOs), on the topsy-turvy Revolcadero where Irene felt the tartness of the *michelada* come up in her throat. She didn't want to get on the roller coaster. She'd had an accident the one time she'd gotten on El Ratón at Western Playland. She'd die of embarrassment if she peed her pants at *la feria.*

A clown with a Polaroid took their picture as they got off the merry-go-round.

"*¿Son hermanas?*" he asked.

"No," said Myrna, and walked away, but Irene wanted the picture.

The clown charged 50 pesos for it. Irene took a five-dollar-bill from her purse and paid him. She was sure he was supposed to give her back some change, but he didn't. She slipped the picture into her pack. A memento of the fair. She was going to frame it and hang it in her room, just to spite her mom. Or maybe she'd give it to Myrna.

They ate mangos *con chile,* steamed corn on the cob covered with mayonnaise, thick *tacos al pastor* with grilled green onions, rainbow-striped cotton candy.

After a couple of hours, Myrna said her feet were tired and they sat down at a table under a big tent. A waiter in a white jacket came up to them. Myrna ordered another round of *micheladas.* Suddenly a girl and her boyfriend sat down at their table.

"*¡Oigan! Cómo se tardaron,*" Myrna said, smiling. "What took you so long?"

Both the girl and the boy kissed Myrna on the cheek. The girl wore her curly, black hair in a ponytail and was dressed in skin-tight Tommy jeans and a shiny black blouse, carrying one of those really expensive Dooney and Bourke little backpacks off her shoulder. The boy was all decked out in western gear, down to the snakeskin boots and the straw cowboy hat.

"This is Irene—*¿cómo te llamas?*"

"Irene Villa, hi," she said to them.

"Hi," said the girl in English. "I'm Amber. This is my boyfriend, Héctor."

"Hi," Irene said again.

Héctor shook her hand.

"So what's up?" said Amber. "You two having a good time?"

The waiter brought their beers, and Héctor ordered two more, plus a round of Herradura shots for everyone, with *sangrita.*

"*¿Sangrita?*" said Irene. "He's ordering a little blood? What is he, a vampire?"

Both Amber and Myrna laughed at that.

"It's an accompaniment to the tequila," Héctor said, stiffly.

"So are you guys best friends?" Irene asked, and then felt really stupid. She took a deep pull on her straw. Somebody had to make conversation.

"We go to El Teresiano together," said Myrna. "Where do you go?"

"Loretto," said Irene.

"Loretto? Really?" Myrna laughed.

"Yeah, what's so funny about that?"

"Oh, nothing. It's just I thought girls like you couldn't afford Loretto."

Irene sucked on her straw again. What did she mean girls like her? *Pochas?*

Amber stepped in right away and said, "Myrna's going to Loretto, too. For the summer, anyway. Her dad can't afford the tuition the rest of the year."

"And Amber's a *pocha*, like you," said Myrna.

Amber cuffed her on the shoulder. "I am not a *pocha*. I was born in D.F. But my brothers are *pochos*," she giggled, "and so is my stepfather. He's from Las Cruces."

"Her mom's high society," said Myrna, wriggling her fingertips like a rich lady.

Amber giggled. "She is not."

"Yes, she is," said Héctor. "Doña Rubí Reyna of the Transportes La Reyna dynasty."

"Héctor, don't say that. You know my mom hates it when people talk about her as someone's daughter. As if she didn't have her own identity."

"Your mom sounds like my sister," Irene said. "She's a feminist."

"That's what I say," said Héctor. "Her mom's got a lot of liberated ideas."

"Héctor!" Amber frowned at him, slapping him on the hand. "*No seas así. Me voy a enojar.* Just because she has a college degree and runs her own business doesn't make her a feminist."

"I don't think she's all that liberated," said Myrna. "She won't even let you go to Cancún with us for vacation."

"I'm working on it," said Amber.

The waiter brought their drinks. Four shots of clear tequila and four little clay cups of something red and a saucer full of lime wedges.

"You guys going to the concert at the *palenque?*" asked Myrna, looking at her watch. "It's almost time for us to go meet my aunt."

"I don't like Pepe Aguilar, he's *cursi,*" said Amber. "And you, Irene?"

She had to admit that she didn't listen to rock *en español* that much. The three of them cracked up.

"What's so funny?"

"Pepe Aguilar sings ballads," Héctor said, catching his breath. "Corny love ballads and *rancheras.* He's not Ricky Martin."

"Oh, I get it." She had to giggle at her own mistake. "The only Mexican music I listen to is Lucha Villa. Anyway, I can't stay for the concert. Curfew, you know."

"Really?" said Héctor. "I didn't know American girls had curfew."

She didn't really have a curfew tonight because she had told her mom she was spending the night with Ivon at Grandma Maggie's house, but she only had eight dollars left and she didn't think that would be enough money for the concert.

"Why don't you spend the night with me at my Tía Raquel's house?" said Myrna.

"Thanks, but I don't think so. My mom's pretty strict."

"*Bueno, salud,* everyone," said Héctor, raising his tequila glass.

The girls followed suit. Irene toasted with them. She knocked back her shot like everyone else but grimaced at the sangrita. It tasted like sour tomato juice with too much Tabasco.

After the third tequila, and who knows how many *micheladas,* Irene found herself sitting in a box with Myrna and her aunt and the men she had met earlier, watching the Pepe Aguilar concert and drinking strawberry margaritas. At one point someone made a stupid bilingual joke about wetbacks who were squatting in an empty house when the police came by to kick them out. One of the wetbacks said the sign in front of the house had told them they could come in: For Sale, the sign said, No Lease. It took her a couple of seconds to figure it out. For-Sale (*fórzale*), force the door open. No-le-ase (*no le hace*), it doesn't matter. Irene burst out laughing, spraying scarlet strawberry juice drops all over her white jeans.

Irene felt like she was in a surreal kind of movie. One minute she was watching this man in a white *charro* outfit crooning about a bad woman who had sold him out for a few coins, "*me vendiste por unas monedas*," in the sweetest male voice she had ever heard. The next minute these roosters with razor blades tied to their talons were tearing into each other and leaving a trail of feathers and blood on the sand.

The next thing she remembered it was almost daybreak and they were walking out of the *palenque*, she and Myrna, arm in arm, like *comadres*. Thank god, Irene had told her mom she was spending the night with Ivon. She'd be in so much trouble if she came home at that hour with tequila breath. Raquel asked her if she could drive. Irene thought that was a funny question.

Somehow all of them ended up at the photographer's brother's house in a *colonia* directly across the river from the ASARCO refinery. Irene thought it was weird that this guy who lived in a *colonia* hung out with someone who had his own chauffeur, but then someone rubbed her butt and she forgot what she was thinking about.

The turquoise-colored cinder-block house was perched on a sand dune close to the levee. Irene was surprised to see so many people everywhere at that hour of the morning: women serving *menudo* in the kitchen, men with beepers and cell phones clipped to their belts walking in and out of the house, trampling the cans of geraniums by the front door. Raquel had to meet with Paco about something and she told Myrna to go wait for her outside. "Take Irene with you," she said, "and don't go near the river."

There were all these guys milling around the riverbank down below. It occurred to Irene that she had never taken a swim in the Río Grande before, so she pulled off her Skechers, noticing for the first time how nasty they'd gotten from walking on the bare ground at the fair. She yanked off her socks, stuffed them into the sneakers, and plunged into the brown water fully clothed. The men on the levee were laughing, calling her wetback and *pocha* and illegal. The water felt so cool seeping through the white denim of her jeans. Something slimy touched her toes, but she didn't pay any attention to it. She breast-stroked and back-stroked back and forth across the river, daring the Border Patrol vans cruising the black bridge to take her in so she could laugh at them and tell them she was an American citizen. At one point she thought she saw Myrna on the riverbank, talking to a guy in a cowboy hat.

15

IVON KNEW HER QUESADILLAS WERE SMOKING IN THE PAN, hot olive oil sputtering all over the clean stove, but she had her eyes glued to the front page of the *El Paso Times*.

Serial Crimes Expert Exonerates Juárez Investigators

At a press conference yesterday, Bob Russell, retired director of the FBI Violent Crimes Unit, spoke on the five-year crime wave of murdered women in Ciudad Juárez. Now a private investigator in the state of Virginia, Russell is an expert on serial killers and has served as a consultant to such films as "Silence of the Lambs" and "Copycat."

Russell exonerated the Task Force on Violent Crimes Against Women organized by the Chihuahua state government to investigate the murders. "They are doing a thorough job, their procedures are on par with investigative and forensic procedures we use in the United States," he said.

Russell indicated that the police alone cannot stop the crimes, and added that the factories need to offer better means of transportation for their workers. "The girls are taken from the industrial parks where they work and dropped off in dark deserted areas where they have to walk the rest of the way to their shantytowns. I wouldn't walk there even if I were armed."

Russell stated that the possibility of a serial killer in Juárez is very real.

The criminologist agreed with the Juárez authorities that the Egyptian chemist, Amen Hakim Hasaan, held as a suspect in the killings since 1995, fits the profile of serial killers like Ted Bundy and could be masterminding the crimes from his jail cell. It is also possible, Russell said, that there is more than one serial killer who may be crossing the border from El Paso to assault women.

She reread the last two sentences until her eyes got blurry. "Un-fucking-believable," she said aloud. How was she going to explain to Brigit that the little boy she had practically agreed to adopt was the biological spawn of a Ted Bundy- or Richard Ramírez-like character?

It wasn't until the fire alarm in the kitchen started blaring that Ivon got up to turn off the stove, then searched frantically for a broom to punch at the alarm button. Yerma, who had been dozing under the table, scooted out of the room, her nails gouging the hardwood floor in her haste to get away from the noise. Ivon could not find a broom anywhere, so she had to drag a chair over, climb onto the counter, yank the cap off the blaring alarm and pull the battery out.

"Ow! Fuck a duck!" she shouted. She'd stepped on the paring knife and cut her toe. Drops of blood gathered on the white tile of the counter. Ivon got down from her perch, favoring her injured foot, and wet a paper towel in the sink to staunch the blood. Just then the phone rang.

"Goddammit! Can't I have my breakfast in peace?" she said to no one. She decided not to pick up. The caller i.d. showed *Samuel Villu*, her mom's number, and she was in no mood to talk to either her mom or Irene right now. Either one was just going to yell at her anyway.

It was almost noon, and she was groggy and hung over. She did not remember what time she had gone to bed, how late she and Ximena had stayed at the Kentucky Club, at loggerheads about Jorgito.

You promised.

You lied to me.

Elsa's going to be devastated.

Brigit will never trust you again.

Why should the child pay for his father's sins?

Why should I pay?

They argued back and forth, raising their voices, crying, pounding their fists into the bar. In the course of their conversation, each of them had probably put away six or seven margaritas.

Ivon remembered stumbling out of the bar with Ximena, but

had no memory of driving across the bridge or getting to Grandma Maggie's house. She recalled talking on the phone with Brigit,
telling her about the graffiti and how she was going to hang out in
El Paso longer than she thought to write that chapter. Brigit had
wanted to know all about Jorgito, said she had already spent $700
at IKEA on stuff for his room. Ivon told her about giving him the
little truck, how he had kissed her and called her "Von." She did-
n't mention the Egyptian. All she'd said was, "Don't take anything
out of the box, yet, Brigit, just in case this Jorgito thing ends up
not working out. The grandmother beats him and he's got all this
bruising on his head. I'm going to have him checked out. I don't
want a kid that's got mental problems." Brigit was still crying
when they hung up.

Ivon scraped her quesadillas out of the pan—the melted
cheese had dripped out and formed a lacey brown crust around
each corn tortilla—and poured half the can of salsa over them.
Taking the plate and the coffeepot over to Ximena's office, where
she'd set up her laptop, she sat down to begin that new chapter.
She ate the first quesadilla, waiting for inspiration to strike, but
the screen remained blank. She connected the phone line to the
computer so she could go online, and ate the second quesadilla.
Still nothing. She pulled up a game of FreeCell. There was a trick
she'd found to arranging the cards. It was almost an intuitive
thing, knowing what cards to move to the free cells and what
cards to arrange in a pattern, moving quickly, not thinking. She
didn't always win, but that wasn't really the objective. The game
helped her concentrate. Of course, she'd made more progress on
her FreeCell skills than on her dissertation.

Poor Juárez, so close to Hell, so far from Jesus. That and *Richy's
Diary* were the only cards she had to go on, for the moment.

Violence against women, she typed on a blank page, and next
to it, *Economic exploitation of the border*, and next to that, *Religion*.
She formatted the page in three columns. She needed to brain-
storm now, let her mind doodle on some free associations, scratch
the surface until she could see the pattern.

*Violence—death—murder—young poor Mexican women—serial
killers—Ted Bundy—Night Stalker—trematode*

*Exploitation—NAFTA—maquiladoras—workers—victims—
Border Patrol?
Religion—church—Father Francis—"so close to Jesus" Could be
a reference to a priest gone astray. He seems to know everything.
Knows about Richard Ramírez—ministered to Night Stalker in
prison—attended his trial—Richy's Diary. Is Father Francis the perp?*

"Wait a minute," she said aloud. "He's Ximena's friend."

But it was sort of suspicious that he knew that nurse at the factory where Elsa had applied and that he hadn't said anything about the Egyptian using the workers for guinea pigs. That was strange. Confession or not, he had a responsibility to report that kind of shit. What kind of social justice activist was he that he didn't report on human rights violations because of his Catholic ode to secrecy? And what about that organization of his—Contra el Silencio? He certainly knew a lot about the murders. He knew the families of the victims, he organized body searches, and he helped build homes for the workers in the *colonias*. And he just happened to know Richard Ramírez, to boot. Father Francis sure was in the thick of things. A creepy feeling started inching up the back of her neck.

Using her cell phone, she dialed information and asked for the Sacred Heart Church. Father Francis answered.

"This is Ivon," she said, "Ximena's cousin. I wasn't expecting you to answer."

"Secretary's day off," he said. "What can I do for you?"

"You know that *Richy's Diary* thing we were looking at yesterday?"

"Yes."

"Do you still have it? I'm doing some research on the Night Stalker right now."

"It's not very useful. You can't really read what it says."

"I was kind of more interested in looking at the picture."

"What's this about, Ivon?"

"Oh, just a hunch. Would you happen to have a picture of him?"

"No, but there's a biography out on him by a guy named Linedecker, I believe. It has a few pictures."

She scribbled the name on her notepad. "You've seen it, the

book, I mean?" she said.

"I don't tend to read biographies of serial killers, Ivon."

She didn't believe him for a second. "Yeah, I guess not. Anyway, thanks for the tip. Sorry I bothered you."

"No bother. I was falling asleep here in the office. How are *you* doing? Ximena told me about Jorgito."

"You know, now that you mention it, Ximena said you knew the nurse at the factory where the Egyptian worked, where Elsa apparently got inseminated."

No response.

She pressed the issue. "Sounds like he was doing some sort of medical testing, right? Don't you think you should've said something, reported it to somebody? I mean, isn't that what you're about, social justice and responsibility?"

"I don't endanger the lives of the people who confide in me in the confessional. That's a binding contract, Ivon, much like doctor-client privilege."

"Okay," she said, "just thought I'd ask. I'm going to write about that in my dissertation and just wanted to check with you and see what you knew. Thanks, anyway, bye."

"Ivon, that might not be the wisest thing to do. You're just speculating."

"I guess I'll just have to talk to somebody who's not bound to secrecy."

Two strikes. The man was guarding his information. Something Ximena seemed to specialize in, too. She drew out a Free-Cell layout in her notebook and placed Father Francis' name in a free cell. She opened up three Internet screens. In the first, she typed the word *Juarez* into the Yahoo search engine. In the second, she searched for Richard Ramírez, and in the third, she did a random search on the *maquiladora* murders. This one kept coming up blank, until she found the right combination of words: *Juarez + women + murder*.

Five minutes later, she had a new category in her Favorites list called Kentucky Club Case Study with three subcategories: Juarez, Serial Killers, and Maquiladoras. She focused on three of them: *Borderlines*, an information source for tourists; *The Night Stalker*

Archives, part of an online Crime Library, and *Frontera Norte-Sur,* an English-language digest of newspaper articles on the U.S.-Mexico border.

The *Borderlines* site not only provided typical tourist information on the region, but also promoted prostitution by informing the potential and obviously male tourists that,

> Every week hundreds of young Mexican girls arrive in Juárez from all over Mexico. Most of these young ladies are looking for work that will be a primary source of income for their families back home. While many will begin their careers in one of the various maquiladora factories in the area, often they end up in the many bars and brothels.

There was even a link called *Those Sexy Latin Ladies,* which would take you to a list of some of the most popular places on La Mariscal. From here you could download a map to the area around the old gymnasium, and there was a downloadable coupon for a free drink at the Sayonara Club. Pictures of young women in bikinis and high heels illustrated the page, and the words *Prostitution is legal here* and *You will not find a place with more beautiful, available, hot-blooded young ladies* flashed in yellow letters.

"Shit," she said aloud, "no wonder there's so many freaks here. They're selling women online." She lit a cigarette.

In the second screen, she found twenty-eight web sites on serial killers. She cross-referenced Richard Ramírez on all of them. The Worldwide Serial Killer Page, Mayhem.net, the Serial Killer Index, and the Crime Library each had an entry on the Night Stalker, but the Crime Library had listed him under "The Most Notorious Serial Killers" and featured a long biographical article about him that included black-and-white pictures from his trials in Los Angeles. Although it was eerie and fascinating to think that Richard Ramírez was only seven years older than she and that they'd grown up practically in the same neighborhood—he had probably gone to Lincoln or Jefferson with some of her cousins— she didn't find anything on him that might indicate he had anything at all to do with the Juárez murders. He'd left El Paso way back in 1984, five years before Ivon had left for Iowa. She did find a quote of his that included the word *trematode*, something he said at his sentencing: "I need not look beyond this room to see all the liars, haters, the killers, the crooks, the paranoid cowards—truly trematodes of the Earth. You maggots make me sick—one and all . . . I am beyond your experience, I am beyond good and evil."

Satanist, drug addict, juvenile delinquent, and high school dropout, native son of south El Paso—where had he learned a word like trematode? Maybe a Black Sabbath or a Judas Priest song. Maybe Anton LeVey's *Satanic Bible*. And, come to think of it, the way he raped and mutilated his women victims was very similar to how some of the Juárez women had been killed. Maybe Richard Ramírez didn't have anything to do with the crimes himself, but what if he had a copycat in town, someone following in the Night Stalker's footsteps. She shuddered and got up to lock the doors.

It was at the Frontera Norte-Sur site where she spent the rest of the morning, digging through its archives section and catching up on the history of the *maquiladora* murders. The archives only went back three years, but she combed each issue for anything at all related to the murders, anything that could shed some light on why the murders were taking place at this particular moment in time. Trained in cultural studies, Ivon always looked for the historical and cultural context of whatever she was researching. She got a nutshell history of the border in the process: the PAN sweep in the state of Chihuahua after decades of PRI monopoly all over Mexico, the dispute between the new PAN administration and the son of a *maquiladora* mogul over the expropriation of some prime property near the airport, the battles against nuclear dumping in Sierra Blanca, the new post-NAFTA senate bill to increase federal funding for the Border Patrol for the implementation of Operation Hold the Line and Operation Gatekeeper, the death of the top druglord of the Juárez cartel and the narco war it started at the changing of the cartel guard, protests on both sides of the Santa Fe Bridge sparked by the violent beating of undocumented immigrants in Riverside, California, the General Motors strike in Ohio that laid off thousands of *maquiladora* workers in Juárez, the hantavirus outbreak along the New Mexico border, the testing of new air defense missiles in White Sands, the unusually high incidence of domestic abuse against women in Juárez, and, interspersed through all of it, story after story about yet another murdered, mutilated, and raped *muchacha del sur*. That, apparently, was part of the profile of the victims; not only did they tend to be thin, dark-haired, dark-skinned young women between the ages of 12 and 25, they were also all poor and many of them had migrated from the south to work at a *maquiladora*. But they were not all Mexican citizens.

In May of 1996, one of the seventeen corpses found between August 1995 and April 1996 was identified as an El Paso girl, the first El Paso girl to be found among the dead in the Juárez *colonia* of Lomas de Poleo. In November 1997, on International Day of No Violence Against Women, the mothers of the then 97 slain women in Juárez held a funeral march and a rally outside of city hall, where they demanded that the authorities bring the killers to justice and end impunity. In February 1998, a group of women representatives from the Mexican legislature visited Juárez to conduct their own investigation of the crimes; they spoke to municipal officials, nongovernmental organizations, feminist groups, the families of the victims, and even the Egyptian in the Juárez jail. A week later, the remains of three more women were found in Lomas de Poleo. By then, the number of victims was up to 109. That same March, three Mexican Americans from Elephant Butte, New Mexico, were arrested for kidnapping and crossing undocumented immigrants and using them as "white slaves," that is, for prostitution. In April, a seventeen-year-old *maquila* worker named Caridad disappeared on her way to work. Most recently, a report issued by the National Commission on Human Rights found the Juárez authorities responsible for a number of irregularities in the investigation of the crimes, including the misidentification of corpses and incompetence in gathering crime scene evidence.

By the time Ivon logged off, she felt completely exhausted. She glanced over her notes: the selling of women online, the Richard

Ramírez copycat, the drug war, white slavery, hantavirus research, political conspiracies. Talk about too much information. Her brain felt like it had been pumped full of helium. Her mouth tasted of smoke and old coffee. She needed to brush her teeth, take a shower, maybe take a nap.

As soon as she disconnected from the Internet, the phone rang again. She walked over to the kitchen to pick it up, not even bothering to look at the caller i.d. display.

"Hi, Ma. You wouldn't be calling to apologize by any chance?"

"Where are you two? I've been calling and calling all morning, and the phone's been busy for hours. The *chiles* are getting cold."

"What are you talking about, Ma? What *chiles?*"

"What time did you girls get home last night? That's two nights in a row *que esa niña* has been out carousing with you."

"Irene's not here, Ma. I haven't seen her since yesterday afternoon."

"*No seas chistosa.* Let me talk to her."

A quiver started in the pit of Ivon's stomach. "She's not here, Ma, really."

"*Mira,* Ivon, I'm in no mood to play these games with you. I've been roasting and frying *chiles* all morning. Irene said she wanted *chiles rellenos* for lunch today, said she was going to spend the night with you after the *feria* and that you all were coming over for lunch. Well, lunch is ready, it's getting cold, and you're not here. Now let me talk to your sister right now."

Ivon's nerves prickled. She was staring at the newspaper, and the phrase *the killer is an American citizen that crosses the border to assault women* beamed out at her as if in neon letters. Again, she thought of Father Francis.

"Ma, I'm not playing with you. I'm telling you the truth. Irene is not here."

"She didn't stay over?"

Ivon took a breath to keep her voice from shaking. "No, Ma. I didn't go to the fair with her last night. I had something to do with Ximena, so I had to change my plans."

"She said you promised to take her. You didn't call to tell her you couldn't go?"

"This other thing was more important than going to the stupid fair."

"More important than your sister?"

"Have you called Gaby? Maybe she went with Gaby. Or with her friends from school. You know how Irene is. She won't stop 'till she gets what she wants. Ma . . . Ma? Still there?"

"*Santo Dios de mi vida*, Ivon. Something's happened to your sister."

"Ma, don't jump to conclusions, okay? I'll be right there. Don't go anywhere. Call her friends. Call Gaby. I'll call the hospitals . . . just in case."

But her mom had already hung up.

16

"I'LL BE RIGHT THERE, M'IJITA. What? Wait, you're breaking up. These goddamn cell phones. There it is. Okay, I'm on Montana right now. I can swing by and pick you up, if you want. ¿Qué pasó? Your mother sounded hysterical. She said something had happened to Irene."

"She didn't come home last night, Tío," Ivon explained. "Ma thought she was over here with me, but I think she may have gone to the fair by herself. I'm calling the hospitals right now. I'll be ready when you get here."

"Okay, don't panic," he said. "I'll page Patrick."

Ivon hung up and ran to the bedroom to change. There was something gnawing at her belly, crawling up into her chest, but she kept pushing it back, not letting it surface in her mind. After she was dressed, she hunted around for the phone book and found it under a pile of newspapers in the living room. She called the emergency rooms at Sierra, Providence, and Hotel Dieu—no record of a girl matching Irene's description. At Thomason, a teenage girl had been brought in at two in the morning with a gunshot wound to the stomach, but no, she wasn't a Hispanic, she was an African-American girl. Uncle Joe's truck pulled up in the driveway just as Ivon ended the call with Vista Hills Medical Center on the east side.

"No luck," she said, jumping into the seat beside him, "although I don't think it's exactly bad luck not to find my little sister in a hospital."

"You got a point, there, m'ijita." He gazed down his bifocals at her. He looked more stooped and weathered than she remembered. "Long time no see."

She kissed him on his stubbly cheek. Uncle Joe was her mother's little brother, Ivon's godfather and strongest supporter during her high school wars with her mother.

"I was getting the pit ready to make some *barbacoa*, since I heard you were in town," he said, "when your mom called, screaming her head off. Scared the dickens out of me."

Leave it to Uncle Joe to be thinking of giving her some sort of welcome dinner. For a second, her eyes got misty.

"So what's really going on, *m'ijita?*" he asked, giving her a sideways glance as he shifted the gears into reverse. "Is your mom just exaggerating, as usual? You know how much she likes to create *telenovelas* in her mind."

"I don't know, Tío. It's pretty scary over there. If Irene really did go to Juárez on her own, with all those young girls her age getting killed . . ."

She punched the inside of the door, angry with herself suddenly.

"I should've called her. She had her heart set on going to that stupid fair with me. We could've gone another day."

"Does she have a boyfriend?"

Ivon shook her head. She didn't think so, but she wasn't sure. She hadn't asked.

"Patrick says it's too soon to put out an APB. We have to wait until she's been missing for 24 hours, and most people turn up in that time. But he's going to call the juvenile detention center and the INS."

"The INS?"

"If she went to Juárez and something happened to her over there, they may be holding her at customs."

"She would've called home."

"Doesn't hurt to check."

"What about the Juárez jail, the Juárez hospitals? I'll never forgive myself if something's happened to my sister, Tío."

"Let's just take it one step at a time, okay, *m'ijita?*"

"Yeah, I know, I'm beginning to sound as paranoid as Ma, but then, Irene's not the type to go off by herself. She's not like me, Tío."

"Thank God," he said.

"She told Ma she was spending the night with me at Grandma Maggie's place after the fair, but I didn't let her know I wasn't going to be able to make it, and I haven't seen her since she dropped me off yesterday afternoon. You think she's just upset at me for not keeping my promise to take her to the fair?"

"That's probably it," her uncle said, patting her leg. Then he chuckled. "I don't know what it is about you Villas who like to go missing in action. Remember when your dad got lost? You were, what, eight or nine years old?"

Seven, Ivon said to herself. She didn't feel like going down memory lane right now, but she knew that her uncle was trying to inject some levity here, changing the subject to keep her from going down the yellow brick road of a guilty conscience. She watched the cars out the window.

"Yep, ole Sammy's past sure caught up with him. You remember what happened between them, don't you? Your Tía Luz and him? You're the one who let the cat out of the bag." Uncle Joe laughed, smacking the steering wheel. "*La luz de mis domingos*," he feigned a sexy, dramatic voice. "*Pinche* Sam. I guess *one* of my crazy *hermanas* wasn't enough for him."

Ivon cringed. She remembered finding the picture, a black-and-white studio portrait of her dad with his hat tipped sideways like a movie star in Tía Luz's rig, dedicated to *la luz de mis domingos*, the light of my Sundays. Ivon and her cousin Mary had been playing at being truck drivers one of the times that Tía Luz was in town, and Ivon had found the photograph under the pillow in the little sleeping compartment behind the seats. Ivon had run into the house with it to show her mom.

"Look, Ma," she'd said, "Tía Luz has a picture of Papi in her truck."

Major hell had broken loose that day. Her mother had slapped Tía Luz so hard she fell down, and then they'd both started crying. When her dad came home from work and saw the rig outside, he didn't even come inside the house. Ivon watched him from the window, walking away from the house in a big hurry, not even taking his car. Ma made her sister promise she would never ever see her husband again or set foot in their house or even show her face in El Paso.

Because Tía Luz was a truck driver (and for that alone, one of Ivon's heroes), it didn't surprise anybody when she left town. But no one heard from her again for more than twenty-five years, until she came to pay her last respects to Grandma Maggie, two years ago.

"Your poor dad was so embarrassed, he disappeared for three days."

Ivon shook her head. *Mujeriega, just like her dad*, her mom had said to Brigit.

They had to wait for the train to pass on Piedras Street. Ivon remembered a poem she had written back in the days when she still wrote poetry, something about how the howling of a train was the sound of lovers leaving.

"He had a few *calaveras* in the closet, that *cuñado* of mine," Uncle Joe was saying. "One of these days I'll tell you the story about why he fell in love with Luz. He told me. It's a pretty good story." He shook his head and stroked the stubble on his cheeks.

Ivon watched the yellow caboose of the Santa Fe line rumbling slowly past the gates.

"And to think he was just up the street the whole time we were looking for him," he continued, putting his truck into gear, "playing dominoes with that judge friend of his. He didn't even come out when he saw the cop cars cruising up and down the neighborhood. That's probably what'll happen with Irene, *m'ijita*. She's somewhere obvious."

Ivon shrugged. "I hope so, Tío. We did have a big fight with Ma yesterday."

"Yeah, I thought there was something y'all weren't telling me."

Her uncle had intended to take Piedras down to the freeway, but there was a detour up ahead where the streetlight was being repaired at Montana, and they had no choice but to go left and follow the detour to Copia. They passed the Furr's Market, and Ivon remembered Raquel.

"Raquel!" she said aloud, as if she'd just found the answer to a puzzle.

"¿*Qué*?"

"We were going to meet a friend of mine at the fair. If Irene went on her own, which is very likely, considering how stubborn she is, she probably met my friend Raquel there."

"Can you call her?"

"I don't have her number, but I know where she works."

"You see, I bet you that's all it is. She was probably mad at your mom over the fight, and mad at you for not keeping your promise, and she spent the night at your friend's house after the fair. Irene's a smart girl, *m'ijita*. She wouldn't do anything stupid."

"That's it," said Ivon, taking a deep breath for the first time since she'd spoken with her mom. Irene went home with Raquel.

And then an eerie thought crossed her mind. No, she didn't even want to think it, but it nagged at her anyway, a weird sensation at the idea that Raquel might seduce her little sister. Why would she do that? It was absurd even to think it. But she remembered how she had met Raquel. Raquel had come to her high school to speak about Mexican art in Ivon's Spanish class. She was her teacher's friend, and Ivon was the teacher's pet. The three of them had lunch together afterward. The whole time, Raquel's black eyes kept weaving a spell over Ivon, and Ivon had not been able to resist later when Raquel invited her to go out for coffee after school.

They went out for coffee a lot. Raquel was a slow seductress. She wanted to know all about Ivon's life, her dreams, her fantasies. She would touch Ivon's hand, stroke her cheek, hold her tight when they hugged goodbye. And always there was that smell of hers, flowery like jasmine, but with a musky undertone that always aroused Ivon, even before she realized what that arousal really meant.

Raquel invited Ivon to the movies, gave her records and watercolor pictures she made. Ivon wrote a poem for her, once, the one about the train. She had dreams about being with Raquel, and it scared her, the passion she could feel imagining Raquel's body against hers. And then, suddenly, one night, coming home after a movie (they had gone to see *Star Trek: The Wrath of Khan*, she remembered), they were making out in Raquel's car, and Raquel had her tongue in her mouth and her hand on Ivon's breast. As if someone had given her instructions on what to do, Ivon had unbuttoned Raquel's blouse and buried her face in the perfumed lace of Raquel's bra. Ivon had been a year older than Irene was now.

Even if Raquel had seduced Irene, she figured, at least she'd be safe. Better in Raquel's arms than a kidnapper's.

17

As SOON AS UNCLE JOE'S TRUCK PULLED UP in front of the house on Barcelona Street, Ivon's mother shot across the porch. Ivon could tell she was *pissed*. She ran down the breezeway and met them at the gate. Without a word, green eyes on fire, she started slapping Ivon right there in front of the whole neighborhood.

"*¡Irresponsable! ¡Egoísta!*" she belted out. "Where is she? Where's your sister?" She hit Ivon's face, smacked at her ears, clawed at her shirt with her nails.

"Lydia! Lydia! *¿Qué te pasa, mujer?*" Uncle Joe yelled out. "Stop that!"

Ivon covered her face with her arms. Uncle Joe had to grab on to her mom's wrists and threaten to hit her back if she didn't stop.

Ivon didn't realize her nose was bleeding until she felt the blood running over her lip. She pinched her nostrils closed and tilted her head back, noticing that the next-door neighbor was watching them from her porch. The neighbor across the street had been taking out the trash and stood glued to the curb watching the spectacle.

"*¡Suéltame!*" her mom ordered, freeing her wrists from Uncle Joe's grip.

"Let's take it inside!" Uncle Joe muttered through clenched teeth. "Making a scandal out here. *¿No te da vergüenza?*"

Ivon felt like she had to empty her bladder. Walking into her mother's house at that moment was the last thing she wanted to do. She could not even bring herself to look at Lydia for fear of railing on her for all of the times she had done this to her as a child, embarrassed her like this in front of her schoolmates, her teachers, her cousins. It had been the reason Ivon had run away from home in the eighth grade and again as a sophomore in high school, after Irene was born.

Locked in the bathroom, she turned on the cold water and watched it pour down the drain. Her hands shook. Blood dribbled into the sink. She scooped the cold water over her face to wash off the blood and staunched her nose with a tissue. She tried to focus on the sound of the water, but it did not drown out her mother's voice. She flushed the toilet, and for the few moments that it took the tank to fill up again, she heard nothing else but water flowing. That's the only sound that calmed her.

Breathe deep, Ivon, imagine you are lying on the beach and you can hear the sound of the surf ebbing and flowing all around you. It was the meditation technique that Brigit had taught her from her yoga class. *Hold your breath in your belly and let it out slowly, like water flowing from your mouth. With each breath you are releasing your anger, Ivon, let it flow out of you and evaporate on the sand of the beach.*

She rinsed her face again and turned off the faucet. At least her hands weren't shaking anymore, but her eyes were red and there were scratch marks on her cheek and neck. Even her T-shirt had gashes and blood stains on it. *Una bestia humana*, that's what her uncle had once called her mom when Ivon showed up on his doorstep after a beating. From then on, that's how Ivon referred to her mom—the Human Beast. Aunt Araceli, Uncle Joe's second wife (rest in peace), had wanted to call someone, report this abuse to the authorities, but Ivon was terrified that they would take her away and hadn't let her. She was thirteen years old. She closed her eyes and took another deep breath.

They were arguing in the living room, and Ivon had the eerie sensation that she was still that runaway teenager and her uncle was there to defend her against her mom's hormonal wrath. Her father never meddled in her mother's affairs. Daughters were a woman's business, not a man's, he said, and he'd leave the house as soon as the arguments started. Later, her dad would come home and hold her, tell her she had to forgive her mother, that the doctor said she was having trouble with her hormones.

"He was drunk, Lydia!" her Uncle Joe was shouting. "Nobody told him to go climbing Cristo Rey in that condition. You can't blame Ivon for that. That's ridiculous!"

"What do *you* know, José? Just because she's your goddaughter, you defend her *a ciegas,* but you don't even know the whole truth."

"I know the whole truth, Lydia. Sam was an alcoholic. He was just looking for an excuse to start drinking again. Ivon did not put the bottle to his lips."

"Oh, sure, she's innocent. Poor Ivoncita, nothing's ever her fault. She's just living her life. As if what she chooses to do with her life doesn't affect the rest of us. That lifestyle of hers killed her father, it killed him to think his own daughter was one of those . . . those *troqueras.*"

"Like our sister Luz? She was the real truck driver in the family, and Sam didn't seem to have any problem with that."

"*¡Cállate!*" her mom hissed. "You think it's easy living with a daughter like that? You think it doesn't terrify me that Irene might grow up to be just like her?"

"We should all be so lucky to have a daughter like Ivon. You think I wouldn't want a role model like her for Gaby? *Lo que pasa* is that you can't ever accept people for who they are, Lydia. You can't ever see the good side to anything. Let it be, *hermana.* She isn't going to change. She doesn't have to change. She's fine the way she is. *Acéptala* once and for all."

"Has she told you what she's doing here, eh, José? Has she told you that she's here to adopt a child? Is that the kind of role model you would want for Gaby? *Se está burlando de nosotros,* just mocking her entire family. Her father's turning over in his grave. *¡Sin vergüenza!*"

"What does this have to do with Irene? Why are you beating up Ivon when she had nothing to do with it? How do you know for sure Irene even went to Juárez? Maybe she went somewhere else. Maybe you drove her out of the house like you drove Ivon out. Why aren't *you* ever responsible for anything, Lydia?"

"I didn't make a plan with her, José. I didn't change my mind and forget to call her. I didn't let her go by herself. Has she forgotten that she's her sister's keeper?"

Breathe deep, Ivon, just breathe deep and let the anger flow out of you like water.

But another voice, her dad's voice this time, came forward: *Now that you have a little sister, Ivon, you have a job to do. You are your sister's keeper from now on. No matter what happens to your mother and me, she will always have you to look after her.* When had he said that to her? It was on the tip of her memory, but she couldn't place it. All she remembered was the feeling it gave her, how it brought forth the childhood fantasy of herself as a knight with a mission to protect the little damsel Irene. Sir Ivanhoe.

Ivon emerged from the bathroom with a purpose. She was pumped up with adrenaline and rage. She couldn't sit around here all day listening to her mother's recriminations. She had to find her sister.

Her mother turned her back on her as soon as she walked into the living room, but Ivon was not going to deal with her mother right now.

"I'm going to Juárez," she said. "I'm going to look for Irene. Can I borrow your truck, Tío?"

"You can't go over there by yourself," he said. "I'll take you."

"No, can you stay here with Ma, please? I know what I'm doing." She jotted her cell phone number on the tablet by the phone. "Call me if you hear anything. Did you call her friends, Ma?"

"She's not with any of her friends," her mother muttered, staring out the window. "She told them . . . you . . . were taking her to the fair."

Ivon heard the catch in her mother's voice. She grabbed the keys from her uncle's hand.

Her uncle followed her to the door. "I have to take something out of the glove box," he said in a low voice.

From the living room, her mom was shouting, "Don't even think of coming back here without your sister!"

I'm never coming back here, Ivon wanted to yell back, but instead she hurried to the truck. She was going to find Irene, bring her home, and never set foot in her mother's house again.

"Your shirt's all ripped, *m'ijita*, here, take mine," he said, taking off his red flannel shirt.

Right away she got a knot in her throat, but she put the shirt on before stepping up into the truck. No matter how hot it was, her uncle always wore flannel shirts, since Ivon could remember. The flannel was old and soft and still warm with her uncle's heat. It smelled of rosemary and smoked mesquite wood.

Her uncle leaned into the passenger side window and pulled a .22 out of the glove compartment. "Don't want you driving in Juárez with a gun in the car," he said, slipping it into the back of his Bermuda shorts.

"I might need it," she said.

"Not on your life," he said.

Uncle Joe had taught Ivon and his oldest daughter, Mary, how to shoot when they were in high school. They would drive out to Hueco Tanks and aim at bottles and snakes. Ivon had a knack for it, bringing the dead snakes home to show her dad, but Mary preferred going to the public library.

Pulling away from the curb, Ivon looked back at the house and saw her wiry uncle standing on the porch in his undershirt, hands buried in his pockets. She caught her mother blessing her from the window.

18

IVON DID NOT REMEMBER HOW SHE GOT THERE. It was as if she had blacked out as soon as she left Barcelona Street and had reawakened in the parking lot of the Pronaf Shopping Center in Juárez. She must have stopped at a gas station or a 7-11 because there were two liters of cold water on the seat beside her, sweating through the white plastic bag, a pack of cigarettes, a pack of gum, and an open bag of corn chips. She took a handful of chips and ate mechanically, not because she was hungry but because she needed something to crush with her teeth. She opened one of the water bottles and took several deep swallows, the cool water coursing down her throat into her stomach, spilling over the sides of her mouth and running down her chin.

"Wake up, Ivon," she talked aloud to herself, "watch what you're doing. Stay alert."

She wiped her chin and neck with her hand, looked in the rearview mirror, and set her jaw. *Find Irene*, that was her mantra right now. *Find Irene. Find Irene.* She would not permit herself to think that anything tragic had happened to her sister. She rolled up the windows in the truck, locked both doors, and stepped out into the hundred-degree heat. Only the truck, a taxi, and a parking attendant were in the lot.

She had parked in front of the Museum of Art and History, a round building surrounded by a moat of water, incongruously placed between a supermarket and the Casa del Sol restaurant, smack in the middle of Pronaf's parking lot. At an angle between the museum and the row of stores that made up the strip mall stood a small building that had the words Instituto Frontelingua embossed on the window glass.

Cerrado, read the sign on the glass door. Ivon checked her watch. Half past one, Mexican lunchtime. She pounded on the glass.

"Raquel!" she called out. "Open the door, it's me, Ivon, are you in there?"

No response. She pounded again, pressing her face against the hot glass. Still nothing. The parking attendant came up to her and told her the school had been closed all day. The man eyeballed her up and down. She glared at him.

Asshole macho piece of shit, she thought, don't you fucking leer at me. She glanced down at her clothes and realized he was staring at the man's shirt she was wearing, shirttails hanging low over her linen pants. No wonder he was looking at her like that. He probably thought she was *una de las otras*. Mexican men weren't used to seeing women in men's shirts, not unless they were *cholas* or lesbians. Either one was bad news in Juárez. As far as Mexicans were concerned, they meant the same thing: traitors. As Americanized Mexicans spoiled by First World liberties and behaviors, *cholas* betrayed their own culture. Lesbians, although every macho's wet dream—to voyeurize or to conquer—of course, betrayed not just their culture, but their gender, their families, and their religion.

The parking attendant walked back to the taxi, and he and the taxi driver sitting behind the wheel had a good laugh about something. Ivon pounded on the door again, but no one came to the door. Finally she gave it up and went back to the truck to get her cigarettes and wait. She decided to give the assholes a show and stood outside the truck with one leg up on the baseboard, smoking with one hand, holding a water bottle with the other. The whole time she stared straight at the taxi.

The heat bored like thorns through the flannel shirt. She could feel her arms and face, her scalp and toes roasting. She put the bottle to her lips and sucked at the water, then took a hit off her cigarette and let it flow out her nostrils. It was making her dizzy, the cigarette and the heat, but she would not give up the pose, even though the men were not paying attention to her anymore.

She heard the tires of a car crunching on the asphalt of the parking lot and turned to look who it was, hoping it was Raquel, but no, it was a shiny green Border Jumper trolley shuttling tourists to the Mexican curio stores in the Pronaf mall. Ivon watched the tourists getting down from the trolley, looking very much like midwestern housewives from Iowa, the lot of them, wearing big sunglasses, flowery dresses, sneakers, and cute straw caps, clutching their purses tight against their hips.

"Señora," he said, standing too close behind her, and Ivon whirled around as though she'd been attacked.

It was the parking attendant. "*¿Qué?*" she nearly spat at him.

"*Allí llegó alguien*," he said, pointing toward the Instituto.

She threw down her cigarette and tossed the water bottle into the front seat of the truck, locked the door again, and hurried up the steps to the entrance. Nothing had changed, the *cerrado* sign was still on the door, but then she saw the lights turning on from the inside.

Pounding on the glass with her flat palm, she heard heels clicking on the floor. All at once Raquel was standing there on the other side of the locked door, staring at her with her black eyes dilated with fear.

"Open the door," Ivon shouted through the glass.

Raquel unlocked the door from the inside. Ivon pushed it open.

"Where's my sister?"

Raquel looked as though she were going to burst into tears.

"Ivon, *espérate . . . no te enojes.*"

"*Dime dónde está mi hermana.*"

Raquel shook her head, swallowing, but didn't say anything.

Ivon grabbed her by the shoulders and pushed her up against the wall. "She met you at the fair last night, didn't she?"

Raquel nodded. Her eyes were two pools of black liquid.

"So where is she? She didn't come home. Did she stay with you?"

Raquel shook her head. "I don't know where she is," she said at last, her voice a trembly whisper. "I looked for her all morning, I swear it."

Ivon felt ants swarming into her stomach. "Don't fuck with me, Raquel. Don't tell me you let something happen to my little sister."

Raquel's face creased into a grimace and she started to cry. "I don't know," she said, tears washing down her cheeks. "I swear to you, Ivon, I don't know where she is."

"How long did she stay at the fair?"

"She was with us, with me or Myrna, the whole time, but things got out of hand when we went to that party."

"You didn't take my sister to a party after the fair, did you?"

Raquel sobbed into her hands.

"Where was this party?"

Raquel mumbled into her hands.

Ivon pulled Raquel's hands off her face. "I can't understand what you're saying."

"At Paco's house," she said, "*Colonia Soledad*. Near ASARCO."

Ivon's mouth dropped open. "You took my sister to a party in a *colonia?*"

"It was getting late, almost sunrise, and I had to get Myrna back to my house before Gabriel came over and found out we had stayed out all night. But Irene wouldn't get out of the river. I told her, Ivon, I told her she had to get out and come with us, but she wouldn't listen . . ."

"What do you mean she wouldn't get out of the river? What was she doing in the river?"

"How should I know? She was having a good time, I guess, swimming back and forth, and she wouldn't come out. It was getting late, and I had to go. I had to get Myrna back, otherwise . . . *pues*, you know how Gabriel can be . . . so I asked this guy I know to watch your sister 'till I came back for her. But when I came back she was . . . she was . . . she wasn't there anymore, everybody had left already."

Ivon's eyes had narrowed into slits. She could not believe what she was hearing.

"You left her there alone?"

"I had to, Ivon, don't you understand, didn't you hear anything I said? I had to get Myrna back before Gabriel . . ."

"You fucking stupid bitch! You left my sister alone in a *colonia?*"

"What was I supposed to do, Ivon? I should never have invited her to go with us, I know that, but it was four o'clock in the morning when we left the fair. The girl was completely drunk. Did you want me to let her drive in that condition? She couldn't drive. She couldn't even remember where she left her car."

"How much did she have to drink?"

"She was at the fair," said Raquel, as if that explained everything.

"Was she doing anything else, any drugs? It doesn't sound like Irene to do something stupid like jump into that polluted river. Even drunk I don't think she'd be that stupid. Somebody must have pushed her in."

"I didn't see her doing any drugs. She was just playing. She was getting a lot of attention from the men. I guess that's why she didn't want to get out."

"And your niece? What was she doing?"

"She was just standing around like everyone else, watching your sister play wetback. That's how Myrna put it . . . she said *la pochita* was playing wetback."

"*La pochita*, that's so rude. How could you have left her there, Raquel? With all the shit that's going on over here, all those girls getting raped and killed."

"I tried, Ivon, but she wouldn't listen. I even asked one of the guys to go in and get her, but there was *migra* everywhere. They would've arrested him for illegal crossing."

"Maybe she got picked up by the Border Patrol," said Ivon.

"Maybe, I don't know."

"You didn't check?"

"It didn't occur to me."

"Well, what if she did get picked up? What if they thought she was an illegal?"

"No *mojado* would be swimming like that, back and forth, like it was a swimming pool. You think *la migra* doesn't know the difference?"

Ivon pressed her hands over her face. The blood was pounding in her temples. For the first time in her life, Ivon thanked God for the Border Patrol. Slow down, Ivon, she told herself, don't jump to conclusions and don't make assumptions.

"Where is this *colonia?*"

"Close to ASARCO."

"And those men? Who are those men that were watching her? Did you know them?"

"I don't know, friends of Paco, I guess. It was Paco who was giving the party."

"Who is this Paco?"

"Just an acquaintance, Ivon. He went with me to look for Irene. We found her car still parked at the fairgrounds, but it had been broken into. The radio and the battery were stolen, so we had to leave it there. Paco called a tow truck. I told him to have the car towed over to my house. I didn't know what else to do with it."

Raquel started sobbing again.

Ivon shook Raquel's shoulders. "Enough, okay, this isn't help-ing. You and I are going to go look for my sister right now."

"But I haven't been here all day, my brother . . ."

"I don't give a shit about your brother or this fucking place," said Ivon. "You're taking me to this Paco's house right now."

"What for? He doesn't know anything."

"I want to talk to him, and to your niece, too, and whoever else was out there having a good time at my sister's expense. Let's go." She grabbed Raquel's elbow.

"Let me at least get my purse and the keys to lock up," said Raquel, pulling her elbow loose.

The security guard had been standing by the front door, lis-tening to everything. "Is there some problem, Señora?" he asked as they came out.

"Here, take this to your wife," Raquel said, handing the man a twenty-dollar bill. "Don't tell my brother you saw me."

"*No, claro que no, como usted quiera. Y muchas gracias.*" He fol-lowed them to the truck and held the passenger door open for Raquel.

"Are you okay to drive?" Raquel said, noticing that Ivon's hand on the stick shift was shaking.

"What do you care?" Ivon answered.

"I don't. All I care about is finding your sister."

"That makes two of us." Ivon slammed the truck into gear and shot out of the parking lot, nearly hitting the Border Jumper as it rounded the corner.

"How do I get there?"

"I told you, it's close to ASARCO. Go downtown and take the road into the *colonias*."

Ivon took Avenida Lincoln back toward the free bridge, dialing her uncle's cell phone on the way. She was going to cut across the Chamizal and drive past the fairgrounds, to see if Irene's car was still in the parking lot.

Her uncle picked up the call on the fourth ring. "It's me, Uncle, but don't tell Ma I'm calling. No, I didn't find her yet, but she did meet my friend . . ." Ivon gave Raquel an angry look, ". . . at the fair. She was with her until early this morning. Listen, it's possible that Irene may have gotten picked up by the Border Patrol, after all. Did you call them yet?"

She told him about the party and how Irene had been swimming in the Río Grande near the ASARCO refinery.

"I know, Uncle, I know. Just tell them that, okay? What was she wearing?" Ivon asked Raquel. From her purse, Raquel took a Polaroid picture and handed it to her.

"That's her and Myrna," said Raquel. "They took it at the fair."

Ivon stared at Irene's face in the picture, the carousel horses in the background. She wasn't smiling like Myrna, but staring straight ahead, lips as red as her blouse.

"White jeans and a red-and-white striped blouse," Ivon told her uncle, and then, remembering something else, she added, "with a post in her tongue. You know, like an earring, only in her tongue."

"How'd you get the picture?" Ivon asked after she'd ended the call with her uncle.

"Myrna had it," said Raquel. "Your sister gave it to her as a souvenir, I guess."

Ivon had turned west on La Ribereña, and Raquel suggested they pull into the fairgrounds to see if Irene's car had been towed yet.

Ivon was already following the sign that read, Expo Juárez.

"It was right here," Raquel said, pointing to a slot that was occupied by a battered brown van. "I guess Paco took care of it already. It's probably at my house by now."

Ivon heard the music of the carousel and remembered taking Irene to Western Playland every birthday since she was eight. It's what Irene always asked Ivon for, her eyes dancing.

"Come on, Pancho, take me on the roller coaster, don't be a chicken, pleeeeese," she'd begged the first year. She'd screamed with the wild abandon of an eight-year-old and gotten so excited she wet her pants. Ivon had pretended not to notice.

Ivon looked at the Polaroid again. It should have been me, she thought, standing next to you in this picture, Lucha. Without thinking, she smashed her fist into the steering wheel.

Raquel touched her shoulder. "*No te enojes*, Ivon," she said, "it wasn't your fault."

19

RAQUEL FANNED HERSELF IN THE SHADE OF THE COTTONWOOD while Ivon paced the levee, looking for signs of her sister. The river stunk of sewer. Beer cans and human feces floated in the black water. "I can't believe Irene was swimming in this shit. There is actual shit here. Look at this!"

"We better hurry," Raquel called out. "I don't want Paco to leave."

Paco's house was small but built of cinder block, more solid than most in this *colonia* of plank and PVC shacks, situated with a view of the ASARCO stacks on the other side of the river. The rusty metal door stood ajar, and the smell of boiled tripe and cigarette smoke wafted through the doorway. Ivon pushed back the sudden wash of bile in the back of her throat. They walked into the house without knocking. A woman with purple- and yellow-streaked hair was in the kitchen pouring Nescafé into a chipped blue pot on the stove. She did not seem surprised to see them.

"*¿Quiubo? Mira, ésta es la hermana de la muchacha,*" Raquel said, by way of introduction. "This is Ariel, Paco's wife."

"*Siéntense,*" said Ariel, and Raquel took a seat at the metal Corona table. Ivon remained standing. Ariel pulled a chair out for her and told her again to sit down. Ivon sat on the edge.

"*¿Quieren café?*"

"I need to know what happened to my sister." Ivon had no time for formalities.

Ariel shook her head. "I don't know what happened to your sister." She sat across from Raquel and lit up a cigarette. "She was here earlier, and then I think she went to the store to get cigarettes."

"She doesn't smoke."

"Maybe she went to get ice cream, what do I know?'

"Did you see her going with anybody?"

Ariel glanced sideways at Raquel. "I saw her flirting with Salvador, and then later I saw her whispering with Armando in a corner. Maybe she went with one of them."

"Don't be so rude, Ariel. Can't you see the girl could be in trouble?" said Raquel.

"You didn't seem real worried about that when you got here."

Raquel ignored her.

"Do you have any idea where she went?" Ivon insisted.

Ariel shrugged and puffed on her cigarette. "Maybe she went into heat. Maybe she wanted to get laid."

"What are you talking about, *pendeja?*" said Ivon. "She's just a kid."

The woman laughed at her, blowing smoke in their faces. "Are you really that stupid, or are you just faking it? And don't be calling me a *pendeja, cabrona.*"

"Do you want money, is that it?"

Ariel laughed at her again. "For what? Are you saying we kidnapped her?"

"Look, I don't want to insult you. She's my little sister. Please, help me."

"*No te hagas,* Ariel, you know how dangerous it could be if she went off with a stranger," said Raquel.

"And whose fault is that, bitch? How many people like you come to a place like this, anyway, unless they need something? Don't think I didn't see your little transaction with Paco. That's all you came for."

Ivon turned to glare at Raquel. "What is she talking about?"

"I'll tell you what I'm talking about," said Ariel. "*La cabrona ésta se la cura.* She's a doper."

Ivon swallowed hard. Raquel glanced at her watch.

Ariel threw her cigarette stub into a Coke bottle on the table. "I bet your sister's nursing her popped cherry right now, if she still had one. Maybe the devil came to the party looking for a *cholita* from El Paso."

"I need to speak to your husband," said Ivon, clenching her fist.

"Paco's asleep. He won't like it if I wake him up."

Ivon pounded the table. "I don't care if he's asleep. Wake him up."

"*Uy-uy*," Ariel smirked. "What a temper. I'm so scared."

Ariel went behind the flowery plastic shower curtain that separated the kitchen from the back of the house.

"You needed a fucking fix?" Ivon hissed.

Raquel kept her eyes on the table.

"She's lying. I was just giving someone a ride. We weren't going to stay very long."

"I guess you stayed long enough for a transaction, huh?" Ivon wanted to smack her. "I wonder what your big brother would do to you if he found out you brought your niece to a crack house."

Ariel came back with a cell phone and a blue denim backpack. She dropped the backpack on the table.

"This was in the outhouse," said Ariel. "Is it hers?"

The bag had a Universal Studios logo stitched to the flap. Ivon had sent one just like it to Irene a few years ago. Ivon's vocal chords were suddenly too tight.

"You can look through it if you want, to make sure we didn't steal anything."

"Where's Paco?" said Raquel.

"He's coming. He said to call the guys."

Ariel dialed a number and Ivon rummaged through the pack with shaking hands. A hairbrush, car and house keys on a Miffy keychain, a khaki wallet with a Mickey Mouse face embroidered on it; inside, she found a five-dollar bill and a picture of Ivon raising her fist in front of the Statue of Liberty, silver jewelry in plastic bags—a bracelet, a yin/yang ring, a filigreed rosary—that Irene must have bought at the fair, a bag of nail polish and lipstick. An empty CD cover of Tori Amos' *From the Choirgirl Hotel*. She remembered Irene waiting for her at the airport, yellow headphones around her neck. No CD player or headphones anywhere in sight.

"What's that? That's horrible," said Raquel. She was staring at the image on the CD cover: a young woman with long hair swirling over her head as though she were floating in water, face pressed against glass, eyes rolled back, hands splayed out. "Looks like she's drowning," Raquel added.

Ivon opened the CD case and the image on the inside was of the same woman, floating facedown, hair swirling over her naked back. She threw the case into the pack before she lost it.

Ariel was dialing another number.

"Gordo? Ariel. *Oye*, by any chance, is that girl who was swimming in the river over there with you? Yeah, the *cholita* from El Paso. Is she there? I didn't say that, *maricón*. I'm just wondering if you saw her or you saw who she went with or what? I thought she went to the store with one of you. Oh, really? No, he's not answering. Okay, call me back if you find out anything." She ended the call.

"He says he went to the store by himself. The girl was still playing wetback when he left."

The cigarette butts floating in the Coke bottle, the bowls of greasy menudo broth, the stench of stale beer and onions, pumped a hot bitter liquid up Ivon's throat. She barely made it to the sink.

"*¡Ay, qué asco!*" said Ariel. "I hope you clean that up."

"*You* clean it up!" Paco yelled at his wife, walking into the room and buckling his belt. His whole body gave off the acrid odor of alcohol. "This place is a fucking pigsty! Give me that phone."

Ivon turned the single faucet of the sink, but no water came out of the tap.

"Leave it," said Paco, handing her a cold Sprite from a metal barrel that served as an ice chest. "Here, sit down and drink this. We'll find her, don't worry. What's her name again?"

Through the barred window over the sink Ivon could see the border highway in the distance and behind it the ASARCO smokestacks and the black bridge. A Southern Pacific train rumbled across the bridge, wheels screeching against the trestles.

It sounded like a woman screaming.

20

![SEEKING INFORMATION](heading banner)

Authorities would like to speak to anyone who may have information on this El Paso teenager. She was last seen in Juárez, Mexico Thursday morning, June 11, 1998.

Irene Feliciana Villa

DESCRIPTION

Date of Birth: January 22, 1982
Sex: F
Height: 5'2"
Weight: 115 pounds
Place of Birth: El Paso, Texas
Hair: Long, Dark Brown
Eyes: Dark Brown
Race: White (Hispanic)
Date reported missing: June 11, 1998

DETAILS

On Wednesday night, June 10, 1998, Irene Villa, a sixteen-year-old senior at Loretto Academy in El Paso, Texas, crossed the border to go to the Juárez Expo Fair. Later, she and some friends from Juárez attended a party at a private residence in Colonia La Soledad across from the ASARCO refinery. Irene was last seen at approximately 6 A.M. the next morning near the riverbank, wearing white jeans and a red-and-white striped T-shirt. She is believed to have been swimming in the river. She has shoulder-length dark brown hair, dark brown eyes, and has a metal stud in her tongue. Her fingernails were painted different colors. Anyone with information is asked to contact the nearest law enforcement agency.

21

novel's opening

SHE LOVES THE WAY HE LOOKS, his golden hair pulled back in a thin ponytail under his cowboy hat, eyes like the sky. He wears blue jeans, a crisp white shirt rolled up to the elbows, a small flag with a star in it pinned to the front pocket. He's so masculine and handsome enough to be in a *telenovela*, except he speaks Spanish worse than the *americanos* who run the *maquila* where she works.

"*Yo soy* from Dallas," he says. "*Tú saber* where Dallas is?"

She has heard the joke before. She isn't that ignorant. She knows that when a man says "Dallas," he is really saying *dar las*, which means he is trying to find out if she is going to give her *nalgas* to him. Her cousin Sergio has taught her these things.

"No," she says, offended. "I don't know anything about Dallas."

"*Me gusta Juárez mejor*," he says, smiling down at her. "*Muchas mujeres bonitas* here."

She blushes under his blue gaze.

Her floor supervisor, Ariel, introduced them at La Fiesta. They had a couple of drinks, spoke in low voices in their dark booth, and when Ariel left he made no attempt to touch her. She feels lucky. Maybe he doesn't want to take her to Dallas, after all. From La Fiesta, they came to La Tuna Country, and now he asks her if she likes to dance. She nods, even though she has not danced with men very much. He tells her Joe's Place just down the street has a bigger dance floor with disco lights. This is what she loves about living in a real city. Discos and dancing and freedom to do what she wants without permission.

It is early still, but in the six months she has lived in this border city, she has come to learn that on Fridays in Juárez, when

147

everyone gets paid, the action begins in the early afternoon. By nightfall, music is blaring out of all the discos, and the streets are filled with drunks and prostitutes hopping from bar to bar. The prostitutes scare her a little—she does not want to become one of them. Ariel tells her there are clients who want young girls like her with no experience and that they pay in dollars, more dollars than she can make in a week at the *maquila*. But she's not interested.

"Some of them don't want to have sex with you," Ariel said. "They're married men, but they're lonely, they're on a business trip and they just want your company. They don't pay as well, but it's still better than what you make. Let me introduce you to El Güero. He's very nice. He'll treat you with respect."

The doorman at Joe's Place seems to know El Güero very well. The waitresses all smile seductively at him, give her the evil eye. He's not a good dancer, he says, but he likes to watch women move, so if she doesn't mind, he'll just watch as she dances. There are other girls who dance by themselves, or with each other, but she feels silly moving on the dance floor with him just watching. But he's so polite. She feels lucky. She wonders if Ariel told him the truth about her, that she is only fourteen years old and a virgin.

Now he is warming up to her on the dance floor and he pulls her against him and squeezes her backside. She can feel something hard poking against her belly. Maybe it's his belt buckle. Her heart is pounding now because she isn't sure if he knows the truth about her and she is afraid of him getting too close. She pulls away from him and goes back to their table, acting offended so that he won't think she's that kind of girl. Besides, her feet ache from standing on high-heeled sandals all ten hours of her shift. She takes her compact out of her purse and fixes her lipstick, adjusts the green butterfly barrette closer to her ear.

"What are you doing?" he says, looming over the table. "What is the problem?" He frowns at her, and she can tell he is displeased.

He slips into the booth beside her, sitting much closer than he did at the other two places. The waitress walks by, winks at him, hands him a folded napkin. Someone is sending him a note, probably a little love note from one of the other women he's charmed, but he doesn't read it right away. He sits right against her and places a hand on her thigh. He tells the waitress to bring them a round. He drinks J&B scotch on the rocks. She hates alcohol—it reminds her of her stepfather. She orders another Shirley Temple.

He laughs at her order. "Tell me your name again," he says.

"Mireya," she says, then remembers she should have given him a false name.

His hand moves down to her knee, fingers skimming the nylon of her pantyhose. Her leg twitches. She doesn't know what to say. He pulls his arm back.

"Are you in school, Mireya?" he asks, moving in to smell her hair.

She shivers. She can smell his cologne. She can tell he wants to kiss her. "I work at the Phillips plant," she says, hoping the conversation will take his mind off touching her so much. "Making television remotes."

Her job is to plug some wires into the remote controls. By the middle of the morning, her right wrist hurts, and by lunchtime she has to support it with the other hand, but she knows better than to complain. *Twenty more girls outside waiting to take your place*, the lineman at the factory likes to yell out at least once a day. *O se apuran o se van a la chingada, ¿eh?* The lineman likes her, though. He's going to recommend her for the beauty pageant next month.

"*Y, usted, ¿cómo se llama?*" She finally feels brave enough to ask him his name.

"They call me the Lone Ranger," El Güero says, "*Llanero Solitario.*"

She creases her eyes at him. "You're not the real Lone Ranger."

He laughs and she sees gold in the back of his mouth. "So you know who he is," he says, trailing his arm over the back of the seat. She can feel the hair on his arm brushing against her bare shoulder, and it makes her shiver.

"No, I'm not the real *Llanero*, but I do make movies. I'm a film producer. Do you know what that is? A film producer? I make *películas.*"

She doesn't know what that is, but she is remembering how

her mother would make extra money by meeting strange men outside the *cine* back in Durango. When her stepfather found out, he
beat her mother so hard she hemorrhaged inside her head and
died. Terrified that he might beat her, too, Mireya had stolen five
hundred pesos from her stepfather's wallet and climbed on the
first bus to Juárez. Her mother's cousin, Sergio, took her in.

"Do you like going to the movies?"

She blinks back her tears. "I don't go very much," she says.
"It's expensive."

"Tonight," he says, "I invite you."

His eyes feel like blue flames on her skin. Another quiver runs
down her spine.

"Not tonight," she says. "I have to meet my friend Ariel here
at nine."

He reaches over and strokes her cheek. "*Te gusta* popcorn and
candy?" he whispers. His breath tickles her ear. "*Te gusta* crystal
meth?"

Her earlobe feels moist and warm with his breath. "*No, gracias*," she says. She doesn't know what crystal meth is. She push-
es her hair back behind her ear.

"That's a pretty thing in your hair," he says, and she's relieved
he's changed the subject. "Was it expensive?"

"Not really. It's just *chaquira*."

His eyes light up. "Shakira? Like the singer?"

She giggles. "No. *Chaquira*: fake jewelry. I gave it to myself for
my *quin* . . ." she catches herself just in time. She can't tell him
she's going to have a *quinceañera* celebration next Saturday—that
would give it all away, and she could even lose her job if they
found out her true age. "For my friend's *quinceañera*," she corrects
herself quickly. "A coworker sells them at the factory. I think she
gets them from the dollar store in El Paso."

"*Muy bonito*," he says, but she can tell he's suddenly distracted
by someone at the bar. That hand of his is getting awfully close to
her private area, and she's not prepared for that. She just wants to
be friends for now. She shifts her leg, moving away just slightly so
he understands he's getting too close. He acts a little flustered when
she pulls away, then spots the napkin on the table and picks it up.

"I couldn't decide between this green one or one that was yellow with red markings," she tells him. "But my friend said the green was shinier and looked better with the color of my hair."

"Mm-hmm. Sounds pretty," he says again, but his eyes are focused on his note. He folds the napkin and slips it into his pocket. The waitress brings their drinks and he tells her, "Tell them not now." Then he pays for the drinks with a ten-dollar bill that he peels off a huge wad of U.S. dollars, no pesos anywhere.

[handwritten: tuh huh.]

"Does somebody want to talk to you?" she says.

"Just friends want to know if they can join us," he says, picking up his drink and swirling the ice around in the glass before drinking it all in one swallow.

She watches the bone in his throat ripple. He has tufts of blonde hair sprouting out from his open collar and on the backs of his fingers. If she weren't so afraid, she'd like to kiss him. She's never kissed a *gringo* before. She sips her sweet cool drink from a straw and plays one of her favorite fantasies in her head: it is her *quinceañera* mass, and she is walking down the aisle in a white chiffon dress, on the arm of her real father. Instead, she and some friends are going to cross over to El Paso to shop at Cielo Vista Mall. One of them knows what bus to take because she works over there on Sundays, cleaning an old lady's house. They're all going to pitch in to buy her a present.

[handwritten marginalia: 4c / vion / the / TV / fantasías / qv / produce / cq]

"Why do they call you the Lone Ranger?" she says.

He winks at her. "*Para mi saber, señorita, para tú encontrar.*"

She frowns at his words. Sometimes it's hard to understand his Spanish. For him to know and for her to find? What does that mean?

"You need good makeup so you can look even prettier," he tells her, directing his gaze at her again.

She loves it when he pays attention to her like that with those blue eyes.

"Do you have good makeup?"

She shakes her head. All she has is an old tube of mascara that has more spit in it than paint, and it runs down her face in the heat of the factory.

"I have a friend who sells makeup," he says. "Good quality

Avon products, very popular with the El Paso girls. I can call her so she can bring you some free samples?"

Her eyes open wide. She feels like a beggar in a bakery. "Free samples?"

"*Absolutamente* free. If you're pretty enough, you can be in one of my movies."

"Really? *¿De veras?*" She cannot believe how lucky she is tonight.

"Let me call her."

He pulls a flat little telephone out of his pocket and punches some numbers. She can't hear what he says because the music gets loud all of a sudden, but he ends the call quickly and puts his phone away.

"She wants us to meet her at her house," he shouts into her ear. "She's busy right now making dinner for her kids."

Little warning bells start ringing in her head, but she's excited about the free makeup samples, and it's a woman with kids. Besides, she knows that Ariel wouldn't introduce her to a bad man. And he's so good-looking.

"Is it far? I have to meet Ariel back at La Fiesta at ten."

"I thought you said you were meeting Ariel here at nine," he says. She is afraid he will hit her for lying, but all he does is laugh. One of his front teeth is chipped.

He shows her his watch, which has three dials and glows in the dark. She has no idea what time it is with all those dials. "No worries," he says, "I'll bring you back in time. Besides, if it gets a little late, Ariel knows where my friend lives."

"She does?"

"Of course. Ariel buys makeup from her all the time."

"*Bueno, pues*, okay," she says, "but I don't want to go to Dallas."

"Dallas?" he says, "you mean El Paso? My friend doesn't live in El Paso. She lives close by, near the stadium."

She slides out after him and notices that a piece of her factory smock is sticking out of her purse. How embarrassing, she thinks, but he doesn't seem to notice. He drapes his arm over her shoulders and guides her through the tangle of dancing bodies on the dance floor. Somebody hands him something as they pass the bar.

"Don't forget the meter's running, Güero!" the bartender calls out.

His car parked in the *estacionamiento* on the same street, is disappointing. She's expecting a sportscar, something shiny and red like the kind she's seen on the *telenovelas,* but instead it's an old white boat of a car with a crack in the windshield. She notices a box of plastic trash bags and a coil of rope on the backseat. There's no radio, just an empty slot in the dashboard where the radio would've gone.

He tells her to put on her seat belt, but something's hanging off the rearview mirror that catches her eye: handcuffs. She feels her stomach jump. The door closes on her side. She reaches for the door handle, but all she finds is a screw. No window crank, either. She can't get out. Now her head starts to pound and her limbs feel suddenly very sluggish. She opens her mouth to yell for help, but her throat has closed and no sound comes out. She hears him talking to the parking attendant who's been watching his car.

She raps on the window to get the attendant's attention. "Señor, help me," she says, but her voice is no louder than a whimper.

He slips into the driver's side and frowns at her. "What are you doing?"

"Let me out," she says. "I don't want to go with you."

"I thought you wanted that makeup. Don't you want to be in my movie?"

"No," she shrieks. "Let me out! Let me out!"

He reaches over and punches her in the face.

"Shut up," he says, pointing his finger in her face. "Shut up, or I'll cut your tongue out, you little whore. It's not time to scream yet."

22

"TELL US THE STORY, MUSE MAN," Detective Ortiz goaded him again.

"Nothing else to do out here, man," added Detective Borunda. "Train's not due for another hour. We could use a little entertainment."

"Yeah, it'll keep us awake, Muse Man. Think of it as a service to the EPPD."

"You guys are driving me nuts already," Pete McCuts finally relented.

The three of them were on train detail. Ortiz and Borunda were part of an undercover operation called Rail Raid that was investigating a spate of thefts from the Southern Pacific line. There'd been more than a hundred robberies this year already, and thousands of dollars of cargo had gotten lifted straight off the trains and moved to Mexico. Rail Raid was a multiagency operation that involved the FBI, the El Paso Police Department, Customs officials, and Border Patrol agents. Ortiz had confided to Pete that there was talk of the robberies being an inside job orchestrated by some INS people.

Pete McCuts had tagged along to learn something about undercover work. He'd just made detective three weeks earlier and, as the son of Judge Anacleto Ramírez, he had certain privileges that few of the other detectives in his unit could enjoy. Just this afternoon, he'd gotten his first Missing Persons case: a high school girl who'd gone missing in Juárez. His commander in the Crimes Against Persons unit wasn't interested in pursuing the matter or using up manpower hours to go snooping around in business across the border. But then his dad called the office and

154

told him the missing girl was related to one of his social workers, and he would appreciate it if Pete got the case. It wasn't technically a case yet because all he had was a statement from the family and a suspicion of foul play, but his name was on the board next to the case number. Now, here he was, on his first undercover assignment, even if he was just a trainee.

"I knew I shouldn't have shared that stupid story with you," Pete said to Marcia Ortiz, who'd been his partner before she got promoted last year.

"Come on, give it up, Muse Man. And tell it the way you told it to me. He takes on his father's voice," she said to Borunda, "it's so funny to hear His Honor Judge Anacleto talking like a *pachuco*."

"Promise you won't make fun of me, okay?" said Pete.

"Don't be such a *maricón*," Borunda chided, and Ortiz cracked up. She knew the punchline already.

It was just past midnight and the crickets were loud along the levee of the Río Grande, where they had parked in a clump of old salt cedars that hid the car from view. They were just across the highway from ASARCO, at the interstate railroad junction between Texas, New Mexico, and Mexico. It was known locally as Calavera, a community of ex-Smeltertown residents controlled by gangs and drug traffickers. Even though ASARCO had shut down operations in January, the air still smelled of refinery soot and chemical fumes.

Pete loosened his tie. "Okay, so this is a story about how I got my name and ya'll better not tell anyone else about it. It's embarrassing."

"Get on with it, *ese*," Borunda said.

Pete cleared his throat. "I was the accidental child of Anacleto Ramírez and a mechanic named Berenice Tinajera, who everyone called Bernie. She lived next door, and her and my Pop would hang out on the weekends, you know, watch games together, he'd mow her lawn, she'd change his oil, that kind of stuff."

"She sounds like a dyke, man," Borunda interjected.

"Shut up, *vato*, let him finish," Ortiz said.

"So anyway, Bernie came over one day with a jar of her famous spiked *limonada* and just straight up proposed to my dad."

Pete felt his father's voice taking over him, as it always did when he told this story. "'¿*Que qué?*' Cleto actually blushed at her words. 'You want me to do what? I thought . . . *pues*, I mean, *pues* . . . you hate men, *¿qué no?*'"

Pete changed his voice. "'Don't give yourself a hernia,' said la Bernie Tinajera, refilling his glass with the tequila and lime juice concoction, which Cleto had to admit had never tasted so good. 'Here, have some more. I put Gran Mañé in it today to make it good and sweet, just like you like it.'

"'I'm not a modern man, Bernie,' Cleto started to say. 'I don't understand any of this women's lib stuff.' It was the seventies and women were doing all kinds of crazy stuff, burning their bras and whatnot, but this, to Cleto's mind, was just about the craziest he'd ever heard.

"'*Mira*,' she said, ignoring his distress, 'I've been taking my temperature every day for two months, now, and I know today's the day. If I want to have a kid, I gotta get laid *ahora*, and don't think I have all day, *eh*? I still got that leaky toilet to fix before Molly gets home.'"

"She's a kick," said Borunda.

"'But, Bernie . . . ' Cleto tried not to sound ignorant, but the truth was he had no idea what her temperature had to do with anything. He couldn't get beyond two simple questions. Since when did women like her have babies or come over to a widower's house on a Sunday afternoon asking to get laid?

"' . . . Bernie, you gotta gimme some time here. I gotta think about this, *mujer!* I can't just unzip my fly and let you have it.'"

"You go, Judge," Borunda hooted.

"Cleto had never measured his words with Bernie. They played dominoes and bingo and watched Monday Night Football together, borrowed each other's tools, argued about the best ways to conquer women. Now he found himself blushing at the reality that Bernie *was* a woman, maybe even a lady, for all he knew, and he had just said something that any lady would find insulting.

"'Besides,' he added, after gulping down his second glass of *limonada*, 'I'm not a young macho, any more, you know. I can't just impregnate on command.' Always Cleto's military training crept into his speech, but in the end, it was Bernie who took command—she could fix anything, that Bernie."

"You go, Bernie!" howled Ortiz.

"Six weeks later, Bernie calls my dad to congratulate him. *'¡Donde pones el ojo pones la bala!'* she says. 'You got good aim, *viejo!* I knew you could do it. Let's celebrate. Come on over, La Molly's making enchiladas.'

"Anacleto was flustered, to be sure. What was he going to tell his family and all? But right away he saw that he had a right to make one condition. 'I just got one proviso,' he said, talking like a judge and blushing on the other side of the phone. 'I get to name it if it's a boy.'

"Anacleto, you see, wrote poetry at the time, even took some poetry classes at la UTEP, and he'd always wanted to name a son after the muses."

"'*Qué proviso ni qué chingazo,*' Bernie said, 'if it's a boy you get to keep it over there, *ése.* Molly said she ain't gonna be cleaning up after no boy, or putting the seat down on the toilet all day for the rest of her life.'"

Ortiz was laughing so hard she said she was going to pee her pants.

"I don't get it," said Borunda. "The name thing."

"Watch," said Pete. "Polyhymnia, muse of the Song; Euterpe, muse of Lyric Poetry; Thalia, muse of Comedy; Erato, muse of Love Poetry—the first letter of each name spells Pete."

"But you said ten muses, man. I used to be an English major before I went into law enforcement . . ."

"You're kidding," Ortiz interrupted.

". . . and I know there are only nine muses."

"Well, nine Greek ones," said Pete, "but there's a tenth one from Mexico. There's Melpomene, the muse of Tragedy; Clio, the muse of History; Calliope, muse of Epic Poetry; Urania, muse of Astronomy; Terpsichore, muse of the Dance; and Sor Juana Inés de la Cruz, the tenth muse of Mexico."

"No way!" said Borunda. "She's not a muse."

"Don't tell my dad that," said Pete.

"Tell him what Bernie said about your name," Ortiz spurred him.

"Bernie wasn't too crazy about Pete McCuts. She said it sounded like a *gringo* name. But he explained the part about the ten muses, and Bernie said, 'Okay, *viejo*, you wanna name your son after ten women, *pues*, it's fine with me, but don't go blaming my ass if your kid turns out funny. *Nada de que* like mother like son, eh?'"

"You're killing me, man," Ortiz said, wiping the tears from her eyes.

"Hey, what the fuck was that?" Borunda sat up suddenly, still as a foxhound.

"It's too early for the train," said Ortiz.

"Ssh! Listen!"

Pete held his breath and paid attention.

"I know I heard something," Borunda said. "This is Calavera country, man. There's some mean Mexicans out here who don't take well to strange cars in their territory. They probably spotted us."

"We better look around," said Ortiz, putting her baseball cap on backwards.

Pete unbuckled his seat belt and was about to get out of the back.

"You stay, you're not dressed for this," ordered Borunda, tying on his headband. "You know how to work the walkie-talkie, right? Call dispatch if we're not back in ten. I'm leaving the keys in the ignition."

"Got it," said Pete.

They racked their Berettas and were gone before Pete could blink. He heard Ortiz cussing at something and Borunda telling her to hush, and then nothing but the sound of cars on the highway, and those crickets.

He could feel the sweat gathering in his armpits and around the starched collar of his shirt. His Auntie Molly insisted on starching and pressing his shirts herself and left them stiff as body casts that itched his neck. He freed the collar button and told himself to focus. Stay loose. Pay attention, Pete.

He kept his eye on the digital clock on the dashboard. Should he call in, just in case? Only three minutes had passed. Give it another five, by then, maybe they'd be back. But where were they?

It was too quiet out there. Four minutes. The sweat was running down his arms. Maybe he should get out and see. He could use a little fresh air. All the windows were rolled down, but the car was shrouded by the branches of the trees, and it felt muggy. Five minutes. Okay, something wasn't right. He better call it in. But what would he say? He'd feel really stupid if they came back and found out he'd called in the troops. Wait it out, Pete. But he couldn't sit there anymore. He had to get out. He couldn't breathe.

Carefully, he opened the door, crawled out, removed his .40 caliber from the holster and pulled the slide back as quietly as he could, and tripped over the roots of a tree.

"Fuck!" he said under his breath, his finger twitching on the trigger.

Calm down, now. Get your ass out there. He stepped out onto the moonlit levee and for a second felt completely exposed in his white shirt, as if instead of the full moon it was a searchlight up there, looking for him. He glanced around to get his bearings. The Southern Pacific tracks were right behind him and ran northwest into Anapra and the foothills of Mount Cristo Rey. Just west of Buena Vista, near the Sunland Park Racetrack, a team of FBI agents and police officers was waiting to jump the train, and a few others had already boarded some of the cars, pretending to be hobos. Ortiz and Borunda had been stationed further south, where the Southern Pacific and the Santa Fe tracks intersected down here in Calavera.

Suddenly a broad shaft of light broke the darkness, and he realized the Santa Fe train had appeared out of nowhere, barreling past him on its way north from the direction of Smeltertown. In the brightness, he saw them, Ortiz and Borunda being chased across the river by men wielding pipes and chains. He watched a pipe come down on Ortiz, the chains loop around Borunda's neck and his body dragged down into the river. Pete raised his gun and fired into the air. He didn't know what else to do.

"They're getting attacked," he shouted into his walkie-talkie. "Officers under attack."

"Who is this?"

"Operation 'Rail Raid,' Calavera unit. Detectives Ortiz and

Borunda are under attack. We need backup. Now."

Instantly, agents and officers were jumping out of the back cars of the train, running toward him.

"They're taking them across the river!" Pete shouted. "Into Mexico."

There was a wild crisscrossing of flashlight beams, but when they reached the riverbank, the attackers had fled. Some of the agents gave pursuit.

"Oh shit," someone said, "here they are." Pete ran to where the officer was pointing his flashlight. Ortiz and Borunda were sprawled on the riverbank on the Mexican side, legs in the water. Pete waded across the river, the water so shallow it barely covered the toe of his boots. Ortiz had been beaten so hard on the head that part of her scalp had torn off and one of her eyes had come loose from its socket. Borunda looked like he had been choked to death. The chains had cut into his neck, and his face in the glare of the flashlights looked bloated and blue, tears running out of the corners of his eyes, his bleeding tongue caught between his teeth.

"They dead?" someone asked.

Pete reached down and felt their wrists. He could feel a pulse on Ortiz.

"She's good," he said.

Someone else was already calling it in. He moved his hand to Borunda's other wrist, but still no pulse, just a white stripe where his watch used to be.

"Marcia, can you hear me? It's Pete. You're gonna be okay, okay?"

"She's unconscious, man, can't you tell?"

"What about him? Does he need CPR?"

Pete touched Borunda's neck in three places and finally felt a vein move. It was a glimmer of a pulse, but enough to prove his heart was still pumping. Pete placed his palm over Borunda's mouth and loosened the jaw muscles to release the tongue. He was barely breathing.

"Both of them," he said, "they're both alive."

"We need a chopper," the walkie-talkie guy said. "I've got two officers down, hurt bad, but alive. Need to get them to a hospital ASAP."

"Fuck, what happened?"

"Shouldn't we pull them out of the water?" said Pete.

"No, don't touch them. We could make it worse."

"We need to keep them warm, they're in critical condition."

"Not our call, man, not our call."

"Well, call someone, goddammit. Borunda's barely got a pulse. He can't stay in the water." Pete realized it was he talking.

"Requesting permission to move the detectives out of the water."

A commotion had started on the Mexican side of the levee. The agents who had gone across were kicking and pushing four handcuffed men back to El Paso, yelling every obscenity in the book.

"*¡No fuimos nosotros!*" one of the men kept saying. "It wasn't us, we're just coyotes. We didn't do nothing."

One of the officers clubbed him in the face. |t, *one violence*

"Chief says we can't move 'em. Here comes the chopper, anyway."

By the time the ambulance and the fire engine and the armada of cop cars arrived, Ortiz and Borunda had already been strapped into the helicopter and gone airborne, taken to the nearest hospital, Providence, just on the other side of I-10.

"Need a lift?" one of the cops asked him when they were finished loading up the suspects with the help of their nightsticks.

"Thanks, but I think Borunda left his keys in the car. I better drive it back."

"Better hurry up, this is a dangerous fucking area."

Long after the troops disbanded, Pete sat in Borunda's car between the salt cedars. He was too stunned to drive anywhere, his hands trembling hard on the steering wheel. He knew he should call his dad and tell him he was okay, but he couldn't do that either.

The thing about law enforcement, son, his dad had said to him when Pete announced he'd been accepted to the police academy, is you have to be willing to risk your life to protect someone else's.

I know that, Pop.

Problem is, I don't think *I'm* willing to risk your life, son.

It's my life, Pop.

Tonight had shown him that his life really was on the line in this job. It could've been him out there, getting beaten to a pulp along with Ortiz and Borunda. If he hadn't worn that shirt and tie, if he'd been part of the team instead of just a trainee along for the ride, he'd be dying in Providence Hospital right now, like his friends.

Pete felt like someone had just pinned him to the mat in a choke hold. Sweat trailed down his face, but no, it wasn't sweat. He realized he was crying.

23

THERE WAS ONLY ONE WAY IVON KNEW TO STAY CALM, to keep her mother's screaming from boring holes into her head. She had to write down what those lawyers had told her, what she had learned. It was the only way of staying focused on what she had to do. She could not allow herself to get caught up in the family fights.

She dated the page and started to write something, but that screaming . . . that ugly animal tone vibrating like that. She couldn't shake it off. Last night, after the detective had left, preparing coffee in the kitchen, and in front of everyone, her mother had wailed that it was Ivon's fault, that she had no right to stand in front of her when she had let something happen to her little sister.

"It's *your* fault, *maldita seas. You* promised to take her to the fair, *you* broke your promise, *you* didn't call her." She kept poking Ivon's chest with every *you.* "*You've* always been a bad example for your sister. She turned out as stubborn and disobedient as *you* are. None of this would have happened if *you* hadn't come to town in the first place. God is punishing us, don't you see? Don't you see what you've brought on this family with your degenerate lifestyle?"

Uncle Joe, Ximena, and Grandma Betty all stepped in to protect Ivon. Aunt Lulu and Aunt Fátima both took her mother's side.

Pobrecita, can't you all see she's terrified? She may have lost her little girl?

I didn't lose her. Esta desgraciada let her get lost.

You're always blaming everything on Ivon, Lydia.

Pretty soon, the protectors and the consolers were at each other's throats, yelling about responsibility and shame.

Maldita seas, damn you, her mother had said. The only other

163

time she'd said that was at her father's funeral.

"M'ijita, defiéndete," her grandmother chided. "Say something for yourself, you're a grown woman now, don't let your mother do that to you no more."

Ivon kissed her grandma's cheek and walked out of the house. She knew there was no stopping her mother's diatribes. It broke her up inside to have her mother cursing at her and blaming her like that, but she had to admit Ma was right. Ivon could've prevented this with a simple phone call. If she had taken Irene along to meet Elsa, she would never have gone to the fair by herself. She would not have gotten kidnapped.

That was a fact. Irene had been kidnapped. She had not run away or eloped, as Aunt Fátima had suggested. Ivon knew all about running away. She knew all the planning it took. There'd be signs, missing clothes, money stashed in a sock, Ma's signature practiced over and over in a notebook so she could forge absence slips or doctor's notes—Ivon's old tricks. She found her sister's diaries under the mattress and read them all in one sitting. It made her eyes sting to read how lonely Irene felt, how much she missed her big sister and her dad, even though she'd been only eight when he died. She read about some nameless boy Irene had a crush on who had taken her to a Cathedral game, and about another one she'd met at the mall, a black basketball player named Gilbert who came knocking at the house to ask her out for a walk and nearly gave Ma a heart attack. Nothing at all about wanting to leave.

She had called Gaby, Uncle Joe's youngest daughter who was the same age as Irene, and talked to Irene's friends and teammates. All of them had told her the same thing, that Irene didn't have a boyfriend, no drug habits, not even cigarette smoking. She hadn't invited them to go to the fair because she was looking forward to hanging out with Ivon, they said. Didn't make her feel any better. It didn't take a genius to deduce that Irene had been taken against her will.

Ivon had to write down what she knew and research what she didn't know. This would keep her focused, would keep her from wallowing in hindsight and guilt.

Saturday, June 13, 1998
Facts:

- Irene disappeared early Thursday morning.
- She was kidnapped from a *colonia* in Juárez.
- Raquel showed me where Irene had been swimming, introduced me to Paco and his wife, Ariel. Paco was apologetic and looked concerned, but the wife kept shrugging and saying she didn't know why we thought they knew anything about it. There were a lot of people at their house that day, she said, they couldn't keep track of everybody. I don't trust her. And I hate Raquel right now. She took my sister to a crack house so she could get a fix. I wanted to kill her yesterday.
- Uncle Joe reported Irene's disappearance to the El Paso police at noon on Thursday, and then again on Friday morning. It wasn't until that afternoon, at 5:35 P.M., that they sent out a detective. The guy assigned to the case (Pete McCuts, son of Ximena's friend, the judge) said that unless we get a demand for a ransom or any other evidence to prove Irene was kidnapped, all they can do is call her a "Missing Person," and since it happened across the border, they have no jurisdiction over there. The Kidnapping unit will not even get the case unless foul play is suspected, or, if "her body turns up," that's how McCuts put it. I wonder if he knows what he's doing. He looks like a high school kid.
- We were told we had to report Irene to this agency in Juárez called PREVIAS, a group of lawyers who screen cases like this and determine if any offense has occurred or if "the girl has simply run off with her boyfriend." Uncle Joe went with me yesterday, and we had to wait six hours before they called our number. Six hours sitting in that hot, crowded little lobby, waiting our turn. All those whose number didn't get called before they closed, and there were at least eight or nine other families that came in after we did, will have to go back on Monday.
- As far as the Juárez police are concerned, because Irene was last seen sitting on the El Paso riverbank, this is probably a case for the American authorities, not the Juárez police.
- Detective McCuts disagrees. He says that Irene was in Juárez

voluntarily, she had gone over to the fair of her own accord, her car was parked at the fairgrounds, she was intoxicated, and even if she was swimming back and forth between El Paso and Juárez, she was voluntarily attending a party across the border. Therefore, she disappeared in Mexico and it's a case for the Mexican authorities. Even if foul play is suspected, and who wouldn't immediately suspect that with all the killings going on over there, McCuts added in this condescending tone, the case is not in the EPPD's jurisdiction, and will not be in their jurisdiction unless we get a ransom note or her body turns up. His conclusion: young girls should not be allowed to go across the border, much less by themselves, and certainly not to imbibe alcoholic beverages without proper adult supervision. In other words, Irene asked for it, and it's our fault, too, for not supervising her properly.

- I searched the INS and the Border Patrol web sites to see if they had any jurisdiction on abduction cases across the border. Found out about the binational task force they've organized with the EPPD and the judicial police in Juárez to help stop car theft, but nothing at all about how to end the kidnapping and killing of women. Something occurred to me while I was online, about how immigration laws, since the Chinese Exclusion Act, have always targeted women of color to prevent them from entering the U.S. and breeding babies of color. Need to research this some more.

- Ma's house is pandemonium. Family fighting with each other, neighbors being nosy, Uncle Joe or Aunt Fátima telling the story over and over. At least Ma isn't alone. Grandma Betty and Great-aunt Esperanza are both staying with her. Aunt Lulu comes over every day with groceries and cooks for everyone. "Your mother doesn't hate you, *m'ijita*," Grandma keeps telling me, "don't believe that for a minute."

Impressions:

- There were so many families at the PREVIAS office, so many missing girls, hundreds more than those who have turned up dead in the desert, I was told. We were the only ones from El Paso. Everyone else was Mexican. Many of them (most?) are not even from Juárez, they're *"gente humilde,"* as my dad used to call them, humble people from the interior that have been lured to this border by the promise of jobs at the *maquiladoras.* It's a daughter or a niece or a sister they come to report, all of them young, like Irene, who didn't come home from their shift—like what happened to Cecilia—or who didn't make it to their shift, or who were last seen at a nightclub on La Mariscal or getting into a bus at the factory.

- I talked to so many families while we waited. The women sit there holding their rosaries, the men just stare straight ahead, eyes hidden under the brims of their hats, nodding occasionally, not saying much. Every single woman I spoke with knows that God will help her family, God will make things right for them. God will bring back the missing girl in their lives. I want to ask them if they have ever wondered why God did this to them in the first place, but that would be rude and mean. Who am I to trample on their hope? Like me, none of them will allow themselves to think the girl they are looking for has been killed, although we all fear and don't say that her life is in danger. You can't function if you think like that.

- *"No sé qué pasó, quién se la llevó, ella no hacía nada malo, era retebuena muchacha,"* that's about all they really say, I don't know what happened, who took her, she didn't do anything bad, she was a good girl. They're all survivors, these people, and they know that to dwell on possibilities like what happened or who is responsible will not bring their girls back. So they put one foot in front of the other and do what they have to do, even if it means sitting in those rickety metal chairs in the PREVIAS office for days on end, waiting their turn.

- The PREVIAS lawyer who took our statement yesterday kept interrupting our interview each time his pager beeped, and we could hear him laughing in the hallway, talking on his cell phone and laughing. They don't give a shit about any of us. The guy told us the state judicial police will get involved only when it has been determined that an offense has occurred. So far all they have determined is that Irene was at Expo Juárez, since we had a photograph of her standing in front of the carousel, that she left her car parked at the fairgrounds, that she went to a party at a *colonia* afterward, that she was swimming back and forth in the Río Grande. That's not a determination on your part, I said, that's the statement we just gave you. "That's the best we can do for now, Señora," he tells me, "until we get more evidence like this photograph, all we can go on is your statement. Most of the time, these missing girls come home in a day or two. If they are American girls like your sister, they like to come over to Juárez to drink and have a good time, and sometimes they end up having a little adventure." I guess getting kidnapped and raped are just adventures to him.

Conclusions:

- I can't wait any more. Authorities on both sides are washing their hands of this situation. So now it's up to me to find Irene on my own. I know she's alive, I can feel it. I don't know why, but I have this faith that Irene knows what to do, that she won't panic, that she'll do what it takes to stay alive. She's scrappy, my Lucha, barrio girl all the way, even with her Catholic high school education. She knows how to pay attention, how to run, how to yell her guts out if she can, how to slam into the instep or ram her knee up into the fucker's balls if he gets that close. I was hard on her, but I taught her to be tough, to defend herself physically and verbally, and I never, *ever* hit her. She's alive out there. I know it.
- STAY ALIVE, LUCHA, STAY ALIVE!!!!
- Today, I want to go back to that *colonia* to talk to Ariel and Paco again. Uncle Joe and I stopped by their house yesterday, after leaving the PREVIAS office, but the place looked abandoned. We went to Raquel's house, too, so I could pick up Irene's car, but Raquel wasn't home either, and I didn't see Irene's car anywhere. I'll have to pick it up today, after my escorted tour of La Mariscal.
- Ximena insists that I can't go to Juárez alone today and has volunteered her brother William, the Mormon, to be my escort. Poor William, he came into town early because one of the out-

of-town kids always has to come in early to help out with the reunion preparations. Ximena needs all the help she can get. This year it's William's turn. He thought he was coming to drive people to the market and move furniture. Never thought he'd have to wander around Juárez with me, looking for a disappeared cousin.

- Father Francis has faxed the police bulletin on Irene to a couple of the NGOs in Juárez who have been advocating for the victims. He also wrote a letter to the mayor complaining about how long it took the police to respond to our report.
- I'm starting to have second thoughts about Father Francis. I don't think he's the perpetrator. The coincidences bug me, but he's been really kind to us, and I can't imagine he could fake that level of caring. He hasn't forgotten about Elsa or Jorgito, either, Ximena says. He's been calling all the hospitals and clinics in Juárez trying to locate that nurse who used to work for the Egyptian.
- It gives me the creeps to look at the flyer I made announcing Irene's disappearance. I blew up the picture she took at the fair so that people can see what she was wearing the day she was taken, and next to that I put her graduation picture, with the information I cut and pasted from that police bulletin.
- Need to stop by the church later to pick up the copies Father Francis made of the flyer. William and I will hand them out everywhere we go today: that *colonia*, the fairgrounds, the red-light district.
- Tomorrow morning I'll go out on the *rastreo* with Ximena and Father Francis and the rest of the Contra el Silencio group. I'm not saying Irene is dead, but I'm not going to pretend it isn't possible, after everything I've seen and heard. I'm not going to leave any stone unturned, even if it means—God, my hands are shaking as I write this—even if it means finding Irene's body underneath.
- I am the only one that Ma can rely on, and I am, as my dad said when Irene was born, my sister's keeper.
- Had to tell Brigit the whole story about Irene last night. She wants to come and be with me, but that would be way too much for me to handle. She was terrified when I mentioned the Night

Stalker. I asked her to order the biography that Father Francis told me about and send it to me. "What're you doing, Ivon?" she demanded. "Why do you want to know about the Night Stalker? You're not going to tell me this is research, are you? What about Georgito?"

• Ximena has talked to Jorgito's mother and told her what's happened, but she's sick, very sick, Ximena says, vomiting blood now. In the back of my head I keep worrying about Jorgito being left in his abusive grandmother's care. I look at my mom and feel the dread she's feeling right now at the thought that some horrible thing may have happened to my little sister. I realize that this is what it means to have children—to worry all the time, to fear something could happen to your child. To lose your mind when something does happen. From the sounds my mom makes when she cries, it sounds like a part of her own body has been wounded.

• Ma and I had another horrible fight this morning. She still won't talk to me or even acknowledge my presence. "Isn't it enough to have one daughter missing?" I yelled. "Is it easier to pretend I don't exist?" "I wish you didn't," she said.

24

THEY THINK SHE DOESN'T UNDERSTAND WHAT THEY'RE SAYING.

"We need another one," the man's voice on the megaphone says. "We need a double, same height, same coloring, same age, same everything. We have to do them together. What's wrong with you fucking idiots, you know the rules. This is supposed to be a nickel, not a penny."

When they don't say anything, he shouts: *"¡Nicle, cabrones! ¿No entienden qué quiere decir un nicle? Dos por nicle, pinches idiotas."*

Two for a nickel.

The man on the megaphone is furious. They've wasted very expensive time, he says. Now that El Diablo isn't around, things aren't the same any more. He has to rely on crack heads now, and they're always making him fall behind. His boss is prodding him in the ass, he says.

"Me anda culeando, el buey, y a ustedes les vale, cabrones, a ver si se apuran o me los voy a chingar a todos, pinches tecatos idiotas, all you care about is that fucking needle. We can't do anything without the other one, so go get me another one today, *igual que ella, igualita,* and don't hurt the merchandise, *¡hijos de su chingada madre!"*

Whatever it is that he's so angry about, Irene knows it's kept her alive, kept them from hurting her the way they hurt the others. She hears their screams and knows they're dying.

She hasn't hyperventilated today. She passed out at first because her allergies kicked up from all the dust under the cot that's bolted to the floor. They stuck a rag in her mouth, and she can't breathe through her nose. Her legs are trussed with rope, wrists tied over her head. The springs of the cot are so close she can reach them with her nose when she lifts her head.

When the megaphone man leaves, the others get on the cot and the mattress sags on top of her, pins her to the floor. They do things, it's like they're having a pissing contest, but they're not pissing. The springs squeak and the mattress bobs up and down on her head. They're taking bets on who can shoot first, and she thinks maybe they're playing Russian roulette, but they sound like they're panting and they say disgusting things like "I'm gonna chop her in pieces" and "I want to shit all over her." The uglier it gets, the more they grunt and egg each other on.

"Stick a knife up her ass."

"Suck her blood till she dies."

Dracula, that's the one who's always talking about sucking her blood. Once he dangled his head over the side of the cot and laughed at her, wagging his tongue like a maniac. She knows who he is. She remembers his gold teeth. He's that driver with the tattoos.

Cancer, that's the one who wants to chop her up.

Armando, the one who wants to take a dump on her.

The one who wants to stick a knife into her behind is called Turi.

I have to remember their names. Memorize their names.

Megaphone man is just called Junior, but she knows who he is, too, the rich guy at the fair. There's a woman, too, dressed in a nurse's uniform, but she's only around for a little while. She's the one who cleans her up, and her hands always smell like onions and bleach.

Irene is naked, so it's easier for the woman to wipe up the piss and the shit that flow out of her. At first she tried to hold it, embarrassed by the smell and the feel of feces on her skin.

The woman has fed and cleaned her four times. From all the time that passes between feedings and the way the light changes in the room, she thinks she's been here two days. She's too scared to be hungry, but her stomach feels hollow, like it's sinking. Her tongue feels like a dry frog is in her mouth.

The room is dark and hot. It reminds her of being in her

cousin Patrick's house. He lives in a trailer out by Ascarate Lake, and the heat seeps through the walls like water.

When the woman comes in, she opens the top part of the windows and lets some air and light into the room, thin stripes of light against the red walls. The glass on the windows is painted blood-red. The walls, the floor, even the cot—everything is painted red. And there's black and white graffiti scrawled all over the walls.

The woman sweeps the floor again—the first time, the broom pulled carcasses of rats out of the corners of the room—and then she drags Irene out by the rope around her ankles and helps her sit up, pulls the rag out of her mouth. She massages Irene's arms and shoulders. The woman wears a skeleton mask, so all Irene can make out are the woman's black eyes behind the mask. She's got purple-streaked hair and chewed-up fingernails. She's wearing Irene's Skechers, and has Irene's headphones wrapped around her neck, Irene's CD player clipped to the waistband of her pedal pushers.

That's my stuff, Irene wants to say, but she keeps quiet.

The woman wipes her down with a cold gray towel that she pulls from a bucket that has a mop in it. There is bleach in the water and it makes Irene's skin sting. But the bleach keeps the rats away from her. The smell of the bleach reminds her of chlorine. The woman has to mop under the bed, too. When she's done cleaning up, she leaves the room, hauling the bucket. She'll be back a little later with a tray.

In the time the woman is gone, Irene drags herself over to the other side of the room, pulling her body across the hot metal floor with her heels, using her knees and elbows for leverage. She tries not to notice the pull of her shoulder muscles, the way her skin burns as she slides. There's a seat under the window back there, looks like a bus seat. When she reaches it, she tucks her legs tight against her body and hauls herself to her knees and then to her feet. Sometimes she gets cramps in her legs from the blood circulating too fast. If she can stand on the seat, she can try to look out the window, maybe she can see something through the red paint.

She sits on the seat to catch her breath. All she has to do is lift her legs and stand up, in one quick motion. It takes all of her strength to pull herself up, her legs are so tired. Pain shoots up her spine, but she presses her lips shut to keep from crying out. All she sees are sky and sand dunes and clumps of sagebrush. Last night she saw city lights and today she thought she saw ASARCO in the distance. It's like the view changes every day.

Irene crawls back to the bed when she hears the woman's footsteps crunching outside, returning. Her heart is pounding, and she's dizzy from all that movement.

The woman spoons this stuff into her mouth. Tastes like salty beans mixed with something weird that chews like meat but doesn't taste like meat. Maybe it's dog or cat that she's eating. Can't think about what else it could be or she'll puke.

The woman sings to her while she eats. *Sana, sana, colita de rana, si no muere hoy morirá mañana.* When she first realized the woman had changed the words to the song, she cried. Her mom used to sing her that lullabye when she got hurt as a kid: heal little frog tail, heal, if you're not well today you'll be well tomorrow. That's how the song goes. The woman has changed it to something ugly, to a song about dying rather than healing. She wants to yell at the woman to shut up, but she's too terrified to say anything. It's better if they don't know she understands Spanish.

When she is finished eating, the woman makes her sit on the shit bucket. She studies the graffiti while she empties herself out. Letters and words that she can't make out, a big pulsing heart, two hands pointing guns at each other, penises and balls, and on the wall behind the bed, something that looks like a chalkboard with three columns. At the top of each column there's a coin painted— a copper penny, a white nickel, and a grey dime—big and exaggerated, the president on each coin smiling wickedly. Under each coin there are lines; the penny category has the most lines, but she can't focus enough to count them.

The woman must be giving her something in her food, because the graffiti on the walls starts to turn really slowly, like the room is moving. She feels like she's on the carousel at the fair. She can almost hear the music. Sometimes she can even hear Pepe Aguilar's voice singing *"me vendiste por unas monedas"*—you sold me for a few coins.

To keep herself going, she sings that line from "Black Dove" that says *I have to get to Texas*. She remembers something about a tiny scary house in the lyrics, too. It's like Tori Amos wrote that song just for her.

She doesn't scream anymore when the men jump on the cot. She just lies there, listening to them, praying her Our Fathers and Hail Marys, trying to breathe really shallow so her allergies don't flare up and close her nostrils again.

25

OUTSIDE OF THE SACRED HEART CHURCH on Fourth and Oregon,
noon mass was just letting out. Father Francis, in his white robe
and Guatemalan-styled stole, stood in the doorway thanking his
parishioners. The older women kissed his ring, the men shook
hands. Ivon told her chaperone-escort-driver-pain-in-the-ass
cousin William to wait in the truck while she went to get the
copies of Irene's flyer from the priest.

Father Francis gave her a hug. "How are you? How's your
mother?"

"You can imagine," she said.

"I mentioned your sister in today's homily and asked the congregation to pray for her."

"Thanks, I'll tell Ma."

Father Francis paused to pump hands with two women in
black lace mantillas. "*Vayan con Dios*," he told them, then glanced
over at the truck. "Is that William? I haven't seen him since he
went away to college." Father Francis waved at William.

"He's such an asshole," said Ivon. "He won't let me drive
because Uncle Joe told him about that incident on the bridge yesterday, where I almost whacked this Camaro with a crowbar when
it cut in line, and now William's saying *he* doesn't want to drive
across to Juárez, either. He wants us to walk over. How am I supposed to look for Irene on foot?"

"Just walk the strip," Father Francis said. "Many of the girls
disappeared from nightclubs on the strip behind Juárez Avenue,
on Ugarte Street, mostly. The Mariscal area. You know that's the
red-light district, right?"

"I used to live here, remember? I know the Mariscal." In the old days, when she was with Raquel, Ivon had had a girlfriend named Magda who worked in one of the bars of the red-light district. The Red Canary, it was called.

"Just talk to the bartenders and the waitresses, maybe they can give you some leads. As long as you're with a man you'll be safe."

Ivon forced herself not to roll her eyes at that comment.

"If you can wait a minute while I finish up here, we can go down to my office, and I'll get you the flyers and give you the names of some of the bars where those girls disappeared. Why don't you wait inside, where it's cooler. Shall we ask William to come in, too?"

"Let him roast out here, what do I care?" said Ivon.

She glanced at the truck. In his missionary shirt and tie, William was fanning himself with a folded-up newspaper.

Ivon walked over to the little booth in the vestibule that had candles and rosaries and prayer cards for sale, little booklets of the church's history, the oldest church in south El Paso. She bought a small votive candle and took it over to the candle stand at the entrance to the nave, placed it in a blue glass holder, and lit it for Irene.

"Give her light," she whispered to the statue of the Sacred Heart of Jesus. She wasn't a believer, but Brigit had taught her the power of visualization and white light.

Finally, the priest greeted an old woman in a wheelchair pushed by a middle-aged woman dressed entirely in black, the last people to file out of the church. He pulled the black iron gates shut, locked them, closed the wooden doors, and locked them, too.

"I remember when churches used to stay open all the time," she said, following Father Francis down the main aisle of the church.

"That was before gang life ruled the barrio," he muttered, crossing himself as he stepped in front of the altar. In the sacristy, he removed his robes with the help of an acolyte. He was wearing jeans and a black T-shirt underneath. Arms thin but well-muscled, flat stomach, he looked like a buff gay man with a tanned face, except for the unkempt hair hanging over the back of his neck.

Father Francis's office was in the basement of the adjoining school. The fluorescent-lighted cubicle smelled of cigarette smoke and fried food. Everywhere she looked, on the bookshelf planks sagging with books, on the cluttered desk, on the file cabinets piled with folders and newspapers, she saw ashtrays brimming with butts and ashes, cans of Pepsi and Kentucky Fried Chicken boxes.

"Sorry about the mess," he said, "our cleaning woman isn't allowed to clean in here anymore because she throws out all my stuff."

Ivon coughed into her hand. He cleared off a chair next to his desk and she took a seat. One side of the room was paneled in corkboard, crowded with layers of colored index cards and photographs of young women.

"Where are those flyers now? I lose everything in this office."

The Missing Girls from El Paso, read the little sign tacked in the middle of the corkboard. Ivon felt queasy when she spotted Irene's police bulletin.

Hi, Lucha, she said silently to her sister's picture. You hang in there, baby, I'm going to find you, I swear to God. Just don't let anything happen to you, okay?

"Okay," Father Francis said, and for a moment she had the eerie sensation that he had read her mind. "Here they are, inside the phone book. How did they get in there? See?"

He held out a stack of bright pink flyers with the headline: *Se Busca, Estudiante de El Paso*. There were two contact numbers: the Contra el Silencio office and a Juárez cell phone number that people could use if they weren't able to make long distance calls to El Paso.

Ivon's eyes got watery staring at her sister's graduation picture in the flyer. Valedictorian, captain of the swim team, senior at Loretto Academy. Ivon couldn't even remember what the girl wanted to major in when she went to college.

"Wait a minute, where's the other picture?"

"I decided just to use that one. The other one . . . well, it makes her look a little . . ."

"A little what? All you can see is her face and the top of her blouse. I wanted people to see what she was wearing the day she disappeared."

"I know, but they never end up wearing the same clothes they were taken in. You don't know how many families thought they had identified their daughters by the clothing the bodies were wearing, only to find out after a DNA test that it really wasn't their daughter, it was just someone wearing their daughter's clothes."

"Okay, but I still don't get what was wrong with that picture."

"It's the lipstick," he said. "Too much red lipstick, and it comes out looking almost black on the copy. Sends the wrong message."

"So you believe that bullshit too, huh?"

"I'm not passing judgment on anyone's life, Ivon. I just know how people react, and if they see a picture of someone that to them looks like a prostitute, they won't have sympathy for her. They'll just think she was a bad girl and she got what she deserved."

Ivon had to concede the point. Know your audience, that's what he was saying.

He sat down at his computer and typed furiously for a minute. "These are the names of the bars you should visit," he said, pulling a sheet out of the printer and handing it to her.

"They're all on or near Ugarte Street, in the area of the old municipal gymnasium, except those two at the bottom. El Nebraska's a gay bar a little further west from La Mariscal, and that last one, well, that one's more of an urban legend than a real place. When that gang named The Rebels was arrested a couple of years ago, that's all they talked about, Casa Colorada. But very few people have actually been there or seen it, so you may not find it. It may not even exist."

"So what am I supposed to do with these flyers, Father? Is anybody going to give me a hard time for handing them out? Can I staple them to electric poles or whatever?"

"Just show the flyer to the bartenders and the girls working at each of these clubs," he said. "Who knows? Maybe someone at one of those places has seen her."

Ivon spotted the Sayonara Club on the list of bars he had given her. "Did you know this club was featured online in a tourist site on Juárez? It had a coupon for a free drink."

"The *Borderlines* site?"

"You've seen it?"

"I've been trying to get them to remove that link to Sultry Señoritas for some time now. Exploiting those half-naked girls and pandering to perverts is all they're doing."

"They're trying to make prostitution look like a tourist attraction."

"My point exactly. But nobody's listening to me."

Ivon gathered up the flyers and got to her feet. "Okay, I better go before William passes out or leaves me stranded. Thanks." She held out her hand to him, but he didn't take it. He looked worried.

"What is it?" she said.

He stared at her, his eyes silver behind the glare of his glasses.

"I have to tell you something. Shimeyna didn't want you to know, but I think it would be wrong not to tell you. After what's happened, you have a right to know."

"What is it?" she said again, impatiently this time.

"Remember that accident she got into the other night?"

"Yeah, when she plowed into a phone pole."

"Well, it wasn't because she was trying to avoid a pedestrian that she lost control of her car. I mean, that's the story she gave, but that's not what happened. Someone tried to run her off the road. Someone in a big truck with Texas plates, that's all she saw."

"And she got arrested for that?"

"Well, she *did* end up driving into that pole, and she *was* under the influence . . ."

"Does she know who it was?"

"We think it's somebody who's upset with Contra el Silencio."

She narrowed her eyes. Was it her imagination or had she seen a guilty look cross the priest's face all of a sudden, like he knew something else he wasn't telling.

"Has this happened before?" she asked.

"We get our share of threatening phone calls. I mean, so does everyone else who's trying to do anything about these crimes . . . but it wasn't until just a few months ago that we noticed we were being followed. Not all the time, usually just after a *rastreo*.

Shimeyna says she's seen that truck before. It's one of those big king cab Chevys with the dual tires on the back, painted a dark green with polarized windows."

"Does she remember the license plate number?"

He shook his head. "Didn't have a number." He reached for a pencil on his desk and wrote out the plate on a post-it note and gave it to her. LONE R★NGR

That star reminded her of something, but she couldn't place it.

"Shimeyna dropped off your sister the first night you were here, right?"

"You're saying she may have been followed to my mother's house?"

He swallowed, raised his eyebrows, and shrugged slightly. "It's possible."

"And you're thinking maybe whoever followed Ximena may have followed Irene into Juárez   is that what you're trying to tell me?"

"It's possible," he said again, lighting a cigarette with nervous hands.

"Damn! It is so fucked up that Ximena didn't tell me this. We could have given that truck description to the police. They would've already tracked down this plate."

"Point is, Ivon, you should keep your eyes and ears open at all times. They may be following you, too."

"But who is 'they,' Father?"

He shook his head. "That, I don't know. But from the make of the truck, you know it's got to be somebody with money. Only the drug pushers drive those kinds of trucks over there. Drug pushers and police. But this one had Texas plates, so go figure."

"Fucking Ximena and all her secrets," said Ivon.

"She doesn't mean to be secretive." he said. "It's her job to hold back information sometimes, to protect people. That's what she's about, you know, protecting people."

"Yeah, but she still should've said something."

He took her hand between both of his. "God be with you," he said. "Just remember, it's a dangerous area where you're going, even during the day, so stay alert at all times. Don't trust anybody.

Don't ask too many questions. Show the flyer, talk about Irene, how young she is, what a good student she is, how your mother is suffering, let people feel how you feel. You never know. It's a small world. Someone may have useful information."

"That's exactly what I need—information," she said. "What you told me the other day, about how I didn't know what was going on in my own hometown, you know why it pissed me off so much? Because it's true. I have a lot of *home* work to do, literally. I did a little research, but I still feel so helpless. Like I don't have the first clue how to begin looking for Irene. If I knew more about these crimes, maybe I'd know what to look for, what to ask other than 'Have you seen this girl'—you know what I mean, Father?"

"I have . . ." he gestured around his office, ". . . tons of information here, more than I know what to do with, as you can see. Clippings, pictures, reports—whatever you need, you can come and look through all of this anytime you want to. It's not light reading, I assure you."

"I'm not looking for entertainment, Father. I'm trying to find my sister."

"Look, I agree with what you're doing. The authorities are clearly just washing their hands of this matter. But you really do have to be extremely careful, Ivon."

He squeezed her hand and, out of habit, she checked out his watch. A cheap black chronograph with a black leather band. *Extremely careful* reminded her of the phrase *exxxtremely lucky*. She couldn't trust anybody, apparently, not even Ximena.

26

"I think that's the best plan, Ivon," said William the Patriarch, placing the cardboard visor over the windshield of Uncle Joe's truck.

"It is *not* the best plan, William, it's going to ruin my plan, actually. This *colonia* La Soledad that we're going to is not walking distance from the downtown bridge, goddammit, and neither is the fairgrounds. And how am I supposed to get to Raquel's house to pick up Irene's car? This is going to fuck up all my plans."

"They have taxis, don't they?"

"Are you fucking out of your mind, William? Can you imagine arriving in a taxi in one of those shantytowns? Let me drive. I'll drive if you're chicken. Move over."

"Has nothing to do with being chicken," William said, but the hollows of his cheeks had gotten flushed. "First, Uncle Joe doesn't want you driving. This is his truck, and I'm responsible for it. Second, if they end up closing the bridge this afternoon, we'll be stuck over there for who knows how long. It's smarter just to walk across. We can park right here."

The World Cup Championship had started in France, and Uncle Joe had warned them that if Mexico won its game today, the Córdoba Bridge would probably close down. Juárez soccer fans took the sport very much to heart, storming the Chamizal Park near the bridge each time Mexico advanced toward the championship, hundreds of fans waving Mexican flags, faces painted red, white, and green. This was causing a major disturbance to the flow of traffic on the bridge, making the lines and the waiting time to get across even longer because customs had to close down for as long as it took to get the revelers under control.

"Even if they close the free bridge, William, they won't close this one or the one in Zaragosa. We can still get back. It's not like you're going to be stranded in Mexico the rest of your life."

"Sorry, Ivon, I've made up my mind," William said, after paying the attendant at the entrance to the border parking lot.

That really pissed her off. He made up *his* mind? She felt her ears burning. Here was the second man making decisions for her today. Maybe she could accept her uncle not letting her drive, especially considering how scattered she'd been these last few days, road rage taking her over at the drop of a hat, but she wasn't going to take any paternalistic bullshit from Mr. Mormon Deacon here, who was younger than she by five years. Even Patrick would've been better, but as a police officer, Patrick said, he wasn't allowed to come across the border on a reconnaissance mission. She was stuck with William. Ximena had promised Brigit that she would not let Ivon go anywhere in Juárez by herself.

"When did you turn into such an asshole?" she said, as he parked the truck.

"I don't really want to spend all my Saturday in Juárez, Ivon. I told Pam and the kids I'd be back to take them swimming at Memorial Park later."

"I hear you, okay, William," Ivon said, "and if we weren't looking for my missing little sister, maybe I'd give a shit about your going swimming with your family. Wouldn't it be nice if we could *all* go to Memorial Park and have a good time today. You didn't have to come along, you know, I don't need a fucking chaperone. I'll go by myself."

"Look, Ivon, you can curse at me all you want, but I'm not trying to be insensitive, just practical. I am not letting you out of my sight. Sorry."

"Fuck!" she said, kicking the door of the truck shut.

The high noon sun baked the back of Ivon's neck in the ten minutes it took for them to walk between the parking lot on El Paso Street, where they had left Uncle Joe's truck, and the turnstile at the downtown Mexican Customs building.

Juárez Avenue looked like a minefield. The asphalt had been completely dug up. In front of the Mexican curio shops, liquor stores, restaurants, and nightclubs, the street was nothing but ditches, trenches, and mounds of dirt and concrete. Wobbly wooden walkways connected one side of the street to the other. The few people walking along Juárez Avenue all looked like high school kids from El Paso or Las Cruces, budding party animals, Ivon surmised, determined not to let street construction get in the way of a Sunday afternoon attitude adjustment in J-Town. A few cigarette vendors and shoeshine boys stood at the corners, but gone were the uniformed attendants gleaning quarters here and there for watching the parked cars, and the kids with the greasy rags and bottles of fake Windex brazenly making a peso here and there by cleaning the windshields of the cars heading north on Juárez Avenue, toward the bridge, toward the Promised Land. Right now, the road to the Promised Land was closed for repairs.

Behind Avenida Juárez lies La Mariscal, a labyrinth of streets and alleys where the brothels are located, where the ladies of the night congregate along the sidewalks or by the canal waiting for customers. Local folklore has it that, although the street was named after some famous General Mariscal, the area is called that because of the pervasive smell of seafood, or *mariscos*, the salty, fishy smell that emanates from all the brothels. It was Magda who had given her this bit of trivia on La Mariscal.

The brothels on Mariscal Street, which runs directly behind Avenida Juárez, are the ones the tourists from across the border go to, a clientele of high school students, college kids, and business-men. The seediest bars, the ones that line the darker streets near the old gymnasium are for the locals and the drug lords. It was here that Father Francis had told her they should go.

Ivon and William stood outside the Kentucky Club looking at the list of names Father Francis had given her: Joe's Place, La Fies-ta, La Tuna Country, La Maledón, Deportivo, Nebraska, Casa Co-lorada. She pulled out the map she'd downloaded from the *Bor-derlines* site to get her bearings on where they stood in relation to the old gymnasium.

"Where did *that* come from?" asked William.

"I pulled it out of my ass," she said, still seething at him.

"Well, put it away. You look like such a tourist."

"Do you have any idea where you're going, Mr. Brigham Young?"

"The priest told you these places were near the gymnasium, didn't he?" said William.

"And I suppose you know where that is?"

"We can always ask."

"Oh, and that doesn't make us look like tourists, huh?" Ivon turned on her heel and walked into the Kentucky Club.

"What're you doing?" William muttered behind her.

She was going to call Raquel on her cell phone and ask her to pick her up. She was fed up with this bantering and had no intention of going anywhere with William.

"I'm going to the bathroom, if you don't mind," she said. "Here." She handed him the map. "Show this to the bartender, ask him if he knows how to get to any of these bars, to point us in the right direction."

"I already know the right direction," he said, but she left him standing there while she hurried to the back. Two women in shiny halter tops sat on stools at the end of the ornate oak bar. One of them was sipping an exotic blue drink, the other was drinking a margarita in a salt-rimmed glass. Both of them winked at her as she passed. She opened her backpack and took out a copy of Irene's flyer.

"*Mi hermanita, la ando buscando, ¿no la han visto?*"

The women shook their heads and gave her back the flyer.

"*No te preocupes, chula,*" said one of them. "*Ha de andar por allí.*"

Por allí, a euphemism for being out in the street, loose with men. No wonder these crimes haven't been solved, thought Ivon. From the prostitutes to the police, everyone thinks it's just about sex, it's just about the girls going off with men, *por allí*.

Ivon walked into the bathroom and felt a moment of deja vu. Just a couple of nights ago, she'd been sitting here reading graffiti and planning out the new chapter of her dissertation. Fucking unbelievable how quickly things can change. She saw some fresh graffiti on the wall, couldn't find the one she was looking for, and then she saw it, but it said something else now: *Poor Juarez, so far from the Truth, so close to Jesus.* The old version, she could still see traces of it—*tan cerca al infierno, tan lejos de Jesús*—had been scratched out with something sharp.

So far from the Truth. Talk about understatement.

She dialed Raquel's number, thinking about the new phrase, what was it that didn't seem right? Five rings, six rings, eight rings. Ivon was about to hang up, but Raquel finally answered on the tenth ring.

"It's Ivon," she said in Spanish. "I need your help. I need to pick up Irene's car. Can you come get me? I'm at the Kentucky Club right now. What do you mean, no? I realize that, okay, but I don't have any choice. And this really is your fault. Half an hour? Don't be late. Okay, forty-five minutes, then. Bye."

It was exactly one o'clock.

When she walked out of the bathroom, the television sports announcer was yelling out G-O-O-O-O-O-O-O-O-L, stretching the word into a manic exhalation, and the Kentucky Club had come alive with *gritos* and waving Mexican flags. Standing at the bar, staring up at the soccer game on television, William looked ridiculously out of place in his black slacks, white shirt, and blue tie.

"Mexico just scored again," said William. "It's 4 to 2 now. Looks like we did the right thing by walking across."

"Do you always feel this good about yourself?" Ivon said, rolling her eyes. "What did you find out?"

"The bartender says to get to these bars all we need to do is take Mejía back to Mariscal Street, and then make a right off Mariscal on Calle Ugarte. He says all these bars, except for this Casa Colorada place are on Calle Ugarte, west of Mariscal. Casa Colorada is actually on an alley off Ugarte, a block south of the gymnasium."

"West of Mariscal, south of the gymnasium—I'm impressed, William."

"Took you long enough," he said, peering over his sunglasses at her. "You okay?"

"Just a touch of sunstroke from walking over the bridge in the middle of the day," Ivon said, slipping onto a stool.

William looked at his gold Mickey Mouse watch. "Don't you

think we better get going? I don't really want to be walking around here longer than we have to."

"Let me pull myself together, okay? I need something to drink."

Ivon did not tell him she was waiting for Raquel. She was looking forward to leaving him stranded there on Juárez Avenue and letting him walk back across the bridge by himself. She thought about the graffiti again. What was it that bothered her? Something obvious that she was missing. Then she got it. It was written in English.

The bartender brought them each a glass of beer.

"I didn't order this," William said, scowling as he pushed one of the glasses away from him.

"Compliments of the ladies at the end of the bar," said the bartender, grinning. He was the same man from the other night.

"No, thanks," William said.

"Thank them for us, but tell them we're in a hurry," Ivon told the bartender. She picked up one of the glasses and drained the beer in one long draught. William just stared at her. The mildly horrified look on his face almost made her choke.

"Since when do whores buy drinks for men? Isn't it the other way around?"

"Maybe it's affirmative action," said Ivon, glancing back at the end of the bar and holding up her empty glass to the two women. They raised their glasses in unison.

"You sure seem experienced at this," William commented.

"Been there, done that," Ivon said. She eyed the Mont Blanc pen in William's shirt pocket and took it without asking. "Be right back," she said and hurried to the bathroom again. She drew a circle around *so far from the Truth* and then an arrow pointing to a question: *Do you know the truth? Call me.* She wrote her cell phone number.

The bartender was talking to William and cleared his throat when she sat down again. "Eh, excuse me," he said in English. He leaned over the bar and gestured for them to come closer. "Forgive me to interrupt, but I think I give you advice, okay? My name is Gregorio Vela."

"Advice is good," William said right away.

"*Pues, miren*, with all respect, it is not a good idea for you . . . for tourists like you . . . to be going to those places on the map. Most of them are not even open right now. The *discotecas* like Joe's Place and La Maledón, they open only at night. The other places, they are bad places, full of thieves and *cholos* and police. Police are all over that street. They are worse than the *cholos* or the thieves. Why do you want to go to those places? Just stay here, okay? Kentucky Club is safe for the tourists, close to the bridge. You can go home easy, no problems with the police here."

William turned to look at Ivon with an irritating I-told-you-so look.

"*Gracias*," Ivon said to Gregorio, talking in Spanish. "It's very kind of you to be concerned, but we're not tourists, we're not here to have a good time." She handed him a copy of the flyer. "We're looking for my little sister. Have you seen her, by any chance?"

The bartender studied the picture and shook his head.

"Will you display the flyer in the bar, just in case?"

The bartender lifted his shoulders in a slow-motion shrug. "Okay," he said. "But now I worry more for you." He stared at her outfit. "Your clothes," he said.

Ivon looked down at her khaki shorts, *Sparks* jersey, and running shoes, and realized she wasn't dressed for walking the Mariscal. Really stupid idea to wear shorts. She wasn't thinking. Just couldn't concentrate on mundane things like clothes right now.

Gregorio taped Irene's flyer to the mirror behind the cash register. Ivon thanked him and decided it would be best to wait for Raquel outside. With all the construction on Juárez Avenue, she wouldn't be able to pull up in front of the bar. They were heading out the door, when the bartender flagged them back.

"Wait, please," the bartender said, still talking in English. "I give you something. If you need any help, go to the Red Canary on the corner of Mariscal and María Martínez." He uncapped a pen and wrote the name of the place on a bar napkin. "My sister Berta used to work there. People there are good people. Tell them Gregorio sent you."

The Red Canary. That was it, that was where Ivon had seen him, all those years ago when she'd visit Magda at that bar.

Gregorio handed the napkin to William, and William shook hands with him. A male bond. William took a five-dollar bill out of his wallet and left it on the bar.

"*Oye, güera*," a drunk called out to Ivon as they walked to the corner. "*¿No quieres verga?*" he moved his hips up and down at her.

She could see his erection through his filthy jeans.

"I'd rather eat shit," she said, and hawked a gob of spit in his direction.

"*Pinche pocha, hija de la chingada,*" he spat back.

William blushed, but didn't do anything.

27

RAQUEL WASN'T GOING ANYWHERE. She stared at her black eye in the mirror. After three days, the swelling had gone down and the color had changed from blackish-blue to an eggplant color tinged with yellow at the edges, but the veins inside the eye were still raw. Ivon had done this to her, she had to remind herself. No matter what she had done afterwards, Ivon had hit her and given her a black eye.

Why did things like this happen to her? Didn't she have any dignity?

She'd been holed up in her house since Thursday, treating the eye with ice packs and ointments, but a bruise like that did not go away in three days and could not really be hidden with makeup. She'd called in sick today and yesterday had bribed her niece Myrna to fill in for her under the pretext that she was having a really bad time of the month. But her brother wasn't going to tolerate any more absences. If she didn't show up to work on Monday, he was going to come over and see her face.

She pressed the ice pack to her eye again. If only that bitch Ariel hadn't said anything about her transaction with Paco. If only Raquel had kept her mouth shut when she saw Ariel tromping around in the girl's blue suede shoes, maybe Ivon wouldn't have gone off like she did. Ivon was already mad at Raquel when she heard about the drug thing. She didn't need to know the shoes Ariel was wearing were her sister's shoes. Why did I say anything? How could I be so stupid?

The shoes were muddy and looked like they'd sat out in the sun too long, but Raquel recognized them right away.

"*Oyes, ¿qué no son esos los zapatos de la muchacha?*" she said to Ariel.

"I don't know," Ariel said, "I found them down by the river. Now they're mine."

"You should give them back to Ivon. They belong to her sister. She was wearing them last night at the fair. Nobody has shoes like that around here."

Ivon and Ariel had had a big fight over those shoes, but Ariel had won. She'd kicked them both out of her house and yelled that if Raquel hadn't been doing business with Paco, maybe nothing would've happened to the little *chola*.

"It wasn't business," Raquel had tried to explain in the truck.

"I can't believe you took my sister to a crack house, you stupid bitch," Ivon said and popped Raquel in the face, swift as a boxer.

Maybe I asked for it, she thought. Maybe she just wanted to lure Ivon back using the same infallible trick she had always used before. Stir up her rage. If the way to some people's hearts is through their stomachs, to get to Ivon's you have to go through her rage, an emotion she carries like a bodily organ. Once Raquel had painted Ivon's rage: a small sac of red and blue veins attached to her navel.

You'd think that at forty-one years of age I'd have learned my lesson, I'd have grown up, she thought, but not when it came to Ivon. She had never been able to get Ivon out of her system, even as she was pushing her away when they were together, even as she was sleeping with men and refusing to go with her when she left for graduate school. She wanted Ivon to stay put, to stop harassing her about coming out and just be happy they had found each other.

Nobody touched her like Ivon. Not even Ximena. Ximena didn't know about Raquel's way of making love. She needed her neck squeezed or her face slapped so she could climax. Ivon loved making her come. It had led to ugliness between them, eventually, ugly kicking and punching fights that brought them both to tears. But afterward, after the rage settled, there was love and tenderness and so much passion.

The trick had backfired on her this time, though. Sure, Ivon had hit her, kissed her through her tears, stroked her, and told her over and over how sorry she was, how freaked out she was because of everything that had happened with Irene and her mother. But that's as far as it went. No lovemaking, no promise of lovemaking, just this black eye.

She closed her eyes, listening to Donna Summer's "Love to Love You Baby" blaring from the stereo and tried to relive Ivon's kiss, those warm lips of hers, the soft tip of Ivon's tongue against her own. Raquel had become instantly aroused. But Ivon noticed her hard nipples and pulled away. Raquel felt so embarrassed.

One thing she knew for sure: she wasn't going to give Ivon the satisfaction of seeing her face today. She had to maintain some dignity, after all. She had no intention of going to pick up Ivon at the Kentucky Club. Maybe by Monday, she'd be able to hide the bruise better so she could go to work. Taking care of herself today and tomorrow had to be her first priority. If she didn't make it to the office Monday, her brother was going to come over after work, pound on the door, see her black eye, and beat the truth out of her. He would kill her if he found out she was seeing a woman again. He would kill Ivon if he knew she was the one who'd hit her.

Years ago, suspicious of her friendship with Ivon, and enraged when he discovered they had rented an apartment together in El Paso, Gabriel had threatened Ivon's life. In the middle of the night he had kicked down the door of their apartment and dragged Raquel to his car.

"*Pinche tortillera cabrona*," he had yelled at Ivon, "you better watch yourself. If I ever see you around my sister again, I'll beat the shit out of you, you dyke bitch."

For Ivon's sake, Raquel had broken it off. Her heart shattered when Ivon left town, but at least she wouldn't have to worry that one day Gabriel would catch up to her lover on a dark street. She'd been alone for a couple of years, unable to bring herself to be with anybody, until Ximena.

Her affair with Ximena had started four months ago. She had seen Ximena at the Casa del Sol restaurant in the Pronaf, where Raquel and her brother ate lunch every day. Ximena, sitting with a priest and some other people, had recognized Raquel right away and came over to the table to say hello, give her a hug, tell her she looked wonderful and that it had been a long time. She introduced herself to Gabriel, and Gabriel gave her his snake-eyed look, glowering at Raquel, but Ximena either didn't notice or didn't care. When she went back to her table, Raquel made it a point *not* to tell Gabriel that she was Ivon's cousin. They had different last names anyway. Just a friend, she said.

The following week, they saw each other again at Casa del Sol. Raquel had stopped by after work to pick up the take-out order she had phoned in, when she spotted Ximena sitting at a table in the bar by herself. Raquel joined her, and they sat together for hours, talking and drinking until closing time, sharing the plate of *flautas* Raquel was going to take home for dinner. She ended up taking Ximena home, instead.

They never talked about Ivon, and unlike Ivon, Ximena didn't fight with her about coming out. Ximena herself was "just experimenting," she said, a phrase that used to drive Ivon into fits of rage. It didn't bother Raquel. Being with Ximena was the closest she got to being back with Ivon, except that Ximena's touch was much too gentle, and most of the time Raquel had to pretend she had felt something. For four months now, they would meet every Wednesday afternoon at Ximena's grandmother's house, have sex, and go out for a late lunch. That was all. That was enough. They respected each other's secrets.

On Wednesday, Ximena had forgotten to mention that Ivon was in town, that Ivon was staying at the grandmother's house and sleeping in the same bed in which they had just made love. When Raquel ran into Ivon at the Furr's market, she had just come from being with Ximena. The whole time they were talking, Raquel was sure Ivon could smell the scent of sex on her hands. She just could not explain why it depressed her so much.

Her heart ballooned when she saw Ivon, and just as quickly, the air drained out of her lungs, and she could barely breathe. Dear God, was it possible that after all these years she still had not buried her love for Ivon? Donna Summer answered for her: *no more tears, enough is enough.*

28

WHEN SHE SLEEPS, SHE DREAMS OF WATER. Sometimes she is in the pool at school, alone, doing her workout, wondering where her teammates are, why the coach isn't blowing her whistle, yelling at her to stay in her lane and speed it up. She is swimming diagonally in the pool and does not want to speed up. She loves the cool blue water, the slow even strokes of her arms, the firm kick of her legs, and the steady rhythm of her face coming out of the water every third stroke to suck on air.

Other times the water is black and slimy, and she knows she's swimming in the river again. Only this time, there are hands down there growing up from the bottom, reaching for her, trying to pull her down. She is naked and the hands probe between her legs, pull her pubic hair, bruise her thighs. No matter how fast she swims, she cannot get away from those hands.

And then she is on dry land again, hunkering under the shadow of a black bridge. A train pumps across the trestles—she can see it clearly, the Southern Pacific, huffing and puffing and blowing its loud oad whistle. Then she hears something snapping, and the screech of the wheels of the train is so sharp it cuts her ears. She sees the trestle breaking and she knows the train is going to crash down on top of her. Her only escape is the river, the black water where the hands are waiting for her. She closes her eyes, her heart pumping like when she's on the last leg of the 200 meters, and when she opens them again, she is back in the pool at school and the coach is blowing her whistle, telling her to stay in her lane and speed it up.

There's a floor vent next to the bed and she can hear them perfectly. Junior and another man are arguing. The other man speaks

English like a Texan. Hearing someone speak English brings tears to her eyes. She wants to make a sound, figures if she can hear them, they can hear her, too. She could try to scream through the rag.

"I told you that girl was my business," says the Texan. "What the fuck are you doing bringing her here?"

"We got an order for two *americanas*," says Junior. He has a thick Mexican accent to his English.

"I'm the one who gives the orders, you asshole. This is my domain, and nobody does American girls without my knowing about it. We agreed y'all weren't going to poach on American girls. I have busloads of wets for you to choose from. And that girl was on reserve, goddammit. I thought I made that clear."

"You want her back?"

"Fuck no. She's spoilt, now. Who placed the order?"

"My partner. It's for the Egyptian. To keep him quiet till he gets transferred."

"Look, asshole, the Egyptian is not my problem. You and your partner and me had an agreement. Did you all forget that?"

"I know, but the Egyptian can ruin everything. He says he's been talking to El Diablo in jail, says he knows the whole story."

"Fucking Diablo and his big mouth! I should have taken care of his ass a long time ago."

"*Mi socio, buey.* My partner is getting the Egyptian transferred out of the Juárez jail as quickly as possible. Son of a bitch is talking too much. He is on the television, he is in the newspaper, soon we will be hearing him on the radio. All we have to do is give him what he wants until he leaves."

"Or else?"

"You know he talks to the press, he holds fucking press conferences from El CeReSo. I'm telling you, our little dot-com *negocio* here is going to become public information if he doesn't get his order filled."

"What the fuck did he order?"

"Two *americanitas,* I told you, plus the bitch at the morgue and her daughter."

"Tell him he can kiss my white ass. Who does he think he is, anyway? I don't give a fuck that the media's on him like flies on shit. You and your partner ain't nothing but a pair of pussies, letting yourselves get pushed around by some jailbird like that. Doesn't one of you own the fucking media, anyway? Listen here, bud, I'm gonna shut your end down if y'all can't play the game. I don't need no fucking pussies on my team. You asswipes can kiss your investment goodbye."

"¡No mames, buey! Fuck you, you cannot shut us down! It is our money."

"Yeah, and who brings in the goods, motherfucker?"

"Look, we are having enough problems right now without El Diablo's crew. Those guys from El Paso you recommended are *idiotas*. They think this is Disneyland over here, they think they can do whatever they want with the *mercancía*, they hurt them bad, and they look like shit when they arrive, all bruised up."

"What does it matter how they look, they're just gonna get melted down, anyway."

"Our clients want to see the real thing. They want a pretty girl, not one with bruises already before we even shoot the scene. Those *cabrones* are just having a good time at my expense. So now I have to give the job to Dracula's people, and they are *la misma cagada* but a different color—getting high all the time, jerking off, getting free fucks. I can't run a business like this. We have to stay on schedule. Our shows are supposed to stream, that means live, *cabrón*, not prerecorded. People are paying to see live action. They know the difference, they're not stupid. We're losing clients. I have enough problems keeping this site going without you threatening to shut us down. And you do *not* want me telling the media what you're doing with those *mojadas*."

"You're threatening *me*, motherfucker? You're threatening to call the media on me? You go ahead and try that, and see how many federal agents from both sides start crawling up your daddy's ass. See how he feels about his little junior playing with fire. Twin Plant Alliance will fucking fry your stupid ass. You and your partner both."

Junior says something she can't hear, and then their voices fade. She hears footsteps coming up the stairs outside the door.

The door opens and she can make out two pairs of male shoes stomping into the room. The whole room seems to move with their weight. One of them walks over to the window and yanks it open. The light flooding suddenly into the room slices into her eyes and blinds her. When she opens her eyes again, she is staring straight at black lace-up boots and khaki-colored pants with a green stripe up the side.

"One more and that's it," the Texan says. "After that, no more American girls, you hear me? The FBI's got that Bob Russell here right now looking through our records to make sure we've got all the registered sex offenders in our database. Fucking shit is heating up, so you stick to your kind and honor the deal we made, *entiende?* Or I *will* fuckin' bust this thing wide open, and your partner's gonna find himself sucking the Egyptian's cock in jail. Don't ever threaten me again, motherfucker, if you don't wanna end up like one of your bitches."

"You want to see her or not? She's got a *chingadera* in her tongue, man."

Junior has not told the Texan that she is under the bed. She thinks she should move her legs and rattle the cot, but she's terrified of their fury.

"No, I don't want to fucking see her. I don't want to know shit. You make sure she's fucking melted down when you're through with her. And the other one, too. I don't want to see a face, I don't want fingerprints, I want them both fucking turned to bacon with a blowtorch. Goddamn unreliable sons of bitches."

The soles of the Texan's boots squeak on the red floor as they leave the room. Her heart is pounding again like it was in the dream when the train was about to crash down on top of her. *Turned to bacon*, she keeps hearing, melted down, no face, no fingerprints. She moans into the rag, spit and snot and tears and piss running out of her.

29

Outside the Kentucky Club, Ivon showed Irene's flyer to anybody who walked by—to the workers jackhammering the street, to the cigarette vendors and the American kids drifting in and out of the bar. William was angry at her dillydallying, and Ivon had to fess up that she was waiting for a friend who was going to take her to the *colonia*, so he might as well go on home.

"Let me tell you something, Ivon," he said, acting all offended, "this isn't my idea of a vacation. I didn't fly down from Salt Lake with my family so that I could wander around this godforsaken city with you. But I gave my word to Uncle Joe and my sister *and* your mom that I would look after you today, and I intend to keep it. Even if you go off with your friend, I'm still coming with you, and that's that. So get over it."

She was stuck with him. Goddammit.

William crossed the street to staple copies of the flyer to the telephone poles on that side. Ivon stood in the square of shade under the green awning of the bar, and a boy walked by selling newspapers.

"*Investigan privilegios del egipcio*," he hawked. "Read about the Egyptian's privileges in the CeReSo."

She flagged the boy down. "Let me see that," she said.

"*El Diario* o *El Norte*?"

"Both."

"*Un peso, güera.*"

She handed him a dollar bill and took both papers, scanning the stories quickly.

"Un-fucking-believable," she said to William when he came back.

"What did I do now?"

"You should see. That sick fucking Egyptian has all these privileges in jail. Ever heard of a prisoner having his own cell phone? Listen to this." She translated a section from one of the stories. "'On Friday morning, Doctor Norma Flores, the medical examiner, was being interviewed about the murdered women of Juárez on the local television show, *Mujeres sin Fronteras*. While the show was still on the air, the host, Rubí Reyna, received a phone call from Amen Hakim Hassan, the prime suspect in the crimes, protesting his innocence to the television audience. Hassan said he was being used as a scapegoat to hide the identity of the true killers. He further stated that 'things were not going to stay as they were,' and that the authorities were making a big mistake in calling him the mastermind. Another caller phoned in immediately after Hassan's call and asked how it was possible for a prisoner to be calling the station, since there are no public phones in the CeReSo? An immediate investigation of the Egyptian's cell was ordered by the mayor's office yesterday afternoon. It was discovered that Hassan has been living in a cell for conjugal visits that is fully furnished and has its own private bathroom facilities. Two cellular phones, a color television, a videocassette recorder, a microwave oven, and other items of luxury were found in his possession. Evidently, the Egyptian is free to do whatever he wants whenever he wants inside the prison. He can make phone calls, watch television, receive visits at all hours, and even has access to his bank account in El Paso, Texas. The warden of *el* CeReSo is also being investigated for possible bribery from Hassan.' Can you fucking believe that shit?"

"Doesn't *cereso* mean cherry?"

"No, stupid, that's *cereza*. CeReSo stands for *Centro de Rehabilitación Social*."

"So jail here is a social rehab center?"

"So they say."

William looked at his watch. "Ivon, we've been out here half an hour waiting for your friend. Shouldn't we get going?"

Clearly, Raquel wasn't coming. Ivon had forgotten how passive-aggressive Raquel could be. Instead of saying, *fuck you, I can't pick you up*, she just didn't show up. First, she'd taken her sister to a crack house, now this. Ivon was going to let her have it.

"Let's go," Ivon said, stuffing the newspapers into her backpack. "We've wasted enough time here." Her legs cut across the sidewalk like scissors.

"That's what I'm saying," said William, trotting behind her.

They stopped at Fausto's, the Mona Lisa, the Panama Club— all places Ivon remembered, although they'd gotten face lifts, on the outside anyway, and sported neon signs and fresh coats of bright paint. William tried to act like he'd seen it all, but Ivon could tell he'd never been to a brothel before.

At the Red Canary, a man in sunglasses and a Hawaiian shirt stood in the doorway and invited them in. "Cold beer, hot women inside," he said, motioning past the fake palm trees at the entrance. William kept his sunglasses on when they went inside, even though it was so dark he tripped over a girl in a bikini who was filing her nails at one of the tables. Like hungry dogs, two men watched the girl from the next table. Celia Cruz music blared from the tall loudspeakers on the stage. Ivon headed directly for the bar. She recognized the woman tending bar, something familiar about her eyes, although she had put on about fifty pounds and was now running the bar rather than escorting the clientele.

"Are you Berta?" William asked before Ivon had a chance to say anything.

She shook her head.

Ivon narrowed her eyes at her. Yes, she knew her, all right. "Magda?"

"*Para servirle*," she said, wiping down the linoleum bar in front of them.

"Berta's brother Gregorio at the Kentucky Club sent us," said William. "Is Berta here?"

"Berta doesn't work here anymore." Magda eyed Ivon like she recognized her, too.

"We're looking for my little sister," Ivon said. "She disappeared from a *colonia* on Thursday morning. Maybe somebody here has seen her." Ivon showed her the flyer.

Magda stared at the pictures, then shook her head and said,

"No, I work here every day and I haven't seen her." She called the waitresses and the other girls and showed them the picture. Bikini Girl hurried over to see what they were looking at.

"*Ya ni pa' qué,*" said one of the waitresses, "*ya la han de haber matado, pobrecita, tan jovencita.*"

Ivon started to cry at that. The woman had spoken aloud what she'd been fearing most: that her sister had been killed already.

Magda brought her a shot of tequila rimmed with salt and garnished with a lime wedge. "*Cálmate,*" she said. "*No le hagas caso a esta cabrona.* Don't pay attention to her." She waved the girls away. "All of you, get back to work."

"Let's go, Ivon," said William, pointing at his watch.

"*Gracias,*" Ivon said to Magda. She squeezed the lime between her teeth and knocked back the tequila.

"She may not have been killed yet," said Magda under her breath. "They don't kill them right away, sometimes. They use them until they don't need them any more. That happened to one of the girls who used to work here."

"Use them for what?" asked William.

Both Ivon and Magda turned to look at him.

"Oh," he said, "sorry."

"What happened to her, the girl who worked here?" Ivon asked.

Magda shook her head, like she didn't want to say.

"Please," Ivon pressed, "it might help me figure out what happened to my sister."

Magda looked left and right, then leaned her elbows on the bar. "She was a dancer," she said, her voice low and husky. "Her name was Julie and she worked here after her shift at RCA. One night three men came in, they were drunk, one of them had a camera, you know, one of those that make movies . . ."

"A video camera," said Ivon, taking notes with William's pen on a napkin.

"The man with the camera told her he wanted two hours with her, but that his friends had to watch. They paid double the usual rate, so the boss let them do what they wanted. That was the last time I saw Julie. Until they found her body ten days after she disappeared, under a bed in a little hotel up the street. Strangled and raped and starved. *Flaquita, flaquita,* like she hadn't eaten the whole time. Police said she'd been dead no more than two days, so they must have used her for eight days before they killed her."

"But you had descriptions of the men, didn't you? Didn't you report them?" asked Ivon. William was trying to understand her story, but Magda spoke too fast for his Spanish skills.

"The police never even came in here to take a statement. I wanted to go to the station, but my boss wouldn't let me, said he would fire anybody who went and talked to the police."

Ivon translated quickly, for William's sake.

"Didn't anybody see the men when they left?" he asked.

Ivon asked Magda, but Magda shook her head. "We don't know how or when they left. They didn't go out the front door."

"Is your boss here?" Ivon said. "We need to talk to him."

"No," Magda said, "he won't talk to anybody. He's dead now. He was gunned down in front of the bar last month."

"Jesus," said Ivon, "why?"

"Some narco-related thing, they said."

"When did the dancer get taken?" asked Ivon.

"Last year, last summer," said Magda.

"Do you still remember what the men looked like?"

Magda shook her head. Ivon could tell she knew more, but the front door had opened behind them and some American boys walked up to the bar.

"I'll keep an eye out," said Magda. "Is there a number to call you?"

Ivon wrote her cell phone number on the back of the flyer. She thought of something else, and wrote out *Poor Juárez, so far from the Truth, so close to Jesus.* "Do you have any idea what this means?" She pointed to what she had just written.

Magda's eyes froze. "No," she said, "I don't read English."

Ivon placed her hand on Magda's arm. "Do you remember me?" she asked.

Magda nodded. "It's been a long time. I never thought I'd see you again."

"Come here," Ivon said. Magda leaned toward her and Ivon

whispered the translation into her ear. She felt Magda shiver. "Please, Magda, if you know what it means, tell me."

"Where did you see that?"

"Graffiti. In the bathroom of the Kentucky Club."

Magda swallowed again. The youngsters started pounding on the bar, demanding drinks. "I don't know," she said, "really, I don't."

Ivon squeezed her arm. "I'll be back. Alone," said Ivon.

"Hey, *puta*, we need drinks," shouted out one of the boys.

Ivon walked up to him and slapped his face.

"What the fuck!" said the kid, holding his cheek.

"Didn't your mother teach you to respect women?" she said.

"Bitch, I'll teach you . . ."

"What can I get you boys?" said Magda, smiling behind the bar. "First round on the house." She winked at Ivon.

William pulled her away from the bar.

"Jeez," said William, out on the sidewalk, "I thought we'd never get out of there. I hope you don't go taking a drink at every place we stop. I don't want to have to carry you over the bridge," he said.

"William," she said, stopping to scowl at him, "do me a favor and shut your stupid Mormon ass up, okay? Do you really think I'm here to party? Asshole."

She walked on ahead, fuming. William stayed close behind.

They passed the huge public gymnasium that took up an entire city block and found themselves suddenly on Calle Ugarte.

William suggested they scout out the street first. It was a short street that started at the corner of Juárez Avenue and 16 de Septiembre, in front of the downtown plaza, and extended four blocks north of Mariscal. It took them exactly eight and a half minutes to walk from end to end of Ugarte. They walked at a fast clip, the women standing in doorways or leaning out of windows calling out to them.

"The three B's," said an older woman in spandex pants and a leather bustier, a rose tattoo splayed across her cleavage. "*Bueno, bonito y barato.*"

"*Yo le hago de a tres,*" said another, inviting them to a three-some.

William blushed each time. Ivon showed them Irene's flyer. No luck.

At one doorway, a barefoot girl no more than ten years old stood in a camisole waiting for customers. Behind her a woman's voice was saying, "*M'ija*, don't forget to wash yourself after each time." The girl pursed her red lips and made eyes at William.

They only found five of the bars they were looking for on Calle Ugarte. La Fiesta and Deportivo were small pickup places, dark and smoky, with naked girls dancing on tiny stages, mostly empty on a Saturday afternoon. Joe's Place and La Maledón were closed, but La Tuna Country was open. Swankier and newer than the others, situated right next door to a public parking lot, it had glass block on each side of the front door and along the back of the bar. On the small checkered dance floor, lots of honky-tonk-looking Mexicans in *vaquero* outfits, cowboy hats, plaid shirts, bolo ties, and boots danced to *banda* music with women in short skirts and backless blouses. Some younger men and women, wearing baggie pants and T-shirts with state abbreviations, such as ZAC for Zacatecas and DGO for Durango, stood clumped near the door.

None of the bartenders or waitresses they showed the flyer to had seen Irene, but at least Ivon was allowed to post the flyer at the entrance to each bar.

The only bars they had still not found were Casa Colorada and El Nebraska. Gregorio had said Casa Colorada was on an alley off Ugarte, but they couldn't find it. They walked the length of Ugarte again and turned into all of the alleys that intersected, but no luck. In one of the alleys they found a graffiti-scrawled red bus from the old public bus system in Juárez. It was parked in front of an abandoned building. The crooked letters on the destination panel over the windshield spelled "La Cruz Roja." More Mexican humor, Ivon thought, naming that decrepit old bus after the Red Cross. William said he could see someone moving around inside the bus and wanted to go see if they knew anything about this Casa Colorada. Ivon didn't think that was a good idea. She could feel eyes following them wherever they went.

A guy on a ten-speed cycle rode by and William flagged him down.

"¿*Qué onda, gringo?* Are you lost?" the guy asked.

There was something about the guy Ivon didn't trust. She was going to pretend they were looking for the Kentucky Club, just to be safe, but William spoke first.

"We're looking for Casa Colorada or El Nebraska."

The guy glanced over one shoulder, then the other, and finally shook his head. "Not around here," he said. "What are you looking for? Something different?"

He underscored the word different and stared straight at Ivon.

"Let's go," Ivon said, pulling William's arm. The guy pedaled off, whistling.

"Would you stop calling attention to us?" Ivon told William.

"Me? I'm not the one walking around half-naked," he said.

"Your tie isn't helping much either," she said. "Can't you take that thing off?"

He ignored her.

Another police car crept by. This was the fourth police car they'd seen, or maybe it was the same one following them around. Ivon figured it would probably be best if people did think they were tourists. Tourists would be safer than people looking for a disappeared girl. She told William they had to hold hands. The police cars stopped following them after that.

"So what do you think, William, about what Magda told us?"

"I think what we're doing is really stupid, I think she was scared of talking to us, and I think we should probably go home now."

"If the guy had a video camera, it's got to be porno," said Ivon, ignoring his whining. She was starting to connect the dots. "It coincides with this other thing we found, this newsletter that Cecilia got at the factory. It had a web address for an extreme site."

"Who's Cecilia?"

"And the thing with Magda's boss getting gunned down for some drug thing . . ."

He wasn't paying attention to her. "Ivon, where are we? I think we're getting further and further away from the gymnasium. I've lost my bearings now, with all the zigzagging we've been doing."

Ivon spotted a couple of transvestites standing on a corner and went to ask them how to get back to the gymnasium. One of them looked like a beauty queen with a tiara and the other was dressed as a gypsy. They made a big fuss over William, calling him *papito,* straightening his tie, and linking arms with him as though they were all *comadres* from a long time back. William's face was already sunburned, but his ears and cheeks got fiery red. The transvestites each bummed a smoke from Ivon. She had to light it for them, too.

Ivon asked them if they'd ever heard of El Nebraska. Father Francis had told her that was a gay bar, and she figured they'd probably know where it was. They said, no, they'd never heard of it, but Ivon could tell they knew where it was.

"What about Casa Colorada?" she asked.

"You're looking in the wrong place, honey," said Beauty Queen.

"No, *muchacha,* Casa Roja isn't even near here," said Gypsy. His accent sounded Cuban or Puerto Rican. He made a dismissive gesture with his hand, waving behind him. "*Está allá, lejísimo, casi hasta Puerto de Anapra.* I heard it's been condemned. It's not open any more. It's just a big nest of *cholos* and drug addicts, now."

"Are you sure it's in Anapra?" Ivon said. "Someone told us it was off Ugarte."

"Where's Anapra?" William said.

"¡Ay, *nene! Las colonias,*" said Gypsy, surprised that William didn't know the terrain.

"Is it close to a place called La Soledad?" Ivon jumped.

Beauty Queen narrowed his eyes at her. "Why are you looking for Casa Roja, anyway?"

"All I know is that my sister disappeared from a house in La Soledad three days ago. She went to a party there and just vanished. We're trying to find her." She showed them the flyer.

"A party?" said Gypsy. "Since when does a *niña* like this party in the *colonias?*"

"What does this word mean?" Beauty Queen pointed at *vale-dictorian* under Irene's graduation picture, her face radiant under the white mortar board.

"That she's the best student in her graduating class," said Ivon, pulling out the photograph Irene had taken in front of the carousel at the fair.

"This is what she was wearing that day. Have you seen her?" Beauty Queen shook his head. "Not me."

"Wait, let me see that," said Gypsy, holding the Polaroid close to his face. "*Mira, a éste yo le he visto antes*, I've seen him before," he said, pointing to the man in a cowboy hat riding one of the horses of the carousel behind Irene. His face was out of focus, but the checks on his shirt and the turquoise studs on his hatband were clearly visible. Ivon hadn't even noticed him in the picture. Something flickered in her memory, as it had earlier in Father Francis' office.

Cowboy hat, she thought. Lone Ranger. Where had she seen that before?

"What's his name?" asked William, but Beauty Queen gave Gypsy a warning look, and Gypsy handed the flyer back to Ivon.

"Maybe not," he said, "he just reminded me of somebody."

"Reminded you of who?" said William.

"Please, *muchachos*," said Ivon, "if you know something that could help us, I'd be very grateful. She's my little sister, you guys. She's only sixteen years old."

"My mother had two children by the time she was sixteen," said Beauty Queen. "Anyway, we haven't seen her. We have to go, we're late for a manicure."

"Good luck. *Adiós, papito*. . . ." Gypsy blew kisses at William and they hustled away.

"Can't you at least tell us how to get to that Casa Roja place?" William called behind them, but they didn't turn back around. William muttered under his breath. "Those fags just wanted money."

Ivon decided to ignore that. The sun felt like a flatiron on the top of her head, and she was starting to feel queasy.

"Now where do we go?" said William.

"How about south of Mariscal and west of the gymnasium?" Ivon ribbed him.

He didn't think that was funny.

"You thirsty or hungry?" she said.

"We've been walking for hours, Ivon. Can't we just go back?"

"Yeah," said Ivon, sighing, "let's go back." It was clear she was going to have to go back to Puerto de Anapra with Ximena or Father Francis. This was just a shortcut to sunstroke.

They followed the directions the transvestites had given them. Two lefts, two rights, and another left later, they were standing in front of the gymanasium again. The building was like a big blue mirage that appeared and disappeared depending on the angle of the sun. Ivon asked a parking attendant about Casa Roja.

"Casa Roja or Casa Colorada?" said the man.

"Don't they mean the same thing?" Ivon asked.

"It's the same color, but it's not the same place," said the man.

They waited for him to say something else. When he didn't, William took out his wallet and offered the man a dollar bill.

"*No, pos, aquí un dólar ya no vale mucho,*" the man said, not finding the dollar enough compensation. He scratched the stubble on his neck and kept his eye on William's wallet. William gave him a ten-dollar bill. He had no more dollar bills left.

"There's a Casa Colorada a few blocks up on Ugarte, in the Arroyo Colorado neighborhood."

"Isn't Ugarte just these few blocks here?" Ivon said, showing him the map she had downloaded.

"*No'mbre,*" said the man, "it's a really long street, goes all the way to the end, like Mejía and María Martínez. On this end it stops on Abacolo Street, three blocks from here, that's why it looks like a short street. But then it picks up again at the corner of San Francisco and goes for five or six kilometers, all the way to the end."

"So how far is this Casa Roja place?" said William.

"I told you, it's Casa Colorada, not Casa Roja. It's about ten blocks up on Ugarte, where it crosses streets named after metals, like Plata and Plomo. If you want, I can call my cousin. He has a taxi and he can take you."

"No, thanks, we'll find it," said William, not willing to part with any more of his money. "Ten dollars," he muttered under his breath when they walked away, "just to go back where we came from."

"See why I said we needed a car?" Ivon said. "Look, I'll pay for lunch, okay? When we're done? There's a place near the Kentucky Club called Fred's that has the best ham and avocado sandwiches you've ever tasted. Deal?"

"That's all I need," he said, dejected, "dehydration and Montezuma's revenge."

Ivon squeezed his hand. It was at least a hundred degrees out here. They weren't even sweating, it was so hot, and she knew they had to get something to drink or else they really were going to dehydrate out there. Her arms and legs were completely sunburned by now, and William's face was as red as a stop sign. Each time a car drove by and moved the air a little, it felt like a gust from a furnace.

Fourteen blocks later, they found the place on an alley between Bronze and Nickel Streets. It didn't look at all decrepit, as the transvestites had described Casa Roja. This was a two-story red-brick "Ladies Bar," with a huge sign that said Casa Colorada. It had security guards at the entrance and a cover charge. Ivon paid the cover, and the man at the door gave them each a paper ticket, good for a free drink each.

At the bar, Ivon ordered an ice-cold Tecate. William asked for a Coke. She downed half the can in thirsty gulps, shuddering as the cold beer hit her hot belly. William slurped all of the Coke out of the bottle through a straw.

"I'll be right back," she said. "Don't say anything until I get back."

There aren't any women's bathrooms in "Ladies Bars" on La Mariscal. The only women expected to be in "Ladies Bars" are prostitutes or dancers, not female customers. Ivon walked into the dressing room in the back and saw a couple of topless dancers in stiletto heels and thongs, smoking and fixing their makeup. One of them had glittery stuff on her nipples, the other had nipple rings. They both stared at Ivon in the mirror.

"Is it okay to leave a flyer here? My little sister disappeared two days ago."

One of the women raised her eyebrows at her reflection in the mirror. The other, lining her pouted lips with a black pencil, just shrugged. Ivon could hear them whispering when she was in the stall.

"*Marimacha*," one of them said.

"I think she liked you," said the other one. They giggled.

There was a bidet and a box of Fab next to the toilet. Ivon knew the detergent wasn't there for the purpose of doing laundry in the toilet.

She took a quick look at the graffiti, thinking maybe someone was leaving clues on the walls of women's toilets. Amid a hodge-podge of sexual innuendoes, dirty drawings, and comments on food coupons and contraceptives, she spotted two remarks that could be useful. Over the screw holes where a toilet paper holder might have been fastened once, inside a box decorated with stars, was the statement: *Aquí no hay cholas ni maqui-locas.* And in tiny letters at the bottom edge of the door: *El nuevo gobernador le chupa la verga a la migra.*

Ivon had to copy those down on the back of a flyer. Good thing she had hung on to William's Mont Blanc. "No cholas or maqui-locas here" and "The new governor sucks the Border Patrol's cock." She remembered the little boy in *las colonias* the other day selling old Barbie dolls as "maqui-locas." Ximena had said that was the vernacular way of referring to *maquiladora* work-ers who become Americanized and turn into whores.

"Do they *turn* into whores, Ximena, or is that just how people perceive them because they have jobs outside the home?"

"Whatever," Ximena had shrugged. "Point is, nobody respects them. Some don't have a choice, you know. They got kids to feed and they can't do that on their pitiful salaries."

The other reference about the Border Patrol receiving sexual favors from the new governor that opened a whole new vein of possible research leads. . . .

Suddenly, the phone rang in her backpack, startling her. The caller i.d. was blocked.

"*Es una fábrica cerca de Jesús,*" said a woman's voice.

"What? Is this Magda?" But the signal had cut off.

She wrote the words down under the graffiti she'd just copied. *It's a factory close to Jesus.* What the hell did that mean?

The bathroom was empty when she came out. When she returned to the bar, two policemen were standing behind William.

"You the people looking for trouble?" one of them asked Ivon.

30

WILLIAM LOOKED TERRIFIED.

"We're not looking for trouble," Ivon said, shoving her suddenly shaking hands into her pockets. "We're looking for my little sister who disappeared."

"You were seen," said the one in green sunglasses. "You and your friend here are selling drugs."

"We're what?" said William, turning around too quickly. In a flash, the other official twisted William's arm behind his back.

"I'm an American citizen," William muttered.

Green Glasses stepped up to him, grabbed his tie; and yanked William toward him until their noses were almost touching. "And we're the judicial police, *cabrón*."

"You were seen selling marijuana cigarettes to two *travestis* earlier," the other cop said. "You're under arrest!"

"But, officer . . ."

Ivon felt a quiver in her gut, but she knew exactly what was happening. "Don't say anything, William. I know what they want."

The cop pulled William's other arm behind his back and snapped the handcuffs on him.

"This is illegal," William protested.

"William, I mean it, shut up!"

"But, officer," William wouldn't let up in his bad Spanish, "I'm an American. I'm a deacon of the Church of Latter Day Saints, I'm a Mormon, I don't take drugs, I don't use alcohol. I have a family."

"Did you hear that? He's a Mormon."

"I hate Mormons," said the other cop, pushing William's face against a wall to pat him down. "They're always coming to the house on their stupid bicycles trying to get us to convert."

He took all the bills out of William's wallet, license and credit cards, too, and tossed the wallet on the floor.

"*¡Vamos pa' fuera, cabrón!*"

Ivon was expecting Green Glasses to shake her down next. He fondled her breasts instead and Ivon had to clench her fists to keep her self-defense training from taking over. He didn't handcuff her, but grabbed the back of her neck as he pushed her out of the bar, his thick fingers reaching almost all the way around her neck. In an assault, do not panic, she remembered her self-defense instructor's voice, remember your center. It took every ounce of willpower she could muster to keep from breaking into a run, or better still, elbowing him in the rib cage and kneeing him in the groin.

The last time Ivon had gotten picked up by Juárez police she had been a drunken twenty-year-old with a broken heart. It had been after Raquel had told her she was not going to move with her to Iowa City, and she'd decided it was over between them and had gone to visit Magda at the Red Canary. She'd been drinking by herself at first, and then she'd run into some people she knew from high school who were bar hopping La Mariscal with a professor from the university. Somehow they'd all gotten into a heated argument, and suddenly Ivon was breaking things and someone called the cops on her. She wouldn't listen when the police told her to settle down or they'd have to remove her from the bar. Instead, she had made a scene, kicking and screaming and punching, her fist through a window. She had the scar on her right hand to show for it. She'd gotten out of going to jail that time by giving one of the cops a blow job in his police car while the other cop wrote up a ticket on each of her friends and collected a so-called fine for disturbing the peace from the professor.

These pigs hauling them out of Casa Colorada were not just ordinary cops—these were state police, *judiciales*. Bribes and blow jobs would be the least of what she was going to have to do to get out of this one.

The lights of the police car parked outside the bar were flashing blue, and it seemed like the whole neighborhood had come out to the sidewalk to watch the arrest. Ivon spotted the drag queens, Beauty Queen and Gypsy, in the crowd. Green Glasses took Ivon's backpack before shoving her into the backseat.

"*A ver qué chingaos traes aquí,*" he said.

The doors slammed on either side of them, and Ivon watched the two combing through her pack. They removed the stack of flyers, the newspapers, the stapler, Ivon's phone, passport, and wallet. They seemed especially interested in the post-it note Father Francis had given her with the customized license plate written on it. Green Glasses folded it up and slipped the yellow note under his watchband.

Ivon touched the money clip in her back pocket. Thank god she'd taken all of the money out of her wallet earlier.

"How much did they take?" she whispered to William.

William didn't answer. He turned away from her, his jaw muscles working.

"Hey, why are you pissed at me? We have to strategize here, you know, these fucks mean business. These aren't just cops, they're *judiciales.*"

"I cannot believe that this is happening to me right now, Ivon."

"In other words it's my fault?"

"I'm a family man, I have a family."

"And I don't? You mean, you don't deserve this, but I do?"

"She's your sister, not mine." That hurt her deeply. "I'll remember that, William. You know, maybe if more people around here thought each one of these girls that disappears was their sister, they might be able to stop these crimes. But hey, if it's not your sister, it's not your problem, right?"

"Shut up."

The *judiciales* climbed into the front seat. The one in the green glasses held up a baggie full of marijuana. "What do you call this?" he said, dangling the baggie in front of the grille that separated them from their captives.

William glared at Ivon like he really believed they had found that dope in her pack.

"Give me a break, they fucking planted that," she told him. To the cop she said, in Spanish, "I didn't have that in there, you put it there."

"Let's see what the captain says at the station," he said.

The other man floored the gas pedal and the car bolted down Ugarte Street.

"I am an American citizen," William yammered on, his voice tremulous. "I demand that you stop this car right now or let me make a phone call to my lawyer."

Mr. Green Glasses turned up the volume on the radio.

"Shut up, William, okay?" Ivon said in his ear. "You're just turning him on."

"This isn't good, Ivon." His eyes looked shiny.

"Just shut up. They love terrifying people. It gets them off."

"I'm not terrified, I'm pissed off," he said, and she noticed that a bit of a white crust had formed in the corners of his mouth.

"Just don't freak out, okay? Look around you. We're not going to any police station. They're taking us out to the desert."

The look in his eyes changed to sheer terror, and for a moment she remembered him as a little boy hiding behind the trash cans in the alley one Sunday afternoon when his father was interrogating the cousins about who had dumped Clorox into the marinade for the *carne asada*. Since he was the only one not in the lineup, William was blamed by all, and he'd gotten a *santa paliza* (as her mother liked to call it), a sound whipping from his father.

Ivon squeezed her cousin's leg. He turned his head again.

The cop car turned north on a street called Avenida de las Víboras and headed in the direction of the river until it dead ended at La Ribereña. Then they headed west, toward the Pollen Hills of Puerto de Anapra.

Short of a blow job, she knew she was going to have to use her mouth to get them out of this one.

"Don't say a word," she whispered to William. "Let me talk to them. Trust me, okay?"

He swallowed hard and nodded, shifting his weight off his handcuffed hands.

"¿A dónde vamos?" she said, loud enough so they could hear her over the radio.

"Did you say something?" said Green Glasses, lowering the volume.

The other man was staring at her in his rearview mirror, smoking a cigarette. They had the front windows rolled down and the hot stench of sewage from the trash dump they were passing mingled with his smoke and gathered in the backseat like a lethal gas. William started to cough.

"I said where are we going? Did they build a new station out here in the *colonias?*"

"What do you know about the *colonias*, eh?" said the driver. "Is that where you do your drug business? Taking advantage of these poor people?"

"Señor, I've already told you, we're not selling drugs, we're looking for my little sister who disappeared on Thursday. My uncle and I made a report at PREVIAS yesterday. They have all the information, there."

"*Mira, mira,*" said Green Glasses, acting like he didn't believe her, but she could tell that naming the agency had bothered him. He and the driver gave each other a look.

"We had to wait all day for them to call our number," she continued. "The lawyer who took our statement . . . I think his name was Licenciado Márquez Ruiz. You probably know him, right? I can't believe how many families were there to report a missing girl. What's going on in Juárez, anyway? Why are so many young women disappearing and getting killed? Who's killing them, do you know?"

"You need to shut your face," said the driver.

But she was on a roll now. "We've been showing my sister's pictures to everybody. We've left flyers up and down Juárez Avenue, in the plaza, in the church, and all over Mariscal. Everyone knows we're looking for my sister."

No one said anything. The radio announcer reported that the Córdoba Bridge had reopened now that the soccer fans had left the Chamizal. They were on the washboard road that Father Francis had taken into Puerto de Anapra the morning they found out about Cecilia, the police car bumping over the ruts and potholes.

"You're making a big mistake," Ivon persisted. "The detective who's helping us look for my sister, he knows we're over here, and if we don't come back, he's going to contact the FBI."

Another sideways glance between the cops.

"Are you going to get her to shut up, or am I, *güey?*" the driver asked his partner.

William kneed her leg, but she played one more card.

"You know that Bob Russell who was interviewed on TV the other day?" she said to William in a loud voice. "He didn't say anything about the *judiciales* kidnapping people."

The cop brought the car to a sudden halt, causing it to swerve on the dirt road.

"Shut your snout!" the driver spit through the grille. "*¡O se me calla el hocico o me la bajo de aquí a patadas!*" He was going to kick her out of the car if she didn't shut up. That was fine with her.

Satisfied that his threat had scared her, he drove on, maneuvering the car around the carcass of a dog in the road.

She took out her money clip and smacked William's leg. She had five twenty's, three ten's, three five's and a one-dollar bill. A hundred and forty-six dollars. Chump change. Tucked in the credit card pocket of her money clip, she noticed something pink. She pulled it out. It was Rubí Reyna's business card.

"How much is our fine?" she said. "We have a hundred dollars in cash here, not counting the money you already stole from my cousin."

William glared at her, as if to say, you're haggling bribe money with *judiciales?*

"Two hundred apiece," said Green Glasses right away

"Oh, wait a minute, here's ten more," she said. "A hundred and ten dollars, and you can leave us here if you want to. We'll walk." She held the money up, the bills arranged like a poker hand.

Green Glasses spat out the window.

The driver eyed the cash through the rearview. "For the amount of drugs you had in your possession, you owe four times that amount," he said.

Her heart was pounding now, knowing they could go either way with the next thing she had to say. Either they took their guns out and shot them right then and there or they let them go. She played her gambit. A fifty-percent chance was better than nothing.

"Maybe my friend Rubí Reyna can make up the difference," she said, eyes focused on the rosary dangling from the mirror.

Both the cops and William turned to look at her at that.

"What did you say?" said the driver, slowing the car with another jolt.

"You know who she is, right? Rubí Reyna? She does that show on Channel 33, *Mujeres sin Fronteras*. I don't know if it interests you, but Rubí's family and my family *se conocen desde hace años*, they go way back."

"*¡Me lleva la tiznada!*" said the driver, pulling over. "*¡Qué pinche puta suerte tenemos!*"

William's quizzical look almost made her laugh.

The driver slammed on the brakes.

"*Se me apean 'horita mismo, cabrones*," ordered the driver, jerking the transmission into park. "*Ándale*," he gestured to his partner, and they both got out of the car and yanked open the back doors.

William and Ivon climbed out. The driver unlocked William's handcuffs.

"*Dales sus mierdas*," the driver told Green Glasses.

Green Glasses returned her backpack, and she looked through it to make sure her passport and wallet were still there. The stapler was missing, so was her cell phone. "Give me back my telephone," she said.

"What telephone?" said Green Glasses.

"Give them the money, Ivon," William said.

"You want this?" she said, waving the money in their faces.

"Better yet, tell your friend Reyna to shove it up her ass," the other one said, and got back in the driver's seat, slamming the car door behind him.

"*Le andas buscando tres pies al gato, eh, y le vas a encontrar cuatro*," said Green Glasses. It was a warning: You're looking for something you're not going to find; a three-legged cat instead of a cat with four legs. A predator with no weakness.

"Here," Ivon said, handing him a copy of Irene's flyer. He had reached out his hand, thinking she was going to tip him, she guessed, but pulled his hand back when he saw it was a sheet rather than a bill she was offering him. A gust of wind blew the flyer out of her hand, and it tumbled off over the desert. *Se Busca, Jovencita de El Paso.*

"*Me la vas a pagar, cabrona.*"

"*Vayan con Dios,*" she said, imitating Father Francis.

"Polite, aren't they?" said William, shading his face in the wake of sand and exhaust left by the *judiciales*' car. "Why didn't they take the money?"

"I guess they didn't like the names I dropped," said Ivon, watching the car go back toward town. She was worried about her phone. What if Brigit tried to call her? She felt nauseous.

"Who is she, this Ruby woman with the television show? And how come you just happen to have her card on you?"

"We met her at the morgue the other day. Ximena and Father Francis are letting her film their body search tomorrow, for a special she's doing on the murders."

"What murders?"

"Long story."

Now she was feeling dizzy and seeing spots. Clear signs of sunstroke.

They were standing just downwind from a small Abarrotes store with a peeling Coca-Cola logo and graffiti scrawled all over the walls. Trucks and buses rumbled back and forth around them, shrouding the makeshift dwellings that lined each side of the road in smoke and dust. Up ahead, on the El Paso side, rose the twin smokestacks of the ASARCO refinery.

William stared at his surroundings, making a 360-degree turn, almost stumbling. "Where are we, anyway?" he said, looking dazed. "I suddenly feel like I'm back in Desert Storm. This place looks like those villages outside Kuwait after a bombing."

"Collateral damage," said Ivon, "good analogy."

"Place gives me the creeps. How do we get out of here?"

"Well, we can't call home," she said. "I say we flag down the first city bus that passes and get back to the bridge."

"I'm kind of traumatized," said William, loosening his tie. "You think they have cold beer at that place up there?"

He pointed to a dilapidated little bar across from the Abarrotes called Cantina Paracaídas. It had a white parachute for a roof.

"Deacon Cunningham," she said, slipping her arm around his waist, more for support than anything else, "there's hope for you yet."

For a moment she felt like his big sister, soothing him after a scare, but the wind fluttered the flyers in her hand, as if to remind her that wherever she was, nobody was soothing Irene, so she pulled away. A sudden dust devil swirled in front of her, blowing sand into her eyes.

A red bus, the same red bus they had seen earlier on Ugarte Street with "Cruz Roja" in the destination panel, nearly ran them over as they crossed the road, blaring its horn and speeding up. They barely had time to jump out of the way.

"¡Idiota!" Ivon yelled out to the driver.

"Did you see that?" said William.

"Fucking asshole. All bus drivers are assholes in this town."

"No, I mean, did you see that face in the window? I swear it looked like Irene."

Ivon narrowed her eyes at William. His face and ears were burgundy-red by now and his eyes looked glazed. "You're hallucinating, *primo*. Let's get you that beer."

"Pam's going to kill me," he said.

"Those cops were going to kill you," she reminded him. "Pam's going to be happy you're alive."

31

"CRUZITO!" JUNIOR'S VOICE BOOMED OUT. He had been standing in the door to the red room when his cell phone rang.

Irene could hear him pacing outside, yelling into the phone.

"Listen to me, will you? *El pinche güero*'s pissed, man . . . Hey, I know that, okay? I know the mayor stole your land. How many times do you have to tell me that story? Stop with the broken record, already. It's your dad you should be yelling at, *pendejo*, not me. I'm trying to help you make a profit and get your stupid land back . . . but the Egyptian is getting in the way, man . . . Look, all I know is that if *el güero* shuts us down, we lose everything we've put into this. You won't get your industrial park, and I won't get my fucking business going . . . Kill him off, pay him off, whatever, man. Okay, then, kiss my ass . . . When all this goes to shit, it'll be your fault, *maricón!*"

"FUCK!" he shouted and threw something against the outer wall of the room. Irene didn't wince at the shouting and the cursing any more. She had grown used to the anger that saturated all of them.

"*¿Qué pasa?*" It sounded like the woman's voice. "We can hear you clear down to the cemetery."

"That fucking asshole. Just because he's the son of the high and mighty Cruz Benavídez, president of the Maquiladora Alliance, he gets to sit up there in his big air-conditioned penthouse office in the Elysian Fields while I'm burning my balls out here having to deal with that fucking *gringo*. I'm tired of this shit, man."

"The bus is here. Six pennies and the other half of your nickel."

"How do they look?"

"How do they always look? Crazed with fear."

"That's good. They need to look that way."

"Are we doing them tonight, then? All of them?"

"All of them. We're using a different warehouse. Turi's rigging it up right now. One of our regulars wants to hear echoes. *Voces con Eco*, we're gonna call the show."

"Even the girl from the fair?"

Irene flinched under the bed.

"Her, especially. Here, take the camera. I was coming to take a picture of her to put online, but you do it. Make her look cute. Legs wide open. Then go take one of her other half. I've got *cabrones* bidding on that nickel already."

32

DETECTIVE MCCUTS RANG THE DOORBELL AGAIN. He was holding an El Paso Police Department duffle bag with the evidence inside a paper bag. He was pretty sure the pants belonged to the missing girl. At least he was hoping they did because then he would have evidence of foul play and he could start his investigation. He was keeping his fingers mentally crossed as he rang the doorbell again. The front door was open and the screen latched from the inside, so he knew there had to be somebody home. Somebody had to be expecting him. He'd told the mother on the phone he'd be here between five and six.

Finally, he heard the dog barking in the backyard. A minute later, the squeak of rubber soles on the hardwood floor, and the daughter walked up behind the screen door. Seeing the daughter right off the bat like that disarmed him for a moment. He liked masculine women—they reminded him of his mother—and this one with her stylish haircut, wide shoulders and narrow hips, cleft in the chin and light brown eyes, he found dangerously attractive. He had barely managed to keep himself from staring when he came over the first time to take their statement. He had almost gawked when she gave him her business card and he saw that she was a Visiting Professor at a college in Los Angeles. She was way ahead of him in the education category.

"Hi," she said, unlatching the screen and pushing it open, "come on in." Her eyes were bloodshot and her face looked sun-burned. Her skin smelled of Noxema.

Pete wiped his feet on the doormat before entering.

"I was starting to worry," he said. "I've been standing out here for ten minutes."

"Sorry," she said, "we were working in the backyard. Ma's washing up. She'll be out in a minute. Want some iced tea? I just made some."

"Sure, thanks," he said.

"Have a seat if you want," she said and went off into the other room.

Pete sat down on the sofa and surveyed the room quickly. He liked to test himself, see how much he could absorb in one quick sweep of the room, then close his eyes, and run a mental checklist before opening them again. Green leather recliner left of the window, an old-fashioned stereo to the right, near the door, furniture upholstered in red and gold stripes, velvet cushions on the sofa, Oriental rug under the gold-leafed coffee table. He popped his eyes open and found the mother standing there, staring at him. He hadn't even heard her come into the room. Some detective, he thought.

He stood up to shake her hand. "Mrs. Villa," he said stiffly.

Behind her came the daughter with three glasses of iced tea on a tray.

"Please sit down, detective," said Mrs. Villa, sitting down on the edge of the recliner.

The daughter placed the tray on the coffee table. She was wearing shorts and a tank top; he noticed she had hairy armpits. All of her looked like she'd spent the day lying out by the side of a pool too long. She took a glass for herself and sat down on the ottoman of the armchair he hadn't remembered seeing. Pete felt awkward about helping himself to the tea—his dad had taught him to wait until he was served—but he was thirsty, so he reached over for one of the glasses.

"I didn't know if you took sugar or not," said the daughter.

The tea had a sprig of mint leaf in it. He preferred lemon, but he wasn't about to get picky. "This is fine," he said, and took a couple of gulps. He put the glass back on the tray. Nobody said anything.

He knew it was his show. "Well," he said, "shall I show you what they found?"

"Please," said Mrs. Villa.

"You need to understand," he said, "that this doesn't mean anything conclusive."

"Can you tell me again who found this?" asked the daughter.

"Border Patrol agents, doing their rounds of the riverbank this morning at approximately 6 A.M. Apparently the jeans had washed up on our side, over by the black bridge. I had to wait till they dried before I could bring them over."

The daughter nodded and sipped her tea.

He unzipped the duffle bag, snapped on a pair of surgical gloves, and pulled the jeans out of the paper bag. He was expecting exclamations of fear or dread, the usual response his CSI buddies said they got when they revealed evidence to families, not the stone silence of these two women. Mrs. Villa, in fact, had her eyes closed.

"Can I see them?" the daughter said.

"You have to wear gloves." Pete handed her a pair from the duffle bag.

She pulled on the gloves—her hands were smaller than he thought they'd be—and held the jeans up to the light.

"They're filthy," she said, "and they've got, like, blood stains or something."

A small cry escaped from the mother.

"We're still waiting on the lab results, but yes, that's my preliminary assessment, as well, that those are blood stains." A spray pattern like that, he didn't tell them, usually indicated a blunt object like a hammer hitting the head and breaking the scalp. Not a gunshot wound, or there'd be a lot more blood.

"Ma," said the daughter, "I've never seen these pants on her, so I don't know if they're hers. You have to look at them, okay?"

Mrs. Villa pressed her lips together and nodded. The daughter took the jeans over to her. The mother started to cry as soon as she saw them.

"A few months ago I hemmed a pair of white jeans for her," she said. "I always fold the hem over with lace."

"We need to see the hem to make sure," the daughter said to Pete.

Pete got up, folded one of the legs up, and sure enough, there was a ribbon of lace stitched to the hem, mud and debris caught in the webbing.

Mrs. Villa screamed when she saw it. "*¡Ay no, ay no!*" she wailed.

The daughter sank to her knees next to the mother's chair, her face ashen.

That was the response Pete McCuts was expecting. He had it now. The case was his. His dad had been throwing his weight around for weeks trying to get Pete assigned to a good case, and now, at last, he had one. He hoped.

He took the jeans and folded them back inside the paper bag. "As I said, this doesn't mean anything conclusive, other than that the evidence does, indeed, belong to the missing person and that it *suggests* possible foul play. Now we can move forward on this case." He thought it best not to tell them that he was going to have to share this information with the guys in Homicide. Pete did Rape and Missing Persons.

"Look, officer . . ." the daughter began.

"Technically, I'm a detective, not an officer," he corrected her.

"Look, McCuts," she said, still on her knees with her arm around her mother's shoulder. "We'd appreciate it if you stopped referring to this as a *case*. This is my sister, her daughter, we're talking about here. Her name is Irene, if you don't mind."

He nodded. "I stand corrected," he said. "The first order of business is to advise the Kidnapping unit of the State Judicial Police across the border that we have reason to suspect that an American citizen has been kidnapped in Juárez. They are going to ask you to repeat the story you have already told to the PREVIAS people and to us."

The daughter's face registered a look that bordered on terror.

"Is something wrong?" he asked.

"The State Judicial Police? You mean the *judiciales*?"

"Yes, kidnapping and homicides are in their jurisdiction."

"My cousin and I got picked up by the *judiciales* earlier today."

Pete cleared his throat. "In Juárez?"

"They didn't like it that we were going around showing Irene's picture to people and asking questions, so they arrested us, tried to pin a phony drug-pushing charge on us and then drove us out to the *colonias* in Puerto de Anapra, where who knows what they were going to do."

Mrs. Villa stared straight ahead, blinking her eyes nervously.

Pete locked his fingers together and rested his chin on his hands. He felt like he was waiting for someone to say grace. "That's not good," he said.

"No shit, McCuts."

"I mean it's not good that you were over there asking questions and showing pictures. You may have already contaminated the investigation."

That wasn't the right expression. It's crime scenes that get contaminated; investigations get jeopardized. Hell, they'd never know the difference.

"So what were we supposed to do, wait until her body turned up?"

"*Por Dios, no digas eso, Ivon,*" the mother said.

"Miss, procedures exist for a reason."

"Technically," she said, "I'm a doctor, not a miss."

Again, he stood corrected. If only she knew how much he liked that, maybe she wouldn't do it so much. "Sorry," he said, "Doctor Villa, procedures exist for a reason."

"Yeah, well, we don't have time for procedures. We've already wasted enough time waiting for you people to do something about this. My sister's been kidnapped, detective, and it's pretty obvious that they took her pants off for a reason. I need to believe she's still alive, I know she is, and with or without your help, I'm going to find her."

The mother started to sob again.

"I'm sorry, Ma," she said, stroking her mother's back. "I know it's hard for you to hear this, but I need to make Mr. McCuts here understand that we're not going to sit around passively waiting for the police to decide if this is in their jurisdiction or not. Irene didn't run off with her boyfriend or run away from home, okay? She was taken against her will—can you all get that through your thick fucking skulls?"

"I see and understand your distress, Doctor Villa . . ." he started.

"Has something like this ever happened to you, McCuts?" she snapped.

". . . Well, maybe I don't know what it feels like to have a family member kidnapped, but I understand your desire to act, to believe that no permanent harm has come to your sister. Hope is a good thing. But as you yourself experienced today, this is a dangerous thing you're doing. It's not a good idea to interfere with those judicial police. They don't take lightly to Americans poking around in their territory, much less, excuse me for saying this, an American woman who has no official capacity to be asking questions or showing pictures. Frankly, I'm surprised you escaped with your life."

The mother cried out, and the daughter narrowed her eyes at him.

"Excuse me," said the mother. "I can't listen to any more of this." She got up and hurried out of the room.

"Ma? Are you okay?" the daughter called out.

"I just need to be alone right now, m'ijita," the mother said over her shoulder. "I need to take my medication."

The daughter sat on the edge of the ottoman and looked at him, disarming him again with her tear-filled eyes.

"How much did you have to give them to let you go?" he asked softly.

"Let's just say I dropped the right names," she said, wiping her eyes with the back of her hand.

"Sorry, I know this is going to come across as rude, but I thought folks with your level of education had more brains," he said. He took his little notebook from the inside pocket of his jacket. "You need to tell me everything that happened, starting from when you left the house."

She gave him the whole story, from Father Francis to the judiciales.

"What about this Father Francis?" he asked.

"He runs that nonprofit, Contra el Silencio . . ."

He didn't let her finish. "Oh, it's that Father Francis of the Sacred Heart Church. I see. Yes, we know all about his organization. Let me guess. It was his idea that you go around conducting your own investigation, am I right?"

"Actually, I was going to do that anyway. Father Francis suggested we go to some bars on La Mariscal, places where some of the victims were taken, ask if anybody there had seen Irene, hand out copies of our flyer."

"What flyer?"

"The flyers I made of Irene's picture with the information from the police bulletin. That's what we went over there to do, distribute flyers."

He stared at her, tilting his head to one side, then press his fingers over his eyes. She'd screwed up the investigation royally now. It was bad enough that she had showed pictures, but that she'd used the APB and left it all over town, practically announcing to every possible perpetrator that the police were on his tail—well, that just screwed everything up now, didn't it?

"I'm going to need a copy of that flyer."

"Here," she said, walking over to a backpack leaning against the recliner. Something else he'd missed in his survey of the room.

He took the flyer from her hand. "And the names of the places you went to?"

She dug the map of La Mariscal out of her backpack and handed it to him.

"How did you come by this?" he said when he had unfolded the map.

"Gee, McCuts, maybe I should do your job for you. Any other information I can give you that you don't have to look for yourself?"

"The longer it takes for me to do my job, the longer it takes to find your sister."

Good one. Now she stood corrected. He put his notebook away, zipped up the duffle bag, and got to his feet. She walked him to the door.

"By the way," he said, looking down at her, "is the situation with your sister's vehicle all squared away?"

"It's at a friend's house in Juárez. I'm picking it up tomorrow."

"Do you have an address that I can put into my report?"

"What do I look like, the phone book?"

"I can't close the report on the stolen vehicle until I get your friend's name and address." He reached in his jacket pocket for his notebook and flipped to the page he was looking for. "El Camino," he read "1978, mustard yellow exterior and interior." He looked up at her. "Nice ride," he said, "is that the original color?"

"You'd have to ask my dad that, and he's dead."

"It's a great color for an Elky. Is it in one piece?"

"Why do I feel like I'm at a car show talking to a low-rider instead of a detective?"

He stashed his notebook. "Just thought I could help in case there were any missing parts," he said.

"Stolen radio and battery," she said.

He could've told her about the web sites on the net that specialized in parts just for El Caminos, or given her the name of a body shop on Texas Street where they could install the radio and make it look like it had always been there. But he didn't.

"And your friend's name is?" He pulled the notebook out again.

Raquel Montenegro, he wrote down, *Instituto Frontelingua, Pronaf*. Somehow the name of the school rang a bell.

Outside on the front porch, he turned to face her. "I need to ask you to please cease and desist from doing any more investigation on this case, excuse me, on your sister's disappearance. Not only are you putting your life at risk, but you could have already jeopardized our leads. So I'm asking you to please sit tight and let us do our job." He handed her one of his cards.

She went inside and latched the screen door. "Does your job include looking for dead bodies in Juárez, detective?"

"Excuse me?"

"That's what the Contra el Silencio crew is doing tomorrow morning, walking the Anapra hills looking for bodies. And I'm going with them, whether you like it or not."

"You're going on a field sweep? What time?"

"Early. We're supposed to meet at the church at 5 A.M."

"Maybe I'll join you," he said. "Keep you from getting into any more trouble."

She slammed the front door.

God, he loved women with a temper.

He trudged over to his car and sat there mulling over the options. He needed to go and talk to the cousin who'd gotten arrested with her today. He needed to call this Montenegro woman and get her side of the story. He needed to talk to that priest, too. Tomorrow was his day off. What was to stop him from crossing over to Juárez to do some shopping, for example? There were things his Auntie Molly needed from the Juárez market. One thing he knew for sure, he wasn't allowed to cross the border in an official capacity. He debated whether to call his commander and request permission to tail the daughter tomorrow into Juárez, but he knew the commander did things by the book and would deny his request, especially now after what had happened to Ortiz and Borunda, who were both in comas after their beatings.

The daughter wasn't a suspect of any kind, so there was no reason for him to follow her. There was no way his commander would let him cross the border, especially packing a weapon. Still, he knew that if the daughter went over there tomorrow morning, she'd probably do the same thing she'd done earlier today: ask questions, pass out flyers, and endanger herself and the investigation.

He really didn't have a choice, did he? If he were worth anything as a man or a detective, he'd do the right thing and keep an eye on her. That's what his dad would do. Tonight he'd finish his interviews and take the evidence back to the office, write up his report, go home, get some sleep, and be back here before dawn tomorrow. For a second, he thought about leaving his gun at home, but what good was he to anyone without a weapon?

Maybe tomorrow afternoon, when he was sure the daughter was back safely from Juárez, he would go to Providence and sit with Marcia and tell her the story of his name again, to cheer her up, give her something to laugh at down there in that darkness she was in right now.

He put the car into gear and headed toward downtown to the Sacred Heart Church. He had decided to begin there because it was closer.

He was turning left on Paisano Street when his cell phone rang. "Hey, Cleetface," he answered without checking the caller i.d. It was just past six, same time each day his dad called him to ask about dinner plans. Cleetface was short for Anacleto. Cleeter, Cleto-Man, Anacleets—Pete had an arsenal of endearments for his father.

"Is this Detective McCuts? It's Ivon Villa."

Right away he felt himself flush. "Sorry, I thought it was my dad." He waited for her to say more. "Can I help you?" he said.

"I'm sorry if I was rude to you. This thing with my sister has me . . ."

"Don't worry about it," he interrupted. Traffic on Paisano was all backed up, so he turned south again, past the Coliseum, and headed for the border highway.

"Look, I need to ask you a question. I don't know if you've heard of this newsletter that apparently some of the victims received before they got kidnapped?"

His ears pricked up. "What victims? You mean the women in Juárez?"

With Marcia Ortiz, Pete had been working on a secret investigation of the Juárez murders, looking specifically into the rape cases. As a law enforcement officer he had access to some classified information that might shed some light on who was perpetrating the sex crimes.

"There was a girl in Juárez whose baby I was going to adopt . . ." She was quiet for a moment. "Cecilia, that was her name. Anyway, she was killed the night I arrived . . . raped and tortured, stabbed to death, baby carved out of her belly, really brutal shit . . . apparently she got a page of this newsletter on her machine a couple of days before she got killed."

"On her machine?"

"Yeah, you know, at the factory where she worked, at the *maquila*?"

"Right, I see. How do you know this?"

"Cecilia brought it home and showed it to her aunt. The aunt showed the newsletter to the police over there, but they didn't think it meant anything, so they didn't collect it as evidence. When we went to Cecilia's house a couple of days ago, when her body was found, the aunt gave the page to my cousin Ximena."

"So you've seen it?"

"Of course, I've seen it. It's called 'Richy's Diary.' It's in English, and we think it has something to do with Richard Ramírez, the Night Stalker."

He was driving past the Córdoba Bridge now and felt a shudder run through him at the mention of the Night Stalker's name. As a kid, reading about the Night Stalker's crimes in Los Angeles, Pete used to imagine that somehow he was related to Richard Ramírez because his dad had the same last name. Anacleto Ramírez. Pete had even written to Richard in San Quentin and asked him if maybe they might be cousins. Richard never wrote back, but all through junior high, Pete was a groupie of the Night Stalker and collected clippings about 'El Paso's very own Jack the Ripper.' He listened to AC/DC and Black Sabbath, and even belonged to the Richard Ramírez Fan Club, until his dad found out and whipped him. His fascination with the Night Stalker is what had made Pete want to go into law enforcement in the first place.

"What's the connection?"

"For starters, he's from El Paso. You knew that, right? Second, there's a quote on the newsletter that sounds like something Ramírez said at his trial. Third, I've been doing some research, and the way some of the bodies have been butchered, the way Cecilia was butchered, sounds a lot like the way the Night Stalker killed his victims."

"What did the quote say?"

"He used a big word, and it's actually like one of the only words you can make out because the newsletter is mimeographed and the lettering is all washed out. *Trematode*, it said."

"'I don't need to look beyond this room to see all the trematodes of the Earth.' Is that the quote?"

Silence. Then, finally, "Were you at his trial, too?"

"Not hardly. I was a seventh grader at the time."

"You know what that Bob Russell said in the newspaper the other day, that some of the evidence in the crimes pointed to a serial killer, maybe someone from El Paso crossing over to assault women because there isn't a death penalty in Mexico. What if it's somebody with a Night Stalker fetish? What if he's reenacting the Night Stalker's crimes in Juárez and reporting them in the newsletter?"

A map flashed in Pete's mind. The map of all the registered sex offenders in El Paso, pinned to the bulletin board in his office. What the citizens of El Paso did not know was that El Paso was the largest dumping ground of sex offenders in the country. More and more of them were being given one-way tickets to El Paso when they got out on parole. That was the main lead that he and Marcia were following in their own private investigation.

"Reporting them to who?" he said.

"I don't know. Maybe that's what turns him on. Writing about the crimes . . . Maybe he relives the killings that way, or maybe he mails the newsletter to Richard Ramírez. He's still alive, you know, still in San Quentin, hasn't been fried yet. Apparently he's getting married."

"Do you have the newsletter?"

"Father Francis kept it."

"So you're alleging your sister may have been kidnapped by this copycat killer? That he was leaving a clue to his identity with that newsletter?"

"It's possible."

Now *that's* what he called a lead. He needed to get his hands on it. Forget interviewing Ivon's cousin, he thought as he pulled up in front of the red-brick, steepled structure that was the Sacred Heart Church, sitting incongruously amid the trash and tenements of South El Paso.

"You're sure it's in the priest's possession?"

"Positive. Unless he threw it out, and he better not have."

"Thanks for the tip," said Pete, signing off.

The phone rang again and this time it *was* his dad. No dinner, tonight, Cleetito, he'd said, I've got some leads on my new case. I'm working late.

Pete had his plan all laid out. He was going to interrogate the priest, confiscate the newsletter as possible evidence, return to the office to study the sex offender map more closely, and see if he could find any more information on what was bringing all those hundreds of child molesters, rapists, wife beaters, and exhibitionists to the Sun City.

Maybe he should take the map home. He sure as hell didn't want any of the other detectives to get the same idea and beat him to the lead. If somebody *were* copycatting the Night Stalker, he might be living in or near Richard Ramírez's old neighborhood, which was, he realized, not too far from the church.

33

ON A CLEAR DAY IN WEST EL PASO, you can see the forty-foot statue of Christ the Redeemer at the top of Mount Cristo Rey. Against the western skyline, the huge white-robed limestone Christ stretches its crucified arms out like a holy bridge between the First World and the Third, like a mirage of faith across the desert. Any day of the week, but especially on Sundays and holidays, you can always spot a few hard-core believers trekking up the craggy dirt trails. In hundred-degree heat or sixty-mile-an-hour winds, people come to pray, do penance, honor a promise, or offer flowers to the miraculous white man, Christ the King.

Eight years ago, Ivon's dad had gone on a Holy Week pilgrimage there and lost his life. She still wasn't sure it had been an accident. Her dad had always demonstrated an incredible talent for the dramatic. Today, almost in the shadow of Cristo Rey, across the river from ASARCO, they were looking for her little sister in Puerto de Anapra.

She lowered her binoculars and wiped her eyes. She felt exhausted after everything that had happened yesterday: all that walking, the *judiciales*, the detective with the evidence, another fight with Ma. She'd barely slept, images of Irene's naked body washing up on the riverbank penetrating her dreams, waking her up in a cold sweat.

"Chelo was our niece, my sister's daughter from Camargo," an older man was saying into the Channel 33 camera. "The skin on her face, everything, was completely melted away, even the ears. She was lying in a pool of her own grease and blood."

"It wasn't a robbery," said the woman standing next to him.

236

Under the black scarf, her face looked pale and drawn. "The engagement ring her boyfriend had given her was still on her finger. A little heart of pearls," she continued. "They confirmed her identity by her dental plates, but we already knew it was her because of that ring."

The man started to cry on camera and Rubí told Walter to cut.

In her pressed beige blouse and khaki pants stuffed inside knee-length sienna leather boots, red hair blazing under her Panama hat, Rubí looked like she was dressed for a foxhunt rather than a *rastreo*. She had wasted no time in setting up her equipment while the Contra el Silencio group got organized.

Other than the priest and Ximena, Ivon, Rubí Reyna and her husband, only seven people had showed up for today's walk. Father Francis had introduced each of them to Ivon before leaving the church that morning. Mr. and Mrs. Serrano, the man and woman Rubí had just interviewed, and whose eighteen year old niece had been one of the first bodies found at a *rastreo*, had joined all the *rastreos*, out of solidarity. Señora García and her two teenage daughters were looking for Marilú, the oldest, who had gone to a disco on Juárez Avenue three months ago and never returned. A young man in fatigues named Max was trying to find his girlfriend, Terri, who'd been kidnapped from the Futurama mall two weeks ago. And there was Gema, a Middle-Eastern woman who spoke Spanish with a thick accent, whose daughter, Stephanie, had disappeared from a shoe store in downtown Juárez.

Once they reached the search site, they were joined by a young woman in blue jeans and an embroidered Mexican blouse who was sticking close to Rubí. Ivon didn't recognize her at first and then realized she was one of the interns who had been assisting the medical examiner at the autopsy.

"I didn't know she was a member of Contra el Silencio," Ivon said to Ximena.

"She's not. She's here on official business. Norma Flores sent her."

Ximena handed out bright orange safety vests and water bottles.

"In the name of the Father, the Son, and the Holy Spirit,"

Father Francis intoned. "We ask you to guide us and protect us today, oh Sacred Heart of Jesus, and if it is your will for us to find one of our missing girls—Stephanie or Theresa, Marilú, or Irene— we ask that you give us the strength and the courage to do your work."

Ivon choked up when she heard her sister's name. The desert wind was starting to kick up, and even at this hour of the morning, with the sun barely rising over the trash-strewn dunes of Lomas de Poleo, Ivon could feel the heat of the sand seeping through the cushioned soles of her Nikes.

"*¡Fúchila!*" said Rubí, fanning her hat over her perfectly made-up face.

Max had been poking his walking stick into a mound of garbage during Father Francis' prayer and had turned up the carcass of a skunk. The stench of it made Ivon's eyes water. One of Señora García's girls vomited on the spot.

"Walter, be sure to get a shot of that skunk," Rubí ordered. "I think we'll start with that." She turned around and flagged down the Middle Eastern lady. "So, the shoe store . . . was it *Las Tres B* near the cathedral? A girl who was a cashier there disappeared last year, too."

Two green buses trundled past on the rocky washboard road below, one leaving, one entering Puerto de Anapra in the constant shuffle of personnel. Ximena's van and the other cars of the Contra el Silencio group were parked in front of a junkyard that sported a banner reading *Something Grand Will Happen to You Today.*

"Now let's all synchronize our watches," Father Francis said. "It is exactly ten minutes to six. We'll meet back here at 11:30, sharp, before it gets too hot. I don't want anybody getting sunstroke. Okay, let's divide ourselves into two teams. Mr. and Mrs. Serrano, Mrs. García, you and your daughters—all of you with me, please. Ivon, Max, and Gema, you go with Shimeyna and the coroner's assistant, Miss Godoy."

For an instant, Ivon remembered Cecilia's body. The wounds, the gallstones, the gaping cavity of her entrails where her baby had nested. And then it was Irene on the autopsy table, wearing filthy wet white jeans. Ximena stood close to her.

"Earth to Ivon," said Ximena, pinching the back of her arm.

"Ouch. Thanks," Ivon whispered, rubbing her arm. She had not told Ximena about the evidence or the detective's visit.

"I don't want you to say anything to that bunch of *metiches*," her mom had said last night. "They're just being nosey. This thing with your sister, it's nothing but a big *telenovela* to everyone."

"Ma, it's not a *telenovela*. This is real and it's happening to all of us, all of the family, not just to you and me. They're trying to be supportive, you know."

"*Qué* supportive *ni qué nada*. They're just coming over to eat my food. Poor Lulu, that's all she does all day, back and forth to the grocery store, cook and clean, cook and clean. I wish they'd stop being so supportive and just leave me alone."

In many ways, Ivon was more like her mom than either one cared to admit.

"Everyone, please stay with your team," Father Francis was saying. "This is very important. You have no idea how easy it is to get lost in Lomas de Poleo, so don't wander off by yourself. If anybody finds anything, or if anybody gets sick and wants to go back early, be sure to report it on your walkie-talkie, and I'll come and find you."

"*Padre, una pregunta por favor*," Rubí stepped up with her microphone in hand. Walter followed with his camera. "Most of our viewers have never attended a *rastreo*, and it would be very informative for them to hear you describe the terrain that we're walking here today. If you please, Father."

Father Francis cleared his throat. "In English?"

"That's fine, we'll do a voice-over translation when we air it," said Rubí. Walter filmed Father Francis with an ancient 8-millimeter monstrosity hoisted on his shoulder. A tag reading *Propieded de Canal 33* dangled from the cord.

Father Francis fidgeted with his water bottle, capping it and uncapping it as he spoke. "In Lomas de Poleo there are three different terrains. First we have what we see at our feet, the sandy terrain. The sand is very loose and makes it difficult to walk, especially when it gets windy and the sand blows. Today, thank God, the wind is calm. Let's pray it stays that way.

"As we get closer to the sierra, we'll come to the next terrain, which is rock and limestone. That's scorpion country, and by the time we reach it, the ground will be very hot, your feet will feel like they're on fire, and it's also very hard on your eyes because of the glare.

"The final terrain at the foothills is the scrub brush and the thorn bushes. That's where the snakes hide, and sometimes, people get their clothes caught on the thorns if they're not careful. Up in the foothills, there's very few houses up there, and you can't see any landmarks like Cristo Rey or ASARCO. The whole panorama can change in a matter of minutes, so it's easy to get lost. And you don't want to be lost in this desert."

A few feet away from where they stood, Walter had set up a Handycam on a tripod. Ivon watched him fish a remote out of his pocket, which he used to control the camera. The lens turned in the direction of the nearest shack and zoomed out as far as it would go. Some local residents had gathered in the dirt street to watch the Contra el Silencio crew, and Walter's camera was recording them without them knowing it.

"Everyone has a good stick, right?" Father Francis said to the group. "I don't want anybody touching anything with their hands. There could be radioactive waste around here. Remember, White Sands is testing missiles again. We don't want anybody getting hurt. So be careful. If anybody spots anything that looks even remotely like human remains, even if it's just clothing, do not go near it. Stop walking. Stay where you are and call it in."

Walter's Handycam was panning slowly over the crate-and-cardboard shacks clustered on Pollen Hills. A colony of makeshift homes in the middle of a landfill. Piles of old televisions with shattered screens. A throng of bloated-bellied, wild-haired children playing in the trash.

The wind whipped up suddenly and the tripod tilted. Ivon rushed over to steady it before it fell.

"Thanks," said Walter, running up behind her. "Close call."

The little LCD monitor on the camera was open, shaded by a rubber guard, the lens trained on the junkyard where they had left their cars under the care of a security guard. Nothing but scrap metal and hollowed-out rusted car shells without tires. She noticed another car parked behind Ximena's van, a silver Honda that she had not seen earlier.

"Okay, everyone, let's get into our groups, please. The day's not getting any cooler," called Father Francis. Rubí and her husband followed the coroner's assistant, and Ivon followed Ximena.

"We're going due north," Ximena said to her team, "toward Cristo Rey. If you get disoriented, just look for the cross on the hill. And watch out for snakes." She opened her umbrella and led the way. Laura Godoy walked beside her.

"Catch up to them, Walter," Rubí said to her husband. "Eavesdrop on their conversation. We might be able to use some of it. Hurry up."

"You saved my neck yesterday," Ivon said to Rubí.

"Did I? What did I do?"

"Your card," said Ivon, and told her what had happened to her and William with the *judiciales.* "If I hadn't kept your card, who knows where we'd be."

"I know where you'd be," said Rubí, "probably right here with a bullet in your head. *Judiciales* are ruthless. They're not afraid of anything, except media exposure, which is why they love me so much, of course."

"Lucky me."

"I was so sorry to hear about your little sister. No girl is safe in this city anymore. It used to be just the girls from the south who were in danger, but now, they'll take anybody. My father was so upset when he heard that my daughter Amber had been at the fair with Myrna and your sister the night your sister disappeared. He wants me to hire a bodyguard to go with Amber when she goes to Cancún next week. Between the drug traffickers and the serial killers, our young women are constant targets in this city."

"I shouldn't have let Irene go to the fair by herself," said Ivon, surprised she was expressing her feelings aloud to a complete stranger. She felt her throat close.

"You'll find her," said Rubí, touching her shoulder. "Do you have any leads?"

Ivon shook her head. "We talked to a bartender at a place on

La Mariscal and she told us about these men with video cameras who came into the bar one night and took one of the girls whose body was found ten days later. Video cameras in a brothel, sounds like pornography to me."

"Well, that's one theory," said Rubí. "We have lots of theories. It's pornography, it's the black market for human organs, it's a serial killer crossing over from El Paso, it's the police, it's a Satanic cult. I don't think it matters anymore what the cause is, people just want the crimes to stop."

"I read about the Egyptian calling in to your show."

"Did you? It scared me to death. The ratings went sky-high."

"Do you think the Egyptian is calling the shots from jail?"

"That's what they want us to believe. I'm sure he has something to do with some of the crimes; he's no innocent, either. But he's no intellectual author, as they're calling him. The masterminds are the ones who are giving him all his privileges."

"Like the warden?"

"He's just a cardboard figure. In Juárez, only two institutions have power: the government and the *maquiladoras*. Even the police are nothing but pawns."

The government and the *maquiladoras*. Were they two separate suits, one of spades, one of diamonds, say? Or were they just two different face cards in the same suit? If they were different suits, they'd stack up separately, but these two had something in common. What was it? The U.S.-educated rich men who ran both of them?

The desert wind was starting to kick up, and Ivon felt a shudder go through her. *Lent in El Paso, Texas, blows forty days of dust devils*, she had read in a poem once, *forty faithful days without contrition*. In Puerto de Anapra it didn't have to be Lent to blow dust devils or to pull the sinners and the penitents out of their houses to search for the dead.

Ivon took her binoculars out of her jacket pocket and located Father Francis' team. The Serranos were slowly climbing the hill just east of the *Water for Puerto de Anapra* billboard. Father Francis and the rest were further up ahead, near a thicket of scrub brush, surrounded by buzzards. Ivon could tell from everyone's body language that something had turned up.

"Ximena!" she called out, "I think they found something."

Her cousin whirled to face her. "Where?" She yanked the binoculars from Ivon's hand and looked west.

"Frank! Come in, Frank," she spoke into the walkie-talkie.

A loud shriek came across followed by static.

"Shit!" said Ximena.

"What was that?" said Rubí.

"They found something," said Ximena.

So is he, then, calling the shots? (almost literally)

34

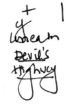

TUCKED INTO THE MESQUITE BUSHES, in a nest of garbage and human hair, the body was lying facedown, legs spread-eagled, wrists handcuffed over her head, a bloodstained blue smock thrown over her head and shoulders. The exposed part of the back, like the legs and the buttocks, had been picked over by scavengers, what was left of the cartilage charred black by the sun. A bottle of J&B had been inserted in her anus. The ground stank of urine and rotted flesh.

"What happened, Frank?" said Ximena, heaving from the sprint across the sand.

"I tripped over the shoes," said Father Francis, pointing to a pair of high-heeled black sandals that lay tossed in the sand at the perimeter of the bushes. "I didn't see them."

"*Dios nos ampare*," said Señora García, clutching her rosary. Her two girls cowered behind her, covering their mouths and noses.

"For God's sake, Walter," Rubí Reyna called out, "get your camera over here!"

Walter caught up to them, lugging the 8-millimeter and the Handycam.

Mrs. Serrano looked like she was hyperventilating.

Ximena reached into her pocket and pulled out a small tin of Vick's Vapor Rub. "Here, Mrs. Serrano," she said. "Put some of this mentholatum in each nostril. Who else wants some?"

"*¿Qué está pasando, pues? ¡Qué horror!*" cried Mrs. Serrano.

"Ivon? Could this be your sister?" said Father Francis.

"I don't think so," said Ivon, acid rising in the back of her throat. "I don't think Irene has streaks in her hair."

244

"Isn't that a *maquiladora* smock covering her?" asked Mr. Serrano. "Did your sister work at a factory?"

Ivon shook her head. She hated it that they were talking about her sister in the past tense.

"Anything special we should be looking for, Ivon?" Father Francis insisted. "A mole, a birthmark?"

"Is she wearing a graduation ring with a turquoise stone?"

Father Francis examined the hands. "Nothing there. And if she was, it was probably stolen. It's not the kind of thing they'd leave on the body."

"They left our niece's pearl ring on the body," said Mrs. Serrano quietly.

"What about her tongue," Ivon said, remembering her sister's piercing. "Irene pierced her tongue. Is there a post in it? Can we see her tongue?"

"A what?"

"It's like an earring in the tongue, Frank," said Ximena.

Father Francis pulled three pairs of surgical gloves from his knapsack and handed a pair to Max and another to Mr. Serrano. "Help me get her out into the open. The rest of you, push these branches back with your sticks."

"Please don't move her," said Laura Godoy.

Walter was biting his fingernails and Rubí nudged him with her elbow. "What are you waiting for, Walter?"

He hoisted the 8-millimeter on his shoulder and started filming.

"The body should be left exactly as we found her, by order of the medical examiner."

Father Francis ignored the intern's comment. "If you don't want to see this, get out of the way," he said. "Ready, guys? Be careful, she might come apart."

"Take the bottle out, for god's sake, Frank," said Ximena.

"No, nothing should be removed," said Laura Godoy. "You may be destroying valuable evidence just by standing in the crime scene."

"You think the *judiciales* collect evidence from the crime scene?" Ximena said.

"Don't touch the hands or the feet," Father Francis instructed the men. "Mr. Serrano, you help me at the shoulders. Max, take the legs. Lift her from the knees."

"*Que no vaya a ser mi hija, por Dios,*" cried Señora García.

The teenagers started to sob. Gema covered her face with both hands. Ivon daubed the mentholatum under her nose, and Ximena pinched her nostrils tight. Please don't let it be Irene, Ivon prayed, echoing Señora García's plea.

Slowly the men lifted the body over the mesquite brush and laid her down on the sand faceup. The bottle dropped out. The scalp loosened from the head. The stench of rotted flesh rose out of the sand like a vapor. Both teenagers vomited.

"Dear God," said Rubí, "it looks like she's still screaming."

Ivon forced herself to stare at the body. The eyes were gone. The face was completely bloated and purple, facial features erased, blistered skin crusted with sand and blood and maggots. Front teeth edged in gold. *It wasn't Irene.* Fluid drained from the ears. A thick black rope burn ran across the neck and teeth marks covered the chest. The bra was pushed up over the breasts. Worms oozed over the torn nipple of the left breast. On the right breast a five-pointed star had been carved into the flesh with a serrated blade.

"Walter," said Rubí behind her handkerchief, "I need close-ups."

"Does anybody recognize her?" Father Francis called out.

"It isn't my sister," said Ivon, feeling like she had to empty her bladder suddenly.

"Shouldn't we look at the tongue to make sure?" said Ximena.

Laura Godoy took a tongue depressor out of her handbag and squatted down by the body, inserting the stick into the gaping hole of the mouth.

"The tongue was either bitten off or eaten away," she announced.

"Max, Gema, Señora García—look closely," said Father Francis.

"Don't push our faces in it, Frank," said Ximena.

"I know this is very difficult for everyone," said Father Francis, "but I need you to look at the body and see if you recognize anything at all."

All but Mrs. Serrano filed by the body, covering their mouths and noses. Nothing. This was not a body any of them recognized. The García girls could not stop crying. *What happened to 'girls'?*

"Naked female body in advanced stage of decomposition found in *colonia* Puerto de Anapra, Sunday, the fourteenth of June, 1998." Still squatting beside the body, Laura Godoy dictated into a handheld cassette recorder. Ivon noticed that Laura's hands trembled. "Body was found lying facedown, handcuffed, with legs extended, head covered, and anally penetrated with a bottle. Against the medical examiner's orders, the members of the organization moved the body out of the crime scene and turned it face-up. Fixed lividity visible on the ventral side shows victim was moved after death. Straight-line ligature bruising on the neck and cyanosis in the face indicate strangulation as probable cause of death. Right breast marked with a satanic symbol probably after death and left nipple severed. Visible bite marks on the thorax. Victim may have bitten off own tongue at time of strangulation. Bruises on the forearms indicate possible struggle with attacker. Victim was approximately fifteen to twenty-five years of age."

The intern pulled a digital thermometer out of her bag and placed it inside the mouth. When it beeped, she looked at her watch and dictated the temperature into her recorder. "Legal time of death is 7:45 A.M. Estimated time of death occurred approximately three to four days ago. Killer was probably a relative or a boyfriend."

"What makes you come to that conclusion, Dr. Godoy?" asked Rubí.

Laura looked at Walter's camera, then back at Rubí. "Usually, when the victim's head is covered in a violent crime like this, it means the perpetrator was someone close to her. Someone who felt guilty about what he had done, so he covered her up."

"Are those animal bites?" asked Ivon.

"Human bites," said Laura. "A number of the bodies in the morgue have had bite marks just like these. Some also had their right breasts cut off and the left nipples bitten off. Only a few have had this satanic marking on the right breast."

"It's called a pentagram, I think," offered Rubí.

"Yes. We've seen it in a few cases, and the marking is always on the right breast."

Ivon thought of Brigit and her Wiccan religion. Brigit had taught her there was a difference between Wicca and Satanism, between positive and negative magic. She had learned over the years of watching Brigit celebrate this solstice and that sabbat, that the pentagram did not symbolize evil, unless it was used, as in this case, in a destructive context.

"But why did they cut off her hair?" one of the teenagers was asking.

Laura shrugged. "The same reason they cut off the breast or immolate the face, as we've seen in some cases, or insert sticks and bottles and other foreign objects into the bodies. Because they can. *Ellos tienen el poder.* And, because they hate women. They want everyone to know they can do whatever they want with a woman's body. They're in control."

"Savages," said Father Francis, raising his right arm to bless the body.

"I have to call the amphitheater," said Laura.

"Here, use this," Ximena handed her a walkie-talkie. "Banda Civil radio will call the police and the morgue."

A few of the residents who had been watching walked over to look at the body. Rubí asked each of them for permission for Walter to include them in the documentary. They heard the same old story. Nobody knew or saw or heard anything. Nobody recognized the body. Two boys made gang signs into the camera. Max kept a pack of skinny dogs at bay with rocks.

"This is Rubí Reyna, your cohost on *Mujeres sin Fronteras,*" Rubí Reyna spoke into the camera, "reporting live from a *rastreo* in Puerto de Anapra. Another victim has been found this morning in Lomas de Poleo. I'm standing here with Doctora Laura Godoy, a medical intern with the medical examiner's office, and the shocked members of the Contra el Silencio group, who have just discovered the mutilated remains of another young woman's body in the desert. This makes it 138 women who have been butchered in this city of death. Doctora Godoy, thank you for speaking to us at this brutal moment. Can you tell us what happened to this poor girl, in your professional opinion?"

Ivon walked away, rubbing the sand out of her eyes. She couldn't look at the body anymore. It wasn't Irene. For as much as she hated to admit it, deep down inside, that's all she cared about right now. It wasn't her sister.

From a clump of nopal cactus five feet away, something white caught her eye. Ivon walked over to it, pulled it out with her stick, and picked it up. An employee identification tag. The name of the smiling girl in the picture was Mireya Beltrán, an operator at the Phillips plant. She was wearing the same color smock as the one that had covered the dead girl's head. Same gold-edged teeth.

"Did you find something, Ivon?" Father Francis and Ximena had followed her.

Ivon showed them the plastic tag. "I think it's her i.d."

"You're not supposed to be touching anything," said the priest.

Ximena looked at the picture. "It's her all right. Look at the teeth."

"God have mercy." Father Francis made the sign of the cross over himself. He took a plastic flask out of his knapsack and walked over to the body, waiting for Rubi to finish interviewing Laura Godoy before he said anything. "We found her identification," he announced to the group. "We know her name. Everybody, please gather around."

He sprinkled the body with water from the flask. "In the name of the Father, the Son, and the Holy Spirit. We beseech you, oh Lord, to bless the ravaged remains of your daughter, Mireya Beltrán, may she rest in the garden of your love now and forever."

Ximena lowered her voice. "At least it wasn't your sister."

"She's someone else's sister, Ximena, someone else's daughter." In the pit of her stomach, Ivon felt the tremor of a deep dread. What would she do, she wondered, if this really were Irene? What would it do to Ma?

Max had pulled a small red flashlight out of his pocket and was shining it on the scalp. "What about that thing in her hair?" he said.

With a gloved finger, the priest rubbed dark blood off something clipped just above the girl's left ear. A green glittery butterfly barrette. "Does this look familiar to anybody?" When he tapped it, a spider crawled out of the dark hair.

Gema cried out. Mrs. Serrano wept in her husband's arms.

"I see something inside the throat," said Max, aiming the flashlight beam into the mouth.

"Please don't do that," protested Laura Godoy. "Don't you think she's been violated enough?"

"I swear to God," said Max, disregarding the intern's comment completely, "there's something shiny in there. Looks like a . . . wait a minute . . ." He hunkered down and nearly poked the flashlight inside the mouth, ". . . Look at that! She's got a penny in her throat."

"Ximena!" Ivon said, smacking her cousin's arm.

"What?"

"Didn't you hear what he just said?" said Ivon. "I told you I saw pennies at Cecilia's autopsy, but you thought I was being delirious."

"She has a penny where?" Rubí scurried over to the body, pressing her kerchief against her nose.

"Right there, see?" said Max. "It's like Abe Lincoln's been shoved down her throat."

Lodged in the back of the throat, a bright copper penny gleamed up at them.

"There's some more around the body," said Ivon, noticing several more pennies in the sand. "Probably fell out of the mouth when they turned her over."

"Don't say anything about this, please," Laura Godoy said, glancing over her shoulder.

"What does it mean?" said Rubí.

"This information cannot be made public." Laura Godoy walked away, but Ivon, Ximena, and Rubí followed her.

"Tell us about those pennies, Laura," said Ivon.

"I could lose my residency," whispered the intern. "Please don't insist."

"I guess I'll have to bring the camera over here," said Rubí.

Laura scratched the back of her head quickly, trying to make up her mind. "You're not leaving me any choice, then, but keep in mind that this could be very dangerous. Yes, I'll lose my residency, but other people, like la doctora Flores, are at even more risk."

"I won't make it public," said Rubí. "Norma's a friend of mine. I wouldn't do anything to put her in danger."

Laura Godoy glanced over her shoulder again. "It's just that some of the bodies," she said, her voice barely above a whisper, "had American pennies inside them when we did the autopsies."

"Inside where?" said Ximena.

"In the vagina, in the rectum, under the tongue. Cecilia had ten of them in her stomach . . ."

Ximena gawked at her. "No way."

". . . The coins had already started to corrode in the stomach lining from the acids and she had subjacent bleeding ulcers."

"They made her swallow pennies?" said Rubí.

"Unless they stuck them in her after they disemboweled her, but I don't think so."

"Somebody's killing these girls with pennies?" Ivon said.

"That's not what's killing them, but it is making them very sick. The ones that had the most prolonged retention in the bowel, longer than four days, had severe zinc poisoning. The ones that had the coins in the rectum and the vagina had to have been dead before the pennies were inserted, otherwise they would have been expelled with the body flush at the time of death."

"What does Norma say about the pennies?" Rubí continued.

"*La doctora* Flores reported it, of course, but she was told to keep that information classified, it cannot be made public, so please don't go saying anything. We're not supposed to say anything. If you mention it on television, they might think the coroner's office told you."

"People have a right to know," said Ivon. "This could be a lead. If anything, it proves that the girls are being kept alive for something, that they're not killed right away."

"I really can't talk about it. The governor has prohibited the release of that information."

A sudden idea occurred to Ivon. "Did the bodies that had the pennies inside, were they *maquiladora* workers, by the way?"

Laura Godoy shook her head and walked away without answering. Ximena and Ivon stared at each other and shrugged.

"Not all the girls who have died were *maquiladora* workers,"

Rubí said to Ivon, "but are you suggesting the pennies somehow implicate the *maquilas?*"

"Max said it best." Ivon repeated what Max had said earlier. "'It's like Abe Lincoln's been shoved down her throat.'"

"Just like the *maquilas* themselves have been shoved down Mexico's throat . . ." added Ximena.

". . . because of NAFTA," Ivon finished the sentence.

"Brilliant," said Rubí, green eyes glittering. "I'll have to follow up on that, but right now, I have to get back to my interview. Walter needs me over there. *Con permiso.*" She hurried back where Walter was filming Father Francis.

Ximena lit up a cigarette. "Jesus! Who could be that sick?"

Ivon squeezed her eyes shut and tried to concentrate. What was it about those pennies? She had seen pennies at the autopsy and somewhere else. She tried word associations: pennies/penis; money/rape. See a penny, pick it up, all day long it brings good luck. What was it? She almost had it.

"Wait till I tell Frank." Ximena walked over to the interviewing area.

"Just make sure he doesn't leak it out to anybody," Ivon warned.

"What I'm saying, Mrs. Reyna," Father Francis said as he stared right into Walter's camera, "is that Juárez is not ready for the liberated woman, at least not in the lower classes. Their traditions are being disrupted in complete disproportion to changes in their economic status. They are expected to alter their value system, to operate within the cultural and political economy of the First World, at the same time that they do not move up on the social ladder. The Mexican gender system cannot accommodate the First World division of labor or the First World freedoms given to women."

"Are you justifying the murders, then, Father?" asked Rubí.

"Of course not. But let's just say I understand the social context for the crimes, which is, ultimately, a Catholic context, you see? The women are being sacrificed to redeem the men for their inability to provide for their families, their social emasculation, if you will, at the hands of the American corporations."

"Are you suggesting, then, Father, that these murders are a

consequence of the North American Free Trade Agreement?"

Father Francis squinted and rubbed his chin. "It's very possible," he said. "People don't migrate north to cross the border, anymore. The jobs are here, now, in Juárez, at one of these three hundred *maquiladoras* they've built all over the city. Young women are lured here in droves, and yet the city can't accommodate them all. There's no subsidized housing for them, so they have to live in these godforsaken shantytowns hours away from their jobs, and their lives are in constant danger. That poor child we found this morning, she's a victim of that infrastructure, do you see? She probably came here hoping to make a good life for herself, hoping to make money to send back home to whatever village she came from, and now she's here, with the buzzards. The twin plant industry has got to take responsibility for the havoc they're wreaking on this border. It's as simple and as complicated as that."

"Thank you so much, Father Francis of the Sacred Heart Church in El Paso, leader of the Contra el Silencio nonprofit organization, for your candid views of what can only be called an epidemic of violence and misogyny in Ciudad Juárez. Cut!"

Walter rested the heavy camera on the tops of his sneakers.

"As soon as the police get here, I want that camera rolling again," Rubí said to him.

"We don't have to stay here in the sun," Father Francis called out to the group. "It's going to take a while for the authorities to get here. Let's go get some lemonade."

Ximena led the way down to the cars.

"We brought oranges, too," said Rubí. "Walter, go and pass out the oranges."

"Now," said Rubí, removing her sunglasses to look Ivon in the eye. She was taller by a couple of inches, and Ivon had to look up to meet her gaze. Bronze eye shadow matched the color of her hair and the outline of her lips. "Let me tell you my theory, and then I want to hear yours. I'm sure you have one."

"I don't have any theories," said Ivon. "I just learned about the crimes a few days ago."

"The whole thing is about economics to me," said Rubí. "I don't buy that FBI man's theory about a serial killer crossing over from El Paso. Juárez has plenty of sexual predators and maniacs of its own, beginning with the police. We don't need help from our good neighbors in the north."

"What I can't understand," said Ivon, "is why they don't just put a bullet in their heads and get it over with, without all the torture and mutilation? I mean, why go to all this trouble unless they're hell-bent on making a point or sending a message."

"And what do you think could be the message? Most of these young women are migrants. They're just lambs among wolves. They're the easiest workers to exploit. They don't unionize, they don't complain, they'll accept whatever wage they get. They have no power, whatsoever."

The phrase *a penny saved, a penny earned* came to Ivon's mind.

"Except one," said Ivon, snapping her fingers. "They can have babies. That's a power that needs to be controlled from the minute they set foot in the *maquiladora* system. Isn't pregnancy reason enough to get fired or not hired at all? Isn't that why the women's periods are monitored so closely at the *maquilas*, because the companies don't want to be paying maternity leave and cutting into their profits? How many potentially pregnant bodies are employed at those *maquilas*? It's probably more cost effective to kill them off."

Rubí's eyes shifted back and forth as she listened to Ivon's argument. "But not all of the victims were pregnant," she interjected.

"That's not the point: they can *get* pregnant, and that's the threat they pose when they come this close to the border. Call it a side effect of NAFTA that has to be curtailed by whatever means possible."

"Fascinating," said Rubí. "*¿No qué no?* I thought you said you didn't have any theories. That gives me an idea for a whole new show. What can I do to persuade you to join me in the studio so we can continue this conversation?"

Ivon shook her head. "I don't think so. I wouldn't want to be putting any theories out there without more research."

"*¡Ay!* You academics are all alike. You've convinced me, anyway. *Bueno,* if you don't mind, I'll explore this line of investigation on my own."

"Be my guest."

"*Oye*, aren't you dehydrating? Let's go get some lemonade. I need to get out of this sun."

Ivon shook her head. She couldn't pull herself away from the body.

"By the way I asked Walter to make a videotape of Friday's show for you," said Rubí.

"Great, thanks. Can you give it to Ximena?"

"No problem."

"Appreciate it," said Ivon, but she was staring at Mireya's mutilated breasts, the *maquila* smock and identification tag next to the body. The irony of it: an assembly worker disassembled in the desert. Dearest mother of god, she thought, maybe that's what they were doing to Irene. It didn't make sense. Her sister was not an assembly worker in a *maquiladora*. But then maybe the kidnappers didn't know that. All they saw was another thin, dark skinned, dark-haired young Mexican woman, and didn't realize she was a Mexican with the privilege of U.S. citizenship. For all the perps cared, she was just another expendable penny.

Holding her breath against the sour stench, she waved the flies away and hunkered down near the body. Using a twig and the cellophane sleeve off her pack of cigarettes, she picked two of the pennies out of the sand. She wrapped them up in the cellophane and slipped them into the side pocket of her backpack. *A penny saved, a penny earned.* Who was making money off the deaths of these girls?

She looked at Mireya's face, but the movement of the maggots turned her stomach and she lost the coffee and *pan dulce* she'd had for breakfast. The water in her water bottle had gotten hot, but at least she was able to rinse out her mouth.

Down by the cars, Father Francis was collecting the safety vests and walkie-talkies while Ximena dragged a bright red cooler from the back of her van and started passing out white cups to everyone. Ivon's mouth watered. Cool lemonade sounded like heaven, right now. But what right did she, or any of them, have to be in heaven when girls like Mireya were so far from the Truth, and so close to Jesus?

Ivon focused the binoculars on the gaunt bearded face of Cristo Rey, the impassive limestone eyes that saw everything and did nothing, and shook her head.

When the police and the medical examiner's van showed up, two and a half hours after the body had been reported, Ivon watched them throw the remains into a body bag, ask a few questions of Laura Godoy, and take some quick pictures of the site. They didn't even bother walking the perimeter. They were in a hurry, they said. They had another body to collect, a fresh kill, they called it, of a young transvestite man found earlier that morning in the "labyrinth of silence," an expanse of desert off the highway to Casas Grandes. The transvestite's mouth had been stapled shut.

Immediately, Ivon thought of Gypsy, one of the *travestis* that she and William had been speaking to yesterday in La Mariscal, the Cuban one who had almost said something about the guy in the cowboy hat in Irene's picture. Ivon remembered that the *judiciales* had taken the stapler from her backpack.

"Another sex crime in Ciudad Juárez," Rubí spoke into the camera. "Another voice without an echo. Two in one morning, bringing the death toll to 139. Who is killing all of these *mujeres y mujercitas* on this border, and why are they being killed? Join us tomorrow when we explore the answers to those questions with our special guests on *Mujeres sin Fronteras*. And in two weeks, another show you will not want to miss, as we take a closer look at the role of pregnancy in the *maquiladora* industry. *Mujeres*, be careful. The devil is loose."

Ivon felt the desert collecting in her throat.

35

"THAT'S IT, THAT'S THE CANTINA where William and I went yesterday after the *judiciales* arrested us," Ivon said from the backseat, pointing to the parachute-covered Cantina Paracaídas on the road from Puerto de Anapra. "I don't know about you guys, but I could use a beer after what we just saw."

Ximena drove past the bar without answering. Ivon couldn't see her cousin's eyes behind her sunglasses, but the furrows in her brow and her abrupt silence were pretty good signs that Ximena was in a bad mood all of a sudden.

"Hey," she said, poking Ximena on the shoulder. "What's the matter with you? I told you I wanted a beer, why didn't you stop?"

"You could've gotten my brother into a lot of trouble yesterday, Ivon."

"Wait a minute. You're the one who pushed him on me. I didn't ask for an escort."

"I told you this *mierda* was dangerous, but no, you have to go poking your nose into stuff you don't know jack-shit about."

"Hello? Weren't we just poking into somebody else's business right now?"

"That's enough, you two," said Father Francis. "Let's try to remember that we're supposed to be praying for Mireya right now."

Ivon ignored him. "I'm the one who should be pissed, Ximena. Why didn't you tell me you were being followed the night you got busted? That you were run off the road. Those are probably the same fucks who took Irene."

Ximena cut her eyes at Father Francis. "You're such a snitch,

Frank." She turned left on Mejía Street and took another left on Avenida Juárez, heading north toward the Santa Fe Bridge.

"Hey," said Ivon, "You have to give me a ride to Raquel's house. I told you I have to pick up Irene's car."

"I don't know where Raquel lives."

"Well, I do."

"Stop fooling yourself," said Ximena. "You just want to get laid."

Ivon scowled at Father Francis, and the priest shrugged in embarrassment.

"What crawled up your ass?" Ivon asked her cousin.

"Forget it. Okay, which way?"

"Toward the racetrack, way the fuck in the opposite direction."

"Great," said Ximena, making a sudden right onto a side street that led to Avenida Lerdo, left on Lerdo, and an immediate right onto La Ribereña.

Father Francis buckled his seat belt and arched his eyebrows at Ivon. Ivon shrugged and stared out at the river.

Heat shimmered off the brown water of the Río Grande, and for a second she remembered the feces she had seen floating in the river. How could you have been swimming in that filth, Lucha? What were you trying to prove? She imagined finding Irene's body in the desert, watching her being dissected at the morgue. She could almost hear the warbling sound in Ma's throat weeping for her little girl. Stop torturing yourself, Ivon.

The van passed houses and grassless soccer courts at a seventy-mile-an-hour clip. When they went by the fairgrounds, Ivon started to cry.

"Look what you've done now, Shimeyna. Can't you see your cousin's in pain?"

"You staying at your mom's again tonight, right?" Ximena said, looking in the rearview.

"I wasn't planning on it. All my stuff is still over at Grandma Maggie's." Ivon wiped her eyes with her shirt.

"Well, you better plan on it from now on. I need the room. Georgie and Tía Luz are flying in from Boston tomorrow."

Not even the anger in her cousin's voice stung her as much as this rejection. She could not figure out what had happened to Ximena all of a sudden. She'd gone bipolar.

Ivon tried to change the subject. "Shit's gonna hit the fan when my mom and Tía Luz see each other."

"Yeah, this whole reunion is turning into one shit storm after another."

"Look, Ximena, I don't know why you're so pissed all of a sudden. Are you afraid of my seeing Raquel, or something? And anyway, what do you care?"

"No, you're right," said Ximena, lighting a cigarette. "I mean, I thought I was helping you and Brigit get the child you wanted. What do I care who you fuck?"

"Fuck you," said Ivon. "Stop the car."

"What?"

"Ivon, please," said Father Francis.

"Stop the fucking car right now or I'll kick the window out."

Ximena pulled over at the entrance to the Chamizal.

"Where's my tape?" said Ivon.

"What tape?"

"The videotape that Rubí made for me. I asked her to . . ."

"It's in your pack," said Ximena.

Ivon dragged her backpack out from the cargo area and yanked the van door open.

"Ivon," said Ximena, "what the hell do you think you're doing? Don't be stupid. It's dangerous around here."

"I don't need any judgmental bullshit from anybody, and I sure as shit don't expect it from you, goddammit!"

Ivon slammed the door behind her. She was going to Raquel's house to pick up Irene's car, not to get laid. Why didn't Ximena believe her? When had Ximena become a judge, anyway?

THE TAXI TURNED SOUTH off La Riberña onto Avenida San Lorenzo. Ivon didn't remember the exact address of Raquel's mother's house anymore, but she knew how to get there. It was in the neighborhood named Las Cuestas, across from the racetrack. It amazed her that so much had changed in this part of Juárez in eight years. There were three new industrial parks out here now, streets and traffic had multiplied a few hundred times, and the area around the church of San Lorenzo had gotten totally developed with Wendy's and Burger Kings and Kentucky Fried Chickens. The shortcut to the Juárez Hipódromo was still there, no longer a side street but a four-lane avenue. Raquel's house, she remembered, was tucked away on one of those elm-shaded streets, in a cul-de-sac named Cuesta Alegre.

The taxi meandered through Las Cuestas until he found the street. The house should have been right there, on the corner, a cute little white-brick house with red awnings and a white wrought-iron gate, a fountain in the front yard. In its place stood a sprawling two-story grey granite mansion with pillars and tiled cupolas that made it look more like a mosque than a house. There was a massive iron door at the street entrance, and a black security fence now encircled the property.

"What the hell . . ." she muttered out loud.

"¿Es aquí?" the taxi driver asked.

"I'm not sure. Can you wait?"

"It's your money, señorita."

She got out of the taxi and walked across the street to read the street signs. Cuesta del Sol and Cuesta Alegre—it was the right corner. She stood there shading her eyes, staring down the block. Every possible architectural style representing a variety of nations: Swiss chalet, French Normandy, Victorian castle, Spanish hacienda, Southern plantation. It was like a miniature version of Embassy Row in Washington, D.C. It could only mean one thing: drug money. This neighborhood face-lift was the kind of exaggerated conspicuous consumption that only sudden amounts of cash could finance. She walked up to a black iron mailbox by the front gate of what she hoped was Raquel's house and pressed a buzzer, spotting the surveillance cameras perched on each corner of the gate.

"Sí, diga," said a voice she didn't recognize.

Ivon couldn't find the speaker anywhere, so she just spoke

into the air. "I'm here to see Raquel Montenegro," she said in Spanish. "My name is Ivon Villa."

"*La señora* is not seeing anybody today."

There it was, the speaker, ingeniously integrated into the granite base of the mailbox stand. "Is she home? Would you please tell her this is an emergency?"

No response. Ivon figured the voice belonged to a maid and that the maid had probably gone to check if *la señora* would receive her. Raquel's mother had always had a maid, and Raquel was so used to having maids that when she lived with Ivon, it never occurred to her to do things like make the bed, clean the kitchen, do the laundry. Anybody who was anybody in Juárez, and many of those who were nobody, had a maid.

She heard the crackly sound of the speaker again. "*Éste . . . fíjese que la señora está enferma. Pide que la disculpe, pero no la puede atender.*"

There was no way that Ivon was going to be brushed off like this. She knew for a fact that Raquel was not sick and no, she was not going to forgive her for failing to attend to her.

"*Mira,*" Ivon said, "I want you to tell Raquel that she either lets me in or I'm going to stand out here honking the car horn until she does."

"What do you want, Ivon?" Finally, Raquel's voice.

"I want you to open this fucking gate and let me in. I need to talk to you."

Silence. Ivon figured she needed to make good on her threat. She trudged back to the taxi and asked the driver to blast the horn a few times. Right away, curtains started to flutter at the neighboring houses. Finally, the front door of Raquel's house opened and the uniformed maid walked down to the gate with a handful of keys. Ivon paid the taxi and he backed out of the cul-de-sac in a hurry.

The inside of Raquel's house was even more conspicuous than the outside. Mediterranean décor with a plant-filled, flagstone atrium (the little fountain that used to stand outside now incorporated into the exotic greenery), arched doorways, and floor-to-ceiling tiled walls that made the house look like one of those opulent castles in Sevilla. She could hear Donna Summer's voice echoing through the house, and instantly, her ears burned.

How dare Raquel be listening to music all safe inside her big house, Ivon fumed, while my sister is in the hands of some maniac, thanks to her.

She had to shove her hands in her pants pocket to keep from losing it.

The maid showed her to a small receiving room off the atrium. Green leather armchairs, a huge bouquet of sunflowers and roses, walls lined with what she recognized as Raquel's art: Dalí-like renditions of a veiled woman wandering in caves and deserts, accompanied by a surreal creature that was half-human, half-crab.

Ivon peered at the creature. The human torso looked both male and female, with pierced breasts and short hair, a beard, and hoop earrings dangling from earlobes and nostrils. The bottom half was all crustacean, huge pink pincers reaching toward the veiled woman. Ivon remembered Raquel used to use the crab as her trademark, because she was a Cancer, she said, and the crab was a symbol of secrets. This crab-woman, mermaid-like figure was an image Ivon had never seen.

"I was just leaving," said Raquel, standing in the doorway. She was wearing a business suit and large sunglasses, her hair pulled back in a tight bun, black bag slung over her shoulder. "I have to go to El Paso to pick up my nieces."

"On a Sunday?"

"They went shopping."

"What happened to your mother's house?"

"This *is* her house."

"Really? It looks more like a mausoleum. Your brother's business must be going well, huh? All those language classes at the *maquilas* must be paying nicely."

Raquel didn't answer. She rummaged in her purse and fished out her keys. "Look, Ivon, I know you're upset that I didn't go and find you yesterday, but my husband came to town unexpectedly. He arrived right after we talked, and I couldn't go. I'm sorry. I tried calling you on your cell phone but it was busy for a long time."

"Would you cut the bullshit, Raquel? You have no idea what you've caused, do you? And it just fucking amazes me that you don't give a shit. You're safe, at home, listening to your Donna Summer. How nice."

"I don't know why you say that, Ivon. I haven't been able to sleep for three nights, worrying about what happened to your *hermanita*. You know I feel responsible."

"Yes, I can tell. You've been so helpful."

"I did what I could, Ivon. I drove up and down for hours looking for her. I took you to Paco's house. I bought a new battery for her car. What else did you want me to do? Go with you to report her disappearance? Put an ad in the paper? What?"

The maid showed up with a tray of refreshments, a pitcher of *tamarindo* water and a plate of *empanadas*. She set the tray on the coffee table next to the vase of flowers. Ivon realized how thirsty and hungry she was after the *rastreo*, but she'd be damned if she was going to take anything from Raquel.

Raquel dismissed the maid.

"I thought maybe you'd show some concern," Ivon continued. "Maybe, yes, you'd go with me to look for her, since it's clear the police on both sides are washing their hands, acting like it's not their jurisdiction. And then today . . . at the *rastreo* . . . we found a body . . ."

"Dear God," said Raquel. "Was it her?"

Ivon shook her head. ". . . and yesterday . . . the detective . . ."

Suddenly the image of Irene's pants flashed in her mind, the red droplets that looked like blood, the streaks of mud and slime crusted on the white denim, the narrow strip of lace her mother had sewn to the hem. She felt her knees go weak and for a second, everything looked black and white. She sat down on the edge of the couch.

Raquel walked over to her. "What is it? The detective . . . what?" She placed an arm around Ivon's shoulders. Ivon shrugged it away. Swiped the tears out of her eyes.

"The Border Patrol found Irene's pants on the riverbank yesterday morning," she said. "The detective brought them over to my mom's house. My mom identified them, and now they're evidence."

"Of what?"

"Now they can say they have proof that something did happen to Irene, that she was kidnapped. The detective didn't say, but obviously, if she doesn't have her pants on, it's also evidence that they've done something to her, raped her, I'm sure, maybe worse." She started to sob.

Raquel embraced her again.

"I need your help, Raquel," Ivon said, tears flooding her face. "Help me find her."

"Here," she said, "lean back, you look dehydrated. Let me get you something to drink. Your face is burning up."

Raquel poured her a glass of the *tamarindo* water. Ivon wiped the tears and snot from her face with one of the cloth napkins, took the glass, and sipped the tartsweet brown liquid.

"Sorry," she said, sitting up again.

Raquel squatted next to her. "For what?" She removed her sunglasses.

"You know I hate to make a fool of myself."

Raquel's eyes misted over. "I know," she said.

Ivon stared at the bruise around Raquel's eye, then reached her hand up and stroked Raquel's temple with the back of her fingers. "I'm so sorry about that," she said.

Raquel turned her face into Ivon's hand and kissed her fingers. "I know," Raquel said again. "It's okay."

She stroked the back of Ivon's neck. Ivon closed her eyes, absorbing the cool softness of Raquel's hand, the light scratch of her nails, the perfumed scent of her wrist. She turned her face toward Raquel's and kissed her, gently at first, then roughly, pulling her close, gnawing at her mouth with a hunger she didn't even realize she felt.

Raquel did not resist.

THE TURQUOISE STONE OF THE RING glinted against charred skin. The hand clawed skyward out of the oven's vent, the nails ripped back, the fingers black and bloated.

"Irene?" she called out. "Irene, baby? Irene?"

The smell of soot and burnt flesh filled her nostrils. Where was everybody? How had she reached the brick plant before the others? Father Francis never left her side. Where was he? How was she going to get the body out of that oven by herself? Please, God, don't let it be Irene. Don't let it be my little sister.

The devil is loose, she heard someone say. *El diablo anda suelto.*

She poked the hand with her stick. The fingers twitched. Now there was a watch on the wrist, a big shiny gold watch with three pennies on the face.

"Irene?" she called out this time, a high-pitched squeal. Something was hammering inside her chest.

"Sshh, it's just a dream, *m'ija. Cálmate.*"

Ivon opened her eyes. It was dark and still. Just the light of the candles on the nightstand and the sound of a helicopter flying overhead.

"I bet she's lying dead somewhere," Ivon said, her throat swelling.

"No, no, she isn't," said Raquel. "That was just a dream. *Ven.* Let me hold you."

Ivon sobbed in Raquel's arms.

The phone rang. Raquel reached over to pick it up, thinking it was her brother calling to check up on her. "No, I haven't seen her." She covered the mouthpiece. "It's your cousin, Ximena," she whispered.

Ivon took the phone and wiped the tears off her face with the sheet. "What's up?"

"You're still there? Your mom's having a conniption fit. Thinks you've been kidnapped, too. She's been calling me every half hour since lunchtime. She even called the detective, but he's off-duty today."

"What do you want, Ximena?"

"You better get your ass over here. Brigit just called from Phoenix. She's arriving in an hour. Meet you at the airport. America West."

Ivon jumped out of the bed so fast she tipped over the ice bucket Raquel had placed next to the bed with bottles of Corona.

"Turn on the light," she said. "I can't see where my clothes are." Her jeans and shirt were on the floor, underwear on the bed, but she couldn't find her socks. She slipped barefoot into her shoes, gritty sand under her toes.

"Where's my backpack?"

"You left it downstairs."

A constant clanging in Ivon's ears. "Where's the car?"

"In the garage, where else would it be?" Raquel had put on her bathrobe by then, and Ivon followed her silently down the stairs. She couldn't look Raquel in the face. Guilt was already hammering loud in her chest.

"Here's your bag," said Raquel. Ivon's backpack was on a bench in the foyer. Ivon dug Irene's Miffy keychain out of the front pocket.

"Okay, where's the garage?"

Without a word, Raquel led her to a side door off the kitchen. She held on to Ivon's arm. "Ivon, wait," she said.

"What?" Ivon turned to face her but could not sustain her gaze. "I have to go, Raquel."

"I still love you, Ivon."

"You shouldn't," said Ivon. "I'm an asshole, and I'm sorry, this was a big mistake."

The garage lights turned on, and Ivon almost broke into tears at the sight of Mostaza. She could see her father sitting behind the wheel, teaching six-year-old Irene how to steer. She paid no attention to the sound of Raquel's sobbing.

36

"ACTION!"

She hears Junior's voice booming out over a megaphone, over the heavy metal music playing in the background. Maybe Marilyn Manson, but she can't be sure. It echoes like they're in a vault, but she can hear coyotes howling in the distance. They've moved her out of the red room into a black closet. A stripe of blue light shows under the door.

"Diablo, I mean Dracula, I said, *action!*" Junior calls out again.

"Wait up!" someone else calls out. "One of these fucking web-cams is busted, again."

"Again? What kind of cheap shit are we using, man?" says Junior.

There's mumbling and cursing, followed by, "Okay, rock and roll. Take One."

"Where's the bitch? I want to see the bitch now! Show me the bitch!"

She's terrified that they're coming for her and feels her bowels contract.

"Here she comes. Here comes the lucky penny."

A girl is crying hysterically. "*A mí no, por favor, a mí no. Tengo hijos.*"

"¡Dracula! Action!"

She hears wild demonic laughter that makes the girl do a staccato of screams.

"Cut! I think she passed out, boss."

"Well, get another one, motherfucker! I want a live one."

"*¿La cholita?*" She recognizes Dracula's high, girlish voice.

267

A sharp pain claws through her intestines.

"You can't have *la cholita, culero,*" Junior says. "She's reserved for the Egyptian. Now, work your prick, man, you're losing it."

Another girl screaming. This one sounds younger.

"There's another lucky penny. Hello, baby!" Junior says.

"No tits, boss."

"Turn her around! Let me see her ass," Junior says. "Okay, let's tie her to the bed facedown. Dracula, give that bad little girl a spanking and then show me some doggie action."

"She pissed herself, boss," Dracula calls out.

"Move out of the way, I want a close-up of that. Camera One, can you pick up the piss on the bed? I don't see it! We need more light there. That's it! I see it now. Hold. Okay, Dracula, take that hood off! Let her have it!"

"In the ass, boss?"

"Fuck the shit out of her, man. Camera Two, keep tight on that prick. Camera One, body shot from behind. That's it. Hump the little bitch. I want to see some spunk in one minute."

She doesn't want to hear any more, but her hands are tied behind her back and she can't cover her ears. The stench of panic is thick in her nostrils. Even as she mutters the words to "Black Dove" over and over—"she never let on how insane it was in that tiny kinda scary house by the woods by the woods by the woods"—she can hear the shrill cries of the coyotes.

"Okay, Dracula, do your thing, man. Let's spend this penny."

37

GODDAMMIT, SHE WAS GOING THE WRONG WAY. She should have been heading north toward the bridge, but had somehow ended up down here near the Benavídez Industrial Park, maneuvering the El Camino between *maquiladora* buses and 18-wheelers.

She made a couple of sharp lefts, hoping to find a way back to La Ribereña, but instead found herself in a completely new development behind the industrial park. Campos Eliseos, it said on a brightly lit billboard up ahead, The Elysian Fields. A clone of the Champs d'Elysée arch had been erected at the entrance to the development on Victor Hugo Street, and behind that were streets called Versailles and Concorde and Saint Germain. She turned on Boulogne, and then again on Orleans and Vendome, passing two- and three-story office buildings and gated communities. A tree-lined park ran the length of Elysian Fields Boulevard. With its fake gas lamps and wrought-iron benches, its poplars and weeping willows and pristine stretches of verdant grass, the park could easily have been transplanted from Paris or the French Quarter in New Orleans.

Across the park stood a five-story marble and glass building with a rotunda at the front entrance and a security-gated parking lot. The billboard in front of the building said World Trade Center and underneath that, in English, *To promote and expand world trade and tourism.*

This was a part of Juárez Ivon had never seen. No cars, no people, it looked surreal, like simulated reality, and for a second she felt like she'd driven into a movie set on the Universal Studios lot.

"Where in the fuck am I?" she said aloud.

The putrid stench of petroleum wafted into the car's air vents.

She noticed the yellow warning signs posted at 10-yard intervals up and down the park that prohibited digging in the ground or building fires, a skull-and-bones image to warn off those who couldn't read that this verdant oasis was not a safe place for picnics or barbecues. She knew where she was now. On the other side of the river, just past midtown El Paso, sprawled the Chevron Oil Refinery. The stench was emanating out of the ground of this idyllic community, constructed over the gasoline pipeline that had been constructed between Chevron and Pemex back in the days of the OPEC crisis. Made sense that this place was called the Elysian Fields, the name in Greek mythology for heaven, which was just another place for the dead.

Out of nowhere, the little boy's voice popped into her head: *Mapi, I thought you were gonna supervise me in the kid's section. I'm starting to feel kinda lonely.*

She stopped in the middle of the empty street, listening to the voice, thinking about Cecilia and the baby, about Jorgito and Brigit, the family they were going to start, the family she'd just cheated on, the family that was breaking up with Irene's kidnapping and her mom so angry at her, she wished Ivon didn't even exist. Her dissertation seemed so unimportant right now. What did it matter if she got a doctorate if her family was falling apart?

"Just find her," she said out loud. "Stop feeling sorry for yourself, and find Irene."

Suddenly she saw headlights behind her and she stepped on the gas pedal.

For Pete McCuts, it had been a long day. The air conditioner had broken down earlier, so his car felt like an aluminum can in a hot oven, with him frying inside. He'd stripped down to his undershirt, but his jeans felt like a second skin, and the rough denim was chafing his crotch. Boots had definitely been the wrong shoes to wear. Luckily, he'd brought a cooler and plenty of Cokes and snacks to keep him going, but the heat was making him feel the weight of his 24-hour day.

He'd had no sleep whatsoever. He'd stayed in his office until three in the morning, home to shower and change and get his supplies together, and back on Barcelona Street by 4:15 A.M. The cousin's van had pulled up in front of the mother's house twenty minutes later, so he'd gotten there in the nick of time.

It was still dark when they picked up the priest outside the church, and he had to be careful not to get too close or they'd see his headlights. There were other cars waiting in front of the church, and after ten minutes, they caravanned down to the bridge, led by the van.

He read through the Richard Ramírez material he'd downloaded from his office computer while he waited for the body search in Anapra to be over. When he saw the police cars approaching the site, he figured they'd found a body. He couldn't see anything with his binoculars. They were too far out. Damn. He would've liked to see it, taken some pictures. But he wasn't even supposed to be there, so he stayed put inside the car, air conditioner running full blast, reading the transcripts of the Richy-the-Rapist trials.

He noted the name and addresses of an apartment complex on Fruta Street called the Truth Apartments, where Ramírez's cousin, a Vietnam vet named Max, had shot his own wife in front of twelve-year-old Richy. According to the court psychologists, witnessing that murder at that susceptible age had probably turned Richard Ramírez into a killer. The cousin, a highly decorated soldier, had been found innocent by reason of insanity caused by post-traumatic stress syndrome, and he was committed to a mental hospital. That was twenty five years ago. Had he gotten out? Maybe there had been other witnesses, maybe a neighbor that still lived at those apartments. Tomorrow, after visiting Marcia and Borunda at the hospital, Pete was going to take a drive in what his detective buddies called "the fruit district," not because it was full of gays, but because the streets had names like Pera and Manzana and Durazno.

His tour of Richard's old 'hood yesterday after talking to the priest had rendered little in the way of clues, although he *had* staked out the two addresses near Richard's childhood home, where a couple of sex offenders lived, and found some suspicious activity going on at one of them. Drug deals going down, he surmised.

Finally, after ten, the group had climbed back into their cars and left the area. Ivon and Ximena and the priest were the last to leave, the priest doling out blessings to a group of women and children who followed them down to the van.

McCuts kept his distance all the way to the bridge, but then the van changed directions and he got caught at the train tracks waiting for a caboose to pass. He figured he'd lost them and was angry he hadn't jumped the tracks.

"You're such a Boy Scout rule-follower," he berated himself out loud, driving in the direction of the free bridge. "So what if the lights are flashing, you idiot, you could have gone across. Now you've lost them." But then he spotted the van stopped on the side of the road near Chamizal Park. He passed them and pulled over, watching Ivon in his rearview mirror as she stormed out of the van, clearly angry about something. She kicked the door and the van took off. He watched Ivon flag down a taxi and stayed close this time, running stop signs and red lights, nearly hitting a pedestrian in front of the San Lorenzo church. He wasn't going to lose her again.

The sunburned skin on his left arm itched. He'd had to wait hours in the blistering heat outside a fancy house in the racetrack neighborhood, sunlight slanting through the window of the car, until it occurred to him to park facing the other direction. Past lunch and dinner, nothing to do but listen to the radio and read the Mexican newspaper he'd bought from a little boy walking back and forth past his car, his patience died out along with his a.c.

By nightfall, he'd almost given up, thinking she might be spending the night in that house, when suddenly she'd come bolting out of the garage in her sister's yellow El Camino. So this was the friend's house where they were keeping the Elky.

He followed her to the industrial park, afraid she was going to meet someone there, and then realized she was driving around in circles like she was lost.

For a moment he was tempted to drive up next to her and let

her know he was there. Maybe he just wanted to talk to her, tell her what he'd found last night scrutinizing the map of the sex offenders in his office. One of them lived on Ivon's mother's street, four blocks down from the mother's house. Another one lived on the street just behind the mother. That whole Coliseum area, all the way down Alameda to Ascarate Park and up into Five Points and Fort Bliss, was congested with sex offenders. Missouri Street, running parallel to I-10, had row after row of halfway houses filled with registered rapists, child molesters, peeping Toms, and pimps. And downtown, in the streets closest to the bridge, in the alleys off St. Vrain and Chihuahua and Kansas Streets, lived an entire neighborhood of habituals who could easily walk across the Santa Fe Bridge and ply their trade on poor young women in Juárez.

He had gotten disgusted with himself and with the whole police force last night, staring at that map, a map that had been staring back at all the detectives in that office for months, and no one had ever drawn a connection between the rising number of sexual perpetrators in El Paso and the escalating sex crimes in Juárez. What disgusted him even more was that people in El Paso were not supposed to know the city was housing all those perverts in its midst. Classified information. Ivon's mother was living practically next door to one. Her little sister could easily have been followed into Juárez and snatched by some American perp.

He was so outraged by this, he was thinking of calling his friend, Diana, at the *El Paso Times,* so that she could expose the hundreds of sex offenders who were making use of El Paso's hospitality.

Tomorrow, after staking out the Truth Apartments, he was going to come back to that Clardy Fox neighborhood, where the mother lived, and systematically visit every single sex offender in the area to see if anyone among them might have a Night Stalker fetish.

But for now, he had to catch up to Ivon.

38

IVON PULLED UP TO THE CUSTOMS BOOTH AND SAID *AMERICAN*, annoyed as hell that at 9 P.M. on a Sunday there was still a line at the Córdoba Bridge. Thirty-five minutes it had taken her to get to the booth. She was not going to make it to the airport on time. What had possessed Brigit to get on a plane, for God's sake? Maybe Ximena had called her. Maybe Ximena had told Brigit Ivon went to see Raquel. How did Ximena know Raquel's number, anyway?

She leaned over and cranked down the passenger window. She was expecting the usual questions: Purpose of your trip to Mexico, bringing any fruits or vegetables? Instead, the INS officer gave her a strange look, walked completely around the car, and punched the license plate number into the computer in his booth.

Ivon sniffed at the steering wheel. She had left the house so fast she hadn't even washed her hands, and now Raquel's smell was all over the inside of the car.

The officer poked his head in the window. "Sir, uh, oh excuse me, ma'am, I need to see the registration and your driver's license, please, ma'am. Did you know you were driving a stolen vehicle?"

"What? Look, there's been a mistake." She sifted through all the junk in the glove compartment but couldn't find the registration anywhere. "It belongs to my little sister, she was kidnapped in Juárez a few days ago, and her car was found at the fairgrounds over on this side. That should all be in the report. I'm just bringing the car home." She handed him her license.

"I'm sorry, ma'am, I have no clue what you're talking about. All I know is that the plates match those of a stolen vehicle."

He punched her license number into the keyboard and stared

at the monitor in his little booth. "We're gonna need to pull you over, ma'am. We have to search the car."

"Call the police department if you don't believe me. Call Detective McCuts, he should have cancelled the stolen vehicle report by now. I'm the one who reported the car missing."

"Follow me, please." He stood in front of the car and directed her into a space in the searching area.

"Fuck," Ivon cursed aloud. This was all she needed. She riffled through the glove compartment again. Where the hell was that registration? Had they stolen that, too?

The INS officer rapped on the hood with his knuckles. "Step out of the car, ma'am. We're bringing in a K-9 unit. We need to look in your purse, too."

"I don't have a purse," said Ivon, throwing her pack on the metal inspection table.

Another agent appeared with two huge German Shepherds on a leash, one white, the other black and tan. Standing on their hind legs, the dogs inspected under the hood, then crawled under the car and worked over each of the tires. Inside the car, they shoved their snouts into the upholstery and under the dashboard and the mats in a kind of frenzy. When they reached the storage compartment behind the driver's seat, the dogs went ballistic. As far as she knew, the only thing stowed behind the seat was the spare, but the dogs were barking as though they'd just discovered a stash of cocaine back there.

"Cut!" said the guy with the dogs, and the animals instantly stopped barking. He clicked his tongue at them, and they clambered down off the car and sat obediently at his feet. Ivon narrowed her eyes at him. He looked familiar. His beige cowboy hat and hairy forearms. The other guy leaned into the car to lift out the spare and a thick manila envelope fell out. Someone had slashed the rubber and stuffed the envelope into the tire. The INS guy opened it and sorted through the contents.

"Hello!" he said, pulling out a handful of pictures. "Looks like she's bringing some pornography across, Captain."

"You don't say," dog-guy said, leering at Ivon. "Would you say we got ourselves a *child* pornographer here, Roy, or just plain ole dirty pictures?"

"They do look real young."

"Anything in her bag?" He led the dogs over to the backpack, and again the dogs went nuts. "Good boys, Silver and Tonto. Cut!" He unzipped the pack and peered inside.

"Well, now, what's this?" He reached in and brought out a videotape.

"Uh-huh," said Roy.

"Know what I think, Roy? I think we caught ourselves anoth-′ er pervert from that porn ring out of Elephant Butte."

"That'd be my guess," Roy said, stuffing the pictures back into the envelope.

Dog-guy smiled and tipped his hat to Ivon with his right hand. She'd seen that expensive watch before. "Told you I'd catch ya later, alligator," he said.

As soon as he said that, she remembered him. The annoying guy with the cowboy hat and the Patek Phillippe on the airplane. The name badge on his uniform said *Capt. J. Wilcox, Chief Detention Enforcement Officer.* J.W., he'd called himself.

"Ivon Villa, right?" he said, blue eyes dancing.

"I don't know anything about those pictures," she said, trying to keep her voice level. "And I'm not stealing this vehicle. It's my sister's car. Your buddy over there doesn't seem to understand that I'm the one who reported the car missing."

"Ain't that a shame?" he said, "The way some people are? Here, Roy, take these bad boys back where they belong. I know this young lady. I'll take her in."

"Take me in for what? I told you, I don't know anything about those pictures."

"I'm off-duty in five," said Roy, handing him the envelope and hauling the dogs off. "See ya at the movies!"

J.W. shoved the envelope and the videotape into the pack, then reached inside the car and pulled out the keys. "Now, then," he said, walking over to her, shouldering the pack, "suppose we go see what's on this video?"

"I'm not going anywhere." Ivon felt her pulse quickening. She glanced around, she wanted to yell out to someone, run away from him, but she'd lost her voice all of a sudden and her limbs felt like wax.

"You got six INS officers watching you right now with long-range rifles pointed at your head," he said. "Better do as I say, Ms. Butch. We got ourselves reasonable suspicion . . ." he patted the bag, ". . . that you are trafficking in contraband images of child pornography. And we *will* use force if you attempt to escape."

"You're full of shit," was all she managed to say.

"Let's go. Arms behind your back." The handcuffs bit into her wrists. Gun drawn, he led her inside the U.S. Customs building.

At that hour, there were few people crossing over on foot, waiting their turn to announce their citizenship, so it was mostly the INS agents gawking at Ivon. She bit her tongue and tried to breathe as normally as possible. But her heart felt like she'd had too much coffee, and the blood was pounding in her head.

"Where are you taking me?"

"Shut up."

"This is an illegal arrest," she said in a loud voice. The gun poked her in the spine, but he didn't say anything. His fingers clamped around her arm. They walked past a cage in the back of the building, and he threw her car keys on the counter.

"Another child molester from Elephant Butte," he said to the two officers inside.

"Suckers just don't know when to quit," said one of them.

"Confiscated a mess of pictures and a video she was bringing across. Taking her in, myself. I'm sick to death of these perverts."

"Want us to impound the car?"

"Yeah, and draw me up a Class A Medical Exclusion Certificate, will ya?"

"A what, sir?"

"You know, for queers."

"Uh, I don't think . . ."

"Self-declared lesbian, right here."

"What the fuck are you talking about?" she muttered.

"Didn't you know," he sneered, "that gays and lesbians are a threat to national security? All psychopaths and sexual deviants are supposed to be excluded."

"I don't think that's in effect any more, Captain Wilcox," said the officer behind the cage. "Not since 1990."

"Look it up in the computer, Lieutenant. You'll see what it says about HIV threats."

"You're the man."

"Owe y'all a beer."

Ivon's ears were on fire. HIV threats?

"Remember I told you on the plane it was a mistake to flaunt your dyke-ness?" he whispered behind her. "Especially in Texas. Shit comes back to haunt you."

He pushed her inside a small cubicle with a table and chairs and a television monitor on a cart hooked up to a VCR.

"Let's see what you got," he said, popping the video into the machine.

"A friend of mine made that tape for me. It's a copy of a talk show in Juárez."

"Right, and I'm Bozo the Clown." He holstered his gun.

The tape showed Rubí Reyna talking to the medical examiner, a display of human bones on the metal table in front of them. He turned up the volume.

"*This one, for example,*" the medical examiner was saying, holding up a shattered skull, "*probably died of cranio-encephalic trauma, which means her head was bludgeoned with a blunt force object. From the relatively clean lines of the wound, we can deduce that it must have been a heavy rock, at least 5 or 6 kilos in weight, or some other heavy flat object used by someone with a great amount of strength. She was probably hit two, no more than three times—see how the damage here shows the cranium being fractured in at least two large pieces? If it had been a bat or something light that hit her, say, the barrel of a gun, the fracture would have looked different, there would be shards along the breakage points, not these clean ruptures of the bone.*"

Ivon shuddered, remembering Mireya's body that morning.

He was sorting through the photographs of naked children in the envelope and not really paying attention to the video. "What's she talking about?" he asked.

Like she was really going to translate for him.

". . . was found four months ago, in February, in the old city dump, along with the spinal column, the remains of a foot inside a shoe, part of the pelvis."

"And the body was never identified?"

"Never. She's one more unidentified skeleton in the amphitheater."

"What about the DNA procedure?"

"Unfortunately, we don't have that technology here in Juárez. The remains have to be sent off to Chihuahua City, and the families just can't afford it."

"I'm bored with this Chinese," said J.W. "Let's see what else is on here." He fast-forwarded the tape past more conversation, commercials, back to Rubí Reyna's face, and suddenly, snow, followed by rainbow-colored bars.

Some words appeared on the screen, like a title.

"Bingo!" he said, rewinding and pausing. "Now, we're talking. Doris Meets El Diablo," he read the title out loud.

"Every week hundreds of young Mexican girls arrive in Juárez from all over Mexico," the voice-over began, a man's voice in English. A panoramic view of the El Paso/Juárez Valley appeared on screen. Twilight, the star glowing on the blue Franklin Mountains in the distance. "Most of these young ladies are looking for work that will be a primary source of income for their families back home. While many will begin their careers in one of the various maquiladora factories in the area, often they end up in the many bars and brothels."

It was the same narrative Ivon had read in that Juárez tourist site on the Internet.

"Wish I had me some popcorn," said J.W., straddling a chair in front of the TV.

Now the scene changed to a long shot of La Mariscal, traffic of cars and pedestrians all around, the bustling nightlife of the red-light district. The camera panned in fast-frame down the street, the neon names of clubs and the faces of women turning like a kaleidoscope until finally the camera froze on the entrance to the Sayonara Club.

"Girls like Brenda, Becky, and Eunice . . ."

Three long-haired girls in glittery thong bikinis and stiletto heels appeared in the door.

"... *are just waiting to meet you. In Ciudad Juárez, prostitution is legal, and you will not find a place with more beautiful, available, hot-blooded young ladies than these.*"

The girls turned their bare backsides to the camera and then turned coyly back, red lips pouting, long red fingernails luring the viewer to follow them into the Sayonara Club.

"*But clubs aren't the only place to meet young ladies in this exciting border town. All over the city, fresh new girls of all ages arrive every day. You'll find them in the stores around the downtown plaza, in a mall or a city park, or even at national monuments.*"

Now a day-shot of the monumental statue of Mexican president Benito Juárez. A young girl, probably no more than ten years old, in long braids and a school uniform, standing at a bus stop near the statue. A white car pulling up in front of her. The driver reaching an arm out toward the girl, holding a dollar bill, the girl climbing inside. Some words appeared on-screen: *'Twas down in Cunt Valley, where red rivers flow, where cocksuckers flourish and maidenheads grow, 'twas there I met Doris, the girl I adore, my hot fucking, cocksucking Mexican whore.*

Another scene change. In the backseat of the car, the girl struggling with the driver. His face not in the picture, but his pants down around his knees. His fingers clamped around the girl's arm, yanking at her, the girl pulling back, refusing, resisting, crying. The camera zooming in on his huge erect penis. The *ranchera* song, "Camarón Pelado," playing loud in the background.

"What's the song saying?" J.W. asked.

"I don't know."

"Bitch," he said, pulling his gun out and pointing it at her head, "you better tell me."

"Peeled shrimp you ask for, peeled shrimp you get."

"Catchy." He kept the gun in his hand.

Now the camera was panning up to the man's tattooed hands wrapping the girl's long braids around her neck and pulling. Her eyes puffed up with fear, tears gushing down her cheeks, she was still refusing to do what the man wanted. More words rolling at the bottom of the screen: *Now Doris popped her cherry when she was but six, swinging upon El Diablo's big prick, the upright slipped in, and she finished her life in a welter of sin.*

He lifted her up and forced her to straddle him. The camera closed on the girl's face as the sharp pain of the penetration registered in her eyes. The man's hands tightened around the girl's neck, knuckles white, veins bulging under the green and blue ink of the tattoos as he choked her.

"That's all she wrote," said J.W.

Ivon's vision blurred, and she clamped her eyes shut to keep from seeing the girl's dead face, tongue squeezed between her teeth, head lolling to the side. The realization of what this was hit her like a fist between the eyes. This was more than pornography. This was snuff.

Next shot: the girl lying faceup in the sand, hair chopped off, still wearing her uniform, arms tucked under the body, one leg bent so sharply the heel was touching the hip, shoes and braids placed neatly beside the body. Nothing but sagebrush all around her, radio towers in the distance. More words rolled on-screen: *Now Doris is dead and buried, and lies in her tomb, while maggots crawl out of her decomposed womb, the smile on her face is a sure cry for more, my hot fucking, cocksucking Mexican whore.*

A cackling *calavera* on a skeletal horse galloped across the screen to the William Tell Overture, followed by: Lone Ranger Productions . . . ★

J.W. turned to smirk at Ivon. "You are one sick bitch," he said, licking his lips. "We're going for a little ride."

She noticed the bulge in his pants when he stood up. He holstered his gun again, and adjusted himself. "Yep, I know just the place for you," he said, walking over to the VCR. He ejected the tape, slipped it back into its case, and stuffed the video and the envelope of photographs back into her pack.

Ivon was trying desperately to sort out these cards in her head. Rubí gave that videotape to Ximena this morning. Did she know what was on it? Or was it Walter? He was the camera guy. Ivon remembered the way he had filmed the *colonia* people this morning without them knowing about it. She felt cold, and yet the sweat smelled rank under her arms.

"I want to talk to my lawyer," she said, heart pounding. "That's my right as a citizen."

"Shut your face," he said, shoving her out the door.

J.W. walked her across the building, out to the gated parking lot in the back, lit up as bright as a dealership, and toward a row of white and green Broncos with Border Patrol logos. He went up to one of them, opened a back door, and pushed her into the seat. No door handles or window cranks, a plastic panel between the front and back seats, like a taxi, two growling German Shepherds in the caged cargo area. He mounted the driver's seat and buckled up.

"Where are you taking me, goddammit?"

He was whistling "Camarón Pelado" as he drove out of the lot.

"You know this is an illegal arrest. I don't have anything to do with anybody from Elephant Butte. I didn't know what was on that video and I sure as shit didn't put those pictures there. Someone planted them, and you know it. I demand to know where you're taking me." She kicked the back of the seat and the dogs growled behind her.

He shook his finger at her reflection. "Temper, temper. I wouldn't upset my dogs, if I was you, they ain't been fed yet."

She shook her head to get the tears out of her eyes. A ball of spikes had formed in her throat. Breathe, Ivon, she told herself. Calm down. Get your bearings.

They were heading west on the border highway, toward downtown. He was packing the inside of his mouth with tobacco.

"Look," she tried another approach, "I don't know anything about those pictures, but I can give you the names of the people who gave me the video." Her voice was shaking. "The woman on the talk show, the interviewer, her name is Rubí Reyna, and she offered to make me a dub of that show she did with the medical examiner yesterday. Her husband, Walter Luna—he's the one who dubbed the tape and Rubí gave it to me this morning at this body search in Lomas de Poleo. This Walter guy is the cameraman for the show, so, I don't know, maybe he's the one who added that disgusting footage, or maybe it was a tech at the station or whatever. I seriously doubt that Rubí knows what's on there, but anyway, call *them* and let me the *fuck* out of here!" She raised her voice too much at the end of that one, and again the dogs growled.

His ice-blue eyes looked almost fluorescent in the neon glow of the dashboard lights. "I see. You're one of them fanatics that likes to go out looking for dead bodies."

"I told you. I was looking for my little sister. We have evidence that she was taken against her will and probably sexually molested, if not worse. Hell, it was the Border Patrol that found her jeans on the riverbank yesterday morning. Don't you all have a log of some kind?"

"Ya'll find anything?"

"She wasn't a thing. She was a human being with a name and a life, you pig." The pain in her throat had moved up into her ears.

"Was the body intact or in pieces? Did Luna film what you found?"

"He was there with two cameras."

"Guess we got our man, then." He spit tobacco juice out the window and took out a cell phone. "Hey, Junior," he said into the phone, "that guy at the station, what's his name? Walter Luna, right? We need to teach that boy a lesson . . ."

So Rubí's husband was involved in this, too? God, how deep did this go?

". . . Either he's stupid and trying to show our shit to other people, or he's a smartass thinking he can get some video action on the side . . . 'Course, I'm sure . . . I know you're busy, asshole. Get your fuck-wad partner to do it. And I mean *now*. Hey, y'all done that nickel yet? Wait for me. I'll be there in ten. Got someone here who wants to watch."

What was he talking about? Watch what?

"Are you shitting me?" he bellowed. "Nobody said nothing about no inspection. The fucking plant is shut down. What are they gonna inspect? Look, I don't give a shit. You stay on schedule. I'll deal with that motherfucker." He dialed another number.

"I don't want to watch anything," she said. Her temples were throbbing.

He ignored her and spoke into the phone. "Get me the foreman."

"I mean it," she said. A part of her already knew what he was referring to, but she was trying to ignore those bells gonging in her head.

"J.W. Hey! What is this shit about an inspection? I don't fucking believe it. Don't those assholes have anything better to do on a Sunday night? I need more warning than this, motherfucker! I got some business to take care of right now. I don't know, tell them you found a leak or something. All I'm asking for is two hours. I'll comp you a show tomorrow night. Whatever you want, you name it . . . Fine. Whatever. We'll be outa there in two hours."

He punched the phone off and threw it across the seat. "Cocksucker!"

"I know where you're taking me," she bluffed. They were heading west on Paisano Street, toward downtown. That's all she knew.

He fixed her gaze in the mirror. "Took you long enough." He spat out the window again. "You know, that little sister of yours is a real cutie-pie. Hope she's not a lezbo, like you. Be a real shame if she was."

"You don't know anything about my sister."

"I know she's one half of a very exciting show." He chuckled.

"Shut up!" she muttered. She concentrated on the names of the shops they were passing on Paisano. Dollar Store, Macdonald's, Vinny's XXX Video, Casa de Cambio, Jail Bonds, the Whatever Lounge. They were not too far from the jail, where she and Father Francis had picked up Ximena yesterday morning.

"I especially like that little doo-hickey on her tongue."

"What?" She felt like she had suddenly run out of oxygen. "You're lying."

"If I'm lying I'm flying," he said.

Oh my God. Connect the dots, Ivon.

"I lost that little bet of ours on the plane, but I hadn't taken a peek at your sister. Now there's star material. She is one cute little lucky penny."

On the plane, he'd given her a roll of pennies, her winnings, he'd called them. She remembered the two pennies she'd taken from the crime scene that morning. They were right there in the side pocket of her backpack, which was sitting on the front seat next to him. *Some of the bodies had American pennies inside them when we did the autopsies,* Laura Godoy had said.

Ivon felt the bottom falling out of her stomach.

"You better not have hurt my sister," she said.

"Or else what? What're you gonna do, Ms. Butch?" He wagged his gun at her.

"You fucking bastard!" She kicked the back of the seat with both legs, and the dogs growled again.

"You kick that seat one more time and I'll give my dogs an early dinner."

Think fast, Ivon, put it together. "I know about the pennies," she said.

He narrowed his eyes at her in the rearview. "I said shut up!"

"Guess you need to rape those girls with rolls of pennies because your dick's too small." She held up her hand so he could see her thumb and index finger making a sign at him in the rearview mirror. "It's that big, right?"

"You want to see how big my cock is, bitch?" he slammed his elbow against the plastic panel, and the dogs snarled. "I'll ram it down your throat if you don't shut up!"

She thought of that graffiti in the bathroom at Casa Colorada. "You know, they're writing graffiti about you in the red-light district, something about how the Border Patrol sucks the Chihuahua governor's cock."

His eyes scintillated in the mirror. "You say one more word, and I swear to God I'll have that little sister of yours melted down to bacon, so shut your fucking cunt."

She bit her tongue.

They had left downtown behind and were heading toward the ASARCO smokestacks on the Border Highway. It was too dark to see it, but she knew that off to the left was the river, and above it, Mount Cristo Rey. Was it just this morning that she'd been staring up at the statue's face from Lomas de Poleo? That impassive limestone face that offered nothing but . . . wait a minute . . . that impassive limestone face of *Jesus.*

Poor Juárez, so far from the Truth, so close to Jesus.

Es una fábrica cerca de Jesús, the voice had said on the phone. A factory close to Jesus. Close to Cristo Rey. What was close to Cristo Rey? She could see the smokestacks of the smelter up ahead near Executive Center.

Suddenly, he floored the gas pedal, and the engine kicked into high gear. "I'll be goddammed!" he said, checking all his mirrors. "Is that car following me?"

Ivon turned her head, but the dogs bared their teeth, so she faced forward again.

"Better not be following me, motherfucker." He zigzagged between the lanes and just past the black bridge made a sudden ninety-degree turn onto Executive Center and then immediately turned south, tires spinning into a street marked with a Dead-End sign.

It was pitch black, but she knew where she was. Executive Center behind her, Interstate 10 to the left, Border Highway to the right. The stench of refinery soot told her they were on ASARCO grounds.

Everything fell into place. ASARCO—the American Smelting and Refining Company—was a copper refinery, a factory close to Cristo Rey. The smelter was shut down, apparently, from what he'd been saying on the phone, but J.W. was using the place for business, and whoever this "foreman" was that he'd been yelling at, J.W. was going to "comp him a show tomorrow night." Clearly, his business was something to watch. Then she saw it, the web address on the bottom of the page of "Richy's Diary." www.exxxtremelylucky . . . What had he called Irene? *A cute little lucky penny*. It all came together.

"You're running a porn site," she gasped. "You're killing women online." Her whole body was shaking.

"Quiet!" he hissed, pulling over and killing the engine and the lights.

39

PETE WAS STARTING TO GET FRANTIC. Where the hell was he taking her? They weren't headed east toward Camp Montana, the Border Patrol's alien processing center and detention facility on the east side. But he had her handcuffed and sitting in the back of his truck like an illegal, with a pair of dogs guarding her back. Something was wrong, very wrong.

He'd been only two cars behind her on the bridge and seen it all. The dogs, the search, the arrest. He'd gone through customs, forgetting completely about his weapon in the trunk, then driven around the corner, and parked on Hammet Street, where he could climb on the roof of the car and watch the parking lot through his binoculars.

All his senses had gone on red alert when he saw the agent leading her to a Border Patrol truck like a detainee. And now, he had no idea where they were going. He'd already established they weren't going to the EPC, and they'd passed downtown, so he wasn't taking her to the Santa Fe facility either.

He took his phone out and speed-dialed dispatch, then changed his mind and clicked the off button. What was he going to say? That he had a hunch about something? That he'd gone across the river to tail someone who'd gotten picked up by the Border Patrol? The phone rang.

"McCuts," he said, trying to sound nonchalant.

"This is dispatch. Caught your number. Thought you might need a call-back."

"Uh, yeah, thanks, I think so."

"McCuts, I'm filling in for someone tonight, I don't want to be here. Gimme a break, okay? Do you need something or not?"

Now his stupid heart was pounding in his neck. "Maybe. Uh, yeah, I'm pretty sure something's not right. I'm tailing someone who's got one of my cases in the back of his truck, in handcuffs."

"I'm drawing a blank, McCuts."

"He's a Border Patrol guy. He arrested her at the free bridge, and then I saw him cuff her and put her in the back of his truck, and now he's taking her who knows where. Can you, uh, can you start me a unit?"

"Maybe she was bringing something across."

"I don't think so. Didn't pat her down, didn't read her her rights, didn't even process her, I bet. They were inside maybe fifteen minutes, didn't look like a real arrest to me."

"Maybe she's an illegal."

"She's not an illegal, she's U.S. And like I said, she wasn't processed. Besides, these guys don't take detainees one by one. They take busloads. Why is he giving her a personal ride? And he should be taking her to Camp Montana but he's not anywhere near it. He's going in the opposite direction."

"You're not even on duty tonight. I don't see your name anywhere."

"Look, there's a woman in trouble. I mean it. I need backup."

"What's your twenty?"

He looked up at the highway signs. "U.S. 85, just past Doniphan Park."

"I don't know, McCuts, it's gonna take awhile. You're way the hell out there."

"How long?"

"An hour, at least. Plenty of time to talk to your supervisor about it."

"Gee, thanks."

"Sure thing."

Shit. He'd been spotted. He'd gotten too close. He slowed down and hung back behind a semi, maintaining visual. He wanted to pursue, but he knew he needed to wait for reinforcements, knew he should've contacted his supervisor and that he couldn't execute a warrant without approval. Now what?

The Border Patrol vehicle had turned east on Executive Center, but there was no sign of it now. It must have scuttled up into the hills leading to Calavera and ASARCO. What he needed was a chopper to scope out the area. He called dispatch again.

"I need air support," he said, "something's going down over here at ASARCO."

"Who is this and what is this call in reference to?"

It wasn't the same woman he'd talked to before, but he thought he recognized the voice. He explained the situation again.

"Were you tailing this person in Mexico, McCuts?"

"She was compromising our investigation, going around showing her sister's APB to people, putting herself in danger. Now she's been arrested by the Border Patrol."

"You sure about this?"

"Something's not right, I know that for sure."

"Okay, but this better not be a wild goose chase. We have an air unit by McKelligon Canyon. I'll send him over, what's your location?"

"I'm right in front of the cement plant on Executive Center, corner with 85."

"That's Calavera territory."

"I know that," he said.

"Okay, that's the rendezvous point. I'm sending out two marked units to meet you. Do not pursue, you're not on duty. I repeat: do not pursue. Patrols are on their way. I don't want anyone in Calavera territory by themselves."

"Ten-four."

"Oh, and McCuts?"

"Yeah?"

"This is your supervisor. Dispatch patched me through. Guess they thought I might need to know what my rookie detective was up to. Next time you feel like bypassing me, Petey Boy, you're going to find yourself on foot patrol handing out parking tickets, I don't care who your daddy is."

"Yes, ma'am. Sorry, ma'am."

"I want your report on my desk in the morning, first thing."

"Yes, ma'am."

"And McCuts? I better not find out you were tailing someone in Mexico, and I sure as hell better not know you took a weapon."

"No, ma'am, that will be in the report."

He clicked off the phone and drove away from the cement plant. The patrols were going to be too late. But at least a chopper was coming. He had to drive up there and shoot his flare gun for the chopper.

He knew Ivon was in danger, and he was going to do something about it, approval or not. He'd reported the situation, he'd requested backup. Just following procedure. Now he had to act. He'd been trained for this.

He swerved into San Marcos Road and shut his lights off, navigating with his flashlight. At the turnoff to the road that led up to ASARCO, there was a *Private Property* sign tacked to an electric pole. He was trespassing in Calavera country. Just like Ortiz and Borunda had been trespassing the other night. They'd be on him like vultures, if he wasn't careful. He pulled over and parked the Honda. His Kevlar vest, the walkie-talkie, and the flare gun were in the trunk. He had his flashlight, his Bowie knife; his gun was good to go. Every inch of his body was pulsing.

40

IRENE COULD NOT REMEMBER how she'd gotten back to the red room. At some point, she must have fainted. She could still hear the howling and didn't know if it was coyotes or the girl. Her stomach cramped, and she rolled sideways to vomit. There was already a pool of it on the floor, the smell and color of rust. She realized she was on top of the cot, not under it. She was naked.

Whenever they left her alone on top of the cot, she did leg crunches, pulling her legs to her chest and raising them over her head to keep the muscles limber and her stomach strong. With these leg chains, she could make pedaling motions. She could even take steps.

All she knew is that she was next. They were coming for her. She could hear them laughing outside the bus: one of the men and the woman who sang the lullabye, who wore the yellow head-phones of the CD player like a headband. The smoke from their joint wafted in through the open window, masking the stench of rotting flesh for a few seconds.

She knew the woman's name now. Ariel, one of the men had called her. She knew something else, too. The red room they were keeping her in wasn't a room at all, but a converted bus, and they weren't in Juárez anymore—the ASARCO smokestacks were right outside the window, so close she thought they must be on the premises. That meant they'd crossed over to the El Paso side. She was back in Texas.

Her skin itched. Ariel must have washed her before bringing her back to the bus. Her wrists were tied in front of her now, but instead of the itchy rope around her ankles, someone had clamped leg irons on her. They were heavy, but at least the chains gave her legs more movement.

A breeze blew into the room and the air felt like ice on her feverish skin. How had she gotten a fever? Something they'd given her to eat had made her sick, but she couldn't remember how long ago that was. Her stomach cramped again, but there was hardly anything left in her gut, just a rank brown liquid.

She closed her eyes and took some deep breaths. This was it. She knew she was next.

She shuddered again, and the shaking of her body reminded her of the bath. Hunkered down in the tin washtub, Ariel pouring cold water over her. At least she remembered the bath.

"Stop shivering," Ariel had said behind her mask, "you're making me nervous."

She couldn't stop. Even her teeth were chattering.

"Stop it!" Ariel flicked her butt with the wet towel. She couldn't feel pain anymore, just the tingling sensation on her flesh.

"I . . . ca . . . ca . . . can't," she said, "I . . . I'm c . . . c . . . cold."

Ariel told her to lean over and rubbed a bar of laundry soap between her legs and scrubbed her hard. The raw skin down there burned from the soap.

"Guess what? You get to go swimming again," Ariel teased her. "The river water is nice and high tonight. You'll float real easy when they're finished." She laughed and rubbed the soapy rag up and down the rest of her body.

Ariel dried her with an old towel, pushed her back on the cot and ordered her to spread her legs as wide as she could so she could take her picture. That's all she remembered. Now she was here, naked on the cot, puking her guts out. And she was next.

"Are you decent?" Ariel laughed, stumbling into the room. She carried a laundry basket full of clothes. "We have to find you something to wear, *algo muy especial para tu viaje especial*," she cackled.

She saw her own striped T-shirt in there, but Ariel selected a different outfit: a short black skirt with a red lame halter emblazoned with the letters JAL. "This should fit," she said, and draped the items over her arm. "Oh, I almost forgot." She took something out of her shirt pocket. "Take this," she said, popping a pink pill in her mouth. "It's almost your turn."

She waited for Ariel to leave, then spit the pill out in the corner where the shit bucket stood, where she spit all the other pills they gave her. She knew that *her turn* meant they were going to take her away to that place where they'd had her, listening to the screaming.

Action! She could hear Junior shouting into the megaphone.

No matter how loud they played the music, she could still hear the howling. Now it was the theme from the Lone Ranger playing loudly over the speakers, the "William Tell Overture" echoing off the red aluminum walls of the bus.

She thought of Ivon and knew her sister would do whatever it took to escape. Kick the woman in the face. Her legs were strong. Choke her with the chain of the leg irons. Ariel was so stoned it would be easy to take her by surprise.

It was her only chance. Either that or *her turn.*

41

J.W. STARTED UP THE ENGINE AGAIN.

He drove around in circles, trying to find something. In the darkness, Ivon could hear the rush of freeway traffic, and beneath that, a wild chorus of coyotes in the canyon. She couldn't tell if the coyotes were in Juárez or El Paso or New Mexico. She was trying to orient herself, figure out what direction the river was in. If she escaped, she'd have to run the opposite way, toward the freeway.

His headlights illuminated a huge skull and crossbones painted against a blood-red background on the side of a white shack.

Underneath the skull it said *La Calavera—El Paso, 1882.*

Ivon knew the place well. In high school, she and her cousin Mary used to come out here on Friday nights to bring groceries and fix supper for Tata Alberto, their great-grandfather, who'd lived in Calavera since Smeltertown was condemned. One of them would read the newspaper to him while the other boiled pasta or made tuna salad. After he'd eaten and they'd washed up and put him to bed, Ivon and Mary would hike up to the old cemetery on the mesa and get high and hold séances. They were horror film freaks and liked to pretend they could summon the dead. Nobody guarded Smelter Cemetery. Not even ghosts.

Now they were climbing up an incline. The dogs started to whine, like they knew where they were going.

"Settle down, boys. It's almost show time!"

At the top of the mesa the Bronco came to the wrought-iron gates of the cemetery entrance. It looked locked, but J.W. got down, rattled something on the latch and pushed the gates open. The truck lights bounced off the tombs. Piles of stones and crucifixes populated the little graveyard. The ground was covered with mounds of thick black soot, and the chemical fumes were so strong they made her eyes water. Here and there plastic flowers and green scrub brush broke through the black ground. A few of the graves were encircled with wood or metal railing. One of them had a Sacred Heart of Jesus painted on the white headstone.

Just below the cemetery, she could see the billboards off I-10, and beyond that, the lights of West El Paso. She knew exactly where she was. There was a railroad track that led out of ASARCO up to the interstate. She and her cousin had discovered it once when a helicopter patrol had flown overhead and interrupted their séance. The moon was waning but still nearly full. Plenty of light to help her plot a course out of Calavera.

"Home, sweet home," he said. "Who's hungry?"

The dogs started to whine.

"Need some *protein*." The dogs started to slobber. He just loved his own jokes.

Now the tires were crunching down the loose asphalt away from the cemetery. In the moonlight, the refinery smokestacks stood like sentinels of death. La Esmelda, Tata Alberto used to call it, the place that gave him stomach cancer and killed Granny Rosemary with tuberculosis. They'd had a house in Five Points for a few years, but when the Great Depression hit, Tata lost his job at the newspaper, and they'd lost their house and their dreams. The cheapest real estate they could find was in Smeltertown.

The Bronco meandered into the plant, moving slowly between the empty office buildings and the abandoned warehouses. ASARCO had become a ghost town, utterly dark and deserted. The only signs of life were the howling of the coyotes in the Anapra hills and the faraway echo of a train. Abruptly, they pulled to a stop in front of a warehouse, and suddenly they were surrounded by what looked like movie lights. Someone was filming a movie up there.

She saw an RV and a couple of horse trailers parked near the warehouse.

"What the fuck is that bus doing here?" J.W. muttered.

Behind the trailers, she saw a Juárez bus, the same kind of bus she had seen yesterday on Ugarte Street. No, it was the same bus.

She recognized the graffiti and the crooked letters on the destination panel spelling La Cruz Roja. It was the same *camión rojo* that
had almost run her and William off the road in Puerto Anapra.

J.W. stepped out of the jeep. "What the fuck's going on, Junior?" he demanded.

The bright lights flashed off, leaving everything yellow in the
acid glow of the moon. From here, Ivon couldn't see the valley or
the canyon or even the cemetery.

"Hey, it's cool!" someone yelled out. "Turn those lights back
on, man!"

J.W. walked around the back of the jeep to let the dogs out. A
skinny guy in baggie pants and a tank top came out of the warehouse and swaggered up to him. He had a beer bottle in one hand,
a megaphone in the other. A long earring dangled from one earlobe.

In the distance Ivon heard a helicopter.

"Junior, you better tell me what the fuck's going on," J.W. said,
pulling Ivon out of the Bronco by the hair. "Why is that fucking
bus here? They shouldn't be here."

The other man scratched his crotch and shrugged at the same
time. "Thought *you'd* sent them, man," he said. "Thought we were
gonna have a live audience tonight!" He burped and laughed like
he was high on something.

"I didn't send shit! Somebody's setting us up! Can't you fucking see that?"

The man fluttered his arms. "It's the fucking Egyptian, man. I
told you he was going to spill the beans if we didn't get him what
he wanted."

"It's not the Egyptian, you stupid fuck. I told you, it's Walter
Luna. Did you call your partner? Did you tell him he needs to
clean some shit up, pronto?"

The guy chugged the rest of his beer and threw the bottle over
his shoulder.

"You call him, man," he said. "I've got a show to finish."

J.W. grabbed the guy by the ear and shone his flashlight on the
earring. From where Ivon was standing, it looked like a desiccat-
ed human nipple.

"Take this stupid shit off, for fuck's sake."

J.W. marched back to the Bronco and took out his cell phone. "Silver and Tonto," he said casually over his shoulder. "Take One."

The dogs closed in on Ivon, growling, their eyes glued to each side of her.

"Don't you wish," she muttered under her breath to the dogs. She could see a hand sticking out of the slats of one of the horse trailers. Her heart started to hammer. The helicopter was getting closer.

Phone to his ear, J.W. stomped off in the direction of the warehouse, complaining about the stink. Holding the megaphone between his legs, the other guy turned to face Ivon and very deliberately tied a green surgical mask over his face. Ivon realized she had seen him before. He waved at her like he wanted her to recognize him. Junior, from the amphitheater, the medical examiner's assistant. The entanglement between perpetrators and public officials was staggering.

"Hurry the fuck up!" J.W. called out to him.

There it was again, that hand sticking out of the horse trailer. Ivon inched sideways and the dogs growled. "Back!" she hissed at them. They growled some more. "Cut!" she said, remembering J.W.'s command to them back at the bridge. They laid their ears back and peeled their teeth.

All at once, the blue and red lights of a helicopter flashed overhead, and someone was yelling out, "Police! Freeze!"

A group of men bolted out of the red bus, busting out in all directions.

"¡Nos calló la chingada!" she heard Junior shouting through the megaphone.

The halogen beams from the helicopter flooded ASARCO, the force of the propeller blades blasting grainy refinery soot all over Ivon.

Turning her back on the helicopter to protect her face, Ivon crouched. The dogs broke away, barking frantically. She stumbled toward the horse trailer.

"Irene?" she called out, "is that you? It's me. Talk to me."

The hand poked out through the slats again, waving frantically. In the bright light she saw ragged fingernails and chipped silver polish. Not her sister's hand.

"*Ayúdeme, por favor*," she heard a woman say.

She ran to the front of the trailer but it was padlocked. "*Tiene candado*," she shouted to the woman. "Is there anyone there with you?"

"*¡Sáquenme de aquí!*" The woman yelled hysterically, pounding the side of the trailer.

More shouting. "We've got you surrounded! Drop your weapons!"

"*La policía*," she shouted to the woman. "Call out to the police. I can't open the door."

She ran up to the second trailer and called out her sister's name. No hands, no voices, just a smell that was becoming all too familiar to her. The fetor of death. She peered into the trailer and held her breath to keep from retching. It was too dark to see, but she knew there was a dead body in there. She turned her back on the door and raised her cuffed hands toward the latch, pulling her shoulder muscles as she stretched, but she couldn't reach it.

"Don't be in there, Irene, don't be in there."

The helicopter swooped overhead, and in the glare of its lights, she saw a white tennis shoe lying outside the trailer, stained with blood.

"Somebody's gonna pay for this!" she clearly heard J.W. shouting. And then a barrage of bullets rang out against the metal blades of the helicopter. Sounded like a machine gun or an automatic. The helicopter rose out of range.

"Shots fired! Shots fired!" a man called out.

Ivon ran toward the red bus. The door faced away from the gunfire, but then somebody shot at Ivon and shattered the windshield of the bus.

"Ivon, get down! Take cover!" It sounded like Detective McCuts. Where had he come from? He was right behind her.

She heard someone racking a round, and two more shots rang out, so close the report deafened her for a moment.

"Irene?" she yelled.

"*¡Cabrona!*" she heard a woman screech from inside the bus.

Another spray of bullets. She heard McCuts cry out and then curse.

"Goddammit, get down!" McCuts barked. She saw him leaning against the side of the bus.

"I have to find Irene," she told him. The door of the bus fell open, and a woman leapt down the stairs, howling like crazy. Ivon stepped in front of her. It was Ariel.

"You fucking bitch," she said, "I knew you were lying."

The woman's eyes darted manically in her bruised face.

"Where's my sister? Did they hurt her? Did they kill her?"

Ariel had raw welts across her neck, as if somebody had tried to choke her, and her face looked like it had gotten pummeled.

"*¡La voy a matar!*" the woman screamed. "*Hija de su chingada madre*, I'm going to kill her myself!"

Ivon snapped her head forward and hit Ariel between the eyes. Blood spurted out of her nose. Ivon hit her again, and the woman stumbled and fell down.

The helicopter had flown up even higher. For a moment, everything was completely still.

"Irene!" Ivon hollered. "Run Irene! Run to the cemetery! Behind us!"

Ivon kicked Ariel in the ribs, and again in the face, knowing that this bitch had been involved with her sister's kidnapping.

"Ivon!" McCuts wheezed behind her. "Enough! Can't you see she's passed out? Here, turn around." She felt him unlocking the handcuffs. He bent down and snapped them on Ariel.

Sirens blazing, lights flashing, a bevy of police cars suddenly swarmed into the plant. "Finally!" said McCuts.

"I think she's alive," Ivon said, huffing. "I think she escaped."

"Did you see her?"

"We have to go after her, McCuts."

She hadn't noticed until then that he was bleeding. He'd been shot in the thigh. His head was shaking from the pain. Blood bubbled out over his jeans.

"Shit, McCuts, you're wounded. You can't go after her. Give me your gun."

"I can't surrender my weapon," he said, jerking his leg up.

"I know how to shoot."

"It's against the rules."

He just stood there on one leg, looking at her, bleeding over his boots.

"Irene's out there, alive, I know it. Help me save her."

He handed her his gun. "It's a .40 caliber," he said. "Don't need to pull the slide back. I already shot someone." She nodded.

He spoke into his walkie-talkie. "Officer down," he said.

Ivon dashed away from the trailers, the gun warm and heavy in her hand. The helicopter pumped overhead again.

42

UNDER THE SEARCHLIGHTS OF THE HELICOPTER, Ivon's shadow stretched out long and thin over the black ground. She was sprinting toward the cemetery. Maybe Irene had heard her and knew what direction to follow. Behind her, even over the shrill cry of the sirens, she heard J.W.'s voice barking out a command to the dogs through the megaphone.

"Silver and Tonto! Away!"

Mother of God, Ivon prayed, keep her alive, don't let the dogs catch her, please, those dogs are trained to kill.

She kept running. She could see crosses and headstones up ahead. The dogs were panting behind her, their paws scuttling through the loose gravel. She gripped the gun in both hands and turned to shoot at them. She had forgotten the recoil of a semi-automatic and lost her balance. The dogs loped off to the side, tracking someone else.

The helicopter lights didn't reach as far as the cemetery, but the moon was high and she could make out the headstones more clearly. Suddenly, she heard a scream. A girl screaming. The dogs had found their target.

"Irene?" she yelled, "Is that you?"

"Help me!" she heard, off to the right. A gritty voice she didn't recognize, speaking English.

"Is that you, Lucha?" Her voice echoed. Down below, she heard ambulance and fire truck sirens.

"Ivon!" her sister wailed. "Ivon, over here!"

She heard snarling, and suddenly a scream. Ivon froze in her tracks. Her hands shook so hard she nearly dropped the gun.

301

"Kick them!" Ivon shouted, running toward the sound of the snarling. "Kick the fuckers!" She was tripping over rocks, over scrub brush and concrete slabs, her shoe caught on some barbed wire. The dogs were going to tear her sister apart if she didn't hurry.

"Talk to me!" she called out. "I can't see you."

But all she could hear now was her sister moaning. She steadied the gun and shot into the air to scare off the dogs. And then she saw it. A shadow streaking across the graveyard, gleaming silver in the moonlight, coming at her. She could hear the rumbling in his throat. Ivon stumbled back. The dog lunged and she pulled the trigger two times. Blood and bone matter spattered her face.

"Irene!" she called out, holding her breath.

No response.

"Lucha?"

Nothing. She fainted, that's all, she's not dead, Ivon told herself. She ran in the direction the dog had come from. And then she saw her. Irene had crawled inside the railing of one of the burial plots, crouched at an awkward angle between a clump of tumbleweeds and the headstone. She was naked and covered with blood. The other dog was standing guard over his prey, his throat warbling.

"Get off her you son of a bitch, I'll fucking kill you!" she told the other dog as she approached. He let her come two feet away before he attacked. She spread her legs, braced herself for the recoil, and pulled the trigger two, three times. The dog yelped and crashed on top of her. For a second she felt stunned, dog blood running hot over her skin. She could not feel the gun in her hand anymore.

"By the woods, by the woods, by the woods," she heard Irene singing in a ragged, high-pitched voice.

Ivon threw off the animal's heavy corpse, scrambled over the railing, and pried the tumbleweed out of Irene's hands.

"I'm here, baby," she said. "You're going to be okay."

"Black dove," Irene continued to sing. "Black dove."

She was hurt. Her baby sister was hurt bad.

"You're not a helicopter."

Ivon could see where the dogs had ripped into the back of Irene's leg from the middle of her thigh down to the heel of her foot, black gnarled flesh and torn veins bleeding over the tombstone. Her knees and elbows were scraped raw.

"But I have to get to Texas." She started to shake.

Dimly, Ivon was aware of more light in the cemetery now, like car headlights beaming in their direction.

"Irene! Listen to me! Can you move?"

The girl stared at her. "Ivon?"

"Yes, it's me, baby. Let me hold you." Ivon kicked the tumbleweeds out of the way and scooted behind her, holding her waist to help her stretch out. The girl leaned back in Ivon's arms, trembling, and Ivon saw raw bite marks all over her breasts. One had nearly torn off the nipple. Stripes of blood poured down her pale belly. The trembling got worse. She was going into shock.

Ivon put her arms around her, careful not to touch her wounds. "How you doing, Lucha?" she said, throat full of needles.

Irene clutched Ivon's hands. "I was lonely every day," Irene said.

Ivon started to sob. A tiny memory she had forgotten. Six-year-old Irene saying goodbye to her at the airport, Ivon leaving for college in Iowa. Not allowing herself to cry, Irene had said, "Pancho, I thought you were gonna help me with my homework. I'm gonna be lonely every day."

It was Irene's voice she heard in that little boy's at the bookstore.

"*¡Aquí están!*" she heard a man's voice cry out.

"Run down and get the ambulance," said a woman in English. "Get those dogs out of here, now."

The air smelled of gunpowder and wet animal.

43

Ivon watched the intern pluck shards of glass, debris, and dog hair out of the raw flesh of her arm. She didn't even remember how she'd gotten that wound. With all that glass embedded in it, it must have happened before the dog attacked her, must have been when they shot out the windshield of the red bus. Her stomach felt woozy from the tetracycline the paramedics had given her in the ambulance. She'd had to get a tetanus shot, too, for the gouge in her chin. She could still feel the dog pouncing on her, the hot spray of his blood over her face.

Something moved out of the corner of her eye, and she looked up. A tall, dark-haired woman in a blue slip dress was approaching the gurney. Brigit—miraculous as her name.

Ivon raised her arms to her, like a child.

"Can't let you out of my sight," Brigit said, blue eyes silvering with tears. She cradled Ivon's head between her hands, and Ivon bawled against her breasts, leaving slobbery tear marks and bloodstains from her chin wound all over the paisley print of her lover's dress.

"What's wrong with your face?" Brigit touched her cheeks very lightly. Ivon didn't answer. She was starting to see big white spots everywhere.

"Combination of sunburn and sandblasting," the intern responded to Brigit's question.

That's the last thing Ivon heard before she passed out.

"WE SEEM TO HAVE A DISCREPANCY HERE, Miss Villa, between what you're saying happened and what the witnesses we talked to at the scene said."

She blinked at the mustache moving in front of her face. Badge, gun, uniform.

"Oh," she said, "you're a cop." She wasn't sure if there were four of them or two of them that she was seeing double. Where was Brigit? Brigit had been standing right there next to her in the emergency room just a minute ago. Her watch said it was almost four o'clock, but she couldn't figure out if that was A.M. or P.M. Her chin itched and she scratched around the bandage.

"She needs to rest," someone said.

She glanced around and realized she was in the waiting room and it was like seeing a carousel full of relatives. Grandma praying the rosary, Aunt Fátima sitting between her son, William, and her husband, Uncle Michael, Gaby curled up on another sofa, her head in her dad's lap, Uncle Joe reading the newspaper, Grandpa and Patrick playing dominoes on one of the coffee tables, Aunt Lulu and her proverbial knitting basket off to the side, even Great-aunt Esperanza was there, nodding off in her wheelchair. The only ones missing were her mom, Ximena, and Brigit. The rest of them were just sitting there staring at Ivon and the policemen.

"Is Irene okay?" she asked no one in particular.

"She's in intensive care, *m'ijita*," Uncle Joe said. "Pulled through the surgery just fine."

"Ma'am, we need to ask you a few more questions," said a freckle-faced cop.

"Look, I already told the other guys what happened," said Ivon. Her mouth tasted like she'd been sucking on nails. "How many times do I have to tell the same story?"

"Like I said, ma'am, there's some discrepancies we need to clear up."

All four officers stood up when an older, heavy-set man with brown hollows under his eyes walked in, followed by Father Francis. They were both carrying Styrofoam cups.

"Judge Ramírez, Your Honor, sir," said one of the policemen.

The judge nodded at them. "Sit down, sit down," he said.

"Did anybody else want coffee?" said the priest. "We brought extra."

Ivon watched the judge shaking hands with Grandma and Grandpa first, then the rest of the family. Mexican manners, no matter what.

"There was a caretaker up there," Mustache Man was studying his notes. "He's the one who alerted the ambulance where you were, and he said he chased away a pack of coyotes that were attacking your sister."

"I'm telling you they were trained dogs," Ivon said, "not coyotes. I shot those dogs myself," said Ivon. "You think I'm making that up? How do you think I got all this blood on me?" She looked down at her shirt. Someone had brought her a clean change of clothes. No blood or traces of violence other than her bandaged arm in a sling.

"We didn't find any dead animals up there, ma'am. No gun, either."

"What do you mean, no gun? It was Detective McCuts' own .40 caliber."

"Excuse me," the judge frowned, "did you say you were using my son's gun?"

"According to her statement, Detective McCuts willingly surrendered his weapon, sir."

The officers looked at each other and shook their heads.

"He'd been shot," Ivon told the judge. "He gave me his gun so I could go after Irene. He knew the dogs were after her."

"How is he? Your son?" Grandma asked the judge.

Father Francis steadied the judge as he lowered himself into a chair next to Grandma.

The man's eyes looked weary. He pinched a scalloped edge around his white cup. "The transfusion went well, and he's all patched up, but he went into a coma from the shock. He'd almost flatlined by the time they brought him in. Massive hemorrhage, they call it. We don't know yet, if it affected any of his organs."

"I didn't realize he'd been hit that bad," said Ivon.

"The bullet perforated a major blood vessel in the groin," said the judge. "He almost bled to death out there. God willing, he's going to pull through."

"If you'd like, I can give him his last rites," said Father Francis. "Just in case."

Aunt Fátima covered her mouth and wept into a wad of tissue.

"I don't think that will be necessary, Father, but I do thank you for donating blood."

"I'm really sorry to hear that, sir," said Ivon.

"Wasn't your fault. He knew better than to give you his gun."

"From what dispatch told us," said Freckles, "he'd been following you all day. His story corroborates what you're saying about the Border Patrol arresting you and taking you out to ASARCO. He didn't know what was going on out there and called in the troops. Looks like he disobeyed orders in all kinds of ways and gave pursuit, probably moved in too soon, before backup got there."

"He helped save my sister's life," said Ivon.

The judge nodded. "Just doing his job," was all he said.

The officers were looking impatient. Freckles kept checking his watch and Mustache Man riffled the pages of his notebook so much it made her dizzy. There were two of them, not four. Ivon's head was starting to clear.

"Look, I don't know why you all don't believe me," said Ivon.

"It's not that we don't believe you, Miss Villa, it's that this is a high profile case involving Border Patrol agents and police officers. After what happened to the two detectives who were almost beaten to death the other night in that same area, people are terrified. We don't want to make it worse now, do we? We've got TV, we've got reporters, every media you can think of downstairs in the lobby, waiting for our briefing. But our chief doesn't want to say anything until we figure out these inconsistencies."

He leafed through his notebook again. "Now, according to the ER doctor, the viciousness of the attack suggests it was a wild animal. That corroborates the caretaker's statement about the pack of coyotes. You're saying different."

"They were *not* wild animals. They were trained fucking canines."

"Jesus, Mary, and Joseph, what language," Aunt Lulu piped in, knitting needles clicking away. "And in front of a judge, too."

"Mom, stay out of it," said two identical women in unison. Ivon hadn't even recognized her cousins Yolanda and Zenaida sitting over by the television.

"Hey," said Ivon, smiling wanly, "it's the XYZ Club."

They wiggled their fingers at her and turned back to watch the television.

"Ma'am, we really need to get this story right," said Mustache Man. "So you're saying you're positive they weren't coyotes?"

"Absolutely positive," said Ivon.

"Can you describe them again, please?" said Freckles.

She was too groggy to put up a fight. "German Shepherds. One white, one black. Silver and Tonto. Taught to respond to movie lingo."

"Movie lingo?" said Freckles.

"Yeah, like 'cut!' and 'take one!' I'm telling you: these were expertly trained dogs, nothing feral about them. They weren't just trained to sniff out cars, either. These dogs were trained to attack and to kill. And this Border Patrol guy, this Captain J. Wilcox, he's a pervert and a stalker, and he staged my whole arrest so he could haul me up to ASARCO and have me watch my little sister getting 'melted down to bacon.' That's how he put it, the sick fuck. He's running an extreme pornography web site, extremely extreme, and I think he uses the dogs to dispose of the women he kills online . . ."

"*Ave María Purísima*," mumbled Aunt Lulu.

". . . I saw women up there locked up in horse trailers, and he kept talking about how he was going to feed the dogs their protein, so I'm guessing he feeds human flesh to those dogs . . ."

"I'm going to need to ask you to keep your voice down, ma'am," Mustache Man said. "With your permission, judge, I'd like to tell this young lady something that I probably shouldn't be telling her but that might explain our confusion here."

Judge Ramírez assented. The lines in his face were etched so deeply, they looked like white scars against his brown skin.

"We already checked with the Border Patrol and the INS about the dogs. There's no K-9 unit that has any dogs named Silver and Tonto. They just do not exist."

Ivon felt her ears heating up. "I see, so maybe I'm just some stressed, hysterical female, and none of what I said really happened. Is that what you're saying?" Her voice caught as if she were going to cry. She held her breath and pressed her fingers over her eyes.

"*Pobrecita*," she heard her grandma say. "She needs to rest."

"Officers," said the judge, "I think that's enough for now. The young lady's given her statement, and now she's entitled to some private time with her family."

"Yes, sir, Your Honor," said one of the cops curtly.

They were gone before Ivon opened her eyes. "Where's my mom?" said Ivon.

"Ximena and your friend went with her to the chapel," said Grandma, walking over to sit next to Ivon. She placed an arm around her granddaughter's shoulders and held her tight. "Irenita is a strong girl, just like her big sister, eh?" Grandma kissed her cheek, squeezing her shoulders at the same time, and Ivon realized how sore the muscles in her upper body felt, as though she'd overdone it at a workout.

"Was your girl badly wounded?" the judge asked.

"They got her in the ICU now," said Uncle Joe. "There was a lot of infection. A lot of cutting and mending. And they found zinc poisoning, too."

"Did they pump her stomach?" Ivon said. "Or x-ray it, at least. She's probably got pennies in there."

"Hush, *m'ijita*." Grandma patted her back.

"I mean it. They need to look in her stomach. The pervert makes them eat pennies."

"They're gonna give her rabies shots," offered Gaby.

The judge shook his head in sympathy. "Will she be able to walk?"

"We're not sure. Depends on how much damage was done to the nerve."

"Did they . . . I mean, was she . . . you know . . ."

"Raped?" said Gaby.

"*Cállate*," Uncle Joe said to the girl. "Nobody was talking to you."

"Of course she was raped!" interjected Great-aunt Esperanza in her gravelly voice.

"They didn't find any traces of semen," Patrick stepped in, "but there was evidence of penetration . . . and a lot of bruising . . ."

"Evidence of what?" shouted Grandpa.

". . . They found wood particles inside her."

"They raped her with a piece of wood?"

"At least she won't get pregnant."

"You're such an idiot!"

"What if she can't ever swim again?"

"Men like that should be castrated," Great-aunt Esperanza declared.

"If it were up to me," said the judge, "they'd get the chair."

"Does anyone want more coffee?"

Grandma was rubbing Ivon's back in circles, and Ivon became aware of a deep sorrow in her bones, like she wanted to cry for days. But she was too exhausted to cry.

"*Bueno*, I need to go check on Pete." The judge lumbered to his feet. "He'll be in room 641 if anyone wants to visit him."

He came up to Ivon and held her hand between both of his. "You're a brave woman," he said. "And I don't think you're making anything up. Pete was working on something that might help explain a few things." He pulled a folded post-it note out of the inside pocket of his jacket and handed it to Ivon. "I found this on his desk. I thought you should have it."

"Thank you," said Ivon, her throat taut. She unfolded the note and read what Pete had scribbled in pencil: *Over 600 rso's in El Paso? Why so many? Why here? Why classified?*

"What's 'rso' stand for?"

"Registered sex offenders. The governor didn't want it made public that there's an inordinate number of sex offenders being given one-way tickets to El Paso."

"One-way tickets? When did El Paso become the dumping ground for perverts?"

"Isn't the border the dumping ground for all forms of pollution?"

"Do they get free reign? Can they cross over to Juárez whenever?"

"They're not supposed to leave town, much less cross over to Mexico. They wear these bracelets that help the police monitor their whereabouts, and their names are on file with the immigration service and the Border Patrol."

"So if they do cross, the authorities would know about it, and they'd get sent back to jail."

"Technically speaking."

"That's a weird coincidence, don't you think? All these sex offenders living in El Paso and all those sex crimes happening in Juárez."

The judge shook his head. "There's a map in Pete's office. You should take a look at it." He started to walk away.

"Can I walk you to the elevator?" she said. She tried to stand up but the room spun.

"Better stay put," the judge said, holding her up. "Come see us later."

"Nobody tells me anything!" Grandpa hollowed after the judge had left.

Patrick changed the subject. "*¿Cómo está su rodilla?*" he asked the old man.

"*¿Que qué?*" said Grandpa.

"*Su rodilla.* How's your knee, homes?"

"*¡No, yo no me surro en la silla!* I may be old, but I don't shit in my chair, *baboso!*"

Everyone cracked up. It was the same joke they'd been playing on Grandpa for years, just because his hearing aid didn't help much anymore and he was always confusing the words *su rodilla* with *surro en la silla*.

If only they hadn't given her all those drugs, she'd be halfway to the parking lot by now. She'd drive over to McCuts' office, wherever that was, and take a look at that map. But Grandma's strong fingers were massaging the back of her head, and Ivon felt suddenly very tired. Her legs twitched and she let her head rest on Grandma's shoulder.

"*Duérmete, m'ijita, duérmete.*"

FROM ELBOW TO WRIST, it felt like she had fire under the skin of her left arm. Someone was pressing a wet paper towel against her forehead, wiping down her cheeks and neck. It took all her strength to open her eyelids. She was lying on one of the sofas of the waiting room.

"Hey, sleepyhead," said Brigit. "They're bringing you another pain killer, okay? You've been groaning and moaning in your sleep for the last hour."

Ivon tried to move, but the pain in her arm paralyzed her for a moment. The *Today Show* was on. All the relatives had left.

"How's Irene?" Ivon sat up too fast, and the room tilted.

"Slow down," said Brigit. "She's resting. They haven't been able to give her the vaccine yet, because of all the infection, so they're zapping her with major antibiotics, and she's passed out. Probably won't wake up till tomorrow, they said. So why don't we go get some rest? You look awful, Ivon, like you haven't slept the whole week you've been here."

"Did my mom leave, too?"

"She went with Patrick and Ximena. They were going to get your sister's car out of the Border Patrol impound, and your mom was going to drive it home. Ximena said she'd catch up to us at Grandma Maggie's."

"I can't deal with all those folks at Grandma Maggie's house right now, Brigit. I'd rather go get a room, somewhere close by."

"Hey, that's fine with me. I've got my luggage in Ximena's van."

A nurse showed up with two white capsules in a white paper cup. "Vicodin and penicillin," said the nurse. "No alcohol." She handed Ivon a prescription for the two drugs.

"They gave her some tetracycline earlier," Brigit told the nurse.

"If you want I can get you tetracycline instead," said the nurse.

"Never mind," said Ivon, tossing the capsules back with some old coffee.

"So, shall we go?" Brigit looked paler than normal.

"Yeah, let's go. But let me look in on Irene, at least."

"Okay, you do that, and I'll go get the van and wait for you outside the entrance."

Ivon got to her feet. "Thank God you're here," she said, leaning against Brigit.

"Thank the Goddess," said Brigit, kissing her forehead. "Oh, I almost forgot. Someone called you on Ximena's phone a little while ago. She's called twice, already, says her name is Ruby. She's in a hurry because she's got a show to do this morning, she says, but it's urgent that she talk to you."

Brigit handed her Ximena's flip-top phone. "This Ruby woman needs you to call her back as soon as you wake up. I wrote the number down."

Ivon dialed the number, and Rubí picked up on the first ring.

"*¿Qué pasó*, Rubí? I have a real good exclusive for you," said Ivon sarcastically.

"Look, we go on the air in twenty minutes," said Rubí, "and Walter isn't even here. I don't have time to talk about this thing right now." Her voice sounded frigid.

"Talk about what thing?" Ivon walked toward Irene's room as she talked.

"I need the videotape back."

Ivon realized something was very wrong. Her guard came up instantly. "You know what's on it, then?"

"No, and I don't want to know. I just need it back, please. It's urgent."

"Why? Are you afraid I might see a little girl getting raped and strangled on camera?"

"Please don't talk about this on the cell phone, Ivon."

Ivon stepped into Irene's darkened room. "The scene didn't look simulated to me," she said, lowering her voice so she would-n't disturb her sister. The girl was deep in a drugged sleep, arms and hands bandaged, leg in a sling, her Curious George tucked under her chin. Ivon walked up to her and, out of habit, placed the back of her hand against the girl's mouth to make sure she was breathing.

"I'm going to have to hang up if you don't stop talking about this, Ivon."

"That little girl was actually raped and choked to death just to get someone off. You should have seen the effect it had on Mr. Border Patrol guy. You do realize that's why I was arrested, right? *La Migra* thought I was trafficking in child pornography. Child smut is more like it. On a videotape labeled *Mujeres sin Fronteras*."

"That's impossible!"

"It's right there on the tape, Rubí, spliced in with your interview with Norma Flores."

"Ivon, please. It's urgent that I get that tape back."

Ivon stroked Irene's forehead.

"I don't have it any more. It got confiscated last night by that nice *migra* that sicced these huge German Shepherds on my sister and me."

A pause. "The *migra* kept it?" Rubí's voice shook. "Do you know what he did with it?"

"To tell you the truth, I was more concerned with saving my sister's life."

Long silence. "What is this all about, Rubí?"

"Can you meet me somewhere? We need to discuss this face to face."

"My little sister has just gotten out of major surgery after a traumatic experience, and you want me to leave the hospital to go meet you?"

Ivon bent over to kiss Irene's cheek. There were scratches and bruises on the girl's face.

"You don't understand, Ivon. My own family is at risk here. If that tape gets broadcast, it'll ruin me. It'll ruin my entire family."

The phone clicked. Ivon dialed Rubí's number again, but she got the voice mail. "Hi, this is Rubí's daughter, Amber. Leave her a message. My mom's busy saving the world right now."

"Are you okay, hon?" The woman at the nurse's station was staring at her with concern. "Can I get you something?"

"No . . . thanks. I was just looking in on my little sister."

"612? Dog bites?"

"Yeah, that's her."

"She's lucky to be alive. Those animals almost chewed off her leg."

"Do you know anything about the surgery?"

"Let's see. I've got her chart right here." She handed the clipboard to Ivon.

She tried to translate the medicalese. From what she could figure, the skin around the bites had become acutely infected, and they'd had to cut away a lot of the tissue and wash out the wounds with several doses of antirabies solution. The tendons from the hamstrings to the Achilles had been damaged. The surgeon had taken skin grafts from Irene's backside to sew up part of the leg. It looked like they were giving her a prognosis of twelve months for the nerve damage on the ankle to heal. She would need plastic surgery to reconstruct the heel and the mangled nipple, and several months of physical therapy to restore full mobility to the leg. The doctor also recommended counseling with a specialist on traumatic injuries.

"Is she in any pain, you think?" Ivon asked the nurse, returning the clipboard.

"She's on a steady diet of painkillers and antibiotics. She ain't feeling no pain right now. As soon as the infection settles down, she'll get her first rabies shot. Now that's gonna hurt."

"How many does she have to get?"

"After the first one, she'll get a second two days later, a third two days after that, and one a week for the next three weeks."

"I just don't see why she's got to have this rabies treatment. Those were not wild animals. Why doesn't anybody believe me?"

"You know, hon, they do things by the book around here. The hospital is required by law to administer rabies vaccines if the animal was feral or not available for quarantine. What're you gonna do? Better safe than sorry."

"Yeah, I guess you're right. Thanks for letting me see her chart."

"She's one healthy girl. A little banged-up, but we're gonna take good care of her. Praise Jesus."

No thanks to Jesus, she's banged up all right, Ivon wanted to say, gang-banged and dog-bitten and lonely every day. She couldn't let herself think about what they'd done to Irene. Made her crazy, made her want to kill someone.

She decided to look in on Pete—he was on the same floor, just down another hallway—and found the door open. The judge was asleep in his chair, chin resting on his tie, holding his son's hand. On the other side of the bed, a butch-looking Mexican woman in overalls and work boots was reading the sports page aloud to Pete.

The woman looked up over her reading glasses and held Ivon's gaze.

"Is he okay?" Ivon whispered. "I'm Ivon Villa."

"*Mi'jo,* that girl you have a crush on is here," she said, and continued to read.

44

AMBER LUNA REYNA WOULD NEVER admit to anyone that she watched her mother's talk show, *Mujeres sin Fronteras,* on weekday mornings. The remote sat right next to her on the bed, just in case her little brothers or Papi Wally or even the maid walked into her room, and she had to pull a quick channel switch.

"Thank you for tuning in to *Mujeres sin Fronteras,* where, as you know, women have no borders, no boundaries, and no check-points," her mom was saying into the camera.

On the outside, her mom's media popularity, especially when she got arrested for disturbing the peace, as she had two weeks ago at the picket of the electric company, embarrassed Amber. She would roll her eyes at her friends every time any of them mentioned they'd seen her mom on TV. Secretly she admired her mom's single-minded ambition and the fearless way she did whatever she wanted to do. But most of the time, Amber just felt abandoned.

Before she became a celebrity, her mom used to take her to school every day. On Fridays, after school, they'd go shopping or to a movie. On Saturdays it was beauty day, and they'd spend all morning at the country club beauty parlor, getting their hair and nails done. Then they'd meet Papi Wally and the boys for lunch at the clubhouse. On Catholic holidays when Amber's school was closed, her mom would take her to UTEP, just to give her a taste of college life. She introduced Amber to all her friends and teachers as her best friend.

Once her mom graduated, everything changed. The campus visits stopped, the shopping and beauty days ended. And then her mom approached Clara Apodaca, daughter of the president of

Channel 33, with this crazy idea of starting a talk show for women. The station managers agreed, thinking it would be a cooking and fashion show that would help them draw advertising to the channel, but Rubí Reyna had another idea. She convinced them that what Juárez needed was a show that focused on professional women and that they could use the show to inform women about the murders and at the same time use the murders to raise the ratings of the show. Now, thanks to *Mujeres sin Fronteras*, instead of spending time with her mom, Amber got to watch her on TV.

Her grandpa Ignacio (Iggy, she called him) was right. Her mom's fascination for these crimes was bordering on the fanatical. "A dangerous obsession with other people's causes," that's what Iggy said, and he would say it straight up to her mom's face. All her mom would do was shrug and say, "It's my life, Papi, you don't control me anymore." Iggy always got furious at that.

Even her grandmother would have something to say, although she was almost always on her mom's side. She would say, "Don't be disrespectful to your father, Rubí. He just means there are consequences to what you're doing. He's afraid you aren't taking those consequences into consideration. You have a family to think about. Your poor father gets an ulcer attack every time he watches your show."

"Tell him to watch something else," her mom would say.

The show's two guests today were enemies, according to her mom, who was feeling very proud of herself for having gotten them to agree to come on the show together. Dorinda Sáenz, the special prosecutor in the case of the murdered women, looked more like a prostitute than a lawyer in her peroxide-tinted hair, tight skirt, and scarlet lipstick. Paula Del Río, founder of an organization that advocated for the protection of women against sex crimes and domestic abuse in Juárez, kind of reminded Amber of her grandmother. Sitting beside them in her pageboy haircut, navy pantsuit, and string of pearls, her mom could have been a model on the cover of *Marie Claire*. Except there was something wrong with her mom today. She looked nervous. She was fidgeting with her pearls, and her eyes kept blinking.

"This is precisely part of the problem that my office is encountering, you see, Rubí," the prosecutor was saying. "I and my team of investigators have instituted a methodical questioning of victims' families, friends, employers, coworkers, neighbors—all to determine a pattern of life that might explain some reasons for their deaths. But political groups like CARIDAD, who do not have the training, the expertise, or the authority to investigate these crimes, are putting forth theories and statistics that have nothing to do with the official story."

The older woman was about to interrupt, but the prosecutor didn't give her a chance to speak.

"Don't get me wrong, I respect the work of your organization, Paula . . ." She gave the other woman a haughty look. "As I respect the time and dedication that other civilian groups have given to organizing field sweeps and helping the victims' families. Part of the reason I accepted this invitation to come on the show, in fact, is to thank you publicly for the service that CARIDAD provides to the community. But I am also here, officially, to implore you to leave the task of the investigation to the authorities. We all realize we have a killing epidemic on our hands, and it is not helping matters for these civilian groups to stir up the public any more than it is already stirred up over these brutal murders. They are creating massive confusion in the community with their political ideas and contradictory theories."

"May I speak now?" said Paula Del Río.

"Please, yes, of course," said her mom.

The camera did an unflattering close-up of the older woman, her pale gray face and long gray hair filling the screen. "CARIDAD and other activist groups like CARIDAD," she spoke softly, "are nongovernmental organizations that formed in response to the lack of interest or concern that the authorities Miss Sáenz is talking about have shown for the families of the victims, or for the victims themselves, who, as you have just heard, are blamed for their own murders, are considered nothing more than ignorant or loose-moraled females putting themselves at risk. Thanks to the *rastreos* of groups like CARIDAD, 8 de Marzo, Mujeres por Juárez, Voces sin Eco, and Contra el Silencio in El Paso, many more victims have been found, and we have been able to answer the ques-

tion 'Where is my daughter?' Although the answer in many cases
has been a tragic one in the form of a dead body turning up in a
deserted lot somewhere."

Amber shuddered. It grossed her out to think of sifting
through garbage dumps looking for dead bodies. Her mom had
done that yesterday—she would do anything for that dumb show
of hers—and had come home totally depressed. Instead of going
over, to Iggy and 'Bueli's house for their Sunday barbecue, her
mom and Papi Wally had spent the rest of the day arguing about
whether or not to let Amber go on her vacation to Cancún next
week. Amber had to call her grandfather to the rescue. Iggy saved
the day, as usual, and even got Amber an extra two days out of the
bargain. Despite their always arguing with each other, when it
came to Amber, Iggy was the only one who could make her mom
change her mind.

"There are infinite complications here, Rubí," the Sáenz
woman was saying. "The meddling of all these groups and the
media that supports them is angering the authorities."

"The authorities have been very comfortable at their desks,
playing with their cell phones and their guns," Paula Del Río
rebutted, "taking statements and profiling victims. Until groups
like CARIDAD got involved, they were not about to bother themselves with the dirty work of looking for the missing girls or finding the perpetrators. If this is what Miss Sáenz calls confusion,
then I suppose she's right. It must be very confusing for the general population to understand why the authorities say there are
only sixty-three victims, when in fact one-hundred-thirty-nine
bodies have been found, and who knows how many hundreds of
others are still missing."

"That statistic is a gross exaggeration," the prosecutor
declared, smacking the couch.

Amber pushed the cotton wads out from between her freshly
painted toenails—a bright fuchsia today, to match the color of the
bikini she was going to buy later with her friend, Myrna. She was
so excited about her vacation, she could hardly wait to board the
plane next Sunday. It wasn't the first time she'd been to Cancún—
her grandparents owned a time-share there—but it was the first

time Amber would travel by herself, without any family watching her like hawks. Myrna's family would be there, but it wasn't the same as having her mom's or Papi Wally's or even 'Bueli's suspicious eyes following her around all day.

She pulled on her white tube top, stepped into her baggie pink overalls, and slipped on her DKNY platform shoes, admiring her fuchsia toes. The phone rang, and she leapt on the bed to pick up the call.

"*Hola, chula.*" It was her boyfriend.

"*¿Quiubo, Héctor?*" She muted the volume on the television.

"I heard that you and Myrna were going shopping today."

"Who told you?"

"You know, I have my spies," he laughed.

She didn't think that was funny. "There's some things we need for our vacation." She decided not to tell him that she and Myrna were going to look for matching bikinis. "Girl stuff, you know."

"Don't you think you should be saving your money for the trip?"

"So I shouldn't buy what I need?" Amber frowned at the phone. This was one of the things that bugged her about Héctor. He thought he had a right to tell her what to do with her money.

"Want a ride?"

So that's why he was calling. He wanted to get an invitation. But she and Myrna had plans and they did not include anybody's boyfriend tagging along after them at the mall.

"No, thanks. Papi Wally's dropping us off on his way to work."

"You want to get an ice cream later, then?"

"Sorry, but we have to go over to my grandparents' house. Iggy wants us to stay for dinner, and we won't get home until late, as usual."

"My cousin is having a *tardeada* on Saturday. I told him we'd go."

She frowned at the phone again and was tempted to hang up on him. "I have to pack for my trip on Saturday, you know. I *am* leaving the next day."

"It's just a *tardeada,* Amber, a few hours in the afternoon. I'm sure you can spare the time. Can't you pack on Friday?"

"Look, Héctor, if you want to invite me to a party, ask me first, don't just assume I can go because you say so. You know I can't stand it when you get all bossy."

She regretted having accepted his offer for a ride to the airport next Sunday. She would've rather gotten picked up by Myrna's mom. But then, she hadn't really accepted. It was more like Héctor had gone and asked her mom's permission to take her to the airport. Her mom had said, "That'll work out great, Héctor, thanks for asking. Walter and I have to go to Chihuahua next weekend to interview the governor."

"You're sounding more and more like your mom, Amber."

"Is that supposed to be a bad thing? Let me know, okay, so I can tell my mom what you really think of her."

"I didn't call to pick a fight with you. Why are you being so rude?"

"I'll see you tomorrow, okay?" she said.

"Have fun shopping."

"*Bueno*, bye," she said, and punched the off button on the wireless phone.

Amber was so looking forward to meeting a cute European guy in Cancún. It would help her make it easier to dump this macho type she'd been dating since her *quinceañera*. Just because she'd let him touch her down there, over her jeans, the night they went to the fair, didn't mean he owned her all of a sudden.

A commercial for Transportes La Reyna del Norte, her grandpa's red-bus fleet with a cheesy crown logo on each side, came on, and Amber went to get her makeup bag from the bathroom. She paused to look at herself in the mirror, double-checking that her blouse didn't make her look fat. Sometimes, she wished she'd inherited her mom's light skin, red hair, and green eyes, instead of her biological father's dark features. The only thing she and her mom had in common was their shoe size and their braces.

With her makeup bag, eyelash curler, tweezers, and magnifying mirror in tow, she sat down on the bed to finish watching the show while she plucked her eyebrows and scrutinized her face for blackheads. The phone rang, but Amber decided not to pick it up, in case it was Héctor calling to bug her again.

Now the camera zoomed in on Dorinda Sáenz, who was looking agitated and ready to pop Paula Del Río in the face. Amber turned up the volume.

"You feminist groups think it's always about patriarchy, and the majority of the people you are advocating for don't even know the meaning of the word. People, especially those poor people who migrate here from the interior, are concerned with making a decent living, getting an education for their children, paying the rent, buying food and medicine. Patriarchy doesn't mean anything to them, and groups like CARIDAD are just using these people and the tragic loss of their daughters to push their feminist agendas and raise money for themselves. You're not even sharing that money with the families of the victims. Convincing people that patriarchy is at fault does not bring us any closer to finding the killer. Besides, we can prove that at least 60 percent of the reported rapes and murders of women in this city have nothing to do with patriarchy. They are the result of gang wars with cholos, robberies, revenge, domestic fights, or crimes of passion."

Paula Del Río was shaking her head, looking at her mom like she could not believe the stupidities the other woman was saying. "The majority of the victims are very poor women from villages and *ranchos* in the interior. They are also very young women, many of them under the legal working age, who manage to get hired with false papers. In a society in which women are second-class citizens and in which the poor are no better than animals, a society where cows and cars are worth more than the lives of women, we are talking about the complete devaluation of the feminine gender, as well as the utter depreciation of the female laboring class. Were these crimes happening to men, were men being kidnapped, raped, mutilated, and dismembered, no matter what their class, we would already know the answers to the question of 'Who is killing the women of Juárez?' The authorities would not be wasting their time doing interviews. They would be out on the streets hunting the killers."

Someone knocked on Amber's door, and right away she changed the channel to an El Paso station. A "breaking news" report was on, the reporter standing in front of the ASARCO smokestacks. The words TRAGEDY AT ASARCO blazed over the screen.

"Amber? You ready?" called Papi Wally. "Myrna called. She's running late so she says she'll meet you at the Starbucks by the mall. I hope you're ready. I don't want to be late again. You know there's always an extra long line at the bridge on Mondays. I'll wait for you down in the car." Although he was sort of bilingual, Papi Wally only spoke to her and the boys in English because everyone always made fun of his Spanish.

"Oh, and you guys will have to call someone to pick you up this afternoon. Your mom and I have a meeting with the Maquiladora Alliance tonight."

"Okay," she said, "we'll call a taxi."

"No, you won't, you'll call your grandmother or your boyfriend. I don't want you taking taxis, I told you that."

"Okay, I'll call the National Guard!" she yelled.

Sometimes Papi Wally could be even more over protective than her mom. She dashed to the bathroom mirror once more to make sure her eyebrows looked even. Narrowing her eyes at her reflection, pouting her lips, she decided maybe it was a good thing she didn't look like her mom. She wouldn't want to trade her smooth olive complexion for her mom's freckled one. Her biological father might be an asshole, but at least he was a handsome asshole. He denied his paternity, but Amber had inherited his complexion, his sexy dimples, and deep-set eyes.

"Benavídez," she whispered her father's surname aloud, "Amber Benavídez." Yuck. She liked her own name better. Not that there had ever been any danger of her having her father's name, since Cruz Benavídez was as old as her grandfather and already married when he took advantage of her mom and got her pregnant. He was the richest man in Juárez, next to Carrillo Fuentes, they said, making his money the clean way through the maquiladoras rather than the other popular occupation in town. Her mom had been sent to live with relatives in Mexico City until the embarrassment passed.

Three years after Amber was born, her mom came back to Juárez, started college at UTEP, and met Papi Wally in one of her journalism classes. The joke was always that it was three-year-old Amber who had proposed to him, asking "will you be my *papi?*"

Papi Wally had no choice but to marry her mom. Now, her little brothers, Jade and Jasper, *were* freckle-faced *güeros* like her mom, and legitimate boys to boot. But Amber was still her grandparents' *and* Papi Wally's favorite, and she knew it. Nobody ever talked about her Benavídez connection.

Amber gathered her black curly hair into a high ponytail and applied another layer of lipstick, still listening to the TV report.

"A missing El Paso girl believed to have been kidnapped after attending the Juárez Expo Fair last week was found seriously wounded, but alive at the scene."

The Expo Fair? Amber ran over to the television. They were talking about that *pocha* girl she had met with Myrna the other night. She sat on the edge of the bed to watch the report.

"The devil is loose," her mom had said when they first heard the news of the girl's kidnapping. "I don't want you going back to the fair ever again, me oiste?"

"But she wasn't taken from the fair," Amber argued. "They said she was taken from a *colonia*. I wouldn't go near a *colonia*. I'm not that crazy."

Her mom stood her ground. Amber let it go. Didn't matter anyway, she'd rather go to Cancún than the stupid Juárez fair any day.

"A shoot-out between the kidnappers and the police resulted . . ." the report droned on, but Papi Wally was tooting his silly horn outside.

She ran to the window and yelled out: "*Ya deja de pitar esa cosa. ¡Qué naco! Ya voy.*"

He'd installed a gizmo that played taps on his car horn. Sometimes Papi Wally was just too tacky for her. She turned off the television and hurried downstairs.

Myrna was going to die when she told her about that jackass, Héctor. She touched her earlobes and realized she'd forgotten to put on the 18-karat Bambi earrings that her grandparents had given her as a going-away-on-your-first-independent-vacation present. She didn't want to make Papi Wally mad, but how much harm would one extra little minute do if she just ran back upstairs and got the earrings out of her jewelry box?

Just as she stepped into her bedroom, Amber heard shots.

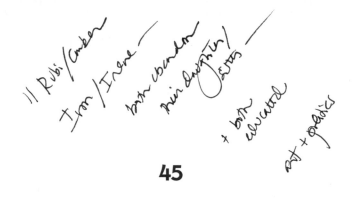

45

Holding the Line, Twenty-One-Gun Salute for Slain Officers

A multiagency sting operation on the Elephant Butte ring of pornographers ended in tragedy last night at the ASARCO refinery, killing two Border Patrol agents and a police officer, and seriously wounding Detective Pete McCuts, son of Judge Anacleto Ramírez of the District of El Paso. McCuts was shot in the leg and remains hospitalized in critical condition.

The bodies of eleven women, believed to be kidnapped victims of the pornographers, were recovered from trailers and warehouses on the site, some in advanced states of decomposition, leading authorities to believe that the women had been dead for at least 48 hours. An ASARCO representative stated that the refinery had shut down operations in January of this year and that the company had no knowledge of any illicit use of the property.

One victim was found alive, the teenager from Loretto High School who was kidnapped in Cd. Juarez last week. She had been trying to run away from the fracas and was attacked by coyotes in the Smelter Cemetery. She was rushed by ambulance to Sierra Hospital and is reported in stable condition. Her family had no comment at this time.

Services will be held Wednesday at 11 a.m. at St. Patrick's Cathedral, followed by a procession to Concordia Cemetery. EPPD Officer Steve García and BP Chief Detention Enforcement Officer Jeremy Wilcox and INS Officer Roy Apodaca will be honored with a twenty-one-gun salute.

They died in the line of duty, holding the line.

"This is utter bullshit!" Ivon yelled, throwing the newspaper down over the litter of bags and banana peels on the floor of Ximena's van. "How dare they say we had no comment? Those ass-holes! They didn't print a word I said. They kept asking me the same stupid questions, and none of what I said made it into the story. I'm calling the fucking *El Paso Times* right now."

She reached for the phone, but Brigit stayed her hand. "Not now, Ivon. No more stress. Your body needs to rest."

"But, Brigit! They're calling it a sting operation! They're saying that this Border Patrol pig was operating undercover. In other words, he was *infiltrating* the porn ring, not running it. That is complete bullshit."

"What do you expect them to say? The Border Patrol is a law enforcement agency, Ivon. Whose side do you think the police department is going to take, especially when their story can be corroborated and yours can't?"

"They're making this depraved maniac sound like a fucking hero! That hero was killing girls and women online, Brigit? Aren't you even the least bit incensed? He has a web site, a newsletter, a dot.com. For all we know, the fucker might not even be dead. They're probably protecting his ass, just like they made those dogs disappear."

Brigit placed her hand on Ivon's thigh. "Calm down. I'm out-raged, okay? But it's not going to do you any good right now to o.d. on more information. Give your brain a rest. We'll go get a room, take a shower, a nap, eat lunch later. Then you'll feel clear-er, and things will make more sense to you."

Brigit reached out to stroke the side of Ivon's face, but Ivon pulled away.

"I can't, Brigit. I can't let this go right now and just chill with you in a hotel room. The judge gave me some information earlier that I have to follow up on, I'm sorry."

Ivon picked up the phone again, and again Brigit stayed her hand.

"I'm not telling you not to follow up on things, Ivon. I'm say-ing take a break, get some rest. Right now, all you're doing is react-ing. You're like a puppet on a string, getting jerked around by every piece of information you hear. You need to get a hold of yourself, Ivon. Figure out how to act, not just react. You're the one who taught me that. You've been through a horrible, stressful ordeal, but Irene is safe, now. You can afford a couple hours of rest, baby."

"Brigit, look," Ivon said stubbornly, "I have to show you something." She dug the post-it note out of the little notebook she always stashed in her back pocket. "See? McCuts found a link that I think is really crucial to figuring out why all those women are being killed in Juárez. Apparently there are over 600 registered sex offenders in El Paso right now. There's a map in McCuts' office that the judge wants me to see." She riffled the pages of the notebook and found Pete's business card. "I have the address right here. It's the police station in Five Points. It's really close to Grandma Maggie's. Please. Let me just stop by there for a minute and check out that map."

"Have you forgotten you're on a schedule, Ivon?"

Ivon stared at her.

"Your dissertation, remember?"

"Oh shit." Ivon had forgotten all about the dissertation.

"Look at the date on your watch, honey."

Ivon checked her watch. June 15. She had exactly two weeks left to finish, or else, goodbye job, goodbye tenure, goodbye real estate. "Shit. Shit. Shit."

"If doing this other work is more important, I'll understand . . ."

"No, don't even say that, Brigit. I hate it when you get all co-dependent on me. You're right. It's June 15th and I'm on a schedule. I can't sabotage our security like this. I have to give it a rest. *Ni modo*."

Even though her brain was telling her it was imperative that she look at that map in Pete's office, that therein lay one of the answers to the riddle of silence that pervaded the murders, Ivon knew she could not allow herself to become obsessed with solving the Juárez murders. She had responsibilities and obligations of her own. Irene was safe, and Ivon had to switch gears now and focus on the dissertation.

"Hotel, then?" asked Brigit.

"Can I at least be alone for a *little* while and get my thoughts in order? Can you just drop me off somewhere, please, and give me, like, an hour to myself? I'll do anything you want after that, I promise."

"One hour, that's all you get," Brigit said, hiding her blue eyes behind sunglasses. "Where do you want me take you? Starbucks?" "No, I need to be outside. Take me to UTEP. There's this spot I've always loved off one of the university parking lots. It overlooks the river and the mountains in Juárez. I used to go there between classes when I was at la UTEP. Did a lot of thinking there."

"One more thing you haven't told me about," said Brigit. "Okay, which way?" Brigit backed the van out of the hospital parking lot.

Ivon gave her directions and looked at her watch again. Ten-fifteen, Monday morning, sunlight pouring out of a pristine blue Texas sky. Not a trace of smog today. The desert air was so clear it looked innocent. By the track at El Paso High School she had a panoramic view of the whole valley. She could almost see the eagle on the huge Mexican flag fluttering over El Chamizal in the distance.

The radio was tuned to a Mexican station. *"On Father's Day, the candidate for the Green Party of the State of Chihuahua will be dropping rosebuds over Lomas de Poleo and Lote Bravo, in commemoration of the dead daughters of Juárez. One-hundred-twenty pink and red rosebuds over the desert, one for each victim."*

"Rosebuds over the desert, that's a great election gimmick," Ivon retorted. "They should at least get their facts right. It's a hundred-thirty-nine, not a hundred-twenty dead daughters of Juárez, you idiots."

"How could there be so many dead women and we not know about it, Ivon?"

"Because who cares about girls from the south?" said Ivon. "Here, turn right on Sun Bowl Drive, and make a left into that second parking lot."

Brigit frowned at the dry scrub brush and mesquite at the back of the lot.

"Are you sure you're going to be safe out here, by yourself?"

Ivon stroked the silky skin of Brigit's thigh and felt a stirring between her legs. The last time she'd made love out here was with Raquel, her first semester of college. Raquel would bring her lunch once a week and they'd sit outside in what even back then Ivon called *mi lugarcito*, eating and watching the traffic on I-10.

Afterwards, they'd go back to the car and make love in the back seat. Just the thought of Raquel and what she'd done yesterday fizzled out Ivon's desire. She removed her hand.

"Don't worry, I'll be fine. Do you want to see my spot?"

Brigit shook her head. "I think I'll go check us in somewhere. We passed a motel on Mesa or Stanton back there. I'll go get your prescriptions filled, too. I'll be back in an hour."

Ivon kissed her, letting her tongue probe between Brigit's lips. "I love you."

"Go over there and do some of that breathing meditation I taught you," Brigit said.

Ivon got out of the car and trudged over to the little hill adjoining the parking lot. She followed a trail to a rocky ledge on the other side, facing the freeway, where she used to sit with her binoculars. It bowled her over to realize that from her spot, she could see straight into ASARCO, the twin phalluses of the smokestacks rising into the azure desert sky, Christ the Redeemer etched clear and white at the top of Mount Cristo Rey in the distance.

So far from the Truth, so close to Jesus.

Sitting here, she had gotten very familiar with the river, its ebbs and tides. When New Mexico wasn't hogging the water up north, the river was deep enough to swim in, and families from the *colonias* would come to play and bathe in the refinery-polluted water. At low tide, when the water was nothing more than a *charco sucio*, as her mother called it, a dirty puddle, *mojados* would cross at their leisure, not even needing to take off their pants. Now, since Silvestre Reyes had implemented Operation Hold the Line, since NAFTA had increased the Border Patrol's budget twelve-fold, the river looked abandoned, except for the *migra* trucks parked all along the levee. She didn't need binoculars to see the green and white vehicles stationed approximately two city blocks away from each other, for miles. Not that anything stopped the flow of the undocumented. The entire border economy, from agribusiness to city hall, from restaurants to laundries, and private homes to public parks, depended on undocumented labor. Operation Hold the Line was just a smokescreen, a way of justifying budget increases for *La Migra.*

So far from the Truth, so close to Jesus. ⟩ *Castillo*

This is what Ivon knew to be the truth: last week at this time she had been packing for her trip to El Paso, coming home to adopt a baby. Her blissful ignorance about what was happening just on the other side of *el charco* was staggering. Today her little sister was a rape victim. Other than getting mauled by dogs, who knew what other horrors she'd experienced, what post-traumatic stress she would have to live with the rest of her life? A detective playing guardian angel to Ivon lay comatose in a hospital bed. And the baby she had come to adopt had gotten murdered and muti-lated, along with his fifteen-year-old mother. She could feel the emotion rising in her chest, and switched tracks. She needed to think like a researcher, right now, look at the bigger picture.

Why were the bodies of one-hundred-thirty-nine *hijas de Juárez* rotting somewhere in the desert or the morgue? Who were they? Other than Irene and the other American girls, the others were called *muchachas del sur*, girls from the south: poor, young migrant women with dollar signs in their eyes and the American Dream of success and U.S. citizenship fastened to their hearts with safety pins. Underpaid, sexually exploited, forced to live in hovels made of *maquiladora* scrap in the middle of the desert, their reproductive cycles under surveillance at the factories where they worked, the tragedy of their lives did not begin when their desecrated bodies were found in a deserted lot. The tragedy began as soon as they got jobs at the *maquiladoras*. As soon as they had to take a pregnancy test with their application, as soon as they had to show their first soiled sanitary napkin to prove they were still menstruating.

She shaded her eyes with one hand and stared at the horizon, the ASARCO smokestacks lined up perpendicular to the white cross of Cristo Rey. A Border Patrol van was heading east on I-10. Holding the line, keeping America safe from invaders and wet-backs . . .

". . . especially women wetbacks," she said aloud, ". . . whose only power is reproductive." Like a FreeCell spread trying to fall into place in her head, she saw an order to her thoughts but she had to see them mapped out on paper. She got to her feet and dug her little notebook and pen out of her back pocket.

"NAFTA's brought thousands of poor, brown, fertile female bodies to the border to work at a *maquiladora*," she spoke aloud as she outlined her thoughts.

North American FREE TRADE Agreement
Maquiladoras
Poor Brown Fertile Female Bodies
Reproductive Monitoring
Pregnancy Tests
Forced Birth Control
No Maternity Leave

"Not all of them will get jobs. Not all of them will keep their jobs. Some might get pregnant. Others fired for being late. Some might get carpal tunnel syndrome or job-related injuries and be unemployable in the factory business."

What to do with all these fertile brown female
bodies on the border?

She chewed the top of her pen and thought about that question. "What happens if they cross over? More illegal Mexican women in El Paso means more legal brown babies. Who wants more brown babies as legal citizens of the Promised Land?"

Undocumented/Crossing over to El Paso
U.S.-born Mexican Babies
What's the price of "free trade"?

"Although we love having all that surplus labor to exploit, once it becomes reproductive rather than just productive, it stops being profitable. How do we continue to make a profit from these women's bodies and also curtail the threat of their reproductive power?"

J.W./Lone Ranger Productions (Texas Ranger)
Exxxtremely lucky penny web site
Women raped, tortured, mutilated, and killed online
Pennies in the bodies
Women expendable as pennies

"Is it just a coincidence that there are over 600 registered sex offenders being given one-way tickets to El Paso, and that nameless, faceless killers are decimating and desecrating the bodies of all these poor brown women in Juárez?"

Serial killers or judiciales?
Gangs or Border Patrol?
All of the above?
A factory of killers?

Pornographers, gang members, serial killers, corrupt policemen, foreign nationals with a taste for hurting women, immigration officers protecting the homeland—what did it matter *who* killed them? This wasn't a case of "whodunit," but rather of who was allowing these crimes to happen? Whose interests were being served? Who was covering it up? Who was profiting from the deaths of all these women?

Her head was pounding as though she'd just downed a triple espresso.

She saw the order of the cards, now. The threat that pregnancy posed to "free trade" revenue. The heavy policing of female reproductive power in the *maquiladoras* to safeguard that revenue. The use of pregnancy tests to filter the desirable from the undesirable, who were still desirable in another context. The overt sexualization of the bodies—not just murder, but violation and mutilation of the maternal organs, the breasts and nipples, the wombs and vaginas. The use of the Internet as a worldwide market for these same organs in easily accessible tourist sites and affordable online pornography. A cost-effective way of disposing of non-productive/reproductive surplus labor while simultaneously protecting the border from infiltration by brown breeding female bodies.

Clipped to Ivon's belt, Ximena's cell phone buzzed, the vibration making her jump.

"Scared me," Ivon said into the phone, not even bothering to check the caller i.d. Had to be either Brigit or Ximena.

"It's Raquel. I'm so upset right now." She sounded like she was crying. "I just heard that Rubí Reyna's husband . . . was shot down outside their house this morning. Execution style."

"Walter Luna?"

"He was going to take Rubí's daughter to the mall in El Paso. He was waiting for her in the car when they drove by."

"Who drove by? Did they get the daughter, too?"

"The girl was still in the house. Can you believe it? My niece, Myrna, was going to drive with them, but I was late picking her up. *Dios mío.* She'd be dead, too."

"When did this happen, Raquel? I talked to Rubí, like . . ." Ivon checked her watch, ". . . less than an hour ago."

A long pause. "Who is this? Ximena?"

"It's me: Ivon. Ximena left her cell phone with me."

Raquel hung up.

"What the hell?" Ivon went to the Received Calls menu and tried to redial Raquel's number, but it came across as "Out of area." She called Rubí's number, but again, she got nothing but the voice mail.

"Hi, this is Rubí's daughter, Amber. Leave her a message. My mom's busy saving the world right now."

Ivon tried not to listen to the voice in her head that was going, "it's your fault, Ivon," blaming herself for Walter's death. She remembered J.W. calling someone and ordering that the Walter Luna mess be cleaned up. You shouldn't have told J.W. it was Walter who dubbed the videotape they found in your pack. Maybe he was and maybe he wasn't implicated in the porn site. You shouldn't have named him, Ivon.

She had to get a hold of Ximena, tell her what had happened to Walter, but her cousin had gone off with Ma and Patrick to get Mostaza out of impound. She had to call someone else. Maybe she could tell Father Francis, and he would absolve her by saying she'd just been trying to keep herself alive in a deadly situation. It was weird for her to be thinking about confession, but she figured staying alive at someone else's expense had to be some sort of mortal sin.

Ivon's hands shook as she scrolled through the directory of names and numbers on Ximena's phone. Searching for Patrick, she ran across three entries for Frank—church, home, and Contra— and two for Montenegro, Raquel—school and private. She found Patrick's number, but held off making the call, taking one more look at the horizon of sky and desert, river and mountains that spelled the ambivalence she called home.

The air was so still, she could hear a radio playing. Maybe someone in the parking lot had the car window open and the sound was carrying. It was Oldies, as usual, Simon and Garfunkel's "The Sounds of Silence."   (c) Portillo

"Fools, said I, you do not know/Silence like a cancer grows."

That's what this was, she realized. A huge malignant tumor of silence, meant to protect not the perpetrators, themselves, but the profit reaped by the handiwork of the perpetrators. A bilateral assembly line of perpetrators, from the actual agents of the crime to the law enforcement agents on both sides of the border to the agents that made binational immigration policy and trade agreements.

The cards fell so perfectly into place, it was almost nauseating.

This thing implicated everyone. No wonder the crimes had not been solved, nor would they ever be solved until someone with much more power than she, with nothing to lose or to gain, brought this conspiracy out into the open.

"And the sign said the words of the prophet are written on subway walls and tenement halls . . ."

Poor Juárez, so far from the Truth, so close to Jesus.

Somewhere out there, under the impassive limestone face of Cristo Rey and the pervasive, fetid fumes of a copper smelter, a prophet was writing on bathroom walls, and rosebuds were dropping like blood over the desert.

The lights started to flash on one then a second and a third of the Border Patrol vans stationed down on the levee. She turned her back on the view: La Migra and las colonias, the smokestacks and Cristo Rey, the river a brown snake meandering between two worlds.

This spot held no more magic for her, now. If anything, it was the spot where the open wound of the border was most visible, that place where, as Gloria Anzaldúa described it, "the Third World grates against the First and bleeds."

Epilogue

"SMELLS LIKE A FUNERAL PARLOR IN HERE," joked Ximena. "Are you all sure there's enough flowers in this room?"

"Don't be mean to Irene," Irene said in a screechy voice, holding up her Curious George like a ventriloquist's puppet.

Irene had been released from the hospital just yesterday, after her third rabies shot, and her bed was a zoo of stuffed animals. Along with the flowers and the stuffed toys, folks had brought balloons, jars of jelly beans, candles of the Virgin of Guadalupe and Don Pedrito Jaramillo, wrapped presents that she hadn't even opened yet. William brought a drawing of Clifford, the red cartoon dog that one of his kids had made for Irene, and Aunt Fátima a holy card of Santo Domingo, patron saint against mad dogs and rabies. Irene had wanted both pieces tacked to the wall above her head, next to the crucifix that had been given to Ma at Dad's funeral.

"*Chiflada.*" Ximena kissed Irene on the forehead and handed her a stuffed hippopotamus with a pink ribbon tied around its belly.

"She's so cute," said Irene. "Look, George, you have a new friend."

"Yeah, like you needed a new friend," said Ivon, sitting cross legged on the floor, trying to revise the first draft of her Juárez chapter.

Once Ivon had allowed herself to fully focus on the work and stopped trying to play detective, the chapter had practically written itself in the five days that she and Brigit had been staying at Ma's place. Ma and Brigit had bonded big-time.

"Looks like you have enough stuff here to open a thrift shop," said Ximena, shoving some of the toys to the side so she could sit at the end of the bed. Something growled.

"What the hell?" Ximena said, startled.

"It's just Samson, under the bed," laughed Irene. "Ma let him come in to visit me."

The dog yelped at the sound of his name.

"Oh, I thought it was Ivon that smelled bad."

"So funny I forgot to laugh," said Ivon.

Ivon was brainstorming on a legal pad about how to integrate Anzaldúa's theory on border identity with Caputi's theory on femicide and the fetishization of serial killers in patriarchal culture. The stitches in her arm were throbbing today, and she'd just taken some more Tylenol.

"Judge Anacleto called earlier," Ximena said. "Pete woke up asking for a margarita."

"Yay!" said Ivon. "We need to take that boy out on the town."

"His mom's giving a big party for him tomorrow. They want us to stop by."

"Can I come?" Irene said.

"No," Ivon and Ximena said in unison.

"You guys are so mean."

"And guess what? I heard from Rubí, too. She sent me an email from some cyber address in Oaxaca. I guess they've gone incognito. Signed it, Ramona," Ximena announced.

"*Todos somos Ramona*," said Ivon. "Could've been anybody."

"It was her. All it said was, 'Tell your cousin that we don't blame her.'"

Ivon put the legal pad down and drew her legs up to her chest, holding her ankles. "I still feel like shit about that," she said. "If I hadn't mentioned Walter's name to that J.W. . . ."

"It wasn't your fault, *prima*. If Walter was in on that lucky penny snuff site, he deserved what he got. He brought it on his own family, not you."

"Don't talk about that, you guys," said Irene, covering her ears with her hands. It traumatized her to hear anything about lucky pennies or pornography.

"Thank God, nothing happened to Rubí or her daughter," said

Ivon. "I couldn't have lived with myself."

"I remember her," said Irene. "She was nice, but her boyfriend acted kind of macho."

"You don't know who we're talking about, Ms. Thing," said Ximena.

"I do, too. Amber, right? I met her at the fair, when I was there with Raquel's niece."

"Did someone say Raquel?"

Her black eyes glittering like ink, Raquel was standing suddenly in the doorway to Irene's bedroom at Ma's house, holding a bright pink gift bag.

Ivon gaped at her. "What are *you* doing here?"

"She came with me," Ximena said.

Ivon stared back and forth between Ximena and Raquel. Something about the way Ximena's nostrils flared when she looked at Raquel and the way Raquel looked down, embarrassed. Ximena knew Raquel's number. Ximena had been acting weird about Ivon seeing Raquel. Smell the coffee, Ivon, she almost laughed. Un-fucking-believable. Brigit was in the kitchen helping Ma make *flautas* for the reunion picnic tomorrow, and Raquel, the woman whose bed she'd been in just a few days ago, was here too, and, it turned out, she was not only Ivon's ex, but also Ximena's girlfriend. She didn't even know her cousin was a dyke. So much for my gaydar, she thought.

"And when did you come out that I wasn't looking?" Ivon whispered to her cousin.

"I brought some *regalitos*." Raquel could be very suave in difficult situations. "This is for *la garrapata*," she said, handing the gift bag to Irene.

Irene pulled out a brand-new compact disc player and some CDs. "Wow! Thanks!"

Ximena must have told Raquel that Irene's disc player had been stolen, as had her graduation ring. Ivon intended to replace the ring as soon as she got some extra cash.

"One of my nieces recommended the music," said Raquel. "I don't have any idea what you girls listen to these days."

Irene examined the CDs. "Maldita Vecindad, Café Tacuba,

Julieta Venegas—cool! I don't have any *rock en español*. Thanks, Raquel."

When she looked like that, her face alight with joy and gratitude, Ivon couldn't help getting a knot in her throat.

"And this is for you, Ivon," said Raquel, stepping out into the hallway for a moment.

"For me?"

Raquel came back into the room with something behind her back. In the background stood Brigit and Ma.

Ivon was still sitting on the floor and didn't even have time to get up before a wiry little body was throwing himself at her, squealing "Von!" One of his fingernails caught in the stitching on Ivon's arm.

"Ouch!" crowed Ivon.

Samson barked. Ximena picked up Irene's Curious George, and said "George, meet your cousin, Jorgito."

Ivon managed to stand up. Brigit and Irene were laughing, and Jorgito was clinging to Ivon's neck tighter than Irene ever had, his little legs clamped hard around her waist. Brigit had come into the room, too, and was holding on to both Ivon and Jorgito. Ma stood stiffly in the hallway, arms crossed, shaking her head in judgment.

"What's going on?" Ivon was having a hard time taking it all in.

"I asked Raquel to pick him up and get him ready to meet Brigit," said Ximena. "He can spend the weekend if you want. Elsa's not well at all. It's time for you guys to finalize your decision."

Jorgito was wearing overalls, a red-striped shirt, and baby-sized Doc Marten sandals like Ivon's. He smelled of patchouli.

Brigit was crying.

"Ma! Get in here! What do you think? Should we do this?"

Ma kind of sauntered into the room. She loved being the center of attention. "You do what you want, *m'ijita*. You always do. But that one . . ." she pointed to Irene, ". . . is going to get that thing out of her tongue right now. It was so embarrassing when Fátima pointed it out to me at the hospital. 'What is that *fierro* doing in your girl's tongue?' she asked me, like I'm supposed to know *las locuras* that you kids get into these days."

People were holding their breath, not sure what would come flying out next from Lydia the Dragon Lady's mouth.

She stood in front of Ivon and took a good look at Jorgito. "Come here, you skinny thing!" she said, opening her arms to him. Ivon nodded at the boy and he went to her. "Let's get you some *flautas*."

"Can I help?" said Brigit, following Ma and Raquel out of the room.

Ivon's eyes met Ximena's. Ximena shrugged.

"What about my dissertation, *ésa?*"

Ximena got up from the bed and threw an arm over Ivon's neck. "Look at it this way, *prima*. You haven't lost a job, you've gained a son."

"I haven't lost my job, *yet*. But I will, if I don't finish."

Ivon looked at the calendar she had drawn on the legal pad. Today was Saturday, June 20th. She and Brigit were flying back to L.A. on Monday, the 22nd. That meant she had exactly eight days to finish the last chapter, write a conclusion, print up the whole manuscript, and submit it to her committee. How the hell she was going to do all that, she didn't know, but it wasn't going to happen sitting here in the midst of all the family madness. Her computer was waiting for her in her old room. Back to the grindstone.

Jorgito toddled into the room, carrying a paper plate with three *flautas*.

Samson leapt out from under the bed.

Irene screamed, "Watch the dog!"

The boy dropped the plate and started to cry.

"You scared him, Lucha," said Ivon, scooping him up with her good arm.

Samson scarfed up the food.

"I didn't mean to. Sorry. I'm paranoid now."

"*No te asustes*," Ivon soothed him. "Samson just loves *flautas*."

Ximena tickled Jorgito under the arm and he giggled.

"He'll be here when you come back," Ximena said to Ivon." In the meantime, I'll have Elsa sign the papers, and I'll make sure Judge Anacleto puts you on his docket."

Mapi, come supervise me in the kid's section.

No rebuttal from her mom's voice in that proverbial ping-pong game in her head.

"Okay, y'all, I gotta split," Ximena said. "We have a big day tomorrow at Ascarate Lake. Everyone, be there or be square."

"I'm not gonna have any fun," whined Irene, "sitting in a wheelchair all day."

"Sure you will. You and Tía Esperanza can sit in your wheelchairs playing Chinese checkers till the cows come home."

Irene threw the stuffed hippopotamus at Ximena.

"Really, she's a lot of fun. She'll make you laugh with stories of the time when she was a soldier in Pancho Villa's army. Oh, Ivon, don't forget your Uncle Joe wants you to help him slice up the *barbacoa,* so get there early."

Ivon had spent yesterday morning helping her uncle salt and season the special roasts he bought for his *barbacoa.* The aluminum-wrapped bundles of brisket would roast in a pit of mesquite wood for two days, beans cooking slowly, thick with ham hocks and garlic, in a cylinder-like pot in the middle of the smoky pit. She could almost taste it.

Then she thought of the families of the murdered women. Were they going to celebrate Father's Day, she wondered, go boating on the lake, break piñatas, and eat barbecue brisket? Just be grateful you have a family, Ivon. Ximena kissed Jorgito on the cheek. He wriggled out of Ivon's arms and went to play with Curious George.

"¡Qué familia!" said Ivon.

Acknowledgments

Never have I felt so much support, good faith, and community effort in the production of a book as I have with this one. The list includes relatives, friends, students, and complete strangers whose own efforts at exposing the crimes and ending the violence inspired me tremendously. All made indispensable contributions to my research. Among my relatives, I have to thank, first and foremost, Lizeth, my niece and research assistant at the University of Texas at El Paso, who in Fall 1999, used her innate archaeological skills to find an archive of Mexican newspaper articles on the murders from 1993 to 1998. That's how it all started, *y sin tu ayuda, mi reina, no hubiera podido hacer este trabajo.* I need to thank Blanca, my cousin and *comadre*, for her networks, connections, and special tours; and, of course, my mother, for her prayers.

Many friends and students sent me e-mail updates on anything related to the murders, and I am grateful to them all. Others provided unique assistance and require special mention: my fellow-Bloomie, Antonia, for finding me the title of the book; my buddy, Emma Pérez aka *la* Sundance, for reading several drafts of the novel, for driving me the length and breadth of Juárez, from Zaragosa to Puerto de Anapra, and especially for the last-minute, late-night, junk-food-laden proofreading session of the galleys; my Border Consciousness student, Miguel, and his dad, for their undercover video skills in La Mariscal; Andy, *la mera-mera detectiva*, who let me pester her with all my questions and made it possible for me to tag along at the autopsy; my friend, Sara, who turned me on to *The Doomed Detective,* Stefano Tani's work on the "anti-detective novel," which helped me figure out the kind of book I was writing; a gentleman named Fred Soza, whom I met after a reading from my Sor Juana novel back in 1995, and who told me about the mnemonic device he had invented to remember the ten Muses (little did you know, Fred, that I would be borrowing "Pete McCuts" one day); and finally, that ragtag team of intrepid Calavera explorers, Yvette, Marina, Irma, and Andy (again), for your last-minute pictures—you guys made it possible for me to wrap up the loose ends.

Special thanks to Deena González, for putting up with my emotional turmoil, lack of housework, and bizarre research trips during the last three and a half years of our relationship, the time it took to write this book (even though we have each gone our own way, I will always treasure our friendship); to Gloria Ramírez, for giving me a room of my own in which to work in her casita in Texas; to Angélica, Heather, Elena, Stacy, Rob, and all the "¡Ni Una Más!" gente who helped me organize the "Who Is Killing the Women of Juárez?" Conference in Los Angeles, under the auspices of the UCLA Chicano Studies Research Center and Amnesty Inernational. ¡Mil gracias a todas y todos!

I thank those seven women journalists of Juárez who first broke the silence about the murders with their invaluable book, *El silencio que la voz de todas quiebra*. My gratitude and respect to all those nongovernmental organizations such as 8 de Marzo, Justicia para las Mujeres de Juárez, and Nuestras Hijas de Regreso a Casa, and to activists like Esther Chávez Cano, Astrid González Dávila, Judith Galarza, and Lucha Castro, who have insisted, from the beginning, on raising the collective Mexican consciousness about domestic abuse and other forms of violence against women. See the webpage for Casa Amiga (www.casa-amiga.org), the only rape crisis shelter for women on the U.S.-Mexico border, for statistical information on the femicides as well as on the number of abused women and children in Juárez. In 2004, for example, there were over 1,500 new incidences of rape, incest, or battery in that border city alone.

I would like to make a special mention of that first collective of families and relatives of the victims, Voces Sin Eco, who organized the first search parties and field sweeps in the early years of the crime wave, and who gave us the now iconic image of the black cross in a pink rectangle as a symbol for justice for *las hijas de Juárez*.

Very heartfelt thanks to Esther Chávez and Vicky Caraveo for taking time out from their incredibly multi-tasked schedules to talk to me and for sharing their archives of information. *Gracias, del corazón*, Norma Andrade, Benita Monárrez, Ramona Morales, Patricia Cervantes, and Marisela Ortiz, for bearing witness to your losses at the UCLA Conference; and *gracias*, as well, to Eve Ensler, Dolores Huerta, Congresswoman Hilda Solís, and all the other activists, artists, scholars, and professionals who spoke at the conference and helped educate the UCLA and greater Los Angeles community about this crime wave against poor brown women in Juárez.

I also want to recognize the pioneering academic work of colleagues María Socorro Tabuenca and Julia Monárrez Fragoso of Colegio de la Frontera, Cynthia Bejarano of New Mexico State University, Kathleen Staudt and Irasema Coronado of the University of Texas at El Paso, Rosa Linda Fregoso of the University of California, Santa Cruz, and Melissa Wright of Penn State Univeristy.

Most of all, I offer my sympathy and admiration to all the mothers of the victims who have tirelessly demanded justice for their dead and missing daughters—for their protests, their marches, and their campaigns to end the impunity.

The Internet proved to be one of the best (and only) resources for some of my research. I would like to thank Greg Bloom and the tireless news hounds and translators at *Frontera NorteSur,* the online news digest for New Mexico State University, for keeping news about the murders available and accessible to the English-speaking public. Thanks to all the other online sources of information on the murdered women of Juárez, including the sites that are now defunct, such as The Sagrario Consortium. Thanks to the organizers of the conferences on the crimes held at New Mexico State University and the Universidad Autónoma de Ciudad Juárez that brought much information and many of the players to light.

And to the Women in Black Art Project (part of the international feminist peace movement) for organizing a march and a protest in Washington D.C. to bring U.S. attention to these heinous crimes.

I am grateful to Lourdes Portillo for the beautiful, sensitive, and disturbing documentary she made on the crimes, called "Señorita Extraviada" (2001). The archival footage in this film as well as the puzzle she constructs to represent the thickening plot that surrounds the murders provided much insight. Thanks for the courage to do this film. I learn from the best.

I also want to recognize journalists Sam Quiñones, John Quiñones, Charles Bowden, Diana Washington Valdez, and Lorena Méndez, and all the other reporters who first brought word of these crimes to an English-speaking audience in such newspapers as the *Los Angeles Times*, the *Washington Post*, the *Christian Science Monitor*, the *San Antonio-Express News*, the *New York Times*, and the *El Paso Times*, and in shows like *20/20* and *America Undercover*. Diana, in particular, has taken major risks in exposing the link between the murders and the affluent "juniors" in Juárez.

To those hardboiled mystery buffs of the Hispanic Detective conference at the Royal Holloway University of London who sat through a very long reading and listened intently to four of my chapters—thank you for all that enthusiasm and positive feedback. Special thanks to Shelley for inviting me, and to Dean Scott Waugh at UCLA and Tom Wortham, Chair of English, for making the trip possible.

To Nick Kanellos and the staff of Arte Público Press, I tender my most sincere appreciation for believing in the integrity of my mission to raise awareness about the crimes and inform the broadest public possible. Y también, for your multiple roles in the book's production.

Partial funding for the research on this project was provided by the UCLA Academic Senate Committee on Research. Thanks to the COR for two years of support.

To learn more about the crimes, or the author, or to sign the online petition to end the violence against women and girls in Juárez, please visit www.desertblood.info.

I hope this book inspires its readers to join the friends and families of the dead and the disappeared women of Juárez. Only in solidarity can we help bring an end to this pandemic of femicides on the border. ¡Ni Una más!